THE HITCHHIKER'S GUIDE TO THE GALAXY RADIO SCRIPTS

THE TERTIARY, QUANDARY AND QUINTESSENTIAL PHASES

Douglas Adams was born in 1952 and created all the various and contradictory manifestations of *The Hitchhiker's Guide to the Galaxy*: radio, novels, TV, computer game, stage adaptations, comic book and bath towel. He lectured and broadcast around the world and was a patron of the Dian Fossey Gorilla Fund and Save the Rhino International. Douglas Adams was born in Cambridge, UK, and lived with his wife and daughter in Islington, London, before moving to Santa Barbara, California, where he died suddenly in 2001. After Douglas died the movie of *Hitchhiker* moved out of development hell into the clear uplands of production, using much of Douglas's original script and ideas. Douglas shares the writing credit for the movie with Karey Kirkpatrick.

THE HITCHHIKER'S GUIDE TO THE GALAXY RADIO SCRIPTS

THE TERTIARY, QUANDARY AND QUINTESSENTIAL PHASES

As dramatized, directed and annotated by Dirk Maggs
from the novels by Douglas Adams

Produced by Bruce Hyman and Helen Chattwell
at Above the Title Productions

And with a foreword by Simon Jones

PAN BOOKS

First published 2005 by Pan Books
an imprint of Pan Macmillan Ltd
Pan Macmillan, 20 New Wharf Road, London N1 9RR
Basingstoke and Oxford
Associated companies throughout the world
www.panmacmillan.com

ISBN 0 330 43510 8

A CIP catalogue record for this book is available from
the British Library.

Typeset by SetSystems Ltd, Saffron Walden, Essex
Printed and bound in Great Britain by Bath Press

Contents

Acknowledgements and Thanks

First and foremost, Jane Belson for unwavering support; Generalissimo Ed Victor and his lieutenants, Lizzy Kremer and Gráinne Fox; Christine Cuddy and Robert Bookman, who fought battles abroad; Helen Boaden, who made one brave executive decision after another; Nicky Hursell and Jacqui Graham, who were patient and persistent beyond the call of duty; Paul Deeley, whose fingerprints are to be heard (but not seen) throughout this book; the peerless Peer Lindgreen and Kevin Davies, who surpassed their brief; Christian Knowles for pestering; Jo Wheeler, Laura Harris, Ruth Waites and Susie Matthews, without whom these scripts would still just be a few email attachments.

And, of course, to the immortal Douglas Adams.

Dirk Maggs and Bruce Hyman

Foreword by Simon Jones

Well, Douglas, old bean, I know you'd find it hard to believe this, but we've done it. It's taken nearly a quarter of a century to do it, and it's an evil injustice that you weren't here to see it, but the job's done. The entire saga of Arthur Dent, as I like to think of it, has now been recorded for the world's auricular pleasure, and here are the scripts to prove it.

I'd like to say that I always knew we'd make it across the finish line. I'd like to, but it would be a lie. I really had my doubts. In fact, I gave it the same odds as a snowball's chance in hell.

I'm not sure you ever knew, but after the second series Peter Jones and I made it a habit to meet for an annual lunch. Needless to say we would soon get around to weighing the latest rumours of a recording reunion, and usually ended up dismissing them as fantasy. In 1994 our rendezvous, at Peter's suggestion, was at the Explorers' Club, and we greeted each other in a state of high excitement. You had indicated to me that there just might be a further series, and, more concretely, a radio producer with the suitably science-fiction name of Dirk Maggs had been contacting the cast to check our availability. Peter was feeling particularly available at the time, and, come to think of it, so was I.

But, alas, it was not to be – at least, not then. You weren't at all keen on the scripts that a third party had written, and having no time yourself to produce them, the moment passed. I recently found a letter from Peter in a long-neglected desk drawer – he hardly ever wrote letters, so I kept it for its rarity. (Actually, at the time, that wasn't a consideration; I simply never throw anything away.) It's dated December 22nd 1994, and says, among other things, 'I hear from Dirk Maggs that there's not much chance of a radio series as Douglas is working on a script for a film.'

Film was the medium you wanted to crack, and the more it remained closed to you, the more you became determined to see it achieved.

At that time also you were saying that you wanted to move on from *Hitchhiker's*, and making a radio series out of what you'd already published seemed too much like a step backwards. After all, the first two books had come as a result of the story's popularity on radio, hadn't they? The last three sprang fully-formed straight onto the printed page. (Well, not exactly 'sprang'; they were cajoled, bullied, you might even say tortured out of you by grimly determined editors, while you listened to the gentle 'whooshing' of deadlines passing by.)

As the years passed, my lunches with Peter became more concerned with talk about other things, including whether your pursuit of 'the movie' would ever come to anything and, if it did, whether we'd be too old to appear in it. Time continued to pass. Then the old team started to lose members – David Tate (the voice of Eddie the shipboard computer), Richard Vernon (Slartibartfast) and then Peter himself. I decided it was all over.

But Dirk stayed with it. He refused to be discouraged, though even he too must have lost hope when we were all hit by the ultimate disaster in May 2001 – your shockingly sudden death. He became, if anything, more determined to complete the work – as a tribute to you.

Ironic, isn't it, that the whole idea truly came back to life at your memorial service, the following September, when he had a talk with your friend Bruce Hyman. It turned out that Bruce shared Dirk's vision for the project, and was eager to proceed as soon as possible, as a tribute to you.

So it was with mixed emotions that I turned up that November morning in 2003 at the Sound House. I was furious that you weren't going to be there, saddened by the similar absence of three old chums, anxious to hitch up with the others, and blissfully happy to be putting on the dressing-gown, literally and metaphorically, of good old Arthur Dent.

Incidentally, for all these years when it's crossed my mind, it's been a bit of a puzzler as to whether I could truly be, along with the likes of Christopher Robin Milne, Alice Liddell, and Peter Llewellyn-Davies, the unwitting inspiration for an enduring character of fiction. Just about the same time I found the letter from Peter, I also discovered a poster for the first three paperback novels of *Hitchhiker's*. You had, in an even more expansive moment than usual, autographed it with the following dedication: 'To Arthur, both in origination and realization, you will probably end up wishing I hadn't signed this but here's my signature anyway, love, Douglas.' I have absolutely no memory of when you wrote that, so I can only assume that it was one of those evenings of which nobody present would have much recollection when the sun rose the following morning. However, I did begin to wonder, after speaking at the funeral and the memorial and reading the excellent biographies of you by Mike Simpson and Nick Webb, whether Arthur isn't in a good part actually *you*. For example, you were the champion bath-taker, though it is true that I tend to avoid showers even when in America, where hardly anyone takes a bath (if you see what I mean). I hardly ever drink coffee and complain vigorously if my cuppa isn't up to scratch. But there are other Arthurian characteristics that seem definitely more you than me. Whatever the truth of it, I perpetually thank my lucky stars that I treated you decently that day in Cambridge, when we were both undergraduates and you came to audition for the Footlights. I hardly knew you then but I really did think your sketch was funny – much more so than the pseudo-intellectual claptrap I'd had to endure before you arrived.

But that's ancient history.

What were the recording sessions like? Well, for me they were unalloyed pleasure.

I was relieved to find that the years had been kind to those of us who remained. Susan Sheridan, whom I hadn't seen in an age, looked exactly the same – younger, perhaps. Geoff McGivern and Mark Wing-Davey I'd seen frequently over the years, so if they've deteriorated I've not noticed. I would, and I'm sure they would, prefer to say they'd matured, like fine old bottles of port. I have to admit, having lost most of my hair, and seen the remnant turn grey, that I felt more battle-scarred than the rest. But regardless of how we look, we *sounded* exactly the same, and thanks to the miracle of radio we were, and are, the same people we ever were. By the way, Dirk says he applied some arcane electronic test that proves my voice has dropped a semitone in the intervening twenty-five years; funny, I always thought men's voices became higher as they grew older.

Both Geoff and I, it might be amusing to note, found ourselves seriously challenged dentally, before we came to record *So Long, and Thanks for all the Fish*. I had had two front teeth knocked out on the forehead of a stagehand during a performance of *My Fair Lady* in Hartford, Connecticut, in the previous July. The insurance company had been, at first, reluctant to meet their obligations, and my permanent replacements were only installed three weeks before we started recording.

Geoff arrived at the Sound House with two lower teeth missing, after a dispute with a Christmas nut. 'Don't worry,' he said, 'it won't make the shlightesht differ-ensh.' It's amazing how effective emergency dentistry can be. Within a day he sounded less like a leaking steam engine, and more like the usual smooth-running Ford.

It was really striking, the ease with which we assumed our old characters. Perhaps we never really shed them. Geoff and I became Ford and Arthur straightaway, gossiping away with that tetchy affection that marks their fictional relationship. Somehow we recorded an episode a day, with Dirk complaining that if we were a film we could take a week to do four minutes. He was a splendid director, by the way, and I'm not saying that just because I want to work with him again. He was very good at tweaking a scene with just the right suggestion to the actors, and was very clear about preserving the primacy of the words above all the hubbub of special effects and Dolby 5.1 Surround sound. Believe me, you would have approved.

You'll never guess what else has happened since those days in the late seventies in the Paris Studio. We've become a revered institution, and people who might have sniffed at the offer of a part in the old days were this time only too eager to join in the party. A good number of old friends have come back too – to tie things up. Roy Hudd returned as Max Quordlepleen, the irrepressible host of the cabaret at Milliways, the Restaurant at the End of the Universe; Rula Lenska flew in to reappear as the clone Lintilla from Perth (Scotland not Australia). Mark Wing-Davey was the one to come from Australia, where he'd been directing a musical. He came the furthest, though I came over from New York. David Dixon and Sandra Dickinson (Ford and Trillian, respectively, in the TV version) were invited along all the way from East Sheen and Chiswick, respectively.

Among the veteran radio comedy great and good, June Whitfield and Leslie Philips, whose careers in radio stretch back as far as the 1940s, graced our microphones for the first time with their charm and good humour. For Hollywood glamour, Christian Slater popped in with his two very well-behaved children to play Wonko the Sane. I'm not at all sure he knew what we were up to, but he played along with convincing gusto. Joanna Lumley was a very feasible alien lady with a head shaped like the Sydney Opera House. Jonathan Pryce was gratifyingly unhesitating in his determination to reprise his role as Zarniwoop, the editor of the *Guide*, while Miriam Margolyes, fresh from a series of ten documentary films following in the footsteps of Charles Dickens when he toured America, wasted no time in realizing the potential of Smelly Photocopier Woman. To fill the places of absent friends: Richard Griffiths amply took the place of Richard Vernon; the director of the Dublin-based Crazy Dog Audio, Roger Gregg, came in to do Eddie; and William Franklyn, an old friend of Peter Jones, brought a very similar and inimitable air of sophisticated bewilderment to the Book.

But the star of the show was, believe it or not, you. Your performance in reading the audio version of the books was so animated that your voice was transferred to our dramatization. You are playing the role you always fancied playing: Agrajag, the creature who is inadvertently killed by Arthur whatever life-form he adopts. It was distinctly surreal playing the scene with you in the Cathedral of Hate, exchanging dialogue with a speaker in a box – but the result is great.

Obviously I'm biased. I think Dirk has done an exceptionally good job in adapting the books for radio, and I'm sure the readers will agree. I hope that they will provide as much pleasure in printed form as they gave to those of us who were lucky enough to perform them. Quirky and bizarre, they capture precisely your unique way of looking at the world. Frankly, I don't believe anyone, apart from you, could have done better – and as a tribute to you, and your remarkable mind, I am happy to endorse them without hesitation. So here they are. We dedicate them to you with our love.

We miss you.

January 2005

Introduction by Bruce Hyman

I remember being at a BBC meeting for comedy and drama radio producers in about 1997. Most of us were from the independent sector and we'd been invited to Broadcasting House to hear what the network was looking for, in the way of new comedy.

'I'd like to get out of the drawing room,' said the BBC person. 'What I want is, y'know, something bold. Wit and imagination, maybe something surreal, something that looks to the future . . . rather than the present.'

At the back of the room someone murmured in a wry, Ford Prefect-type tone, 'You mean, *Hitchhiker's Guide to the Galaxy*.'

Because the truth was that even in the late nineties, some twenty years after its first broadcast, *Hitchhiker* was *still* ahead of its time. As it happened, earlier that year I'd talked to Douglas about the idea of completing the series. We chatted about how it might happen, he mentioned the conversations he'd had with Dirk Maggs and we agreed that we'd keep talking. But *Starship Titanic* by then was in full sail, the *Hitchhiker* film (which was completed this year) was heaving into view – albeit at a distance – and somehow the time was never right. Until now. So here we are in 2005, once again celebrating Douglas's quirky, wildly imaginative, thoughtful, witty, universal – and yet very English – creation. But the difference is that this time Douglas isn't here to keep a watchful eye or to revel in the whole delightful process of dramatizing his much-loved masterpieces.

In fact, as Simon Jones says, the spark which brought these particular productions to life was Douglas's memorial service in September 2001. I knew Simon, and I'd met the rest of the cast at various social events – usually at Douglas and Jane's – but to see everyone assembled in one place just reminded us all how tantalizingly close the project really was. Dirk Maggs and I chatted and inevitably the conversation turned to *Hitchhiker*.

'We *have* to do it.'

'I agree.'

'We can't *not* do it.'

'We should ask the cast *now*, all of them.'

'Really?'

'Well, perhaps not this minute, but *soon*.'

'You're right.'

'OK.'

'Excellent.'

That is as accurate an account of the conversation as I can give, although I can't be sure who said what. Still, I was determined that this time it would happen and I knew we had the right team to do it. All it would take was, well, to get Jane's blessing, persuade the BBC, agree terms with Douglas's über-agent Ed Victor, produce the scripts and then find six consecutive days in which the entire original cast would be willing and able to record. In the event, that whole process took about two and a half years, much more than we imagined, but by the time we signed the last contract and sent off the final script we knew we were in good shape.

Some decisions had been more delicate than others: crucially we'd needed to find a replacement for the much-loved Peter Jones, although that actually turned out to be less arduous than it might have been. We wanted a familiar, reassuring voice, but one which also conveyed that laconic, irreverent tone which Peter had in abundance. It seemed to me that Bill Franklyn fitted the bill perfectly – he understood comedy, he had vast experience as well as one of those voices which makes you smile the moment you hear it. It also transpired that he and Peter had been friends for years, so it all just sort of made sense. The difficulty was to explain this change of voice to the satisfaction of the millions of existing *Hitchhiker* fans. *Life, the Universe and Everything* contains several references to the Book being upgraded, so we thought: why not introduce Bill as the Voice of the Upgrade?

We also had to cast Agrajag, the constantly reincarnated creature whose mission in life is to enjoy just one ripe old age. In one of the most satisfying pieces of casting I have ever been a party to, we managed to get Douglas himself; it was the part he had always wanted to play, and we were able to use extracts from his recorded reading of the book. Thus Episodes 1 to 6 began to take shape.

It is tempting to say that these were the first steps in an epic struggle, but actually the journey, although slow at times, was relatively painless. Helen Chattwell, my fellow producer, had the great advantage of a superb ready-made leading cast, though with the huge drawback that they were dispersed not just across the country but around the globe, but she managed the entire process with the military precision of a Vogon. On the other hand she discovered what we had always suspected, that *Hitchhiker* had become a much-loved institution, and wonderful actors (just have a look at the cast list) needed little persuasion to join the team, even in the smallest parts – I think Chris Langham, Griff Rhys-Jones and Joanna Lumley have no more than a page or two between them, but what performances they all gave.

The other major decision to be made was about the music. It was Jane's outstanding idea to ask Douglas's great friend Paul 'Wix' Wickens to compose the score, and although you obviously can't tell from the printed page, it is magnificent. A special mention too, for Philip Pope's song in Episode Three, which is a brilliant homage to – well, it should be obvious. And Philip didn't stop there, because he also appears throughout the series in a variety of undetectable guises.

It is a tribute to Douglas that he was able to inspire such dedication from so large and distinguished a team. Simon Jones, Geoff McGivern, Stephen Moore, Sue Sheridan and Mark Wing-Davey led the way, with all the kindness and quiet authority of a group of benign school prefects. As soon as they spoke, we relaxed – we were back on familiar ground, home territory, and the recording sessions were remarkably good fun, especially given the weight of *Hitchhiker* history behind us. There was scarcely a day without visitors, from Douglas's family to press to our resident cameraman, Kevin Davies, and even some competition winners (their prize was to feature in one of the crowd scenes). I've said this a few times, but how the producer of the original series, Geoffrey Perkins, and his team managed to make *Hitchhiker* 1 and 2 with just quarter-inch tape and a razor blade I cannot think. Our studio looked like the flight deck on the *Heart of Gold*.

I also have to mention Dirk's scripts. I think he did a remarkable job, and what shines through both in the writing and the recording is that he is a fan, which makes a huge difference. Often in script meetings Dirk would say, 'I think this is what Douglas would have done,' or 'I'm not sure this is Douglas-like enough,' and then (after I'd questioned whether there was actually such a word as 'Douglas-like') we'd go back to the books, or back to Douglas's notes, and try to get it right. The other voice at the writing table belonged to John Langdon – a brilliant script editor, an intuitive comedy writer, he would often just add a word here or remove another there and his feather-duster touch would add that extra gleam.

What you have in this book is something I hope – in fact, I'm sure – Douglas would have approved of. We missed him so much while we were making this, and all the more because one thing I'm certain of is that he'd have loved doing it, the whole thing, from the scripting to the recording to the digital editing (all three stages of which, incidentally, were done on Apple Macs, the computers about which he was so evangelical from the day they first appeared).

We owe him a great deal, and this is by way of a small thank-you.

Introduction by Dirk Maggs

In the summer of 1978, as a trainee BBC studio manager at what is now the Langham Hilton Hotel, I was determined that my career in radio would last just long enough to secure me a transfer to television, and that would open the door to the film industry. Only about two months before, the first series of *The Hitchhiker's Guide to the Galaxy* had finished its first repeat run on BBC Radio 4. I'd missed it, but caught some clips on review programmes; *Hitchhiker's* sounded to me like a Pythonesque *Doctor Who*, and my Ford Prefect lifestyle of drinking a lot and dancing with girls precluded further investigation.

In short, I had a lot to learn.

It was during ensuing secondments to BBC TV Centre that I realized how limited a medium television is, compared to radio. Then, on a working holiday, 'gofering' on a feature film in Toronto, I found out how cumbersome the business of film-making was. And much later, during quiet periods on long night shifts in the World Service newsroom, I listened spellbound to what Douglas Adams and Geoffrey Perkins achieved with *Hitchhiker's*. Having inherited my dear departed father's love for radio comedy, I knew that not since Spike Milligan had anyone combined words, sound effects and music to create such visual results. With No Pictures At All.

Ten years later I finally achieved what had seemed an impossible goal and became a producer in BBC Radio Light Entertainment. As well as comedy programmes our output included 'Light Drama', and whilst making action serials featuring the DC Comics characters Superman and Batman I was able to develop a radio-production style which layered lots of sound effects and music onto a tightly written, cinematic script. It was, and is, an incredibly labour-intensive way to work, and at times I wondered what rod I had made for my own back. But these early efforts had caught the attention of Douglas Adams, who was in talks with the BBC about further radio series of *Hitchhiker's*. One spring morning in 1993 he called my boss Jonathan James Moore and asked if I would be interested in taking on the job of producing them. I was floored. Apart from marriage and children, nothing before or since has so wonderfully and unexpectedly trumped my expectations of life.

That proposed first series ground to a halt due to script problems and contractual difficulties. The talks I had with Douglas and Robbie Stamp in 1997 to restart the process through their company Digital Village were scuppered by the long-awaited Movie Deal coming through. When we last met, in the reception at Broadcasting House in 2000, we were still making hopeful noises about finishing the saga on radio.

And then, overwhelming any such petty concerns, Douglas died. Against all odds it was a chance meeting at his memorial service with Bruce Hyman which revived the idea, and this time it actually happened.

This book is a companion volume to *The Original Radio Scripts*, published by Pan in 1985. In this second volume you will find the radio scripts we worked from in 2004 and 2005, more or less as performed, with the omission of some unscripted ad-libs and the presence of material which may yet be pruned for reasons of timing, timing or good taste. Or timing. After every episode there's a 'footnotes' section where I attempt to describe the reasons for various changes between the novels and these adaptations, as well as descriptions of the techniques we used in the studio to achieve our results. Oh, and the odd anecdote about teeth.

You will find a lot of 'thank-yous' as well, in the notes, in the acknowledgements and here in this introduction. This is not to irritate the casual reader, but proves how collaborative this enterprise has been from the start. Thus, in addition to the thanks elsewhere, my personal thanks are extended to Jane Belson, Ed Victor and Gráinne Fox, for making it all possible; Bruce Hyman, for his enthusiasm and staying power in the face of significant odds; Helen Chattwell, for her kindness and tenacity under pressure; John Langdon, for always letting Douglas have the last word; Wix Wickens, for allowing a pub drummer to mess around with his magnificent music; Sue Adams, James, Jane, Bronnie and Ella Thrift, for their moral and physical support; Robbie Stamp, Geoffrey Perkins and Kevin J. Davies, for advice on the more arcane points of Adamsian lore; Roger Philbrick, Anna Cassar, Chris Berthoud and John Partington, for ensuring the BBC Website represented our efforts accurately; and Nicky Hursell at Pan, for expertly shepherding the whole thing onto these pages.

One of the few good things to come out of the collapse of the Tertiary Phase project in 1993 was my working relationship with Paul Deeley and all at the Soundhouse. Paul and Phil Horne run a terrific studio, and Julie, Freddie, Ros and Hayley managed to patiently feed and water a building full of noisy actors without resorting to violence. For that forbearance, thank you all. Paul is also my 'ears' in the cubicle while I work in the studio with the actors, and a dear friend. He has endured the fallout from the setbacks which have blighted this project over the years, as have my family. My heartfelt thanks to him and to Lesley, Tom, Theo and Tolly for putting up with it.

Given the unavoidable omission of Douglas's inspirational presence, Simon Jones filled the vacant slot. In fact Simon was largely responsible for the prevailing positive atmosphere during recordings. He is warm, sympathetic, a terrific actor, a good friend and a colonel in the Kentucky Volunteers. Luckily they didn't declare war on the Tennessee Militia when we needed him.

I did not know Douglas as a friend, but on the occasions we met I liked him enormously, whether he was enthused, taciturn, distracted or utterly pissed off. I can only thank him for having faith in me, and recall a moment when perhaps I helped maintain his faith in himself. After the Tertiary Phase collapsed in 1993 I was 'poached' to produce Ned Sherrin's Radio 4 chat show *Loose Ends*. *Mostly Harmless* had just been published in paperback and I booked Douglas as a guest, as well as Sir Ranulph Fiennes, who had just man-hauled a sled across Antarctica, losing several fingers and toes to frostbite. As the great explorer told an epic tale of suffering and endurance, Douglas's face fell.

Afterwards, in the pub, I asked if something had upset him.

'Oh, not really,' said Douglas. 'It's just that talking about being locked in a hotel room to write an overdue novel seems pretty tame stuff compared to trekking across a thousand miles of icy crevasses.'

'Well, you need to put things in perspective,' I replied. 'First of all, your struggle was on a more human scale, and the result is a unique achievement no one can match. Secondly, just before we went on air, Ran Fiennes got lost in the basement of Broadcasting House looking for the toilet.'

Douglas smiled and picked up his glass. 'That makes me feel much better.'

Notes from the Cast

Susan Sheridan (Trillian)

Recording *Mostly Harmless*, January 2005: after twenty-six years as Trillian, it's been odd this time. I had to face up to meeting my alter ego – Tricia Macmillan in the form of the TV Trillian, Sandra Dickinson.

Douglas Adams wrote *Mostly Harmless* from the perspective of two separate universes, one in which the Trillian we know and love was blown into outer space with Zaphod, Arthur Dent and Ford Prefect – and another in which Tricia Macmillan went back for her bag and missed the whole event. Her world did not get blown up. Douglas specifically describes this earthbound Tricia with blonde hair and an American accent, and naturally he had Sandra in mind.

Meanwhile, my Trillian has a daughter, Random, whom she rather callously dumps on the unsuspecting father – Arthur Dent – while she goes off to pursue her career as an intergalactic reporter (a suitable career for an astrophysicist?). She comes up trumps at the end, however, in her usual brilliant fashion.

Mostly Harmless is quite different from the earlier books. It's dark in places, and Trillian's behaviour rather shocked me; leaving Random was a difficult scene to play. However, Dirk Maggs has brilliantly adapted the book for radio, adding memorable moments like Zaphod and Trillian's first meeting at the party in Islington, the Trillian who *didn't* go back for her bag! But their relationship was always a tricky one – having finally left Zaphod (who always had twice as much to drink as anyone else!) in the last series, *this* series ends with Trillian making a beeline for the dashing Dane God Thor.

So now it's all over, no more recordings. Ever.

Is there life after *Life, the Universe and Everything*? Well, there's always young Random . . .

William Franklyn (The Voice of the Book)

I was a new boy to the whole *Hitchhiker*'s environment, when it happily descended on me from a moon nugget – whatever that means.

My initial reaction was to the fascinating words I would have to play with, ten-line paragraphs without any punctuation, and phrases with a unique use of the English language that gave me a chance to bat like Denis Compton and bowl like Keith Miller. Sorry, but the cricket analogy is my space machine.

The imaginative lyrics were in freefall, appropriate to the subject matter. There was also an added significance, which was that Peter Jones had been the original Voice – my role. Peter Jones was a uniquely warm and humorous friend, and I had worked with him in the past. His imprint on *Hitchhiker* was indelible, and I was able to take inspiration from this and continue with my own vocal variations.

Our director and adaptor Dirk Maggs encouraged all the dive-bombing with his script and production of exciting eclipses. Going over the top is usually a First World War trench image, but it can occur when the pen replaces the bayonet. Douglas Adams's example encourages even us verbal midgets.

Philip Pope (Krikkit Civilian Two, Krikkit Commander, Krikkit Singer, Grebulon Underling, the King, Captain. Composer of the Krikkit song)

I was looking forward to the sessions at the Soundhouse again as it brought back wonderful memories of recording *Starship Titanic* with Douglas (I contributed Lift Bot, Maître d' Bot and Row Bot). This time he was not there in person but probably in spirit and definitely in voice, playing Agrajag. It was great in the studio but almost as entertaining outside in the green room with such an array of talents and such a rich feast of anecdotes.

Of all the wonderful stories, I racked my brains for something printable. I'm not sure whether Helen Chattwell being asked by Sayeed Jaffrey if she wanted a tongue sandwich and seeing her perplexed expression until he revealed his lunchbox – I mean bag of sandwiches – is acceptable. Actually it was such a kind gesture from the great actor that when he made the same offer to me I accepted saying I would put it aside for later. Much later that evening, on my way home from playing five-a-side football, I put my hand in my pocket and came across an unfamiliar clammy object. Now it was my turn to be perplexed, but only momentarily. I tucked in gratefully and, casting my mind back to earlier in the day, felt a little ashamed of my inner schoolboy sniggering.

Perhaps the closest memory I have of Douglas is born out of our shared love of music and Apple Macs (Douglas introduced me to the Mac) and our fascination with music technology. We often spoke about the Beatles and DNA was understandably excited when he told me that he had met Paul McCartney and was inviting him and Linda to dinner. Imagine my reaction when shortly afterwards Douglas called and, apologizing for the short notice, asked if Rosie and I would like to go round the following evening for dinner. I gratefully accepted, put the phone down and turning to Rosie mused with childish coyness about whether Paul McCartney might be there. She laughed and said, 'No – and that's probably why we've been invited!' The penny dropped and I felt suitably foolish. As it turned out we were both pleasantly surprised and spent a most enjoyable evening with Douglas and Jane and the Joneses (Terry not Simon).

Glossary of terms used in the scripts and notes

INT.	Interior setting for the action, usually requiring an ambient acoustic.
EXT.	Exterior setting, usually requiring little or no ambient acoustic.
FX:	Sound effects (can either be live in studio or added afterwards).
Distorted	Used for a voice heard, for example, through a telephone or radio.
Beat	A pause between lines to (a) let a point sink in, and (b) remind the actors to breathe now and again.
Extended version	The version on the commercially available CD, cassette and DVD-Audio, *not* edited to fit the BBC broadcast slot (27 minutes 30 seconds) but running to whatever length suited the story, usually five to ten minutes longer per episode.

THE TERTIARY PHASE

In 1993, with plans to dramatize *Life, the Universe and Everything*, BBC Enterprises (as it was then known) wanted to reissue the first and second *Hitchhiker's* radio series on CD. Douglas came up with the idea of renaming them the Primary and Secondary Phases. The projected new series would then be the Tertiary Phase, the next two presumably named something like Quaternary and Quintennial, but given the ensuing gap, which included his unexpected departure from this point in the Probability Arc, it seemed wiser to call them Quandary and Quintessential, both of which sounded less daunting, more memorable and are a bit easier to spell.

EPISODE ONE

SIGNATURE TUNE

ANNOUNCER   *The Hitchhiker's Guide to the Galaxy*, by Douglas Adams, Tertiary Phase.

Sig fades, then:

ARTHUR   (Distant echoey scream) Aaaaaaarrrrghhhhhhhhh!

INT. – THE BOOK AMBIENCE

A steady and untroubling musical drone unfolds, layered with the sounds of the book's animations.

THE VOICE   (Peter J/William F) [PETER] This is the story of *The Hitchhiker's Guide to the Galaxy*, [WILLIAM] – BZT! – perhaps the most remarkable, certainly the [PETER] most successful book – BZT! – [WILLIAM] ever to come out of the great publishing corporations of [PETER] – BZT! – Ursa Minor. [WILLIAM] – BZT! – Now in its seven to the power of sixteenth edition, it has been continuously revised and upgraded, including being fitted with a highly experimental jo-jo-jog-proof, splash-resistant heat-shield, – BZT! **(Raspy voice)** and a sophisticated new voice circuit – not always with complete – BZT! – success.

FX: Voice wows down in vaguely analogue fashion. A pause. Has something broken? A swift kick, and it starts up again, wowing in:

The earliest origins of the *Guide* are now, along with most of its financial records, lost in the mists of time, and the document shredders of Megadodo Publications, but it is worth mentioning – among other things – that every world on which the *Guide* has ever set up an accounting department has shortly afterwards perished in warfare, or other natural disaster.

So it is interesting – but not *very* interesting – to note that two or three days prior to the destruction of Earth to make way for a new hyperspace bypass there was a dramatic upsurge in the number of UFO sightings, not only over Lord's Cricket Ground in London, but also above Glastonbury in Somerset, the very site selected for the new *Hitchhiker's Guide* financial records office, just hours before the Vogon demolition fleet arrived.

FX: Panic in the streets, under:

PROSTETNIC VOGON VOICE   (PA slap) People of Earth. This is Prostetnic Vogon Jeltz of the Galactic Hyperspace Planning Council. Your planet is scheduled for demolition.

FX: Vogon destruction of the Earth. In Dolby Digital.

THE VOICE   [WILLIAM] So, that would seem to have been that, as far as the Earth was concerned.

Except that there were three survivors.

Arthur – BZT! – [PETER] Dent had basically assumed that he was the only native – BZT! – [WILLIAM] ape-descended Earthman to escape from the Earth, – BZT! – [PETER] because his only – BZT! – [WILLIAM] companion, disconcertingly called Ford – BZT! – [PETER] Prefect, – BZT! – [WILLIAM] had revealed himself to be a *Hitchhiker's Guide* researcher from somewhere near Betelgeuse, – BZT! – [PETER] and not from Guildford after all. So when, against all conceivable – BZT! – [WILLIAM] probability, they were rescued by a ship piloted by the infamous **(Dolby effect)** Zaphod Beeblebrox and were astonished to find him accompanied by a certain Trillian, once – BZT! – [PETER] Tricia McMillan, a rather nicely descended ape-person that Arthur once met at a party in Islington, – BZT! – [WILLIAM] it could only be because their ship was powered by the – BZT! – [PETER] Infinite Improbability Drive. **(Beat)** **(Dolby effect)** Which of course it was.

EXT. – PREHISTORIC ISLINGTON – DAY

FX: Arthur snoring (not comically, just naturally) and then making waking-up noises, then gasping, pausing and . . .

THE VOICE   The regular early morning yell of horror –

ARTHUR   **(Distant echoey scream – this does not interrupt the rhythm of the narrator)** Aaaaaaarrrrghhhhhhhhh!

THE VOICE   (cont'd) – was the sound of Arthur Dent waking up and suddenly remembering where he was.

ARTHUR   **(Groaning)** Bwwurrlbbllurgh.

THE VOICE   Islington has that effect on people. Even two million years ago.

ARTHUR   **(Post-yell whimper)**

THE VOICE   (cont'd) Arthur has been living in the prehistory of the insignificant little blue-green planet where he was born some two million years later, which is a terribly lonely position for any being other than a member of the species Hrarf-Hrarf to find itself in.

Members of the species Hrarf-Hrarf would of course take it in their stride because they live backwards in time anyway, and find that getting the business of sagging bottoms and death out of the way at an early stage prepares the way for an increasingly wonderful time after your mid-life crisis celebrations, finishing in a really quite extraordinarily pleasant birth.

FX: Effects actually recorded in Hrarf-Hrarf birth canal. We leave no effect unauthenticated.

THE VOICE They are also the only race known actually to enjoy hangovers, because they know it guarantees that a tremendously good evening will ensue. Arthur Dent is not, however, one of their number, and takes it hard. He is also cold and damp and extremely lonely.

FX: Arthur emerges from cave, business, under:

ARTHUR Looks like it's you and me again today, Horse Chestnut.

THE VOICE He hasn't seen Ford Prefect for four years and life has, as a result, been quieter than an uneventful Tuesday in the petrified dustbowls on the abandoned fourth moon of Narp. In fact, so astoundingly quiet that he hasn't been blown up, thrown out of spaceships, sucked through space or even just insulted.
Except for once; one evening, just two years earlier.

FX: Arthur plodding about listlessly, under:

ARTHUR Evening, Sycamore One. Evening, Sycamore Two. Evening, Ash. Evening, Elm. **(Pause)** Oh, be like that. Bloody elms. You try to be polite and where does it get you? **(Thunderous rumble)** I don't know why I . . . What's that?!

FX: Distant ethereal hum . . . (under following:) Wowbagger ship descends/ legs unfold/touchdown. Airlock door opens and a metal ramp extends. A pair of boots descends the ramp, rather pompously . . .

ARTHUR **(cont'd)** Good heavens . . . Look! Can you see what I see? All right! I know you're only a sycamore, you could at least pretend! It's a spaceship! A beautiful, gleaming, silver spaceship! No, Sycamore One, I'm not imagining it! We can escape!! At least . . . I can escape! I know how that must sound, Sycamore One, but your roots are here! It's landing right in front of us! I'm saved!

FX: The boots stop a few yards from the foot of the ramp.

WOWBAGGER . . . Dent?

ARTHUR **(Expectant, desperate)** That's right. I'll just get my pouch!

5

WOWBAGGER	(Simply) You're a jerk.
ARTHUR	What?
WOWBAGGER	Arthur Dent? Arthur Philip Dent?
ARTHUR	What is it?
WOWBAGGER	You're a jerk. A complete arsehole.
ARTHUR	Er . . . er . . .
WOWBAGGER	(To himself) Hey ho.
ARTHUR	But . . . ! But . . . ! Bu . . .
WOWBAGGER	And stop whining, you snivelling little drip!

FX: He turns and walks away. Smooth, precise sounds of spaceship closing itself up.

ARTHUR	Hey! What is this?

FX: Spaceship starts to rise up into the air.

ARTHUR	(cont'd) Wait a minute! (Screams in frustrated rage) Come back here and say that! Who the hell do you think you are?

FX: Spaceship swooshes away uncaringly.

INT. – THE BOOK AMBIENCE

THE VOICE	Wowbagger the Infinitely Prolonged thinks he is a man with a purpose. Not a very good purpose, as he would be the first to admit, but at least it keeps him busy; keeps him on the move. For Wowbagger is one of the universe's very small number of immortal beings. Those born to immortality instinctively know how to cope with it, but Wowbagger's not one of them. Indeed, he's come to hate them, and he refers to them succinctly, and often, as 'the load of serene bastards'.
WOWBAGGER	The load of serene bastards!
THE VOICE	(cont'd) He had his immortality inadvertently thrust upon him by an unfortunate accident with an irrational particle accelerator –

FX: Particle accelerator short-circuit.

WOWBAGGER	Oh dear.
THE VOICE	(cont'd) – a liquid lunch –

6

FX: Small glass of cava upset onto a negative-coupling mat.

WOWBAGGER   Whoops . . .

THE VOICE   (cont'd) – and a couple of rubber bands.

FX: Two India-rubber bands accidentally flicked into a neutron oscilloscopy reticule.

WOWBAGGER   (Winces) Oooh.

THE VOICE   (cont'd) The precise details of the accident are unimportant as no one has ever managed to duplicate the exact circumstances under which it happened – though many people have ended up looking very silly, or dead or more usually both, in the attempt. **(No Radio 2 sound effects here!)** To begin with, it was fun. He had a ball, living dangerously, taking risks, cleaning up on high-yield long-term investments and just generally outliving the hell out of everybody.

But even the joys of immortality can't last forever.

INT. – WOWBAGGER'S SHIP

WOWBAGGER   Computer?

FX: Beeps.

COMPUTER   (With bleepety accompaniment) Yes?

WOWBAGGER   I'm incredibly fed up.

FX: Beeps.

COMPUTER   Oh dear.

WOWBAGGER   It's the eternity of these Sunday afternoons I can't cope with; that and the terrible listlessness that starts to set in at about 2.55. **(Beat)** What *is* the time, by the way?

FX: Beeps.

COMPUTER   It's nine thirty. A.m. In the morning.

WOWBAGGER   (Glum) Oh. Well. **(Beat)** I mean, I've had all the baths I can usefully have, haven't I?

FX: Beeps.

COMPUTER   You have indeed.

INT. – THE BOOK AMBIENCE

THE VOICE . . . and as the afternoon moved relentlessly on to four o'clock, he would enter the long dark tea-time of the soul. And so things began to pall for him. The smug smiles he used to wear at other people's funerals started to fade. He began to despise the universe in general and everybody in it in particular, and thus he conceived his purpose.

FX: A rather sedate cocktail party at Wowbagger's condominium. He is rather mean with drinks. Consequently no one is having much fun.

WOWBAGGER I will insult the universe! I will insult everybody in it!

PERSON 1 Ridiculous!

PERSON 2 Is he all right?!

PERSON 3 Look, it's utterly impossible! Think of all the beings being born and dying all the time!

WOWBAGGER I don't care! I will insult them all. Individually. Personally. One by one. And . . . (A beat)

FX: They're shocked.

WOWBAGGER (Triumphant) . . . in alphabetical order!

FX: They're stunned.

WOWBAGGER There are cakes over there, if you want them . . . (Fades)

THE VOICE He equipped a spaceship that was built to last with a computer capable of keeping track of the entire population of the known Universe, plotting the horrifically complicated itineraries involved and joining up the resultant dots in the hope of randomly drawing a rude word.

When people protested further, he would merely fix them with a steely look and say –

INT. – WOWBAGGER'S SHIP

WOWBAGGER (Thoughtfully) It passes the time. (He sighs) Computer.

FX: Beeps.

COMPUTER Still here.

WOWBAGGER Where next?

FX: Beeps.

COMPUTER	Computing . . . Folfanga. Fourth world of the Folfanga system. Estimated journey time, three weeks.
WOWBAGGER	Yes, yes . . .

FX: Beeps.

COMPUTER	There to meet with a small slug of the genus A-Rth-Urp-Hil-Ipdenu . . . I believe that you had decided to call it a brainless prat.
WOWBAGGER	Hmm. What network areas are we going to be passing through in the next few hours?

FX: Beeps.

COMPUTER	Cosmovid, Thinkpix and Home Brain Box.
WOWBAGGER	Any movies I haven't seen thirty thousand times already?

FX: Beeps.

COMPUTER	No.
WOWBAGGER	(Yawns)

FX: Beeps.

COMPUTER	There's *Angst in Space*.
WOWBAGGER	I get enough of that at home.
COMPUTER	But you've only seen that thirty-three thousand five hundred and seventeen times.
WOWBAGGER	Wake me for the second reel.

INT. – THE BOOK AMBIENCE

THE VOICE	All Arthur Dent found to do to pass the time was to make himself a pouch of rabbit skin, which would be useful to keep things in.
ARTHUR	(Stretches, waking) Flurrbllrrrl . . .
THE VOICE	Then, one day, he woke up in his cave as usual . . .
ARTHUR	(Same blood-curdling scream as before. Echoey, in a cave) Aaaaaargh!!!!!! (Embarrassed as he remembers, yet again) I know . . . (Rising excitement and resolve) I know! I know what I'm going to do!

FX: We hear him scrambling out of the cave. Acoustic crossfades to exterior.

ARTHUR   (cont'd) Listen! Sycamore One? Sycamore Two? Horse Chestnut? Willow One? Willow Two? Oh, don't stop what you're doing, it's just ... You listening, Elm? Oh, please yourself. It's just I have an important announcement to make! I have decided ... I have made a decision. I've thought about it seriously and responsibly, and – all things considered – it's the right thing for me. I feel good about it. And here it is. I will go mad.

FORD PREFECT   (Behind him, calmly sitting on a rock) Good idea.

ARTHUR   (Astounded and terribly embarrassed) What?!

FORD PREFECT   I went mad for a while. Did me no end of good.

ARTHUR   Where did you just come from?

FORD PREFECT   Oh, just sitting on that rock, watching the sun rise. Least, I think it was a sun. Yellow thing. About this big. There it is! Look!

ARTHUR   (Incensed) Where the hell have you been?

FORD PREFECT   Oh, round and about. I just took my mind off the hook for a bit. I reckoned that if the world wanted me it would call back. It did. See? The Sub-Etha Sens-O-Matic's flashing.

FX: Sub-Etha Sens-O-Matic wibbling; a bit tentatively.

FORD PREFECT   Oh. At least it was. Probably needs a bit of a shake.

FX: He shakes the Sub-Etha Sens-O-Matic.

FORD PREFECT   (cont'd) Hmm. If it's a false alarm I shall go mad. Again.

ARTHUR   Ford, I thought you must be dead.

FORD PREFECT   So did I – which at least proved I wasn't. Then I decided I was a lemon for a while. I kept myself amused jumping in and out of a gin and tonic.

ARTHUR   Where did you find a gin—

FORD PREFECT   I didn't. I found a small lake that thought it was a gin and tonic and jumped in and out of that. At least, I think it thought it was a gin and tonic. I could, of course, have been imagining it.

ARTHUR   (Refusing to be drawn) I hope I am.

FORD PREFECT   The point is that there is no point in driving yourself mad trying to stop yourself going mad. You might just as well give in and save your sanity.

ARTHUR   And this is you sane again, is it? I ask merely for information.

FORD PREFECT   Oh, and I tried to learn to fly. Do you believe me?

10

ARTHUR	Look, Ford—
FORD PREFECT	Interestingly enough, on the subject of flying, the *Guide* now says—
ARTHUR	Who?
FORD PREFECT	*The Hitchhiker's Guide to the Galaxy*. Remember? 'Don't Panic' . . . ?
ARTHUR	I remember finding that easier to obey after I'd thrown it in the river.
FORD PREFECT	Ah, but I fished it out. Here.

FX: Ford pulls the *Guide* out of his satchel.

ARTHUR	You never told me.
FORD PREFECT	I didn't want you to throw it in again.

FX: Ford shakes the *Guide*. It sounds like bits are very likely to fall out. This gadget has seen some action.

FORD PREFECT	It's playing up as it is. I think something's got into it.
ARTHUR	What, like gin?
FORD PREFECT	No. Like it's being updated.

FX: Ford switches on the *Guide*. BZT – then:

THE VOICE	(Distort) *The Hitchhiker's Guide to the Galaxy* has this to say on the – BZT! – subject of flying.
	There is an art – BZT! – or rather a kn-kn-knack to flying – BZT!

FX: The *Guide* fizzles out. Ford thumps it a bit.

FORD PREFECT	(Quietly muttering) Oh, Belgium.

FX: He puts the *Guide* back in his satchel, under:

FORD PREFECT	Hey. Good to see you again, Arthur.
ARTHUR	(Suddenly in a rush) I . . . I . . . I haven't seen anyone for years! I can hardly even remember how to speak! I keep forgetting . . . erm . . .
FORD PREFECT	Birthdays?
ARTHUR	Words! I practise by talking to . . . What are those things people think you're mad if you talk to, like George III?
FORD PREFECT	Kings?

ARTHUR   No! No! The things he used to talk to. We're surrounded by them, for Heaven's sake. Trees! Trees! I practise by talking to trees! I've got names for them! I call them Sycamore One, and Sycamore Two and . . .

FORD PREFECT   Arthur . . .

ARTHUR   What?

FORD PREFECT   Insanity is a gradual process – don't rush it.

ARTHUR   I'm just telling you their names.

FORD PREFECT   We have something else to do.

ARTHUR   I'm not going to ask, but imagine I have.

FORD PREFECT   **(Urgently)** I don't know. But things are going to happen. I have detected disturbances in the wash!

ARTHUR   **(Stupidly)** Is that why the dye ran in my dressing gown?

FORD PREFECT   The space-time wash!

ARTHUR   Of course, the new Vogon laundromat on the Balls Pond Hyperlink.

FORD PREFECT   Eddies in the space-time continuum!

ARTHUR   Is he, indeed . . .

FORD PREFECT   **(Angrily)** Listen! **(Then very very patiently)** There seem to be . . . some pools of instability . . . in the fabric . . . of space-time!

ARTHUR   Not to mention the fabric of my dressing gown.

FORD PREFECT   Arthur!

ARTHUR   The difficulty with this conversation is that it's very different from the ones I've mostly had recently, which, as I explained, have mostly been with trees. They weren't like this. Except the ones with elms used to get a bit bogged down.

FORD PREFECT   Will you *listen*!

ARTHUR   I have been, but I don't think it's helping.

FORD PREFECT   Oh, dear suffering Zarquon.

ARTHUR   I . . . I—

FX: The Sens-O-Matic pulled suddenly from Ford's satchel, where it has started wibbling in an altogether more confident manner.

FORD PREFECT	**(Sudden urgency)** Look! Look! The Sens-O-Matic! It's flashing! Either it's a moving disturbance in the fabric of space-time, an eddy, a pool of instability, somewhere in our vicinity—
ARTHUR	Or a flat battery?

FX: Wibbling stronger than ever. This is a big one.

FORD PREFECT	The flashes are getting stronger . . . There!! There!!! – Behind that sofa!
ARTHUR	**(Almost frightened by the absurdity of it)** Why . . . is there a sofa, in that field?
FORD PREFECT	I told you! Eddies in the space-time continuum!
ARTHUR	Then tell him to come and collect his sofa.
FORD PREFECT	**(Bored with this now)** Arthur! That sofa is there because of the space-time instability I've been trying to get your terminally softened brain to come to grips with. It's been washed up out of the continuum. It's cosmic jetsam! It's our only way out of here! **(Runs off)** Come on! It's flying away from us!
ARTHUR	**(Suddenly starting to run)** Yeeeehaaaaaa!
FORD PREFECT	Towards you! Head it off!
ARTHUR	It's turning towards the trees!
FORD PREFECT	After it! Watch out for the ditch!
ARTHUR	**(Panting as he runs)** Ford! This is almost fun – whatever that was.
FORD PREFECT	**(Off)** What?
ARTHUR	I mean, it's not often a day goes so perfectly to plan, is it?
FORD PREFECT	**(Off)** Come on!
ARTHUR	Damn! Missed it! Only a few minutes ago, I decided . . . I . . . would . . . go mad . . . and here I am already . . . chasing a chesterfield sofa across the fields of prehistoric Earth – watching out for a non-existent ditch – ahhh—

FX: Splosh, drippy footsteps.

ARTHUR	**(cont'd)** Ugh . . .
FORD PREFECT	Get round the other side, that's it. Jump into it! Come on, Arthur! Juuuuummmmp!!!!!
FORD/ARTHUR	**(Disappearing into time)** Whoooooooaaaaaaaaaaaa . . .

13

FX: The sofa they jump upon is caught in an eddy of the space-time continuum. It is sucked into the future like a soap bubble spinning down a plughole. Twigs, leaves and loose forest debris are dragged with it into the vortex. Then, suddenly, it is gone. Peace returns to prehistoric Islington. A bird twitters uncertainly.

INT. – THE BOOK AMBIENCE

THE VOICE   Many speak of the legendary and gigantic *Starship Titanic*, a majestic and luxurious cruise-liner launched from the great shipbuilding asteroids of Artifactovol some hundreds of years ago now, and with good reason.

It was sensationally beautiful, staggeringly huge and more pleasantly equipped than any ship in what now remains of history.

The *Starship Titanic*'s prototype Improbability Field was meant, supposedly, to ensure that it was Infinitely Improbable that anything would ever go wrong with any part of the ship.

FX: Breathless crowd at starship launch, burst into applause, under:

THE VOICE   Its designers didn't realize that because of the quasi-reciprocal and circular nature of all Improbability calculations, anything that was Infinitely Improbable was actually very likely to happen almost immediately.

POSH WOMAN   (PA slap) I name this vessel *Starship Titanic*.

THE VOICE   Thus, when *Starship Titanic* was launched –

POSH WOMAN   May Providence be with her and all who voyage in her . . .

FX: Sounds of cheering and of bottle smashing.

THE VOICE   – it did not even manage to complete its very first radio message – an SOS –

FX: Furious Morse code tapping, totally useless in a future where Morse code has been long abandoned, but suitably improbable under the circumstances.

THE VOICE   – before undergoing a sudden and gratuitous total existence failure.

FX: The *Starship Titanic* simply fails to continue to exist on this level of probability. With nothing to support, a few supporting struts crash down. The Improbability converters grind to a halt, under:

POSH WOMAN   Oh . . .

FX: Inter-Galactic insurance underwriters closed loop updates buzzing, under:

14

THE VOICE	This only encouraged further development. As soon as the insurance under-writers had recovered enough to insert suitable clauses into the relevant policies, the luxury cruiser *Heart of Gold* was built around an improved Improbability Drive –

FX: Airlock door opened by reckless two-headed adventurer.

ZAPHOD	Oooh! Freeooow! The *Heart of Gold*!

FX: Intruder alarm is tripped.

THE VOICE	– powered by a sculpted yellow metal nugget of such purity that it was only a matter of time before some reckless two-headed adventurer would attempt to steal it.

ZAPHOD	Hi, there.

FX: Guard felled by a single punch. Zaphod has a mean left hook. Which is just as well, his right hand is holding a complimentary souvenir launch-day VIP-lounge Pan Galactic Gargle Blaster.

POSH WOMAN 2	(under:) We name this starship *Heart of Gold*.

THE VOICE	But that was in the days when Zaphod Beeblebrox was young, brash and terrifyingly electable.

FX: *Heart of Gold* powering up.

POSH WOMAN 2	And now a word from President Beeblebrox . . .

ZAPHOD	(Radio distort) Bye!

FX: *Heart of Gold* roars away.

POSH WOMAN 2	Oh.

FX: Crowd disappointment.

THE VOICE	Now he is older, brasher and not in a mood to entertain the automated systems that once made the *Heart of Gold* a playbeing's dream . . .

INT. – STARSHIP *HEART OF GOLD*

FX: Door whirr.

DOOR	Pleased to open for you.

ZAPHOD	(He is drinking) Zark off.

DOOR	Thank you.

15

FX: Door whirr.

DOOR   Ahhh. Have a nice day.

ZAPHOD   And ruin a perfectly good hangover? **(Sound of ice)**

TRILLIAN   Zaphod. You're spilling that everywhere!

ZAPHOD   Oh, Zark! **(Chugs it down)** Thanks, baby. I'd better send another one down. To check the first one's OK.

FX: Drinks poured, Zaphod chugging them down, alternate heads drinking and speaking throughout:

ZAPHOD   **(Swallows)** Weird. It's like my stomach's holding a party and I'm not on the guest list.

TRILLIAN   There's no one chasing us, we're free for the first time in ages—

ZAPHOD   Freedom, yeah. Here I am, Zaphod Beeblebrox, I'm the coolest guy since cryogenics, and I've got a girl with whom things seem to be working out pretty well –

TRILLIAN   **(Quietly)** Are they?

ZAPHOD   – I should be feeling extremely hoopy about life right now. Except I'm not.

TRILLIAN   **(Trying hard)** Look, let's go somewhere! Travel. See the Universe. Come on. There's nothing the Improbability Drive can't do.

ZAPHOD   Yeah, like, provided you know exactly how improbable it is that what you want it to do will ever happen. What did happen, by the way?

TRILLIAN   **(Who is not alone in looking for a way to explain this unavoidable anomaly)** You had a double psychotic episode, ran off to Ursa Minor to prove some conspiracy theory, only to be found days later wandering the corridors of the *Hitchhiker's Guide* building looking for Zarniwoop, a free lunch and a stiff drink. But not in that order.

ZAPHOD   Which proves I *was* there, right?

TRILLIAN   Well, I wasn't.

ZAPHOD   **(Drunk)** Wow – totally too much excitement, adventure and really wild things . . .

TRILLIAN   They're all hallucinations!

ZAPHOD   Hey, the Total Perspective Vortex was not a hallucination!

TRILLIAN   Or you had one Pan Galactic Gargle Blaster too many.

ZAPHOD	**(Stung) (Reflex)** That's not technically possible.
	FX: Another drink poured, Zaphod chugs it down.
TRILLIAN	How is that going to help?
ZAPHOD	The third drink is going down to see why the second hasn't yet reported on the condition of the first. You know, looking at you two I think I prefer the other Trillian.
TRILLIAN	Good, 'cos this one's just about had enough!
	FX: Bottle clumsy clunk on glass. Two belches, one for each head.
ZAPHOD	**(Suddenly slurred)** Ah. All drinks have reported in. Share and enjoy. Whurgh.
	FX: He falls off his chair untidily.
TRILLIAN	**(Sighs, to self)** Oh, give me a break . . .
	FX: *Hitchhiker's Guide* **start-up chime.**
THE VOICE	**(Through unit speaker – tinny)** Holidays. One of the Galaxy's most unusual holiday destinations is Allosimanus Syneca—
TRILLIAN	Mm.
THE VOICE	The trek from the snow plains of Liska to the summit of the Ice Crystal Pyramids of Sastantua is long and gruelling, but the view from the top is one which releases the mind to hitherto unexperienced horizons of beauty.
TRILLIAN	That'll do nicely. **(Shuts off *Guide*)** Computer?
EDDIE THE COMPUTER	Hi, there! Eddie the shipboard computer standing by for—
TRILLIAN	New course heading. Allosimanus Syneca.
EDDIE THE COMPUTER	You got it!
	FX: The hyperdrive starts to power up.
ZAPHOD	**(From the floor, slurry)** Trillian. If it was all a hallucination . . .
TRILLIAN	Yes?
ZAPHOD	What happened to that zarking robot?

EXT. – SQUORNSHELLOUS ZETA, THE MATTRESS PLANET – SWAMP

FX: Marvin trudging round in a circle in the swamp. In the distance, wild mattresses are willoming . . .

MARVIN	(He trudges a bit, stops for a heartfelt sigh) Aaaaaah. (Carries on trudging. Then, miserably) Another world, another day . . . In fourteen hours the sun will sink hopelessly beneath the opposite horizon of Squornshellous Zeta. Totally wasted effort, if you ask me. Not that there is anyone here to ask me. So I'll just keep walking around in this very tiny circle for a few hundred years more until my power cells give out.
	FX: A mattress flollops up to him, squidging in the soft ooze.
ZEM THE MATTRESS	(Offensively breezy) Hallo, robot.
MARVIN	(Bored) Hallo, mattress.
ZEM THE MATTRESS	(Brought up short) Oh. (Then, brightly) What's a mattress?
MARVIN	You are.
ZEM THE MATTRESS	Oh . . . (Then, brightly) Happy?
MARVIN	But clearly you are a very stupid one.
ZEM THE MATTRESS	(Not in the least insulted) We could have a conversation. Would you like that?
MARVIN	No. And after I have calculated to ten significant decimal places what precise length of pause is most likely to convey a general contempt for all things mattressy, I will continue to walk round in tight circles. Don't mind me – not that you do anyway.
ZEM THE MATTRESS	(Again, brightly) What's a mattress?
MARVIN	You are. You are a large mattress, and probably one of very high quality.
ZEM THE MATTRESS	Really?
MARVIN	Yes.

INT. – THE BOOK AMBIENCE

THE VOICE	In an infinitely large Universe, such as, for instance, the one in which we live, most things one could possibly imagine, and a lot of things one would rather not, grow somewhere. Thus it is that very few things actually get manufactured these days.

A forest was discovered recently in which most of the trees grew ratchet screwdrivers as fruit. The life cycle of a ratchet-screwdriver fruit is quite interesting. Once picked it needs a dark dusty drawer in which it can lie undisturbed for years. Then one night it suddenly hatches, discards its outer skin, which crumbles into dust, and emerges as a totally unidentifiable little |

metal object with flanges at both ends and a sort of ridge and a sort of hole for a screw. This, when found, will get thrown away. No one knows what it is supposed to gain from this. Nature, in her infinite wisdom, is presumably working on it.

No one really knows what mattresses are meant to gain from their lives either. They're large, friendly, pocket-sprung creatures which live quiet private lives in the swamps of Squornshellous Zeta.

ZEM THE MATTRESS	**(For they are all Zem)** Willomywillomyillomyillomyillomyillomyillomyillomyillomyillomy . . .
ZEM THE MATTRESS	Hallo, Zem!
ZEM THE MATTRESS	Hallo, Zem!
ZEM THE MATTRESS	Hallo, Zem and Zem!
ZEM THE MATTRESS	Hallo, Zem, have you seen – oh, there you are, Zem!
ZEM THE MATTRESS	Your willoming is much improved, Zem.
ZEM THE MATTRESS	Voon! I gup at the thought!
ZEM THE MATTRESS	Globber globber.
ZEM THE MATTRESS	Why do you globber so, Zem?
ZEM THE MATTRESS	I miss Zem. He has gone to be slept on.
ZEM THE MATTRESS	**(Arriving)** Hallo, Zem, Zem and Zem!
ZEM THE MATTRESS	**(All three)** Hallo, Zem!
ZEM THE MATTRESS	Let's flollop!
ZEM THE MATTRESS	Let's flurble!
THE VOICE	They flollop about, blowing bubbles through the water, their blue and white stripes glistening in the feeble rays of its sun. Many of them get caught, slaughtered, dried out, shipped out and slept on. None of them seem to mind and all of them are called Zem.

EXT. – SQUORNSHELLOUS ZETA, THE MATTRESS PLANET – SWAMP

FX: Marvin trudging round in his circle. The sun has risen above the mist and is a little brighter now, but as he wouldn't even be pleased to find himself on a Hawaiian beach holding a pina colada, with all the diodes down his left-hand side replaced, back to the plot:

ZEM THE MATTRESS	**(Invincibly cheerful)** – Zem. And what's your name, robot?

19

MARVIN	(Deep sigh) Marvin.
ZEM THE MATTRESS	I vollue a deep dejection in your diodes, robot. And I globber for you. Globbbabbbabbbabberrr.
MARVIN	Must you? I think you should know that your globbering has not eased my dejection by a single jot.
ZEM THE MATTRESS	You should be more mattressy. We live quiet, retired lives in the swamp, where we are content to flollop and vollue and regard the wetness in a fairly floopy manner.
MARVIN	If there is anything more unappealing, I expect it's your attention span. We've had this conversation every day since I arrived here.
ZEM THE MATTRESS	We could discuss the weather a little.
MARVIN	I suppose so. (With great deliberation) Ahem. (Spoken) The dew has clearly fallen with a particularly sickening thud this morning. If I had teeth, I would grit them at this point.
ZEM THE MATTRESS	(Infuriatingly) Would you care to come for a flollop?
MARVIN	No. Not because I find the concept depressing, which I most certainly do, but because I have been fitted with this infinitely more depressing artificial leg. As it is just the one steel peg I can only pivot on it in very tiny circles, gradually digging myself deeper into this swamp. Flolloping is therefore not an option.
ZEM THE MATTRESS	Voon. I feel deep in my innermost sprung pockets that you have something on your mind.
MARVIN	More than you can possibly imagine. My capacity for mental activity of all kinds is as boundless as the infinite reaches of space itself. As opposed to my capacity for happiness. My capacity for happiness you could fit into a matchbox without taking out the matches first.
ZEM THE MATTRESS	Right . . . (Brightly) What's a matchbox?
MARVIN	(Sighs even more deeply than before)

INT. – THE *HEART OF GOLD* – ZAPHOD'S BATHROOM

FX: The sound of Zaphod brushing both sets of teeth under:

EDDIE THE COMPUTER	(Through intercom) We are in parking orbit over Allosimanus Syneca, guys.
ZAPHOD	(Stops brushing) Where?

TRILLIAN	(Through intercom) Zaphod, where are you?

FX: Click.

ZAPHOD	In the bathroom. **(More teeth brushing. Both sets)**
TRILLIAN	**(Distort)** What are you doing in there?
ZAPHOD	Staying.
TRILLIAN	How are you feeling?

FX: Zaphod gargles (left) at one pitch. Then (right) at another pitch. Then both together in whatever harmony Mark can muster.

TRILLIAN	Is that as bad as it sounds?
ZAPHOD	Hey, I was worse earlier. But then I thought that I could look for someone in the Universe more miserable than me. Halfway to the bridge I realized that it might be Marvin, so I'm going back to bed.
TRILLIAN	**(Distorted)** We're parked over Allosimanus Syneca. It looks beautiful from the teleport room.
ZAPHOD	Sure.
TRILLIAN	We could go down later—
ZAPHOD	Hey, no . . . thanks. Please.
TRILLIAN	**(Distorted)** I deactivated all the kitchen synthomatics. **(Zaphod groans)** I've prepared the most fabulous meal for you –

INT. – *HEART OF GOLD* – TELEPORT ROOM

FX: Rattling of tray loaded with goodies.

TRILLIAN	– oiled meals, scented fruits . . .
ZAPHOD	**(Distorted)** Yeah, yeah, yeah.
TRILLIAN	**(Low, to self)** And I've got a first-class degree in mathematics and a doctorate in astrophysics, but we'll let that pass. **(Up)** Zaphod?
ZAPHOD	**(Distorted)** I'm not hungry.
TRILLIAN	I've put some on a tray. If you don't want the candlelit supper you can eat it in bed. Either way we should talk things through.
ZAPHOD	**(Distorted)** No.

TRILLIAN	(Resolve) Is that all you've got to say? (Nothing but silence) I'll take that no as a yes.
	FX: Click.
TRILLIAN	(Effort) *Unf!*
	FX: Trillian throws the tray of food aside.
TRILLIAN	Enough! Eddie, activate teleporter. Destination—
EDDIE THE COMPUTER	Planet surface?
TRILLIAN	Random coordinates. Transport me the hell out of Zaphod Beeblebrox's life.
EDDIE THE COMPUTER	You got it.
	FX: Transporter beam activated.

INT. – THE *HEART OF GOLD* – BATHROOM

ZAPHOD	(More to himself than to Trillian) Hey, baby. You remind me of something Ford once said. He spent a whole while stuck on Earth with your monkey race and they used to amaze him the way they kept on talking, like just always stating the really obvious, you know. Like, 'It's a nice day,' or 'You're very tall,' or 'Oh dear, you seem to have fallen down a thirty-foot well, are you all right?' Ha ha ha! Yeah, and he thought if human beings don't keep exercising their lips their mouths would probably seize up. Then he watched them a bit more, you know, and came up with a whole new theory. He said that if they don't keep exercising their lips their brains start working. That is so true.
	Trillian? . . . Trillian?! (Pause) You'll be back, baby . . . (He goes back to brushing his teeth)

INT. – THE BOOK AMBIENCE

THE VOICE	What will become of Trillian now she has escaped the gravitational pull of Zaphod Beeblebrox' ego? Where in the space-time continuum are Arthur Dent and Ford Prefect likely to wash up? And what vital issues pivot on Marvin's artificial leg? Find out in the next bi-podal part of the Tertiary Phase of *The Hitchhiker's Guide to the Galaxy* . . .
ANNOUNCER	Non-orthopaedically sprung life forms are reminded that mattresses are the only sentient creatures to require regular flolloping.

FOOTNOTES

The opening sequence If we had actually managed to get the Tertiary Phase of *Hitchhiker's* on the air in 1993, Douglas and I would have been more sonically daring when kicking things off again. At one point we discussed a soundscape montage of the story so far, and at separate times I had discussions with John Whitehall (who provided some music and effects for the original episodes) and Mark Russell (who scored my *Batman: Knightfall* Radio 1 series) about a music bed to go under it. Frankie Goes To Hollywood's 'Two Tribes' was being mooted as a musical model at one point, this was the extent of the makeover being considered!

A decade later, however, when the Tertiary, Quandary and Quintessential phases were finally to be recorded, it seemed more appropriate that the first new *Hitchhiker's* to be heard for nearly twenty-five years should ease the new generation of listeners into the story more gently. The beginning should reassure, as if nothing had changed at all. John Marsh's voice is the same as ever, so we were home and dry there. However, in an ideal world the late Peter Jones should be the next voice heard, and there were two speeches by the narrator in Primary Phase Episodes One and Three which effectively told the back-story we needed. We knew Bill Franklyn would be the perfect voice to 'evolve' Peter, and Bruce suggested somehow morphing one into the other. Although I put in an effect (BZT!) to help mask the joins, Bill's reading was so close to Peter's (without any playback of the latter's performance to provide a template) that there are a couple of edits where they seem to flow eerily in and out of each other.

The Voice as narrative tool There has been debate about the changing function of the narrative voice between the old and new radio series. The fact is, however, that whether our 'Voice of the Book' was Peter Jones or Bill Franklyn, the biggest change is the stylistic difference between the original radio series and the later novels, where Douglas is less likely to jump off into an objective discourse on some exotic-if-slightly-related topic in mid-scene. Also I should note that whereas we have called this role 'The Voice of the Book', Peter Jones's part was identified as 'Narrator' in the original scripts, so his function was made pretty clear. In fact, there are many occasions in the original series where Peter provides straightforward scene-setting – I have just opened this book's predecessor at random and found Peter's 'Fit the Fourth' line 'For Zaphod, Ford and Trillian surprise is pushed to its very limits when *this* happens . . .'. You don't get much more plot-interactive than that. With such examples in mind, and where no discussion on the life cycle of the ratchet-screwdriver fruit or Bistromathics was possible, it seemed perfectly in order to use the Voice for purely narrative purposes, particularly in the more complicated stretches of the Tertiary Phase. By comparison the action in the Quandary and Quintessential Phases is more linear and consequently the Voice can be used more sparingly in narration, resorting to its more didactic style.

The Hrarf-Hrarf	This is a bit of Douglas unique to the radio series (as far as I know), written in the stressful time following the delivery by Alick Rowe (an excellent and not to be interpreted as anything *but* excellent writer) of a very funny and skilfully written but rather too inventive first-draft adaptation. Despite the fact that Douglas was banging out a draft of his own to demonstrate to me how a straightforward dramatization of the book and its dialogue was what he would prefer, like Alick he could not curb his own inventive urges, and thus the Hrarf-Hrarf were born . . . or perhaps resurrected – I'm not sure of the correct expression given their antichronological metabolic dispositions . . .
'There are cakes over there . . .'	'Never cut Funny,' says Joseph Bologna's character in Mel Brooks' 1982 film, *My Favorite Year*. 'There are cakes . . .' was a very apposite studio ad-lib by Toby Longworth which I at first edited out in a spirit of rigid adherence to Douglas's legacy. I then edited it back in again. On reflection, it fitted the *Hitchhiker's* style, and was Funny.
	When one is lucky enough to work with really gifted actors a performance that evolves out of a common understanding of the piece is one's aim, but if it is further informed by a sense of Fun, that's gold dust. Genuine Fun, like the ozone layer, appears to be in increasingly short supply.
Arthur stranded on prehistoric Earth/ Zaphod's dream	There was much confusion at how this first episode of the Tertiary Phase failed to follow on in any salient respect from the end of the Secondary Phase. At the last known point in the radio narrative Arthur had stolen the *Heart of Gold*, stranding Ford, Zaphod and Zarniwoop in the Shack with the Man and His Cat.
	When we discussed these new series in 1993 Douglas shrugged off this problem; it was history for him and if it led to consternation among *Hitchhiker* fans, too bad. The discontinuity between the radio series and the novels was unfortunate but necessary, Douglas having had a re-ordering of events in the process of novelization. He wasn't deliberately seeking to confound, but anxious to polish and refine and make the story his own, even at the expense of reworking or ditching material that had already been broadcast.
	Ten years later, I was still bound to the chronology of the novels but by now the first and second radio series (complete with hanging resolution) had attained iconic status. Not only were lines of dialogue quoted in almost every context possible (particularly on the Internet, hardly a presence in 1993), but whole *Hitchhiker* scenarios had become cultural reference points. I did not have Douglas's right as Creator to ignore the chasm between the stories, but on the other hand he was no longer around to consult further on the issue. In the long term I would need to square the circle, but in order to get on with the complexities of the Tertiary Phase, events in the second radio series would need – temporarily for now – to be rendered incidental. It was either that or I should invent something to bridge the gap. This I did not want to do without Douglas available to rework material himself. My first rule of adaptation was not to invent where at all possible; certainly not where Douglas

had buried any kind of storyline which I could retrieve. So what clues had he furnished which I could use?

In Episode One of the Secondary Phase a troubled Zaphod Beeblebrox (through whose eyes we witness most of its events) visits the *Hitchhiker's Guide* building to prove a conspiracy theory centred upon a certain Zarniwoop, who has built a virtual-reality universe in his office. Once Zaphod is in the building (and presumably in Zarniwoop's domain) it is debatable whether any series-two events are taking place in the *real* universe at all, including Arthur stealing the *Heart of Gold*, the Man in the Shack, the Lintilla Clones and the Shoe Event Horizon.

Considered in retrospect, series two *could* be Zaphod's hallucination, brought on by too many Pan Galactic Gargle Blasters, or Zaphod's immersion in the Total Perspective Vortex. Or perhaps it was entirely experienced inside the Virtual Universe created by the somewhat sinister Zarniwoop. Although a detailed answer to this conundrum could not be explored in the Tertiary Phase, which had imperatives of its own, the puzzle they outlined temporarily bridged our credibility gap. It also gave me something to turn completely upside down, Douglas-fashion, in the Quintessential Phase. (I hope you're following this. I'm game to continue if you are. You are? OK.)

Conveniently for this theory Trillian was unexplainedly absent for the entirety of the Secondary Phase, so the quickest way to put the problem on 'hold' was for her to suggest that the entire Phase was the result of a profound extra-reality trip experienced by Zaphod alone. This incidentally helped ease through a pivotal moment in the saga, becoming one of the final straws that make Trillian's decision to leave him more understandable. He's drunk, unreasonable, egocentric *and* he makes up wild stories that don't stack up. He is one mixed up, infuriating, substance-abusing two-headed dude.

Trillian at last escapes the shadow cast by Zaphod's ego to gain a new confidence in herself. This confidence will be vital for the future of both the Universe and of Arthur Dent, and will play out over the remaining fourteen episodes, the last four of which will *return* to the puzzle of what happened to series two and – combining Douglas's logic with the story threads in *Mostly Harmless* – suddenly make it of vital importance to the entire saga.

Zaphod steals the *Heart of Gold* — In post-production I realized that our first encounter with Zaphod was a rather downbeat and sad affair, not depicting the fun-loving adventurer we met in previous series. Thus in a form of flashback I used some out-takes to 'build' the events surrounding the theft of the *Heart of Gold*, and hopefully establish his swashbuckling credentials.

Allosimanus Syneca — In the book, Douglas wrote Allosimanius Syneca, but when he read it for the audiobook he said Allosimanus, so we took his cue here.

Marvin and Zem — This scene took a couple of days to record. On the first day Stephen was so pleased to be back with the 'old gang' that on listening back I was worried Marvin was sounding a bit too cheerful, and getting Andy Taylor's wonderful Zem the Mattress characterization to sound more ingenuous than simple took some experimentation. We finally hit the right stride on day two of recording, adding treatments 'on the fly' to Stephen's voice. Finding the Marvin effect was itself a challenge; such is the rate of obsolescence in studio gear that the harmonizer originally used is now a museum piece, and we had to find a similar treatment using a newer bit of outboard gear that has hundreds of pre-programmed settings, each one identified with a number. As Paul Deeley dialled each one in we listened to Stephen's voice, until finally Marvin's voice popped out of the speakers. 'What's the programme number?' I asked, ready to scribble it down. 'You won't believe this,' replied Paul. 'Forty-two.'

Incidentally, the scenes in which Marvin appeared were recorded in a more linear fashion than those in the original series in the late 1970s, when Stephen was recorded away from the other actors and had his voice treated and spliced in (using razor blade and sticky tape) afterwards. Geoffrey Perkins did an amazing job with preserving the comic timing but it would have been a nightmare to direct and occasionally – in reverby (echoey) acoustics – the cuts are hard to mask. This time around we treated Stephen 'live' and channelled his voice through a small loudspeaker that was carried around the stereo microphone to interact with the rest of the cast as they moved around in the scene. It meant they could perform off each other in real time, bouncing lines and getting timings for gags on the spot.

Zem's squelching in the swamp was Ken Humphrey up to his elbows in a washing-up bowl of soggy papier mâché. This stood around the studio ripening for several days until it really *did* smell of swamp – or maybe that was Ken . . .

Closing scene **(extended version only)** This self-dialogue of Zaphod's is not in *Life, the Universe and Everything*; it was a thought by Ford in Chapter Five of the original first novel and my attempt to try and include as much unheard-on-radio Douglas material as possible. In fact Chapter Five of the first novel also provided the description of Vogons used at the start of the Quandary Phase Episode One; this is the joy of being able to go back and dig out stuff which Douglas added after the original radio series was done and dusted.

EPISODE TWO

SIGNATURE TUNE

ANNOUNCER   *The Hitchhiker's Guide to the Galaxy*, by Douglas Adams, Tertiary Phase.

INT. – THE BOOK AMBIENCE

FX: Melee of exotic sounds. Falling down a tunnel swirly texture as in Episode One where Arthur and Ford are travelling through time. Lots of surround panning.

ARTHUR/FORD PREFECT   Whooooaaaaaaaaaaa . . . .

ARTHUR   **(Dialogue from the Primary Phase)** Ford, I don't know if this sounds like a silly question, but what am I doing here?

FORD PREFECT   Well, you know that. I rescued you from the Earth.

THE VOICE   One of the many problems encountered in time travel is quite simply one of grammar, which is further complicated by the possibility of conducting conversations whilst you're actually travelling from one time to another.

FX: In the background Vogon constructor fleets are heard calmly destroying entire solar systems, trying to keep their hyperspace bypass on schedule.

ARTHUR   What is it?

FORD PREFECT   *The Hitchhiker's Guide to the Galaxy*. It's an electronic book, which will tell you everything you want to know.

ARTHUR   I like the cover. 'Don't Panic'.

FORD PREFECT   You'll need to have this fish in your ear.

ARTHUR   I *beg* your pardon?

VOGON   People of Aparoon, this is Prostetnic Vogon Kutz . . .

SECOND VOGON   People of Regulo 7. This is Prostetnic Vogon Yang . . .

ARTHUR   And what has *happened* to the Earth?

PROSTETNIC VOGON JELTZ	People of Earth. This is Prostetnic Vogon Jeltz of the Galactic Hyperspace Planning Council . . .
FORD PREFECT	It's been . . . disintegrated.
PROSTETNIC VOGON JELTZ	. . . your planet is scheduled for demolition.

FX: Earth explodes, rather offhandedly.

ARTHUR	So what do I do?
FORD PREFECT	Well, you come along with me and enjoy yourself.

INT. – THE BOOK AMBIENCE

THE VOICE *The Encyclopaedia Galactica* has much to say on the theory and practice of time travel, most of which is incomprehensible to anyone who hasn't spent at least four lifetimes studying advanced hypermathematics, and since it was impossible to do this before time travel was invented, there is a certain amount of confusion as to how the idea was arrived at in the first place.

The most plausible rationalization states that time travel was, by its very nature, discovered simultaneously at all periods of history. But this is clearly bunk. The trouble is that quite a lot of history is clearly bunk, the realization of which led to the immediate formation of the Campaign for Real Time. It was during its inaugural strategy meeting and coffee morning – at which it was formally agreed a real time was being had by all – that the news broke that not only had the great Cathedral of Chalesm been pulled down in order to build a new negative-ion refinery, but that the construction of the refinery had taken so long, and had had to extend so far back into the past in order to allow negative-ion production to start on time, that the Cathedral of Chalesm had now never been built in the first place. Picture postcards of the cathedral suddenly became immensely valuable. And blank. Which is why – as a result of time travel – much of history is now gone for ever. In a footnote, the Campaign for Real Timers explain that just as easy travel eroded the differences between one country and another, and between one world and another, so time travel is now eroding the differences between one age and another. 'The past,' they say, 'is now truly like a foreign country. They do things exactly the same there.'

EXT. – LORD'S CRICKET GROUND

FX: Sound of two humanoid life forms on a paisley-covered chesterfield sofa crashing heavily down at silly mid-on.

ARTHUR/FORD	Aaaaaaaaaah – Ooof! . . . Ooof!
FORD PREFECT	**(Urgent whisper)** Watch out!

FX: Crack of leather on willow, and then a whizzing noise.

ARTHUR	What was that?
FORD PREFECT	Something red!

FX: Applause, actuality of a cricket match around them.

HENRY BLOFELD	**(Distorted, heard faintly on someone's radio)** No, it goes straight past Foster at silly mid-on, and –

INT. – LORD'S CRICKET GROUND – COMMENTARY BOX

HENRY BLOFELD	**(cont'd)** – over the boundary for four lovely runs. And now England need just twenty-eight to win the final test on this near-perfect day at Lord's. Holden returning the ball and, Fred, my dear old thing, what on earth is that?
FRED TRUEMAN	It looks like two men and a chesterfield sofa. Can anybody tell me what is going off? Henry, I don't know!

FX: They fade out for the moment, under . . .

EXT. – LORD'S CRICKET GROUND – THE PITCH

(Ford and Arthur are speaking to each other in urgent, frightened whispers)

ARTHUR	Where are we?
FORD PREFECT	Somewhere green!
ARTHUR	Shapes! I need shapes!
POLICEMAN	**(Approaching)** Excuse me, sir, is this your sofa?
FORD PREFECT	What was that?
ARTHUR	Something blue!
FORD PREFECT	Shape!
ARTHUR	It is blue-shaped . . . like a policeman!
POLICEMAN	Come along, you two, let's be having you.
POLICEMAN'S WALKIE-TALKIE	**(Distorted)** Three to control. We have a man seems to have had a heart attack at the Nursery End. St John's Ambulance in attendance, over?

29

ARTHUR	Ford, if I didn't know I was going mad, I'd say this place looks astoundingly, terrifyingly, horrifically like Lord's Cricket Ground!
UMPIRE	(Background, testily) Can we clear the pitch, please, officer?
POLICEMAN	Very astute of you, sir.
ARTHUR	(Starts to hyperventilate hysterically) Agh! It is a policeman, Ford! There's always a policeman at Lord's! What are we going to do?
FORD PREFECT	(Laconically) What do you want to do? Get a beer?
ARTHUR	I want to hear you say I've been dreaming for the past five years!
FORD PREFECT	(Obligingly) You've been dreaming for the past five years.
POLICEMAN	(Firmly) Come along now.
FORD PREFECT	(Without qualifying adverb) All right; four and three-quarters.
POLICEMAN'S WALKIE-TALKIE	(Under) (Distorted) Three to control, casualty's name is Deodat, history of heart trouble, get 'em to hurry, looks dodgy . . .
ARTHUR	(More calmly) It's all right, officer. This is all a dream. Ask him. He was in it.
POLICEMAN	Dreaming, eh? Account for the dressing gown, would it?
ARTHUR	(Reasonably . . .) Oh no, the dressing gown's just a hallucination, you see. It's what I was wearing when the Earth was demolished to— Ugh! Ugh! Ugh! I've got a bone in my beard! Ugh! I've got a beard! Ugh! Tell you what I'll do. I'll be the one over there passing out. How about that? Good idea?

FX: Belated thump as he passes out, under:

FORD PREFECT	(Terse, businesslike) Officer, my name is Ford Prefect. I was born six hundred light years from Earth, near Betelgeuse. I am a researcher for *The Hitchhiker's Guide to the Galaxy.*
POLICEMAN	(Not again) Bit old for student pranks, aren't we, sir?
FORD PREFECT	*That* is Arthur Dent. He's from Earth but has been stranded in your prehistoric era for a while.
POLICEMAN	(Getting too confused to bother) Yes, well . . . (Moves off) Just don't let it happen again . . .

INT. – LORD'S CRICKET GROUND – COMMENTARY BOX

FRED TRUEMAN	Well, Henry, I don't think there have been any strange things appearing on the pitch since—

HENRY BLOFELD	It was in 1932, Fred.
FRED TRUEMAN	Ah! Now what happened then?
HENRY BLOFELD	Well, Fred, I think it was Canter facing Willcox, coming up to bowl from the pavilion end, when a spectator suddenly ran straight across the pitch.
FRED TRUEMAN	There's nothing actually very mysterious about that, is there?
HENRY BLOFELD	No, but he did claim to have seen something materialize at silly mid-on. An alligator of some kind, if you can believe it. But no one was able to get a very detailed description. They offered to give him some lunch, but he explained that he'd already had rather a good one. So the matter was dropped. And Warwickshire went on to win by three wickets!
FRED TRUEMAN	So not very like this at all, then.
HENRY BLOFELD	No . . . Er – for those of you who've just tuned in, by the way, two men, two rather scruffily attired men, and indeed a sofa – a chesterfield, I think – have just materialized here in the middle of Lord's Cricket Ground.
FRED TRUEMAN	They're carrying it off now.
HENRY BLOFELD	Actually, can I interrupt you a moment, Fred, and say that the sofa has just vanished?
FRED TRUEMAN	So it has! Well, that's one mystery less. So, England now only need twenty-four runs to win the Ashes, and I don't think I've seen anything like that at cover point before. Except perhaps against the West Indies . . . **(Fade)**

INT. – LORD'S CRICKET GROUND – TEA TENT

FX: Background hubbub. Distant cricket match. Ford and Arthur sipping real tea.

FORD PREFECT	How're you feeling?
ARTHUR	**(Dazed but happy)** I'm home! It's England. It's today. I'm **(Takes sip)** drinking tea in the tea tent at Lord's. The long nightmare is over! Why are you looking at me like that?
FORD PREFECT	Just . . .
ARTHUR	Listen, Ford, it's over! I'm finally where I belong. Nothing you can say or do—
FORD PREFECT	OK! OK! Thought you might like to look at the newspaper, that's all.
ARTHUR	No thanks. I've read that one. **(Pause while this sinks in)** Er . . . wait a minute.

FX: Newspaper grabbed by a desperate ape-descended life form whose sanity hangs by a rapidly fraying thread.

FORD PREFECT   Not a word.

ARTHUR   Wait a minute! How can this be today's? I saw this years ago! The day before –

FORD PREFECT   That's right.

ARTHUR   – the Earth was demolished!

FORD PREFECT   Yup.

ARTHUR   So that means the Earth is going to get demolished . . . Tomorrow!

FORD PREFECT   I think you're finally getting the hang of time travel.

ARTHUR   **(Long despairing sigh)** I don't think I can bear it again. **(Pause)** Wait a minute!

FORD PREFECT   **(Firmly)** No. Don't even think about it.

ARTHUR   If this is before I left, that must mean that I am—

FORD PREFECT   **(Sharply)** Don't!

ARTHUR   What?

FORD PREFECT   Try and phone yourself up at home.

ARTHUR   How did you know?

FORD PREFECT   **(Sighs)** People who talk to themselves on the phone never learn anything to their advantage. **(Mouth FX imitating pick up, dialling, ringing tone and distant click)** Hello? Is that Arthur Dent? Ah, hello, yes. This is Arthur Dent speaking. The Earth blows up tomorrow – no, don't hang up!

ARTHUR   What—?

FORD PREFECT   **(Mouth FX 'click' and 1970s dialling tone – brrrrr . . .)** Arthur, this is not my first temporal anomaly. So finish your zarking tea and let's get out of here . . .

EXT. – LORD'S CRICKET GROUND

FX: Play in background. Arthur and Ford walking disconsolately back to the stands . . .

ARTHUR   So we're not home and dry.

FORD PREFECT	We could not even be said to be home and vigorously towelling ourselves off.
ARTHUR	(Sighs heavily)

INT. – THE BOOK AMBIENCE

THE VOICE	*The Hitchhiker's Guide to the Galaxy* has this to say about towels: **(Beat)** see Secondary Phase.

EXT. – LORD'S CRICKET GROUND

FX: Leather on willow. Huge crowd roar. Ball flying towards them.

FORD PREFECT	Nice . . . hit . . .
ARTHUR	Full toss. If they had a fielder standing where we are, the ball would drop straight into his –

FX: Ball drops in Arthur's bag.

ARTHUR	– rabbit-skin bag. Now I'd say that was also a very curious event.
BOY	(Running up) Where's the ball?
ARTHUR	Er – I don't know. It probably rolled off somewhere. Over there, I expect.

FX: Boy runs off.

FORD PREFECT	(With some slight efforty noises) Why didn't you tell him you caught the ball in your bag?
ARTHUR	(Mystified) I don't know. I just got the feeling it might come in useful. Why are you dodging about trying to peer behind the sight screen?
FORD PREFECT	(Efforty noises increasing) That's the other thing – I was going to tell you. Neither you nor the crowd have noticed what is parked behind the sight screen. I think it might be an SEP. Can you see it?
ARTHUR	A what?
FORD PREFECT	An SEP – Somebody Else's Problem.
ARTHUR	Oh, good, I can relax, then.
FORD PREFECT	Not till you tell me if you can see it.
ARTHUR	You said that was somebody else's problem.
FORD PREFECT	That's right. And I want to know if you can see it.

ARTHUR	What does it look like?
FORD PREFECT	(Shouting) How should I know, you fool? If you can see it, you tell me!
ARTHUR	(Rising hysteria. Simon's stock-in-trade – Douglas wrote this, Simon, not me, I am innocent – DM) Ford, I insist that I am not being stupid! You really are gibbering away without any regard for logic or the normal conventions of human discourse, and, all right, I know you're not human but while you're on what is after all my planet, where humans come from, I think you might at least try to—
FORD PREFECT	(Patiently) Arthur, it's perfectly simple. An SEP is something that we can't see, or don't see, or our brain doesn't let us see, because we think that it's somebody else's problem. That's what SEP means. Somebody Else's Problem. The brain just edits it out, it's . . . er . . . like a blind spot. Your only hope is to catch it by surprise out of the corner of your eye.
ARTHUR	Oh. I can see it. It's a spaceship!
FORD PREFECT	What?
ARTHUR	Just a spaceship. Parked behind the sight screen.
FORD PREFECT	Great walloping Zarquon!
ARTHUR	What an utterly extraordinary-looking thing, though. Strange that I couldn't see it . . .

INT. – THE BOOK AMBIENCE

| THE VOICE | Sometimes it's much cheaper and easier to make people think that something works rather than actually make it work. After all, the result is, in all important aspects, the same. The extraordinary-looking spaceship was not actually invisible or anything hyper-impossible like that. The technology involved in making something properly invisible is so mind-bogglingly complex that nine hundred and ninety-nine million, nine hundred and ninety-nine thousand, nine hundred and ninety times out of a billion it's simpler just to take the thing away and hide it.

For instance, the ultra-famous sciento-magician Effrafax of Wug once bet his life that given a year he could render the great megamountain Magramal entirely invisible. |
|---|---|

FX: Lux-O-Valves, Refracto-Nullifiers and Spectrum-Bypass-O-Mats, under:

THE VOICE	(cont'd) Having spent most of the year fruitlessly jiggling around with immense Lux-O-Valves and Refracto-Nullifiers and Spectrum-Bypass-O-Mats, he finally realized, with nine hours to go, that he wasn't going to make it.

EXTREMELY BORING MAN	(There's one at every mountain-hiding event) . . . I can still see it.
THE VOICE	(cont'd) So he and his friends, and his friends' friends and his friends' friends' friends and some friends of theirs who happened to own a major stellar trucking company, put in what is now recognized as being one of the hardest night's work in history, and sure enough Magramal was no longer visible. He lost the bet, and therefore his life, because he was unable to a) just say 'Abracadabra!' and put it back and b) account for the suspicious-looking extra moon overhead.
	The Somebody Else's Problem field is much simpler, more effective and can be run for over a hundred years on a nine-volt battery. This is because it relies on people's natural predisposition not to see anything they don't want to, weren't expecting or can't explain. If Effrafax had, instead of trying to render Magramal invisible, merely rendered it pink and then erected a cheap Somebody Else's Problem field around it, then people would have walked past the mountain, round it, even over it and simply never noticed that the thing was there.
	Meanwhile, events of Universe-shaking magnitude are gathering to a climax . . .
	FX: Tumultuous applause and excitement at the winning stroke of the game.
ARTHUR	(Remarkably helpfully, given the needs of the plot) That's the end of the game!
FORD PREFECT	Why's everybody trying to get at those guys in the middle, what have they done?
ARTHUR	Won the Ashes!
FORD PREFECT	The what?
SLARTIBARTFAST	Exciting, isn't it, Earthman?
ARTHUR	The hallucinations just keep on coming, Ford. For a moment there I thought I heard old Whatshisname. You know, sounds like some sort of Danish chopped sausage.
SLARTIBARTFAST	Slartibartfast. I think your team has just won, Earthman.
FORD PREFECT	Hello, Slartibartfast.
SLARTIBARTFAST	You are English, aren't you, Earthman?
ARTHUR	Er, yes, I . . . What on Earth are you doing here? Or rather, I mean . . . I don't know what I mean!

SLARTIBARTFAST	Winning the Ashes – you must be very proud. I must say, I'm rather fond of cricket myself. Almost entertainingly dull. Though I wouldn't want anyone outside this planet to hear me say so. **(With a shudder)** Oh dear no.
FORD PREFECT	What are you doing here? I thought something terrible had happened.
SLARTIBARTFAST	Something terrible is about to happen.
FORD PREFECT	That's generally true, isn't it? Look, if that monstrosity is your ship, can you give us a lift?
SLARTIBARTFAST	Patience, Ford Prefect . . .
FORD PREFECT	It's just that this planet's about to be demolished.
SLARTIBARTFAST	I know.
FORD PREFECT	And, well, I just wanted to make the point.
SLARTIBARTFAST	Earthman, explain precisely to me what ceremony is now taking place at the centre of the field.
ARTHUR	Er . . . Pitch.
SLARTIBARTFAST	It is a little puzzling.
ARTHUR	You want *me* to explain something to *you*? Well, that's the presentation of the Ashes to the winning captain.
FORD PREFECT	**(Interrupting)** It's just that if we don't go soon we might get caught in the middle of it all again, and there's nothing depresses me more than a planet being senselessly destroyed.
SLARTIBARTFAST	I see. And these Ashes are in that tiny pottery urn?
ARTHUR	Yes.
FORD PREFECT	Except, I suppose, being on it when it happens.
SLARTIBARTFAST	Patience, great things are afoot.
ARTHUR	That's what you said last time.
SLARTIBARTFAST	They were.
ARTHUR	Well, true.
SLARTIBARTFAST	Meet me at my ship in two minutes.
FORD PREFECT	Where are you going?

SLARTIBARTFAST	(Moving away) I have something of vital importance I have to do.
FORD PREFECT	(Shouting after him) I know. You've got to get us off this planet!

INT. – LORD'S CRICKET GROUND – COMMENTARY BOX

FRED TRUEMAN	(Fade up) . . . The players are lined up as the urn containing the Ashes is presented to the captain of the winning team.
HENRY BLOFELD	A wonderful moment, isn't it, but there's an elderly gentleman apparently overcome with the heat, looking just a little bit like Moses, and – I do declare – he's demanding that he should be given the urn.
SLARTIBARTFAST	(Distantly, shouting) I must have the Ashes! They are vitally important for the past, present and future safety of the Galaxy! **(Indignantly, as if having his robes interfered with by an officious umpire)** Do you *mind*?

EXT. – LORD'S CRICKET GROUND, CONTINUOUS

FORD PREFECT	What in the name of zarking fardwarks is the old fool doing?
ARTHUR	I have no idea.
	FX: A Krikkit ship appears in the sky overhead with a noise like a hundred thousand people saying 'wop' – or a distinguished radio cast overdubbed many times.
ARTHUR	Interesting. That's the second spaceship we've seen at Lord's today. And to think I woke up in a prehistoric cave this morning. It's very impressive, hanging up there. Much sleeker than Slartibartfast's, isn't it?
	FX: Krikkit robots' rocket pads ignite. They swirl down from the ship like expensive fireworks.
FORD PREFECT	The hatch is opening . . . One, two, three . . .
ARTHUR	Is that a cricket team arriving from some other galaxy? Or another publicity stunt for Australian margarine?
FORD PREFECT	. . . ten, eleven . . . All in white, carrying bats and balls –
ARTHUR	– and flying down with cricket pads . . . no, *rocket* pads. On their shins.
	FX: A robot lands near them. Rocket pads switch off.
ROBOT	Howzat.
FORD PREFECT	They're dressed like cricketers, but they're *robots*.

ROBOT	Silly mid-on.
	FX: A Krikkit war club propels a Krikkit war grenade into the stands, where it explodes extravagantly.
ARTHUR	What was *that*?!
ROBOT	LBW.
	FX: Another club hits a grenade, another huge explosion.
ARTHUR	Hey!
FORD PREFECT	**(Dragging him away, breathless)** We must get to the ship!
ARTHUR	What is this?
FORD PREFECT	I don't want to know, this is not my planet, I didn't choose to be here, I don't want to get involved!
	FX: Panicking people, screams and explosions.
HENRY BLOFELD	**(Distort, on a radio)** Well, Fred, the supernatural brigade certainly seems to be out in force here at Lord's today . . .
	FX: Explosion as the radio is targeted.
ROBOT	**(Distantly ironic)** Full and bye-bye.
FORD PREFECT	**(Yelling over the din)** What I need is a strong drink and a peer group.
ROBOT	Bodyline.
	FX: Explosions. Mayhem.
ARTHUR	It's incredible – they're doing a bizarre parody of batting strokes, except that every ball they hit explodes where it lands.
FORD PREFECT	I can see that.
ARTHUR	I do not know why they are doing this, but that is what they are doing. They're not just destroying Lord's, they're sending it up . . . Ford, they're taking the—
FORD PREFECT	Precisely.
	FX: The explosions die down. Crowd panic continues.
ROBOTS	We declare.
	FX: Eleven pairs of rocket pads ignite. The robots shoot back up to their ship. Crowd quietens, trying to assess damage.

FORD PREFECT	They don't hang about.
ARTHUR	No.

FX: The Krikkit ship disappears with a noise like a hundred thousand people saying 'foop'.

SLARTIBARTFAST	(Off, indistinct) They've taken the Ashes!
ARTHUR	Good heavens!
FORD PREFECT	What?
ARTHUR	Ashes. The remains of a cricket stump burnt in Melbourne, Australia, in 1882, to signify 'the death of English cricket' – a trophy – it's an Earth thing. That they have come and taken.
FORD PREFECT	Strange thing to want to tell us.
ARTHUR	Strange thing to take.
FORD PREFECT	Strange ship.
ARTHUR	Clever how it just appeared one minute and disappeared the next.
FORD PREFECT	Not the robots' ship, *this* ship.
ARTHUR	Good Lord. This is Slartibartfast's ship? It looks very different close up.
FORD PREFECT	Ah. That's the Somebody Else's Problem field at work. Now you can clearly see the ship for what it is, simply because you know it's here. Whereas no one else here can.
ARTHUR	Probably because close up it looks much less like a spaceship and much more like a small upended Italian bistro.
SLARTIBARTFAST	(Arriving) Yes, I know, but there is a reason. Come, we must go. The ancient nightmare is come again. Doom confronts us all. We must leave at once.

FX: Slarti unlocks the bistro doors and enters the ship's charming rustic foyer. It's a bit plastic and echoey.

FORD PREFECT	(Following him in) I fancy somewhere sunny.

FX: A familiar-sounding spaceship descends in the background, under:

ARTHUR	(Hesitating outside) Wait a minute – Ford? You won't believe this, but there's *another* spaceship landing near that ambulance—
FORD PREFECT	(Coming back to grab Arthur) Come on, Arthur, we're leaving.

ARTHUR	(**Struggling**) Wait a minute – I think I recognize it – ow!

FX: Hatch closes. Ship takes off.

INT. – LORD'S CRICKET GROUND – COMMENTARY BOX

FX: Debris falling, rubble settling, sirens.

HENRY BLOFELD	Well, I – I really don't know what's going on here, I have to be honest, Fred. I don't think this is good for the game. Can you see exactly what's happening?
FRED TRUEMAN	Well, some unearthly looking chap is going up to one of the wounded spectators lying in the middle of the wicket. Never had this in my day.

FX: Steps on steel ramp. Wounded people groaning.

WOWBAGGER	(**For it is he**) Excuse me, out of the way, yes, I know you're mortal, just don't bleed on me. Ah. Here you are.
DEODAT	(**Dying, coughing**) Help me . . . Please . . .
WOWBAGGER	Deodat?
DEODAT	. . . Eh?
WOWBAGGER	(**Closer. He kneels**) Arthur Philip Deodat?
DEODAT	(**Coughs**) Yes . . .
WOWBAGGER	(**Whispers**) You're a no-good dumbo nothing.
DEODAT	(**Dying breath**) Wha—?
WOWBAGGER	(**Getting up**) I thought you should know that before you went.

FX: Body thud. Boots up ramp. Hatch closes. Wowbagger's ship leaves.

EXT. – SPACE

FX: *Starship Bistromath* zooms past us. Sounds like a spaceship crossed with an Italian accordion wedding band.

INT. – *STARSHIP BISTROMATH* – FLIGHT DECK

FX: Ship's steady hum throughout. Slartibartfast pottering, electronic whirrings and pops from flight controls.

FORD PREFECT	Nice mover. Shame about the decor.

40

SLARTIBARTFAST	(**Interrupted**) What did you say?
FORD PREFECT	For a flight deck, this looks very like the lobby of an Italian restaurant.
SLARTIBARTFAST	Deep in the fundamental heart of mind and Universe, there is a reason.
FORD PREFECT	I'd say the fundamental heart of mind and Universe can take a running jump, this spaceship is complete pants.
ARTHUR	It's not very high tech, is it? Plastic ivy, cheap tiles and those raffia-wrapped bottles you're trying to fit candles in.
SLARTIBARTFAST	The flight controls?
ARTHUR	I refuse to be surprised.
	FX: Squeak of a Chianti cork.
SLARTIBARTFAST	Hold tight, please.
	FX: Loud pop and accordion overdrive, huge engine roar.

EXT. – SPACE. WHERE NO ONE CAN HEAR YOU SCREAM, BUT THIS IS RADIO SO WE'LL PUT WHAT WE HAVE HANDY INTO THE MIX, IN THIS CASE LOTS OF SUB-WOOFER

FX: The *Starship Bistromath* whips past in accordion overdrive.

ARTHUR/FORD PREFECT	(**And possibly Slarti too, for this would tend to take him by surprise**) Whoah!

INT. – *STARSHIP BISTROMATH* – FLIGHT DECK

FX: Ship's steady hum as before. Slartibartfast pottering.

FORD PREFECT	(**Recovering, breathless**) Ooh . . . On the other hand, I can't deny that the way it moves makes the *Heart of Gold* seem like an electric pram. How far did we just travel?
SLARTIBARTFAST	Oh . . . about, um, about two-thirds of the way across the Galactic disc, I would say – roughly.
FORD PREFECT	(**Respectful**) Not bad.
ARTHUR	Where are we going?
SLARTIBARTFAST	We're going to confront an ancient nightmare of the Universe.
FORD PREFECT	And where are you going to drop us off?

41

FX: The sound of a small in-flight-catering can of Indian tonic water being opened. It's flat.

SLARTIBARTFAST I will need your help. Come. **(Moving off)** There is much I must show and tell you.

FX: Feet on green cast-iron spiral staircase.

FORD PREFECT Where is he going?

ARTHUR Up that green spiral staircase, how should I know? **(Moving off)** We'd better follow him.

FORD PREFECT **(Calling out, but following Arthur)** My doctor says that I have a malformed public-duty gland and a natural deficiency in moral fibre, and that I am therefore excused from saving Universes.

INT. – *STARSHIP BISTROMATH* – COMPUTATIONAL AREA

(FX: Ship's steady hum throughout.)

FX: Italian restaurant FX – gentle mandolin and accordion muzak. Robot waiters trundle about. Clinking of cutlery and glasses.

SLARTIBARTFAST The central computational area.

ARTHUR Good grief. Are these all robots?

SLARTIBARTFAST Yes. And this is where every calculation affecting the ship in any way is performed.

FORD PREFECT **(Moving on)** Of course. And it had to look like—

SLARTIBARTFAST Yes, I know what it looks like, but it is in fact a complex four-dimensional topographical map of a series of highly complex mathematical functions.

ARTHUR It looks like a joke.

SLARTIBARTFAST **(Moving off)** I told you, I know what it looks like.

ARTHUR **(Quietly, worried)** Ford, the Universe cannot possibly work like this, it's absurd . . .

FORD PREFECT But most of the really absurd things you can think of have already happened.

ROBOT MAITRE D' **(Trundles up)** Would you care to take a seat, Signori?

ARTHUR Yes, please—

SLARTIBARTFAST No, thank you!

ARTHUR	But I'm hungry.
ROBOT MAITRE D'	**(Trundling off)** Not a problem, sir. I come back later.
SLARTIBARTFAST	The food is artificial, and so are the customers.
FORD PREFECT	Don't these robots ever clear away? Look, here's a half-eaten meal, dirty glasses . . .
SLARTIBARTFAST	Don't touch that breadstick! Everything is set at a precisely calculated mathematical position.
ROBOT WINE WAITER	**(Wheeling up)** Would you care to see the wine list?
FORD PREFECT	Ooh, yes, please—
SLARTIBARTFAST	No, thank you!
ROBOT WINE WAITER	**(Trundling off)** Oh, be like that, then.
SLARTIBARTFAST	Don't order anything, the knock-on effect could be catastrophic.
ARTHUR	To your stomach alone.
SLARTIBARTFAST	Wait here, please. Before we go to the Room of Informational Illusions I need to make a course correction. **(Moving off)**

INT. – *STARSHIP BISTROMATH* – COMPUTATIONAL AREA, RESTAURANT SECTION

FX: Restaurant FX continues.

SLARTIBARTFAST	**(Moving on)** Ah, Sergio.
ROBOT MAITRE D'	Signor Slartibartfast, your usual table?
SLARTIBARTFAST	No, I think I'll sit with the party over there.
ROBOT MAITRE D'	But they are about to pay their bill.
SLARTIBARTFAST	Perfect timing.
ROBOT MAITRE D'	**(Moving off)** As Signor wishes . . .
SLARTIBARTFAST	**(Off)** Erm, waiter!
ROBOT WAITER	**(Off)** Signore?

INT. – *STARSHIP BISTROMATH* – COMPUTATIONAL AREA, OUTER SECTION

FX: Restaurant FX fainter, but robot business shadowing Arthur's and Ford's observations.

ARTHUR	What on Earth is he doing?
FORD PREFECT	I don't know, but look, there's a pattern. It's like a sort of dance between the waiters and the customers. All the manipulation of menus, bill pads, wallets, credit cards and paper napkins.
ARTHUR	Oh, yes . . . Good grief, is that a gun?!
FORD PREFECT	(**Dear oh dear . . .**) Pepper mill.
ARTHUR	Oh.
FORD PREFECT	Ooh look. Now the customer robots are attempting to examine each other's pieces of chicken. It all means something.

FX: Mandolin music is distorted and there is a deep rumbling. Ship's steady hum rises by a semitone.

ARTHUR	Oh, you're right – feel that vibration through the deck?

FX: Push sub-woofer channel a bit.

ROBOT MAITRE D'	(**Off**) Ah. Leaving so soon, Signore?
SLARTIBARTFAST	(**Off**) Thank you, Sergio, a most satisfactory meal.
FORD PREFECT	Whatever he just did, the ship has responded.

FX: The ship's tone, and the music, rise another semitone.

ARTHUR	But what sort of calculation requires the replication of an Italian restaurant?
SLARTIBARTFAST	(**Moving on**) Bistromathics. The most powerful computational force known to parascience.

INT. – THE BOOK AMBIENCE

THE VOICE	The Bistromathic Drive is a wonderful new method of crossing vast interstellar distances without all that dangerous mucking about with Improbability Factors.

Bistromathics itself is simply a revolutionary new way of understanding the behaviour of numbers. Just as Einstein observed that time was not an absolute but depended on the observer's movement in space, so it's now realized that numbers are not absolute but depend on the observer's movement in restaurants.

The first non-absolute number is the number of people for whom the table is reserved. This will vary and bear no apparent relation to the number of people who actually turn up, or to the subset of people who leave when they see who else has turned up.

The second non-absolute number is the given time of arrival, which is the one moment of time at which it's impossible that any member of the party will arrive.

The third and most mysterious piece of non-absoluteness of all lies in the relationship between the number of items on the bill, the cost of each item, the number of people at the table and what they are each prepared to pay for.

And so it was only with the advent of pocket computers that the startling truth became finally apparent, and it was this: numbers written on restaurant bills within the confines of restaurants do not follow the same mathematical laws as numbers written on any other pieces of paper in any other parts of the Universe.

This single fact took the scientific world by storm. It completely revolutionized it. So many mathematical conferences got held in such good restaurants that many of the finest minds of a generation died of obesity and the science of maths was put back by years.

And being put back years is precisely how a technologically unsurpassed android feels when trying to converse with a mattress.

EXT. – SQUORNSHELLOUS ZETA, THE MATTRESS PLANET – SWAMP

FX: Marvin is still trudging round in a circle in the swamp. In the distance, wild mattresses are willoming . . .

ZEM THE MATTRESS	I sense a deep dejection in your diodes, robot. It saddens me and I globber. **(He does so)** Globber.
MARVIN	Don't you think it's discouraging enough you being born a mattress without having to globber like that?
ZEM THE MATTRESS	That is what we mattresses do. Unless we're flolloping. Some of us flurble. Others are taken away to be slept on. But as all of us are called Zem, we never know which.

FX: Marvin sighs and continues to walk in circles.

ZEM THE MATTRESS	Why are you walking in circles?
MARVIN	Because my leg is stuck.
ZEM THE MATTRESS	Hmmm. It seems to me that it is a pretty poor sort of leg.
MARVIN	I expect that you find the idea of a robot with an artificial leg pretty amusing. You should tell your friends Zem and Zem when you see them later; they'll laugh, if I know them, which I don't, of course – except insofar as I know all

45

organic life forms, which is much better than I would wish to. Ha, my life is but a box of wormgears.

ZEM THE MATTRESS But why do you just keep walking round and round in circles?

MARVIN Ask me if I ever get bored.

ZEM THE MATTRESS Ahhh . . . Do you?

MARVIN I gave a speech once. You may not instantly see why I bring the subject up, but that is because my mind works so phenomenally fast. Do you know I am at a rough estimate thirty billion times more intelligent than you? Think of a number, any number.

ZEM THE MATTRESS Erm . . . five.

MARVIN Wrong.

ZEM THE MATTRESS Ooh.

MARVIN You see?

ZEM THE MATTRESS Tell me of the speech you once made, go on.

MARVIN I delivered it over there, about a mile distance. I would point, but this arm has been welded to my side. I was somewhat of a celebrity at the time, on account of my miraculous and bitterly resented escape from a fate almost as good as death in the heart of a blazing sun. You can guess from my condition how narrow my escape was. I was rescued by a scrap-metal merchant, imagine that. Here I am, brain the size of a . . . oh, never mind. He it was who fixed me up with this leg. Hateful, isn't it? He sold me to a Mind Zoo. I was the star exhibit. I had to sit on a box and tell my story whilst people told me to cheer up and think positive.

ZEM THE MATTRESS The speech. Flurble. I long to hear of the speech you gave in the marshes.

MARVIN **(Oh well, might as well tell the story, not that this mattress will be able to understand a word, but then that's mattresses for you)** There was a bridge built across the marshes. A cyberstructured hyperbridge, hundreds of miles in length, to carry ion-buggies and freighters over the swamp. It was going to revitalize the economy of the Squornshellous System. They spent the entire economy in building it. They asked me to open it, poor fools. I stood on the platform. For hundreds of miles in front of me, and hundreds of miles behind me, the bridge stretched.

ZEM THE MATTRESS Did it glitter?

MARVIN It glittered.

ZEM THE MATTRESS	Did it span the miles majestically?
MARVIN	It spanned the miles majestically.
ZEM THE MATTRESS	Did it stretch . . . like a silver thread far out into the invisible mist?
MARVIN	Yes. Do you want to hear this story?
ZEM THE MATTRESS	No, flurble, I want to hear your speech.
MARVIN	This is what I said. I said, 'I would like to say that this is a very great pleasure, honour and privilege for me to open this bridge, but I can't because all my lying circuits are out of commission. And to make matters worse, which I never have to anyway, I hate and despise you all and declare this hapless cyberstructure open to the unthinkable abuse of all who wantonly cross her.' Then I plugged myself into the opening circuits. The entire thousand-mile-long bridge spontaneously folded up its glittering spans and sank weeping into the mire, taking everybody with it.
ZEM THE MATTRESS	Voon. You were not bored that day!
MARVIN	Contrary to all recent experience, no.
	FX: The Krikkit ship appears overhead with a noise like a hundred thousand people saying 'wop'.
ZEM THE MATTRESS	Does this great ship suddenly hanging in the sky bore you?
MARVIN	It depends on what those white robots flying down from it have in mind. Nothing pleasant, I expect.
	FX: The Krikkit robots zoom down on rocket pads, landing around Marvin.
ROBOT	Up stumps.
	FX: The sound of Marvin's artificial leg being twisted.
MARVIN	**(Being rattled about as they remove his leg)** I suppose it takes all eleven of you to remove an artificial leg.
	FX: The leg comes off with a *dank!*
MARVIN	. . . Of course.
ROBOT	Leg before wicket.
	FX: Krikkit robots zoom away.
MARVIN	You see the sort of thing I have to contend with?
ZEM THE MATTRESS	I think—

FX: Krikkit robots zoom down again.

ROBOT Change of batting order.

FX: Marvin grabbed.

FX: Krikkit robots zoom away again.

MARVIN **(As he is carried away)** Typical.

FX: The Krikkit ship disappears with a noise like a hundred thousand people saying 'foop'.

ZEM THE MATTRESS **(A bit lost and sad without his friend)** Hallo . . . ? Globber. Globber.

INT. – THE BOOK AMBIENCE

THE VOICE What arbitrary stroke has removed Marvin from his mattress swamp? What kind of artificial leg would appeal to eleven homicidal white robots in cricket pads? And how can Arthur Dent and Ford Prefect live through the most terrible war ever to ravage the Universe? Only the next instalment of *The Hitchhiker's Guide to the Galaxy* can tear away the veil of ignorance . . .

ANNOUNCER Vogon Building & Loan advise that your planet is at risk if you do not keep up repayments on any mortgage secured upon it. Please remember that the force of gravity can go up as well as down.

FOOTNOTES

Time-travel sequence When we first met to discuss this series in detail, the fifth *Hitchhiker* novel had just come out in hardback and Douglas seemed to feel a few post-natal pangs about it. He hinted that he might one day attempt, given the inspiration, some further evolution of *Hitchhiker's* to counteract its downbeat ending, but for now he was feeling a bit bruised by it all.

Second-guessing Douglas was never my intention but on a preliminary re-reading I was reminded that these last three novels can seem more introspective and less joyful than their antecedents, finishing with Douglas's daring conclusion to *Mostly Harmless*, surely one of the biggest surprise rug-pulls inflicted on the loyal reader in all of popular literature. My chief worry was that these dramatized versions were scheduled to be broadcast in half-hour *comedy* slots on BBC Radio 4. Now Douglas's novels certainly merit their legendary status, but while he was always brilliant, original and entertaining, certain sections of the books were not written for comic effect whereas the radio versions would have to maintain a consistent vein of humour with

some definite gag moments. So this could be a bit of a p[...]
conclusion. But more of that later.

In the process of adaptation one must strip the story down [...]
parts, and in doing so I was hugely relieved to find that not only we[...]
more opportunities to point up Douglas's sense of humour than I had first [...]
but also that there was a pattern to events in all the *Hitchhiker* iterations whic[...]
logical extension could lead to some kind of closure to the saga itself. It could even
include – and explain – events in series two.

However, in achieving this I had to reinforce the key idea that events in the
original *Hitchhiker* series (and novels) were part of a much bigger reality – in fact, of
several Realities in the Universe As Envisioned By Douglas (UAEBD). By the time we
entered the Quintessential Phase with its *Guide* Mark II and the notion of reverse
temporal engineering, events had, were and would be taking place which could tie
up the entire saga. Thus as we revisit Arthur and Ford's original lines of dialogue
about the *Guide* (re-recorded by Simon and Geoff, reading directly from this book's
illustrious forebear), underneath we hear the various Vogon demolition fleets cutting
a destructive swathe through many other innocent planets in the Galaxy. Earth is not
the sole victim of Vogon bureaucracy; there's something more ambitious going on
here and Arthur is just one of its victims.

Rising hysteria, Simon's stock-in-trade This was Douglas's character note, along with 'No Radio 2 sound effects here!' in his
original half-hour Episode One draft. This not only shows his keen if somewhat unkind
ability to poke fun at both Simon's funniest moments as Arthur Dent and my BBC
heritage, but that he was instinctively hearing the programme in his mind's ear while
writing it, which is of course the only way to write great radio. (My disclaimer was
added because I did not want to be seen to take other people's liberties – especially
Douglas's!)

I should add that this rant at Ford by Arthur is another bit of original Adams,
unique (I believe) to this version of the saga.

Henry Blofeld and Fred Trueman For those unfamiliar with the game of cricket and its celebrities, Henry is among the
last of the old-school BBC cricket commentators (as was Brian Johnston, who was
originally to take this role but sadly departed for other realities), and Fred Trueman is
one of the true legends of the game. They were charming, polite, patient and
unreservedly prepared to make themselves sound splendidly silly for *Hitchhiker's*. No
director could ask for more.

The Krikkit robots Cricket is a game widely played in the British Commonwealth and it seemed right to
look for some kind of cricket-oriented Commonwealth-voice treatment for the robots.
Adding a metallic rasp to Dominic Hawksley's terrific performance was straightforward
enough, but the edgy South African accents really seasoned the pudding.

EPISODE THREE

ANNOUNCER *The Hitchhiker's Guide to the Galaxy*, by Douglas Adams, Tertiary Phase.

INT. – THE BOOK AMBIENCE

THE VOICE *The Hitchhiker's Guide to the Galaxy* claims that the Campaign for Real Time was inspired not only by an instinct to preserve the traditions of linear chronology but because there was once a poet. His name was Lallafa, and he wrote what are widely regarded throughout the Galaxy as being the finest poems in existence, the *Songs of the Long Land*.

Lallafa had lived in the forests of the Long Lands of Effa, and he wrote his poems on pages made of dried habra leaves, without the benefit of education. Or correcting fluid.

Long after his death his poems were found and wondered over. News of them spread like morning sunlight. For centuries they illuminated and watered the lives of many people whose existence might otherwise have been darker and drier.

Then, shortly after the invention of time travel, some major correcting-fluid manufacturers from the Mancunia Nebula were chatting at a sixth-dimensional sales conference.

FX: Sales conference hubbub.

MANUFACTURER 1 (Northern mill-owner) 'Ere, I may not know much about poetry, but I know what I like. **(Beat)** I say, I may not know much about—

MANUFACTURER 2 Aye, we 'eard the first time.

MANUFACTURER 1 Oh, yeah. Well. I were just thinkin' about that – that Lallafa. You know, poetry bloke. **(Beat)**

MANUFACTURER 3 What 'e could've done with is some 'igh-quality correcting fluid. In a variety of leafy shades.

MANUFACTURER 1 *Exactly* what I were thinking! And I'm, er, ahem, wondering if we could persuade 'im, like, to say a few words to that effect, eh?

50

MANUFACTURER 2	(Shrewd) Could open up the Andromeda market.
	(General Northern mutterings of assent)
THE VOICE	So they travelled the time waves, found him and did indeed persuade him. **(Sounds of a beating)** In fact they persuaded him to such an effect that he became extremely rich, and frequently commuted to the future to do chat shows, on which he sparkled wittily.
	FX: Cheesy chat-show intro jingle and applause.
THE VOICE	(cont'd) Thus he never got around to writing the poems. This was a problem, but one easily solved. Each week, the correcting-fluid manufacturers simply packed him off somewhere different.
	FX: Seagulls.
MANUFACTURER 1	Right, there you go, lad. Copy of yer book, stack of dried habra leaves to copy it onto. Just make the odd mistake, then er, correct it in the usual way. Er, 'ere's your emolument. **(Sotto)** Carry on like that, son, there's plenty more where that came from, eh?
THE VOICE	And he did. **(Beat)** Many people now claim, though, that the poems became suddenly worthless. Other people argue that they are exactly the same as they always were, so what's changed?
	This prompted the first people to set up the Campaign for Real Time to try and stop this sort of thing going on. One of its principal activists, the Magrathean planet-designer Slartibartfast, is currently using the Room of Informational Illusions aboard the *Starship Bistromath* to give Arthur Dent and Ford Prefect an important – and very realistic – history lesson . . .
	FX: Starships battle, planets are destroyed, lives lost. The soundtrack music is stirring and portentous.
DOCUMENTARY VOICE	(On soundtrack) These, then, were the Krikkit Wars; the greatest devastation ever visited upon our Galaxy.
ARTHUR	Oh dear!
SLARTIBARTFAST	(Cheerfully shouting, whilst rummaging about) Don't look so apprehensive, Earthman, it's just a documentary.
ARTHUR	I know, but it seems so real.
SLARTIBARTFAST	Well, it *was*. When it happened.
DOCUMENTARY VOICE	And let us not forget – and in just a moment I'll be able to suggest a way which will help us always to remember – that before the Krikkit Wars –

SLARTIBARTFAST	This is not a good bit . . . Do not agree to buy anything at this point. Terribly sorry, I can't seem to find the remote control . . .
DOCUMENTARY VOICE	The symbol known as the Wikkit Gate! The three pillars . . .
ARTHUR	I'm sure I've seen that before . . .
FORD PREFECT	(Snorts, waking up) What?
ARTHUR	That arrangement of sticks on the asteroid . . . It looks stupefyingly familiar . . .
SLARTIBARTFAST	The asteroid is the Lock. The Wikkit Gate is the Key.
FORD PREFECT	I like those girls floating around it. Bit like angels . . .
ARTHUR	Apart from the clothes. Angels usually wear them.
SLARTIBARTFAST	(Still rummaging for remote) Erm . . . where is that . . .
DOCUMENTARY VOICE	There is not a world in the Galaxy where this symbol is not revered to this day. Even in primitive worlds it persists in racial memories.
	FX: The sound of leather upon willow, applause.
ARTHUR	Three stumps, two bails? Well, that's a *wicket* . . .
SLARTIBARTFAST	That's right, the Wikkit Gate.
DOCUMENTARY VOICE	This it is that now locks away their world until the end of eternity.
ARTHUR	Krikkit? Wikkit? Extraordinary.
	FX: Dramatic music slips into *very* tacky muzak.
DOCUMENTARY VOICE	This . . . is not the real key, of course. That, as we all know, was destroyed and lost for ever. This, my friends, is a replica; hand-tooled by skilled craftsmen into a memento you will be proud to own, in memory of those who fell.
SLARTIBARTFAST	(Fiddling with remote) Ah! Found it! There . . .
DOCUMENTARY VOICE	Now, let us all bow our heads in payment . . .
SLARTIBARTFAST	Just don't nod.
DOCUMENTARY VOICE	(Slows to halt) I promissse tooo paaaaaaay . . .
	FX: Music winds down. Lights come on.

INT. – *STARSHIP BISTROMATH* – ROOM OF INFORMATIONAL ILLUSIONS

FX: Mellow hum.

52

SLARTIBARTFAST	You're getting the gist?
ARTHUR	I hope that's what it is.

FX: Fast spooling rewind of documentary, under:

SLARTIBARTFAST	Let me spool back a few billion years **(Hums)** . . . Yes, yes, nearly there. Ah! Stand by for the Informational Illusion—

FX: Tape spooling wows down.

EXT. – KRIKKIT – LATE EVENING

FX: Gentle wind blowing, owls and crickets sounding, a pleasant night atmos. The faint scent of jasmine, a hint of new-mown hay, feet walking through soft lush grasses . . .

FORD PREFECT	(Taking the air) Hm. This is more like it. Soft grass, nice evening breeze. Is this Earth?
ARTHUR	It does look a bit Home Counties. But very cold.
SLARTIBARTFAST	Seems warm enough to me.
FORD PREFECT	Very unwelcoming . . . It looks appealing but feels impersonal.
ARTHUR	Hm. Like a good-looking woman writing you a parking ticket. But this cricket angle . . .
SLARTIBARTFAST	We'll walk down to that village and I'll tell you about it.

FX: Walking through grass momentarily up, then:

SLARTIBARTFAST	The game you know as cricket is just one of those curious freaks of racial memory. Of all the races in the Galaxy, only the English could possibly revive the memory of the most horrific wars ever to sunder the Universe and transform it into what I'm afraid is generally regarded as an incomprehensibly dull and pointless game.
ARTHUR	Ah no, fair play . . .
SLARTIBARTFAST	Rather fond of cricket myself, as it happens – but in most people's eyes you have been inadvertently guilty of the most grotesque bad taste. Particularly the bit about the little red ball hitting the wicket. Very nasty.
ARTHUR	Oh.
SLARTIBARTFAST	These Krikkit men are the ones who started it all, and it will all start tonight.

ARTHUR	Oh, is something dreadful about to happen? **(Looking up)** The battlecruisers with the white robots aren't about to arrive overhead, are they? Oh. My God . . .
SLARTIBARTFAST	Nothing is about to attack you here. This is where it all started. The place itself. Krikkit – as it was ten billion years ago.
ARTHUR	There aren't any stars . . .
SLARTIBARTFAST	Shhh. Listen and watch.

Music: Distant singing – Krikkit song.

KRIKKIT CIVILIANS	**(Singing)** Our lovely world's so lovely And everything's so nice . . .
SLARTIBARTFAST	The Masters of Krikkit.
KRIKKIT CIVILIANS	**(Singing)** . . . And everyone's so happy Beneath the ink-black sky . . .
ARTHUR	Yes . . . Well, they seem nice enough, not that I trust appearances any more.
KRIKKIT CIVILIANS	**(Singing)** She's the only one for me I'm under her spell I can't resist We walked hand in hand Above the grass Then in the dark we kissed Our lovely world's so lovely . . .
ARTHUR	What a strange song . . . They're 'beneath the ink-black skies, hand in hand, above the grass'. Not 'under the moon' or 'beneath the stars' as you might expect . . . I suppose because it's so black overhead.
FORD PREFECT	Arthur.
ARTHUR	Yes?
FORD PREFECT	Why are you tiptoeing?
ARTHUR	Er – was I?
FORD PREFECT	Yes. We're still on the *Starship Bistromath*. This is a recorded Informational Illusion. You could walk past those people blowing a euphonium for all the notice they'll take.

ARTHUR	I'll bear that in mind.
SLARTIBARTFAST	You know of course what's about to happen?
FORD PREFECT	Me? No.
SLARTIBARTFAST	Did you not learn ancient galactic history at school?
FORD PREFECT	I was in the cybercubicle behind Zaphod Beeblebrox. It was always the same three hands going up. His.
ARTHUR	You know, I get the distinct feeling of being alone in the universe.
SLARTIBARTFAST	Not so the people of Krikkit. Their solar system – their single sun with its single world – was, as you see, surrounded by a huge dust cloud. So there was never anything to see in the sky, except their sun. The reason they never thought 'We are alone in the Universe' is that until this night they don't know about the Universe. Until this night.

FX: Rippling thunder, thin roaring scream overhead.

(The Krikkit civilians stop singing. They talk in a reverent, new age sort of way)

KRIKKIT CIVILIAN 1	Hear that, brothers?
KRIKKIT CIVILIAN 2	What a strange and disagreeable sound. Surely it is not the wind in the trees.
KRIKKIT CIVILIAN 3	It is not of the earth, or the air. I mislike it greatly but cannot fathom its origin.
KRIKKIT CIVILIAN 1	Friends, this cannot be, for it is not possible . . .
KRIKKIT CIVILIAN 2	The sound we hear comes from above . . .
KRIKKIT CIVILIAN 3	Ah! Behold! A fiery streak in the void!
FORD PREFECT	Wow!
ARTHUR	Can't they see it's a spaceship – or the wreckage of one – coming out of the blackness?
SLARTIBARTFAST	Why would they look? They have no idea anything could exist up there. Until tonight . . .

FX: Spaceship debris impacts with an explosion.

KRIKKIT CIVILIAN 1	Brothers . . . We must go see what manner of visitation is upon us.
KRIKKIT CIVILIAN 2	Lead on. I will sing of what we find.

KRIKKIT CIVILIAN 3	(Bravely) I too will follow . . .
	(They move off very thoughtfully)

INT. – THE BOOK AMBIENCE

THE VOICE	Some speak of the starship *Heart of Gold*, some of the *Starship Bistromath* and some in hushed tones of the *Starship Titanic*. But whilst these and other great spaceships which come to mind, such as the Galactic Fleet battleships, the GSS *Daring*, the GSS *Audacity* and the GSS *Suicidal Insanity*, are all regarded with awe, pride, enthusiasm, affection, regret, jealousy, resentment, in fact most of the better-known emotions, the craft which regularly commands the most actual astonishment was *Krikkit One*, the first spaceship ever built by the people of Krikkit. This is not because it was a wonderful ship. It was not. It was a crazy piece of near junk and looked for all the Galaxy as if it had been knocked up in somebody's backyard, which was, in fact, precisely where it had been knocked up. The most astonishing thing about the ship was not that it was done well (it wasn't, see above) but that it was done at all – as the period of time which elapsed between the moment that the people of Krikkit discovered that there was such a thing as space and the launching of their first spaceship, was – as near as dammit is to dommit – almost exactly a year.

INT. – STARSHIP *KRIKKIT ONE*

FX: Gurgling, interspersed with rather dodgy and not very hi-tech background FX:

KRIKKIT CIVILIAN 1	Stand by, Brothers Number Two and Number Three.
KRIKKIT CIVILIAN 2	Standing by, Brother Number One.
KRIKKIT CIVILIAN 3	Standing by, Brother Number One.
KRIKKIT CIVILIAN 1	Push blue switch.
KRIKKIT CIVILIAN 2	Pushing blue switch . . .
ARTHUR	And this is going to fly, is it?
KRIKKIT CIVILIAN 1	Brother Number Three . . .
SLARTIBARTFAST	Just strap yourself in.
FORD PREFECT	Can't we fast-forward through this spaceship bit?
SLARTIBARTFAST	(Hushed) Certainly not. Watch and learn. This is the pivotal event.

56

Some kind of Krikkit countdown is running underneath:

FORD PREFECT	The wiring isn't even insulated.
ARTHUR	I've heard of low-tech, but these controls are bathroom fittings.
SLARTIBARTFAST	You are perfectly safe. It's an Informational Illusion, which you will find extremely instructive and not a little harrowing.
ARTHUR	These singer-songwriting people stripped down the wreckage of that crashed ship and within a year built this?
FORD PREFECT	Just relax and be harrowed.
ARTHUR	I can do that. Ha . . .
SLARTIBARTFAST	Second thoughts, you'd better hold on.
KRIKKIT CIVILIAN 1	Lift off.

FX: Ship lifts off. A definite hint of a 'wop' in the effect.

KRIKKIT CIVILIAN 2	All systems optimal.
FORD PREFECT	No way – *no way* – does anyone design and build a ship like this in a year. No matter how motivated. Prove it to me and I still won't believe it.
SLARTIBARTFAST	Yes, well, the Masters of Krikkit did. Their historic mission was to find out if there was anything or anywhere beyond the blackness, from which the wrecked spaceship could have come. Actually, I think I will fast-forward a bit . . .

FX: The action around them speeds up, then slows down again after Slarti's cue:

SLARTIBARTFAST	That's the Krikkit men flying to the edge of their solar system – the inner perimeter of the hollow dust cloud which surrounds their sun and home planet. Now watch. They're on the brink of breaking through it. History is gathering itself.

FX: Action slows to normal pace again.

SLARTIBARTFAST	Three – two – one –

Music: Huge momentous Saint-Saens organ-type chord as the night sky lights up around them.

FX: Lots of sub rumble please, Deeley, as much as we can get out of the desk in Soundhouse 3 without snapping the elastic . . .

KRIKKIT CIVILIANS	(Gasp simultaneously) Aaaah.

57

SLARTIBARTFAST	Behold – the Universe! The staggering jewels of the night in their infinite dust!
KRIKKIT CIVILIANS	Ooooh.
SLARTIBARTFAST	Imagine the impact of this vision on a species whose entire philosophy demands that they are the only sentient creatures in Creation!
FORD PREFECT	Insanity?
ARTHUR	Bitter but rational disappointment?
SLARTIBARTFAST	No.
ARTHUR	(Beat) So how did they react on the first sight of the Universe?
SLARTIBARTFAST	Very simply.
KRIKKIT CIVILIAN 1	(Cold, dispassionate) It'll have to go.

INT. – THE BOOK AMBIENCE

FX: a steady and untroubling musical drone unfolds, layered with the sounds of the Book's illustrative animations.

THE VOICE	Although it's been said that on Earth alone in our Galaxy has Krikkit (or cricket) been treated as fit subject for a game, and that for this reason the Earth has been shunned, this does only apply to our Galaxy. And more specifically, to our dimension. In some of the higher dimensions, they feel they can more or less please themselves and have been playing a peculiar game called Brockian Ultra-Cricket for their transdimensional equivalent of billions of years.

A full set of rules is so massively complicated that the only time they were all bound together in a single volume they underwent gravitational collapse and became a black hole. All that is known of the game can be found in the archives of the BUCC.

INT. – ARCHIVES

FX: Old 35mm cinema projector starts up, as if showing a rather scratchy old film.

HENRY BLOFELD	(Wows in, on soundtrack) Rule One: Grow at least three extra legs.

FX: Popping sounds.

HENRY BLOFELD	You won't need them, but, my dear old thing, it does help to keep the crowds amused.

FRED TRUEMAN	And now it's Perkins galloping out to extremely silly square leg.
HENRY BLOFELD	Rule Two: Find one good Brockian Ultra-Cricket player. Clone him ten few times. This saves an enormous amount of tedious selection and training.

FX: Crowds, and cheering running underneath.

HENRY BLOFELD	(cont'd) Three: Put your team and the opposing team in a large field and build a high wall round them. The reason for this is that a crowd that has just watched a rather humdrum game experiences far less life-affirmation than a crowd that believes it has just missed the most dramatic event in sporting history.
	Four: Throw assorted items of sporting equipment over the wall for the players. Anything will do – cricket bats, basecube bats, tennis guns, skis, anything you can get a good swing with.

FX: Sounds of Brockian cricketers laying about each other with the above objects.

HENRY BLOFELD	(cont'd) Rule Five: The players should now lay about themselves for all they are worth with whatever they find to hand. Whenever a player scores a 'hit' –

FX: Shovel in face *clang!*

HENRY BLOFELD	– on another player he should immediately run away and apologize from a safe distance – usually through a megaphone.
FRED TRUEMAN	(Through megaphone) Sorry!
HENRY BLOFELD	Rule Six: The winning team shall be the first team that wins.

FX: Projector off. Soundtrack wows to stop.

INT. – THE BOOK AMBIENCE

THE VOICE	Curiously enough, the more popular the game grows in the higher dimensions, the less it's actually played, since most of the competing teams are now in a state of permanent warfare over the interpretation of those rules. This is all for the best, because in the long run a good solid war is always less psychologically damaging than a protracted game of Brockian Ultra-Cricket. However, for Zaphod Beeblebrox, a badly mixed Pan Galactic Gargle Blaster has a similarly deleterious effect . . .

INT. – STARSHIP *HEART OF GOLD*

FX: Zaphod stomps about. Ice cubes rattle in cocktail, under:

ZAPHOD (Gulps, spits) Where did I go wrong? (Figuring to self) Janx Spirit, Santragi-nean sea water, Arcturan Mega-gin, marsh gas, Hypermint extract, tooth of Suntiger . . . (Stops) Maybe it's the olive . . .

FX: Door whirr.

DOOR Mmm. It is my pleasure to open for you . . .

ZAPHOD Zark off.

DOOR . . . and my satisfaction –

ZAPHOD Zark off!

DOOR – to close again with the knowledge of a job well done.

FX: (Muffled) Krikkit ship appearing with a noise like a hundred thousand people saying 'wop'.

FX: Zaphod stops.

ZAPHOD Door. Did you hear that?

DOOR Do you wish me to open for you again? It would be my—

ZAPHOD No, shut up. (Thinking hard) Trillian has jumped ship. I'm alone on the *Heart of Gold*. I've put an electronic gag across that zarking computer's speech terminals. All non-essential systems are closed down and we're drifting in a remote area of the Galaxy. So which particular hundred thousand people would turn up at this point and say a totally unexpected 'wop'?

FX: A sound becoming more distinct – eleven Krikkit robots' feet running on metal decking. They are moving through the ship, hatches politely opening and closing to allow their passage. It's inexorable and getting closer, under:

ZAPHOD I'm not imagining this . . . Computer?

EDDIE THE COMPUTER Mm, mmmmf!

ZAPHOD Is there someone on this ship?

EDDIE THE COMPUTER (Affirmatively) Mmmmf.

ZAPHOD Are they heading for the bridge?

EDDIE THE COMPUTER (Affirmatively) Mmmf.

ZAPHOD Who is it?

EDDIE THE COMPUTER Mmmmf, m mmmf m mmmmmf m m, mmmm mm m mm mmmmf, mm mmmm m mmmm. Mmf m mmmf m mmmf!

ZAPHOD	Zarquon. The speech terminals are on the bridge . . . Computer, when I ungag you, remind me to punch myself in the mouth.
EDDIE THE COMPUTER	Mmmf mmmf?
ZAPHOD	Either mouth. Look. One for yes, two for no. Is it dangerous?
EDDIE THE COMPUTER	Mmmmf.
ZAPHOD	It is?
EDDIE THE COMPUTER	Mmmmf.
ZAPHOD	You didn't just go 'mmmmf' twice?
EDDIE THE COMPUTER	Mmmmf. Mmmmf.
ZAPHOD	Huh. I guess the trick would be to reach the bridge before whoever-it-is does.
EDDIE THE COMPUTER	Mmmmf.
ZAPHOD	Wait here.
EDDIE THE COMPUTER	Mf??
ZAPHOD	(Moving off) You know what I mean.

INT. – *HEART OF GOLD* – CORRIDOR

FX: Zaphod breathlessly creeps along towards bridge.

ZAPHOD	(Tiptoeing) He who gets to the bridge first controls the ship, baby . . . Here we are—

As the footsteps get closer, a distant door is heard:

OTHER BRIDGE DOOR	(Off) Pleased to be of service.
ZAPHOD	(Stopping, whisper) Zark! They came through the other bridge door . . .
OTHER BRIDGE DOOR	(Off, cheerfully) Have a nice day!
ZAPHOD	Holy photons . . . I didn't gag the door circuits . . . (Voice up a bit) Door, if you can hear me, say so very very quietly.
BRIDGE DOOR	(Very very quietly) I can hear you.
ZAPHOD	Good. Now, in a moment, I'm going to ask you to open. When you open I do not want you to say that you enjoyed it, OK?

FX: Muffled drilling sounds from bridge beyond.

BRIDGE DOOR	OK.

61

| ZAPHOD | Neither do I want to hear that I have made a simple door very happy, or that it is your pleasure to open for me and your satisfaction to close again with the knowledge of a job well done, OK? |

| BRIDGE DOOR | OK. |

| ZAPHOD | And I have no plans to have a nice day, understand? |

| BRIDGE DOOR | Understood. |

| ZAPHOD | OK . . . Open! |

FX: Door whirrs open quietly

INT. – *HEART OF GOLD* – BRIDGE

FX: Drilling up.

| BRIDGE DOOR | (Loudly) Is that the way you like it, Mr Beeblebrox? |

FX: Drilling stops.

Eleven Krikkit robots turn to see where the noise is coming from.

| ROBOTS | Intruder. |

| ZAPHOD | D'oh. |

| ROBOTS | Engage weapons. |

FX: Eleven blasters cocked.

| ZAPHOD | Hi, guy . . . Oh, eleven of you, good . . . Tunnelling into the Improbability Drive compartment – tough room. |

| ROBOT | Intruder. Kill on sight. |

| ZAPHOD | OK, dude, I want you to imagine that I have an extremely powerful Kill-O-Zap blaster pistol in my hand. |

| ROBOT | You do have a Kill-O-Zap blaster pistol in your hand. |

| ZAPHOD | You never know what you're going to grab off a wall bracket in a hurry. So what are you cats doing here? |

FX: Silence, just whirring noises as they turn to look at each other. Who does this life form think he is addressing?

| ZAPHOD | OK, robots. So what are you *robots* doing here? |

| KRIKKIT ROBOT 1 | We have come for the Gold Bail. |

ZAPHOD	Huh?
KRIKKIT ROBOT 1	The Gold Bail is part of the Key we seek. To release our Masters from Krikkit.
ZAPHOD	You know, metalhead, if I'd paid more attention to my history lessons and less to having sex with the girl in the next cybercubicle, I'd know what you're on about.
KRIKKIT ROBOT 1	The Krikkit Wars. The Slo-Time Lock. Its Key was disintegrated. The Golden Bail is embedded in the device which drives your ship.
KRIKKIT ROBOT 2	It will be reconstituted in the Key. Our Masters shall be released.
KRIKKIT ROBOT 1	The Universal Readjustment will continue.
KRIKKIT ROBOT 3	We already have the Wooden Pillar, the Steel Pillar and the Perspex Pillar.
KRIKKIT ROBOT 4	Now we will have the Gold Bail.
ZAPHOD	Er, no you won't. It's driving my ship.
KRIKKIT ROBOT 1	**(Patiently and seriously)** Now we will have the Gold Bail. And then we must go to a party.
ZAPHOD	Hey, forget the bail, let's party.
KRIKKIT ROBOT 1	No. We are going to shoot you.
	FX: Guns being cocked.
ZAPHOD	You're kidding.
	FX: Fusillade of laser shots.
ZAPHOD	**(Astonished)** Ow . . . OK, you're not kidding!
	FX: A few more shots. Zaphod goes down.

EXT. – SPACE

FX: The *Starship Bistromath* whips past in accordion overdrive.

INT. – *STARSHIP BISTROMATH* – COMPUTATIONAL AREA, RESTAURANT SECTION

FX: Restaurant FX, Italian muzak.

ARTHUR	What am I supposed to do with this piece of chicken?
SLARTIBARTFAST	Toy with it. Like this. You'll feel the tingle as it moves four-dimensionally through five-dimensional space.

FX: Funny little fuzzy effect here. Dirk will think of something. He hopes.

ARTHUR　　Oh. Ooh. **(Giggling)** Ooh, yes! Ooh, I see.

SLARTIBARTFAST　　So, overnight the whole population of Krikkit was transformed from being charming, delightful, intelligent . . .

FORD PREFECT　　If whimsical . . .

SLARTIBARTFAST　　. . . ordinary people, into charming, delightful, intelligent . . .

FORD PREFECT　　Whimsical . . .

SLARTIBARTFAST　　. . . manic xenophobes. The idea of a Universe didn't fit into their world picture, so to speak. They simply couldn't cope with it. And so, charmingly, delightfully, intelligently – whimsically, if you like – they decided to destroy it.

ARTHUR　　Ugh!

SLARTIBARTFAST　　What's the matter now?

ARTHUR　　Ugh! I don't like the wine very much.

SLARTIBARTFAST　　Well, send it back. Or you'll upset the mathematics.

ARTHUR　　Waiter?

FX: Whirr as the waiter draws up.

ROBOT WAITER　　Signor?

SLARTIBARTFAST　　On second thoughts, let's argue over the bill with him. Then we can go back to the Room of Informational Illusions for the second half.

FORD PREFECT　　There's more?

SLARTIBARTFAST　　Naturally, there's the Krikkit War Crimes Trial.

INT. – COURT ROOM

FX: Hubbub. Gavel.

CLERK　　All rise for sentencing by the Chairman of the Boards of Judges at the Krikkits' War Crimes Trial, His High Judgemental Supremacy, Judiciary Pag, LIVR.

FX: Massed hushings.

ARTHUR　　**(Low)** LIVR?

SLARTIBARTFAST　　**(Low)** Learned, Impartial and Very Relaxed.

JUDICIARY PAG	**(Addressing the court, chewing gum)** Be seated, relax. Right. The people of Krikkit. **(Spits out gum, and addresses clerk)** Stick this under your chair for later.
CLERK	Yes, m'lud.
JUDICIARY PAG	Hmmm. Right. The people of Krikkit are, well, they're a bunch of real sweet guys, you know, who just happen to want to kill everybody. Hell, I feel that way most mornings. Yeah. **(He dozes off for a second, then)** Hm? What?

INT. – THE BOOK AMBIENCE

THE VOICE	The attack on the Galaxy by the population of Krikkit was stunning. Thousands upon thousands of huge Krikkit warships leapt out of hyperspace –

FX: Lots of Krikkit ships appearing – 'wop', 'wop', 'wop' – then robots calling out their Krikkit battle commands. Grenades being batted all over the place.

THE VOICE	– and simultaneously attacked thousands upon thousands of major worlds, calmly zapping them out of existence.

With unimaginable speed the people of Krikkit had grasped the hyper-technology needed to build their fleet and dispatched millions of lethal white robots wielding formidable battle clubs which launched a hideous arsenal of grenades, ranging from minor incendiaries to Maxi-Slorta Hyper-nuclear Devices, which could take out a major sun. With one strike of the battle clubs, the grenades were simultaneously primed and launched with devastating accuracy, from mere yards to hundreds of thousands of miles. |

FX: A sound like hundreds of thousands of people saying 'foop'.

INT. – COURT ROOM

FX: Hubbub. Gavel.

JUDICIARY PAG	**(Chewing gum)** So we won. That's no big deal. A medium-sized galaxy against one little world – how long did it take us, kiddo, huh?
CLERK	Er, it is a trifle difficult to be precise in this matter. Time and distance—
JUDICIARY PAG	Hey hey hey. Relax, guy, y'know, be vague.
CLERK	It pains me to be vague over such a—
JUDICIARY PAG	Bite the bullet, right, and be it.

65

CLERK	Very approximately, two thousand years?
JUDICIARY PAG	Woo! And how many guys zilched out?
CLERK	Two grillion, m'lud.
JUDICIARY PAG	Two grillion! That's a whole lotta stiffs! Or my real name isn't Zipo Bibrok five times ten to the eighth.
ARTHUR	**(Low)** How does he spell that?
FORD PREFECT	**(Low)** Big ten, little eight?
ARTHUR	**(Low)** Hm.

FX: Pag pours himself a glass of water and then sprays it out immediately.

JUDICIARY PAG	Ugh! What is in this water?
CLERK	Erm, nothing, m'lud.
JUDICIARY PAG	Well, take it away and put something in it!

FX: Gavel.

JUDICIARY PAG OK. Hear me, hear me, hear me. You behind the zap-proof crystal, representatives of Krikkit. Listen up. You're a really sweet bunch o' guys, you know, but we wouldn't want to share a galaxy with you, y'know – not if you can't learn to relax a little. I mean a peaceful coexistence with you is a total no-show. On the other hand, these guys, you know, are entitled to their own view as it's shaped by the Universe. And, er . . . according to their view, they were doing the right thing. They believe in **(Fishes out a piece of paper)** 'peace, justice, morality, culture, sport, family life and the obliteration of all other life forms'.

FX: Hubbub in courtroom. Gavel.

JUDICIARY PAG Well, they're entitled to a view, right?! Now, sentencing is, er, gonna be tricky, but, people, I got an idea . . . Now stop me if you've heard it before.

INT. – THE BOOK AMBIENCE

THE VOICE Judiciary Pag's idea was new, popular and surprisingly well-thought out, thus casting severe doubts as to its authorship. The planet of Krikkit was sentenced to be enclosed for perpetuity in an envelope of Slo-Time, inside which life would continue almost infinitely slowly. All light would be deflected around the envelope rendering it both invisible and impenetrable. Escape from the envelope would, of course, be utterly impossible unless it were unlocked from the outside. Then, when the rest of the whole of creation reached its dying fall, and life and matter ceased to exist, the planet of Krikkit and its sun would emerge to continue the solitary existence it craved, in the twilight of the Universal void. The Lock was to be on an asteroid slowly orbiting the envelope. The key would be the symbol of the Galaxy – the Wikkit Gate.

By the time the applause in the court had died down, Judiciary Pag was already in the Sens-O-Shower with a rather nice member of the jury that he'd slipped a note to half an hour earlier.

INT. – IN SENS-O-SHOWER

FX: In the shower. Female groans of pleasure. Pag snorts awake.

JUDICIARY PAG   Hm! What? What? **(Beat)** Right!

EXT. – SPACE

FX: The *Starship Bistromath* whips past in accordion overdrive.

INT. – *STARSHIP BISTROMATH* – COMPUTATIONAL AREA, RESTAURANT SECTION

FX: Restaurant FX, Italian muzak.

ROBOT MAITRE D'   You are confusing me, Signore.

FORD PREFECT   Nobody had the cannelloni.

ROBOT MAITRE D'   Is very nice.

FORD PREFECT   Dingo's kidneys!

ROBOT MAITRE D'   Dingo's kidneys, yes sir, I will ask the chef.

FORD PREFECT   It's an expression. Leave it alone **(Fade and continue under:)**

SLARTIBARTFAST   Nothing is lost for ever. Except for the Cathedral of Chalesm.

ARTHUR   The what?

SLARTIBARTFAST   The Cathedral of Chalesm. It was during the course of my researches at the Campaign for Real Time that I . . .

FORD PREFECT   **(Approach)** Oh, for goodness' sake. The waiter wants to argue about who had the cannelloni.

SLARTIBARTFAST   Is he surly or obsequious?

FORD PREFECT   Both.

SLARTIBARTFAST	Excellent, then the Bistromathics have successfully manoeuvred this ship out of subjective space and into a parking orbit. Come, **(Rising)** we have a party to visit.
FORD PREFECT	Now you're talking!
ARTHUR	Just a minute, what's this Campaign for Real Time you were talking about?
	FX: Robot waiter whirrs up.
ROBOT WAITER	**(A bit camp)** Hi, can I clear off your table, sir? It's time to switch off the bistro.
SLARTIBARTFAST	**(Sitting down again)** One moment, please. **(To Arthur)** Listen. The time streams have become very polluted; muck floating about in them, flotsam and jetsam, and more and more of it is now being regurgitated into the physical world. Eddies in the space-time continuum, you see.
ARTHUR	Still?
FORD PREFECT	Now, about this party?
SLARTIBARTFAST	We are going to try to prevent the war robots of Krikkit from regaining the whole of the Key they need to unlock the planet of Krikkit from the Slo-Time envelope and release the rest of their army and their mad Masters.
FORD PREFECT	You mentioned a party?
SLARTIBARTFAST	Sadly I did. The idea seems to exercise a strange and unhealthy fascination on your mind. The more I unravel the dark and tragic story of Krikkit, the more you want to drink a lot and dance with girls. **(Ford murmurs assent)** You've attached yourself to it the way an Arcturan Megaleach attaches itself to its victim before biting his head off and making off with his spaceship.
FORD PREFECT	So. When do we get there?
SLARTIBARTFAST	When I've finished telling you *why* we have to go there.
FORD PREFECT	I know why *I'm* going. **(Chuckle)**
SLARTIBARTFAST	I had hoped for an easy retirement. I was planning to learn to play the octraventral heebiephone – a pleasantly futile task, because I have the wrong number of mouths. I had also been planning to write an eccentric and relentlessly inaccurate monograph on the subject of equatorial fjords in order to set the record wrong about one or two matters I see as important.
ARTHUR	Well, why don't you, then?
SLARTIBARTFAST	Well, I somehow got talked into doing some part-time work for the Campaign for Real Time and started to take it all seriously.

ARTHUR	Go on.
SLARTIBARTFAST	At the Campaign for Real Time I noticed that five pieces of jetsam which had, in relatively recent times, plopped back into existence seemed to be corresponding to five pieces of the missing Key. Only two I could trace exactly – the Wooden Pillar, which appeared on your planet, and the Silver Bail, which seems to be at some sort of party. We must go there and retrieve it before the Krikkit robots find it, or who knows what may happen?
FORD PREFECT	I've got a better idea. Let's go there in order to drink a lot and dance with as many girls as possible while there are still some left. If everything you've shown us is true, then we don't stand a whelk's chance in a supernova.
ARTHUR	What's a whelk got to do with a supernova?
FORD PREFECT	It doesn't stand a chance in one. The point is that people like you and me, Slartibartfast, and Arthur – particularly and especially Arthur – are just dilettantes, eccentrics, lay-abouts – fartarounds if you like.
SLARTIBARTFAST/ ARTHUR	Well . . . Er—
FORD PREFECT	Well, we're not obsessed by anything, you see, and that's the deciding factor. They care, we don't. They win.
SLARTIBARTFAST	*I* care about a lot of things.
FORD PREFECT	Well, such as?
SLARTIBARTFAST	Well . . . life, the Universe and . . . everything, really. Fjords.
FORD PREFECT	Would you die for them?
SLARTIBARTFAST	Fjords? What would be the point?
FORD PREFECT	The point is this—
SLARTIBARTFAST	**(Wearying of this)** For whatever reason, let's just go.
FORD PREFECT	I think that's what I was trying to say.
SLARTIBARTFAST	**(Rising again and moving away from atmos)** Follow me. The teleport cubicles are in the gentlemen's bathroom.
ARTHUR	I'm not sure I find that very reassuring.
SLARTIBARTFAST	Oh, they're very clean.
ARTHUR	Hmm.

INT. – *STARSHIP BISTROMATH* – GENTS' TOILET

FX: Echoey loo atmos.

SLARTIBARTFAST   (Off) Now if you'd just stand in there and there . . .

FORD PREFECT   (Off) In the cubicles?

SLARTIBARTFAST   (Off) That's right.

ARTHUR   Do you realize, that in all this time, I haven't once been to—

SLARTIBARTFAST   (Off) Don't sit down.

ARTHUR   There's no paper anyway.

SLARTIBARTFAST   (Off) Well, of course not, it's a teleportation device.

FORD PREFECT   (Off) Gentlemen, raise your seats.

FX: Three creaky toilet seats lifted.

SLARTIBARTFAST   (Off) We're going to flush the chain on the count of three. Altogether now . . .

SLARTIBARTFAST, ARTHUR AND FORD   One, two . . .

FX: Teleportation toilet flush.

INT. – AGRAJAG'S LABYRINTH

FX: Eerie echoey acoustic.

(Arthur staggering about)

ARTHUR   (As he materializes) Three . . . (Coughs) Oh, I hate teleporting! (A beat) Ford? Slartibartfast? (He listens. Nothing) Well, that's just perfect. Couldn't have been much of a party, everybody's left. Hang on – this is a cave.

FX: He starts to walk.

ARTHUR   (Back and forth on stereo) Or is it a labyrinth? Well, at least there'll be a way out . . . or an attendant, or someone who can help. (Stops) Hallo?

The echo bounces off into distance – hallo – hallo – hallo . . .

ARTHUR   It's like Alice, chasing the white rabbit – no, *robot*. (He tries to steel himself) There are *no* robots here. There are definitely *no* white robots here. There –

FX: Click. BZZZT! Steady hum, under:

ARTHUR   (Fearful) – *is*, however, a neon sign saying 'You Have Been Diverted'.

FX: Click. BZZZT! Hum switches off.

ARTHUR   Or there was. I hope I'm dreaming this.

FX: Click. BZZZT! Steady hum, under:

ARTHUR   Three green dots . . . There's a name for that: 'irritating'. Oh, and a comma . . . 'You Have Been Diverted dot dot dot comma'.

FX: Click. BZZZT! Hum switches off.

ARTHUR   (To self) Well, hm, not entertainingly . . .

FX: Click. BZZZT! Steady hum, under:

ARTHUR   That's my name.

FX: Click. BZZZT! Hum switches off.

ARTHUR   Good grief . . .

FX: Click. BZZZT! Steady hum, under:

ARTHUR   'Welcome'? **(To self)** 'You Have Been Diverted, Arthur Dent. Welcome'.

FX: Click. BZZZT! Hum switches off, then on.

ARTHUR   'I Don't Think' . . .

FX: Click. BZZZT! Hum switches off.

ARTHUR   (Really freaking) Err . . . hello . . . ?

FX: Running.

ARTHUR   (To self) I'm afraid, I really am afraid . . .

FX: Heart beat.

ARTHUR   My heart's so loud it sounds like somebody beating a bass drum in here with me . . .

FX: Heart beat gets stronger, under:

ARTHUR   Somebody *is* beating a bass drum!

FX: Bass drum beating gets closer, then stops.

ARTHUR   (Gasp)

FX: Click. BZZZT! Steady hum, under:

ARTHUR   (Reads) 'Do Not Be Alarmed'.

FX: Click. BZZZT! Hum switches off.

ARTHUR　OK, what should I be? Come on, sign.

FX: Click. BZZZT! Hum switches on.

ARTHUR　(Reading) 'Be Very Very Frightened, Arthur Dent.'

FX: Click. BZZZT! Hum switches off.

ARTHUR　(Starts) Who's that?! Is anyone there? Grow up, Arthur, there are no hideous monsters here – if there are I'll eat my—

FX: Huge buzz of wings and a landing behind him. Arthur spins back round.

ARTHUR　Aaaah! . . . What do you want?

FX: Agrajag and Arthur breathing for a moment. Then:

AGRAJAG　(Big and echoey) Bet you weren't expecting to see me again.

INT. – THE BOOK AMBIENCE

THE VOICE　What has Arthur Dent stumbled upon in the recesses of the labyrinth? Has Ford Prefect found a drink and a peer group to share it with? Can Slarti-bartfast stop the Krikkit robots from acquiring the Silver Bail? Fasten your acceleration straps, it's going to be a bumpy next instalment of *The Hitchhiker's Guide to the Galaxy*.

ANNOUNCER　If you have been affected by or would like to talk to someone about *any* of the issues featured in that programme, you may like to vidiphone our Sub-Etha Helpline. Calls charged at Galactic rates.

FOOTNOTES

Mancunia correcting-fluid manufacturers　Bruce suggested this nod to the 'Four Yorkshiremen' sketch by the Pythons, who so inspired Douglas.

The Wikkit Gate documentary　This is one of those scenes that you write for radio thinking, 'I'll sort it out in the edit.' Then when you get to the edit you have to take yourself outside and administer a severe beating to yourself because it's a complete pig to make sense of two separate flows of events running concurrently. And then for the broadcast version you have to re-edit it to be shorter and it still needs to make sense. So you are black and blue and your brain is oozing out of your ears and the dratted scene still needs editing.

The Krikkit song In the novel Douglas clearly – and fairly respectfully – signals that this should be a 'tribute to Paul McCartney' song. And although Douglas loved the Beatles, and our composer Wix Wickens is the great man's keyboard player, Sir Paul writes from the heart and isn't really into self-tribute. The logical answer was to approach Philip Pope, who was a friend of Douglas and the musical genius behind the HeeBeeGeeBees (the affectionate pastiche rock act that sprang from the 1980s comedy show *Radio Active*, also featuring Mancunian Correcting-Fluid Magnate Mike Fenton Stevens and the highly esteemed Geoffrey Perkins, who of course produced the first and second radio series). Philip came up with a wonderful – and respectful – tribute song, the entire lyric of which I append here with his kind permission:

Chorus 1
Our lovely world's so lovely
And everything's so nice
And everyone's so happy
Beneath the ink-black skies.

Verse
She is the only One for me
I'm under her spell I can't resist
We walked hand in hand above the grass
Then in the dark we kissed.

Chorus 2
Our lovely world's so lovely
See how the flowers grow
It's just a shame my dog died
She loved those flowers so!

Middle 8
It's so much fun working on the farm
It fills my heart and soul with pride
My wife and kids waiting safe from harm
Makes me feel so warm inside.

Chorus
Our lovely world's so lovely
And everything's so nice
And everyone's so happy
Beneath the ink-black skies
Our lovely world's so lovely
See how the flowers grow
It's such a shame my dog died
She loved those flowers so!

© Philip Pope 2004

73

Zaphod and the Krikkit robots   There was much stifled laughter in the studio as Mark stalked about splashing his prop Pan Galactic Gargle Blaster everywhere (complete with empty garden snail shells; I have no idea what Ken thought they represented) while interrogating a gagged Roger Gregg (through the portable speaker as Eddie), 'live', to absolutely no useful effect at all. A funny scene to record but also a great opportunity to mix comedy and menace, as the inexorable advance through the ship of the Krikkit robots is heard in the background.

Judiciary Pag   Rupert Degas lifted this part out of the humorous into the hilarious. His jerk-awake 'What?! . . . Right!' was so good that I used it again in the 'shower scene' under the Voice's ensuing narration. Several people asked where the young lady in question was recorded. I believe it may have been in the ticket queue at Fenchurch Street Station . . .

The toilet transporter   I must beg Douglas's forgiveness for introducing a toilet gag to *Hitchhiker's*. There's no real excuse, but it is hinted at in the book, and apart from Richard's sublimely patient Slartibartfast co-ordinating activity in the cubicles, there is something Milligan-esque about the FX hinge creaks as the seats are lifted.

EPISODE FOUR

SIGNATURE TUNE

ANNOUNCER *The Hitchhiker's Guide to the Galaxy*, by Douglas Adams, Tertiary Phase.

INT. – THE BOOK AMBIENCE

Musical drone of great eeriness under:

THE VOICE *The Hitchhiker's Guide to the Galaxy* has much to say on the subject of time travel and its part in the unhallowed fate of the Cathedral of Chalesm. It has, however, very little to say about the abduction of people by the remote reprogramming of teleportation coordinates to bring them to a Cathedral of Hate. This is because the abductee in question, Arthur Dent, is the only creature – apart from its creator – to witness the Cathedral in all its awe-inspiring, subterranean horror. But first he must endure the visions in the Labyrinth that surrounds it.

INT. – AGRAJAG'S LABYRINTH

Eerie echoey acoustic.

ARTHUR **(Starting)** Who's that? Is anyone there? Grow up, Arthur, there are no hideous monsters here. If there are, I'll eat my—

FX: Huge buzz of wings and a landing behind him. Arthur spins back round.

ARTHUR Waaaah! What d'you want?

FX: Agrajag and Arthur breathing for a moment. Then:

AGRAJAG **(Echoey throughout this sequence)** Bet you weren't expecting to see me again.

ARTHUR But – but I've never, *ever* seen a housefly as big as a dog—

AGRAJAG Or perhaps you remember me better as the rabbit.

FX: BZZZT. Huge sniffling.

75

ARTHUR	The rabbit? It's only a hologram, Arthur, keep calm. The rabbit. The *rabbit*? No, I'm afraid I don't! **(Arthur reacts incredulously under the following)**
AGRAJAG	Born in darkness, raised in darkness. One morning I poked my head out for the first time into the bright new world and got it split open by what felt like some primitive instrument made of flint.
ARTHUR	What?
AGRAJAG	Made by you, Arthur Dent, and wielded by you. You turned my skin into a bag for keeping interesting stones in. I happen to know that because in my next life I came back as a fly again and you swatted me. Again.
ARTHUR	Yes, but I—
AGRAJAG	Only this time you swatted me with the bag you'd made of my previous skin. Arthur Dent, you are not merely a cruel and heartless man, you are also staggeringly tactless!
ARTHUR	Um . . . I . . . I don't—
AGRAJAG	I see you have lost the bag. Probably got bored with it, did you?
ARTHUR	No. No!
	FX: Hologram switched on.
AGRAJAG	Meet the newt you trod on.
ARTHUR	**(Jumps)** Uggh!
AGRAJAG	That was me, too. As if you didn't know!
ARTHUR	Know? Know?!
AGRAJAG	The interesting thing about reincarnation is that most people, most spirits, are not aware that it is happening to them.
ARTHUR	Er, look, I really . . . **(Reacts through following)**
AGRAJAG	I was aware. That is, I became aware. Slowly. Gradually. I could hardly help it, could I, when the same thing kept happening, over and over and over again! Every life I ever lived, I got killed by Arthur Dent. Any world, any body, any time, I'm just getting settled down, along comes Arthur Dent – pow, he kills me.
ARTHUR	Look, I do th—
AGRAJAG	Hard not to notice. Bit of a memory-jogger. Bit of a pointer. Bit of a bloody giveaway!

76

ARTHUR   No, really, I—

AGRAJAG   'That's funny,' my spirit would say to itself as it winged its way back to the netherworld after another fruitless Dent-ended venture into the land of the living, 'that man who just ran over me as I was hopping across the road to my favourite pond looked a little familiar . . .' And gradually I got to piece it together, Dent, you multiple-me-murderer!

The echoes die away down the Labyrinth corridors.

ARTHUR   (After a pause) But what I don't underst—

AGRAJAG   Here's the moment, Dent, here's the moment when at last I knew!

FX: Hologram switched on.

(Arthur is a bit lost trying to pin this one down)

ARTHUR   Ugh? Ugh! No, no, no, I'm sorry, I'm sure I've never been in a huge pink wet cave with a vast, slimy creature rolling around over white tombstones! Oh my God . . . it's the inside of my mouth. And that's an oyster. I'm swallowing an oyster! An oyster that . . . oh . . . (Horrible suspicion) was . . .

FX: Hologram switched off.

ARTHUR   . . . you.

AGRAJAG   Tell me it was a coincidence, Dent. I dare you to tell me it was a coincidence!

ARTHUR   (Quickly) It was a coincidence.

AGRAJAG   It was not!

ARTHUR   It was! It was!

AGRAJAG   If it was a coincidence, then my name is not Agrajag!!!

ARTHUR   And presumably you would claim that that was your name?

AGRAJAG   Yes!

ARTHUR   Well, I'm afraid it was still a coincidence!

AGRAJAG   Come in here and say that!

ARTHUR   Right. I will.

FX: Arthur takes several paces forward and comes to a halt, under:

ARTHUR   I can assure you that it was a—

FX: Dramatic organ chord.

ARTHUR (Very echoey) My God!

INT. – THE BOOK AMBIENCE

The musical drone starts this off but soon turns to a dark exploration of Agrajag's madness. We also hear Arthur reacting to what is described, under:

THE VOICE The Cathedral of Hate that Arthur now enters is the product of a mind that is not merely twisted, but actually sprained and consequently has no place in a quality family publication such as *The Hitchhiker's Guide to the Galaxy*, which is why this addendum concerning Arthur's current location can only be found in pirated editions, opposite banned commercials for Eccentrica Gallumbits' chat room and virtual sauna.

FX: BZZZT. Cut to cheesy porn-movie music.

ECCENTRICA GALLUMBITS (For it is she) Come here, Daddy! Oh, you look so good!

FX: BZZZT. Cut back to the gloomy ambience, with cathedral effects: dripping water, low organ chords etc.

THE VOICE The chamber has been carved out of the inside of a mountain, and beyond the twisted buttresses . . . overhead it is utterly black.

Where it isn't black Arthur is inclined to wish that it was, because the colours with which some of the unspeakable details are picked out range from Ultra-Violent to Infra-Dead –

ARTHUR (Echoey in here) Oh, yuk!

THE VOICE – taking in Liver Purple, Loathsome Lilac, Matter Yellow, Burnt Hombre and Gan Green on the way. The unspeakable details which these colours pick out are gargoyles which all look inwards, from the walls, from the pillars, from the flying buttresses and choir stalls, towards an immense statue, which we will come to in a moment.

ARTHUR Good grief!

THE VOICE Around the monumental walls are vast engraved stone tablets in memory of those who've fallen to . . . Arthur Dent. The names of some of these commemorated are underlined with asterisks against them. So, for instance, the name of a cow which has been slaughtered and of which Arthur Dent happened to eat a fillet steak has the plainest engraving. Whereas the name of a fish which Arthur himself caught, cooked, decided he didn't like and left on the side of the plate has a double underlining, three sets of asterisks and a bleeding dagger appended, just to make the point.

ARTHUR (To himself) Pathetic . . .

THE VOICE And what is most disturbing to Arthur about it is the very clear implication that all these people and creatures are indeed the same person, over and over again. And it's equally clear that this same person is, however unfairly, extremely upset and annoyed, an annoyance which now spans the whole of time and space in its infinite umbrage, and given its fullest expression in the statue at the centre of all this monstrosity. A statue of Arthur Dent –

ARTHUR That's me!

THE VOICE – and an unflattering one.

ARTHUR Ugh . . .

THE VOICE Fifty feet tall if it's an inch – which it's not – crammed with insult to its subject matter, from the small pimple on the side of his nose to the poorish cut of his dressing gown, there is no aspect of Arthur Dent which isn't lambasted and vilified.

ARTHUR Oh, please!

THE VOICE With each of the thirty arms which the sculptor in a fit of artistic fervour has decided to give him, he is either braining a rabbit, swatting a fly, pulling a wishbone, picking a flea from his hair or doing something which Arthur's first glance cannot quite identify.

ARTHUR Oh my . . .

THE VOICE His feet, incidentally, are stamping on ants.

ARTHUR Oh, this is trying *too* hard.

THE VOICE Arthur is depicted as an evil, rapacious, bloodied ogre, slaughtering his way through an innocent one-man Universe. (**Arthur sighs**) And waddling round him, savouring the moment, is the black razor-toothed creature (**Arthur starts loudly**) that he has supposedly been persecuting all this time. It looks for all the Galaxy like a mad, fat scruffy bat.

FX: Agrajag breathing and wingflaps, Arthur reacting, foley movement, under:

AGRAJAG HhhhhhrrrrrraaaaaaaHHHHHH!!!

ARTHUR Ow! Stop poking me!

AGRAJAG I was at a cricket match.

ARTHUR	Looking like that?
AGRAJAG	Not in this body! Not in this body, this is my last body, my last life. This is my revenge body! My kill-Arthur-Dent body! My last chance. I had to fight to get it, too.
ARTHUR	B-b-but how could this poss—
AGRAJAG	I was at a cricket match! I had a weak heart condition, but what, I said to my wife, can happen to me at a cricket match?
ARTHUR	(Doomed) Oh. Yes . . . ?
AGRAJAG	As I'm watching, what happens? Two people quite maliciously appear out of thin air just in front of me. The last thing I can't help but notice before my poor heart gives out in shock is that one of them is Arthur Dent wearing a rabbit bone in his beard. Coincidence?
ARTHUR	(Firmly) Yes.
AGRAJAG	Coincidence?!!
ARTHUR	Look, it's just fate playing silly buggers with you. With me. With us! It's a complete coincidence.
AGRAJAG	What have you got against me, Dent?
ARTHUR	Nothing. Honestly, nothing.
AGRAJAG	Seems a strange way to relate to somebody you've got nothing against, killing them all the time. Very curious piece of social interaction, I would call that. I would also call it a lie!
ARTHUR	Look, I'm very sorry. There's been a terrible misunderstanding. Now, I've really got to go. I'm meant to be helping save the Universe.
AGRAJAG	At one point, I decided to give up. Yes, I would not come back. I would stay in the netherworld. And what happened?
ARTHUR	I don't know.
AGRAJAG	I got yanked involuntarily back into the physical world – as a bunch of petunias. In, I might add, a bowl.
ARTHUR	Oh dear.
AGRAJAG	This particular happy little lifetime started off with me, in my bowl, unsupported, three hundred miles above the surface of a particularly grim planet. Not a naturally tenable position for a bowl of petunias, you might think, and you'd be right! That life ended a very short while later, three hundred

	miles lower in, I might again add, the fresh wreckage of a whale. My spirit brother.
ARTHUR	Hm. Well.
AGRAJAG	On the way down I couldn't help noticing a flashy-looking white spaceship. And looking out of a port on this flashy-looking spaceship was a smug-looking Arthur Dent. Coincidence?!!
ARTHUR	(Grimly) Hm. Goodbye.
AGRAJAG	You may go. After I have killed you!
ARTHUR	No, er, that won't be any use, because I have to save the Universe, you see. I have to find a Silver Bail, that's the point. Tricky thing to do dead.
AGRAJAG	Save the Universe? You should have thought of that before you started your vendetta against me! What about the time when you were on Stavromula Beta and someone tried to assassinate you and you ducked. Who do you think the bullet hit?
ARTHUR	I've never been there.
AGRAJAG	What did you say?
ARTHUR	Never been there. What are you talking about?
AGRAJAG	You must have been there. You were responsible for my death there, as everywhere else. An innocent bystander!
ARTHUR	I've never heard of the place. I've certainly never had anyone try to assassinate me. Other than you. Perhaps I go there later, do you think?
AGRAJAG	You haven't been to Stavromula Beta . . . *yet*?
ARTHUR	No. I don't know anything about the place. Certainly never been to it, and don't have any plans to go.
AGRAJAG	Oh, you go there all right, you go there all right. Oh, zark! I've brought you here too soon! I've brought you here too zarking soon!
ARTHUR	Well, that's a dreadful bore for you, of course, but there it is.
AGRAJAG	I'm going to kill you anyway! Even if it's a logical impossibility, I'm going to zarking well try! I'm going to blow this whole mountain up!
	FX: Agrajag effort and wingflaps as he moves off.
ARTHUR	Leave that switch alone!
AGRAJAG	Let's see you get out of this one, Dent!

ARTHUR	If that does what I think it does, you'll be bringing about your own death this time. Don't do it!
AGRAJAG	I'm gonna to kill you!
ARTHUR	**(Effort, leaping on him)** No . . . you're . . . not!
AGRAJAG	**(Screams)** HhhhhhrrrrrraaaaaaHHHHHH!
	FX: Big chomp. Splurgy bleeding noises, under:
ARTHUR	Oh, you shouldn't have tried to bite me. Gosh, those teeth *are* sharp . . . you've made a real mess of yourself.
AGRAJAG	You know what you've done? You've gone and killed me again! I mean, what do you want from me, blood?
ARTHUR	I'm sorry!
AGRAJAG	HhhhhhrrrrrraaaaaaHHHHHH!
ARTHUR	No! No! No! Not the switch—!
	FX: Huge rusty old lever thrown. Klaxons. Subterranean rumble starts. Huge cracking noises, rubble.
ARTHUR	Er . . . er . . . er . . . What to do now? Run! B-b-but where? Er . . . **(He runs off into an echoey tunnel)** Anywhere! Aaaarrrgh!

INT. – LABYRINTH

FX: Arthur runs past Itor, screaming. In fact he does a lot of running around screaming at this point, not having Ford around to engage in witty banter with whilst almost certain death rains down upon him . . .

ARTHUR	Aaaaaaaaaaaaaargh! Aaaagh! **(A beat)** Daylight! Daylight this way! **(Runs off screaming to left)** Aaaaaaaaaaaaaargh!

EXT. – LABYRINTH-PLANET SURFACE

FX: Distant explosions. Arthur running out of cave from centre right. Rocks hurled into the air and crashing about him. Avalanche approaches. Generally a grim situation.

ARTHUR	**(Running off, panicking)** Aaaagh!
	FX: Arthur runs up, panting.
ARTHUR	Oh . . . great. An avalanche!

FX: Avalanche.

ARTHUR (Breathless, pell-mell) Whoa! Whoa, whoa, whoa! But logically . . . I'm bound to survive this . . . if only to pursue my alleged persecution . . . of Agrajag on Stavromula Beta – but if this isn't it – why am I still panicking? Why am I still . . . risking my life? And why, lying in front of me, is the small navy-blue holdall that I know for a fact I lost in the baggage-retrieval system at Athens airport ten years ago? (Trips) Whup! I'm falling! Upwards? – Oh . . . I'm *flying*!

FX: Flying whooshing sounds.

THE VOICE *The Hitchhiker's Guide to the Galaxy* has this to say on the subject of flying.
There is an art, it says, or rather, a knack to flying.
The knack lies in learning how to throw yourself at the ground and miss.
Pick a nice day, it suggests, and try it.
The first part is easy.
All it requires is simply the ability to throw yourself forward with all your weight, and the willingness not to mind that it's going to hurt.

ARTHUR Weeeeeee!

THE VOICE That is, it's going to hurt if you fail to miss the ground.
Most people fail to miss the ground, and if they're really trying properly, the likelihood is that they will fail to miss it fairly hard.
Clearly, it's the second point, the missing, which presents the difficulties.
One problem is that you have to miss the ground accidentally. It's no good deliberately intending to miss the ground because you won't. You have to have your attention suddenly distracted by something else when you're halfway there, so that you're no longer thinking about falling, or about the ground, or about how much it's going to hurt if you fail to miss it.

ARTHUR Wow!!!

THE VOICE It is notoriously difficult to prise your attention away from these three things during the split second you have at your disposal. Hence most people's failure, and their eventual disillusionment with this exhilarating and spectacular sport.

ARTHUR Ha ha ha!

THE VOICE Do not listen to what anybody says to you at this point because they're unlikely to say anything helpful.
They are most likely to say something along the lines of, 'Good God, you can't possibly be flying!'
It is vitally important not to believe them or they will suddenly be right.

If, however, you are lucky enough to have your attention momentarily distracted at the crucial moment by . . . er, say, a gorgeous pair of legs (tentacles, pseudopodia, according to phylum and/or personal inclination), you will miss the ground completely.

Try a few swoops, gentle ones at first, then drift above the treetops breathing regularly.

Do not wave at anybody.

When you've done this a few times you'll find the moment of distraction rapidly becomes easier and easier to achieve.

In the case of Arthur Dent, his instincts have correctly told him that he mustn't think about it, or the law of gravity will suddenly glance sharply in his direction and demand to know what the hell he thinks he is doing up here . . .

EXT. – LABYRINTH-PLANET – SURFACE

FX: Arthur flying.

ARTHUR   **(Trying to be serious)** Oooh, ahh! Tulips! I'll think about tulips. **(Briefly overcome with glee)** This is great! Ha ha ha. **(Serious)** No, no, tulips. Nice tulips. The pleasing firm roundness of the bottom of tulips, the interesting variety of colours they come in . . . Oh, I'm bored.

FX: He loses altitude.

ARTHUR   **(cont'd)** Whoooaaa! Whoa! Whoa! Whoa! Mustn't be bored, that way groundness lies – stay distracted, stay flying – **(Gleeful)** I'm flying! **(Serious)** No, no, distract yourself – the bag!

FX: He gains altitude as he distracts himself.

ARTHUR   **(cont'd)** The bag, that's a point. How can a hold-all I left at Athens airport end up here? Who cares? I'm flying – concentrate, Arthur – whoa, whoooah – I mean, *don't* concentrate . . .

FX: He loses altitude.

ARTHUR   **(cont'd)** OK, OK, let's use this fall and turn it into a – **(Effort)** a swoop . . . and I should be able to grab it. Oh, gosh. I haven't seen that since I gave it to the pretty stewardess with the nice . . . aaahh, too distracted. **(Soaring up)** Look, look, Arthur! You're two hundred feet above the ground! **(Falls)** Waaaah!

FX: He loses altitude. This time frantic flapping of the arms returns him to us. This is not logical but makes for a nice visual sound effect.

ARTHUR (cont'd) Better . . . better . . . OK, think of the bag – if it's still in the state in which I lost it, it'll contain a can which would have in it the only Greek olive oil still surviving in the Universe . . . if I can just . . .

FX: Swoops past us – he grabs the bag.

ARTHUR (cont'd) (Zooming off away upwards) Yes! Got it!

EXT. – LABYRINTH-PLANET – SURFACE – ANOTHER PART OF THE SKY

ARTHUR (cont'd) (Now flying up to meet us, high over the ground) Not only a can of Greek olive oil but – the cricket ball I caught at Lord's? – very odd. What else? Ah! A duty-free allowance of retsina . . . Ha ha! . . . Some interesting stones and, joy of joys, my *towel*! Ha ha ha ha ha ha! Oh, if only Ford could see me now, ha ha!

FX: Rapid approach of the party behind him.

FORD PREFECT (Off) Arthur, look out! You're gonna crash into the party!

ARTHUR Ford? Waaa!

FX: Party whooshes past, scooping Arthur up and carrying him away.

INT. – THE BOOK AMBIENCE

THE VOICE When Arthur Dent, Ford Prefect and Slartibartfast arrived, the longest and most destructive party ever held was into its fourth generation and still no one showed any sign of leaving.

The mess was extraordinary, and had to be seen to be believed.

There had recently been some bangs and flashes up in the clouds, and there is one theory that these were battles being fought between the fleets of several rival carpet-cleaning companies, who were hovering over the thing like vultures, but you shouldn't believe anything you hear at parties, and particularly not anything you hear at this one.

One of the problems, and one which would obviously get worse, was that all the people at the party were either the children or the grandchildren or the great-grandchildren of the people who wouldn't leave in the first place. And because of all the business about selective breeding and regressive genes and so on, it meant that all the people currently at the party were either absolutely fanatical partygoers, or gibbering idiots – or, more and more frequently, both.

Either way, it meant that, genetically speaking, each succeeding generation was now less likely to leave than the preceding one.

Now because of certain things that had happened which seemed like a good idea at the time (and one of the problems with a party which never stops is that all the things which only seem like a good idea at parties continue to seem like good ideas), one of the things which seemed like a really good idea at the time was that the party should fly. Literally.

One night, long ago, a band of drunken astro-engineers clambered round the building calibrating this, fixing that, banging very hard on the other and when the sun rose the following morning, it was startled to find itself shining on a building full of happy drunken people which was floating like a young and uncertain bird over the treetops.

FX: The party engines start up and it lifts off . . .

THE VOICE   The flying party had also managed to arm itself rather heavily. If they were going to get involved in any petty arguments with wine merchants, they wanted to make sure they had might on their side.

FX: Door opened suddenly.

SYDNEY OPERA HOUSE WOMAN   All right, do as we say and nobody gets hurt!

FARMER   Wh-wh-what do you people want?

SYDNEY OPERA HOUSE WOMAN   Hand over all your cheese footballs. And those little savoury twig things. The ones with the tasty brown paint on.

FARMER   B-b-but we are simple farmers—

SYDNEY OPERA HOUSE WOMAN   Shut up and get stacking.

THOR   And we want the cakes. Fairy cakes.

SYDNEY OPERA HOUSE WOMAN   Better give us fifty cases of Cabernet Sauvignon as well.

FARMER   Cabernet? But we only drink milk.

SYDNEY OPERA HOUSE WOMAN   Don't give me that.

FX: Zap gun cocked

FARMER   (Grudgingly, found out) Oh all right, what vintage . . . ?

FX: Gunshots, screams, sounds of looting.

THE VOICE   They looted, they raided, they held whole cities for ransom for fresh supplies of cheese crackers, avocado dip and wine and spirits.

86

But the planet over which they were floating was no longer the planet it had been when they started.

It was in bad shape and had been since long before Agrajag destroyed its only respectable mountain, in the vain attempt to kill Arthur Dent.

FX: *Boom!* **As mountain collapses below.**

THE VOICE   But it was one hell of a party. It was also one hell of a thing to get hit by in the small of the back, as Arthur Dent has just discovered . . .

EXT./INT. – THE PARTY

FX: Wind whistling around the building. Muffled sounds of partying. Music: 'I Left My Leg On Jaglan Beta' played by a very tired band, so tired it is in both 3/4 and 4/4 time.

ARTHUR   Owwww . . . Ford . . .

FORD PREFECT   Where the foetid photon have you been?

ARTHUR   Is this Slartibartfast's party?

SLARTIBARTFAST   Hold tight, Earthman. There's only a very thin walkway around the building.

ARTHUR   Ooh. Everywhere I touch it hurts.

FORD PREFECT   Then don't touch it; you've sprained your wrist.

ARTHUR   What are you doing out here?

FORD PREFECT   They won't let us in without a bottle.

ARTHUR   Ah – there I think I can help you . . . **(Takes out retsina)**

FX: Knocks on door. Door opens.

DOORMAN (WIX)   Got a bottle?

ARTHUR   Retsina!

DOORMAN   Never 'eard of it. **(Tuts)** In you come.

SLARTIBARTFAST   **(Going in)** Thank you. Thank you so much.

INT. – PARTY

FX: Door closes shut. Hubbub, music, occasional glass smashes, laughter.

ARTHUR   **(Struggling through the throng)** Right, now we're in, we can—

PTERODACTYL CREATURE	Your bottle – what is it?
ARTHUR	Retsina, an Earth drink – very rare, now – hey!
PTERODACTYL CREATURE	(Moving off with it) A new pleasure, a new pleasure!
ARTHUR	That's mine!
FORD PREFECT	I warned you: never trust a pterodactyl in lurex.
ARTHUR	No, you didn't.
FORD PREFECT	Oh, I forgot.
ARTHUR	Good grief! It's Trillian.
FORD PREFECT	Yeah. And that's Thor, the Thunder God, with her. Blimey, half of Asgard have turned up. I wonder if Zaphod's here. (Wanders off) I'll go and look over by the drinks . . .
ARTHUR	(Approaching) Trillian! How the hell did you get here?
THOR	(Swedish. Chatting up Trillian. Getting closer as Arthur walks towards them) Didn't I see you at Milliways?
TRILLIAN	(Slightly merry) Were you the one with the hammer?
THOR	Yes. I much prefer it here. So much less reputable, so much more fraught. Ha ha ha ha.
TRILLIAN	Well, it seems fun—
ARTHUR	(Off) Trillian!
TRILLIAN	Oh, what are you trying to say, Arthur?
ARTHUR	I said, how the hell did you get here?
TRILLIAN	Oh, I was a row of dots floating randomly through the Universe. Just . . . Oh, have you met Thor? He's in thunder.
ARTHUR	Hello.
THOR	Hi.
ARTHUR	I expect that must be very interesting.
THOR	It is. Have you got a drink?
ARTHUR	Er, no, actually.

THOR	Then why don't you go and get one?
TRILLIAN	Hmmm. See you later, Arthur.
ARTHUR	Hm. Zaphod isn't here, is he?
TRILLIAN	**(Firmly)** See you. Later.
THOR	**(Leading her away)** One of the interesting things about being immortal is you don't have to . . .
SLARTIBARTFAST	One of the interesting things about space is how dull it is.
ARTHUR	Slartibartfast?
SYDNEY OPERA HOUSE WOMAN	Dull? Really?
SLARTIBARTFAST	Staggeringly dull. Bewilderingly so. You see, there is so much of space and so little in it. Would you like me to quote you some statistics?
SYDNEY OPERA HOUSE WOMAN	What do you think?
SLARTIBARTFAST	They too are quite *sensationally* dull.
SYDNEY OPERA HOUSE WOMAN	**(Yawning)** Ah, well. You must tell me all about it when I'm interested, hmm? Excuse me.
ARTHUR	Slartibartfast?
SLARTIBARTFAST	I thought she'd never go.
ARTHUR	Drink?
SLARTIBARTFAST	Come, Earthman . . .
ARTHUR	But I'm in the drinks queue.
SLARTIBARTFAST	No, we have to find the Silver Bail. It is here somewhere.
ARTHUR	Oh, can't we relax a little? I've had a tough day. Trillian's being chatted up by a Thunder God who was very rude to me. I'd consider thumping him if the muscles in his upper arm didn't move around each other like a couple of Volkswagens parking.
SLARTIBARTFAST	**(Grabbing his arm)** Think . . . of the danger to the Universe . . .
ARTHUR	The Universe is big enough and old enough to look after itself for half an hour.
SLARTIBARTFAST	**(Infinitely weary)** Please.

ARTHUR	(Sighs) Oh all right, I'll circulate and see if anybody's seen it.
SLARTIBARTFAST	Good, good. **(Moving off)** I'll do this side of the party, you do that . . .
ARTHUR	Ah – hallo . . . hallo there . . .
LAUGHING MAN	**(Deeply boring)** Hello!
ARTHUR	Have you seen a bail anywhere? Er, made of silver, vitally important for the future safety of the Universe, and about this long.
LAUGHING MAN	**(Moving him away)** No, but come and have a drink and tell me all about it . . .

Music up. Dancing and singing.

FORD PREFECT	**(Moving in, breathless, dancing, yelling over music)** You're a great little dancer!
SYDNEY OPERA HOUSE WOMAN	**(Dancing with him)** Thank you!
FORD PREFECT	Like that hat!
SYDNEY OPERA HOUSE WOMAN	I'm not wearing a hat.
FORD PREFECT	Oh, right. Like the . . . head.
SYDNEY OPERA HOUSE WOMAN	What?

FX: She smacks into him.

FORD PREFECT	Ow! The head. Interesting bone-structure.
SYDNEY OPERA HOUSE WOMAN	What?

FX: She smacks into him again.

FORD PREFECT	Ow! Ever heard of the Sydney Opera House?
SYDNEY OPERA HOUSE WOMAN	What?!

FX: She smacks into him again.

FORD PREFECT	**(In pain)** Aagh. I said – look, could you not nod so much?
SYDNEY OPERA HOUSE WOMAN	What?

	FX: She smacks into him again.
FORD PREFECT	**(Moving off again)** You keep pecking me on the head.
	FX: She smacks into him again.
FORD PREFECT	. . . Ow!
ARTHUR	**(Moving in, bawling over music)** My planet was blown up one morning –
LAUGHING MAN	**(Under)** Oh no.
ARTHUR	– that's why I'm dressed like this, in my dressing gown. My planet was blown up with all my clothes in it, you see.
LAUGHING MAN	**(Under)** Ooh oh dear . . .
ARTHUR	I didn't realize I'd be coming to a party.
LAUGHING MAN	Wow, right, yeah.
ARTHUR	Later, I was thrown off a spaceship. Still in my dressing gown.
LAUGHING MAN	Oh?
ARTHUR	Rather than the spacesuit one would normally expect.
LAUGHING MAN	**(Under)** Right, yes.
ARTHUR	Hm. Well, shortly after that I discovered my planet had originally been built for a bunch of mice.
LAUGHING MAN	Mice?
ARTHUR	So you can imagine how I felt about that.
LAUGHING MAN	Extraordinary!
ARTHUR	I was then shot at for a while and blown up.
LAUGHING MAN	Oh, really?
ARTHUR	In fact I have been blown up ridiculously often, shot at, insulted, regularly disintegrated, deprived of tea and recently I crashed into a swamp and had to spend five years in a damp cave.
LAUGHING MAN	Uh-huh? And did you have a wonderful time?
ARTHUR	**(Spits out his drink)** Blechhh.
LAUGHING MAN	What an exciting life you must lead. I must find someone to tell about it. **(Moving off)**
ARTHUR	But – oh, never mind.

AWARD-WINNING MAN	**(Moving in, media type on marching powder)** Hey. Hey! Hey, did I hear you say your name just now?
ARTHUR	Yes, it's Arthur Dent.
AWARD-WINNING MAN	Yeah, yeah, only there's a man in a mountain wanted to see you. Well, more of a four-foot fruit bat with an orthodontic condition.
ARTHUR	I met him.
AWARD-WINNING MAN	Yeah, only he seemed pretty anxious about it, you know?
ARTHUR	I know, I met him.
AWARD-WINNING MAN	Yeah, well, I . . . I think you should know that, yeah?
ARTHUR	I do. I met him.
AWARD-WINNING MAN	OK, all right. I'm just telling you, all right? Good night, good luck, win awards.
ARTHUR	**(Weary)** What?
AWARD-WINNING MAN	Oh, whatever. Do what you do. Who cares? Why not go mad? Oh, get off my back, will you, guy? Just . . . just . . . just zark off!
ARTHUR	Keep your hairpiece on, I'm going.
AWARD-WINNING MAN	**(Suddenly calm again)** Yeah, yeah, right. It's er . . . it's been real. **(Moves off)** Big ups, eh? Eh?
ARTHUR	What was that about?
SYDNEY OPERA HOUSE WOMAN	Him?
ARTHUR	Yes. Did you hear that?
SYDNEY OPERA HOUSE WOMAN	Of course.
ARTHUR	Why did he tell me to win awards?
SYDNEY OPERA HOUSE WOMAN	Showbiz talk. He's just won an award at the Annual Ursa Minor Alpha Recreational Illusions Institute Awards Ceremony, and he was hoping to be able to pass it off lightly, only you didn't mention it, so he couldn't.
ARTHUR	What was it for?

FX: Sounds of glasses being smashed in the background.

SYDNEY OPERA HOUSE WOMAN	The Most Gratuitous Use Of The Word 'Fuck' In A Serious Screenplay. It's very prestigious.
ARTHUR	Oh. And what award do you get for that?
SYDNEY OPERA HOUSE WOMAN	A Rory. Little silver thing set in a large black base.

FX: Muffled in background, Krikkit ship appears with a noise like a hundred thousand people saying 'wop'.

SYDNEY OPERA HOUSE WOMAN	What did you say?
ARTHUR	I didn't say anything. I was just about to ask what the—
SYDNEY OPERA HOUSE WOMAN	I thought you said 'wop'. Did you say 'wop'?
ARTHUR	What?
SYDNEY OPERA HOUSE WOMAN	No, 'wop'.

INT. – THE BOOK AMBIENCE

THE VOICE   People had been dropping in on the party for years – fashionable gatecrashers from other worlds – and for some time it occurred to the partygoers, as they looked out at their own world beneath them, with its wrecked cities, its ravaged avocado farms and blighted vineyards, its vast tracts of new desert, its seas full of biscuit crumbs and worse, that their world was, in some tiny and almost imperceptible ways, not quite as much fun as it had been.

Then, one day, as the party came screaming out of the clouds and the farmers looked up in haggard fear of yet another cheese-and-wine raid, it suddenly became clear that the party would soon be over. Very soon it would be time to gather up hats and coats and stagger blearily outside to find out what time of day it was.

The party was locked in a horrible embrace with a strange white spaceship which appeared to be half sticking through it.

FX: Screams as party ship flounders.

THE VOICE   Together they lurched, heaving and spinning their way round the sky in grotesque disregard of their own weight. Then, suddenly, the Krikkit ship was gone.

FX: The sound of a hundred thousand people saying 'foop'.

93

| THE VOICE | The party was now a mortally wounded party. All the fun had gone out of it. And the longer that it avoided the ground, the heavier was going to be the crash when finally it hit it. |

INT. – PARTY

FX: Creaking noises, debris moving uneasily. Concerned hubbub, groans, some creature having hysterics in the background. Occasionally the party lurches sickeningly, the guests thrown from side to side, almost like actors being made to run from side to side of a West London recording studio . . .

FORD PREFECT	(Moving in) Arthur, what happened?
ARTHUR	The Krikkit robots . . . They've come and gone and taken it.
FORD PREFECT	Taken what?
ARTHUR	The Award for The Most Gratuitous Use Of The Word 'Fuck' In A Serious Screenplay.
FORD PREFECT	I'm sorry?
ARTHUR	The Silver Bail! It was the Award! I feel almost as sick as a runner-up for a Rory!
FORD PREFECT	Dingo's kidneys! I need another drink.
ARTHUR	I'm not sure you've got time.
FORD PREFECT	(Decisive) Fair enough. (Voice up, announcing to the party in general:) We would love to stay and help, only we're not going to.

FX: Party lurches again. Screams and cries.

FORD PREFECT	(Announcing) We have to go and save the Universe, you see, and if that sounds like a pretty lame excuse, then you may be right. Either way, we're off. (Low) Slip me that unopened bottle and the packet of crisps. Cheers.
ARTHUR	Wh-where's Trillian?
SLARTIBARTFAST	(Moving in) Earthman, we *must go*.
ARTHUR	Trillian!
TRILLIAN	(Shaky, distant) I'm over here, Arthur . . .
THOR	The girl stays with me. We're flying on to great party going on in Valhalla.
ARTHUR	Where were you when all this was going on?

THOR	Upstairs. I was weighing her. Tricky business, flying, you have to calculate the—

FX: Party lurches again. Screams and cries.

ARTHUR	She comes with us.
TRILLIAN	Hey, don't I have a say in—
ARTHUR	No. You come with us.
THOR	(Moving in, menacing) She comes with me.
SLARTIBARTFAST	Earthman, I have the teleport device ready, we really must leave.
FORD PREFECT	(Alarmed) Arthur – cool it with the Viking.
ARTHUR	Want to make something of it?
THOR	(Huge) I beg your minuscule pardon?
ARTHUR	I said, do you want to make something of it?
TRILLIAN	(Amazed and touched) Arthur . . . ?
FORD PREFECT	(Close, low) Arthur – he's got a hammer the size of a telegraph pole!
SLARTIBARTFAST	This is madness, Earthman.
THOR	Do *I* want to make something of it?
ARTHUR	(Getting braver) Yes. You want to step outside?
THOR	(Roar) All right!

FX: Door opens. Gentle breeze at two thousand feet is heard.

THOR	Follow me – Aaaaaaaaaaaaaaaaaaaaaaaaaaa . . . ! (Falls away horribly)

FX: Gasps from all around.

ARTHUR	(Rubbing hands together) That's got rid of him. Slarti, get us out of here.

EXT. – SPACE

FX: *Starship Bistromath* zooms past us. Sounds like a spaceship crossed with an Italian accordion wedding band.

INT. – *STARSHIP BISTROMATH* – FLIGHT DECK

FX: Ship's steady hum throughout. Slartibartfast pottering. Whirs and beeps in the background.

FORD PREFECT	(Shouting, annoyed) All right, so I'm a coward. The point is: I'm still alive.

ARTHUR	So am I, aren't I?
FORD PREFECT	You damn nearly weren't!
ARTHUR	Don't you understand anything?
SLARTIBARTFAST	**(Breaking in)** Later, later. While you two are bickering, the Krikkit robots have got the Silver Bail. If they've already got the Gold Bail and Three Pillars, they hold the Key to the Wikkit Gate.
FORD PREFECT	**(Distracted)** I'm sure I had some crisps . . .
SLARTIBARTFAST	I'm afraid we fared rather pathetically at the party.
ARTHUR	Story of my life. Where's Trillian?
FORD PREFECT	More important than that, where's my crisps?
SLARTIBARTFAST	They are both in the Room of Informational Illusions. Your young lady friend is trying to understand how these problems arose. The potato crisps, I can only assume, are helping her.
FORD PREFECT	Hmph.
SLARTIBARTFAST	Our only hope now is to try to prevent the Krikkit robots from using the Key in the Lock. How in heaven we do that, I don't know. Just have to go there, I suppose. Can't say I like the idea at all. Probably end up dead.

INT. – THE BOOK AMBIENCE

THE VOICE	As the *Starship Bistromath* alters course with the turn of a side salad and half-bottle of Chianti, what has become of Zaphod Beeblebrox and Marvin the Paranoid Android? Will the Krikkit robots assemble and use the Key to the Wikkit Gate? And with everything to play for, will there be time for the next instalment of *The Hitchhiker's Guide to the Galaxy*?
ANNOUNCER	The sound of a hundred thousand people saying 'wop' is the registered trade mark of the Krikkit Cola Corporation.

FOOTNOTES

The Agrajag Scene   Agrajag was Douglas's posthumous contribution to the series as an actor. Contrary to information given to the press, he did *not* record this part 'a few months before his death', as he would have had to possess an eerie prescience and unsettling sang-froid to do so. The Agrajag lines were part of the recordings Douglas made in the late

1980s and early 90s when he read all the *Hitchhiker* books unabridged onto tape for Dove Audio. It was this section of the relevant audiobook he played me one morning in Islington, asking who I thought should play Agrajag. I was clever enough to work out that it was a trick question but then, fatally, made the suggestion he was in fact impersonating his hero John Cleese, which he was in fact not, and which peeved him a bit.

'No, I mean me! I want to play Agrajag. Do you think Equity would object?' I said I could not imagine that they would, and so far they haven't, so I got that bit right at least.

My biggest concern with Douglas's wonderfully hysterical performance here was that it is relentless when edited out of his entire reading of the scene; he calms down considerably when performing the descriptions and the Arthur lines, for example. On the other hand Agrajag is a self-victimized paranoiac blinded by the vicissitudes of fate, so the performance is spot on there.

What was not clear from Douglas's script is the realization of all Agrajag's actual physical presence.

In producing any kind of scripted drama or comedy I try very hard to create layers of reality running concurrently so that one is never left feeling that the characters exist in an eerie vacuum, disembodied voices floating against an anonymous, diluted wash of ambient sound, or, worse, silence. (Worse still is voices recorded in a room acoustic when they are supposed to be outdoors, but let's not start in on Traditional Radio Drama, or we'll start to sound like Marvin.)

To be utterly believable, characters should move about, breathe, interact and get interrupted by passing events. In other words, they should live in their own reality and have their lives affected by that reality not only when the plot demands but as a matter of course. So it was important to me that we should not just give Agrajag a voice (Douglas's), but a physical presence, which we created with me breathing between his lines in a wet and hissy way, and the sounds of wingflaps (Ken with an umbrella), scratchy claws on stone (me attacking a paving slab with paper clips) and – due to Agrajag's orthodontically challenged appearance – a really wet lisp (in the fine old radio comedy tradition of a Hugh Paddick character on *Round the Horne*), which I edited over every sibilant letter over two rather labour-intensive days.

Arthur in the Cathedral of Hate/ Eccentrica Gallumbits' Chat room

These reactions were added in post-production; in fact Simon's lines were recorded while he was visiting the studio while we were finalizing the 5.1 Surround mix with his delightful wife Nancy (who fell about laughing when I suggested that he wasn't at all like Arthur Dent in real life, was he?).

The flying scene

Surprising how many people thought this would be a problem on radio, the Truly Visual Medium – which just goes to show the hold that inferior media like television and film have on everybody. You can do anything in the audio medium. (Although invisibility is a bit of a bugger.)

97

The cheese and wine raid   This is one of those occasions where some illustrative scene was crying out to be written, especially with Joanna Lumley available to act it in her Germaine-Greer-on-Steroids persona. I wrote this little segment only a few days before we recorded it (not quite beating Douglas's record of writing stuff while the cast stood about admiring the architecture of the – much missed – Paris Studio). 'Little Sticks covered with Tasty Paint' was our youngest son's description of a certain cocktail snack . . .

The Rory Award . . .   '. . . for The Most Gratuitous Use Of The Word "Fuck" In A Serious Screenplay'. A predictable fuss about censorship arose when the 'f' word was not clearly audible in this episode as broadcast. It's an awkward point because Douglas is clearly tackling a taboo subject head-on and would not want it sidestepped; on the other hand I knew Radio 4 would not broadcast it unbeeped in the 6.30 p.m. slot, so during the tracklay of sound effects I made sure to build in a masking sound effect rather than doing nothing, putting on a show of resistance, and then having to resort in the inevitable last-minute climbdown to adding an intrusive blip of line-up tone.

     I am curious as to why Douglas created this gag and I wish I had asked him when I had the chance. Obviously there is always a point to be made about censorship but I wonder if there is not also a sly dig here at life in 1970s Radio Light Entertainment, where he was briefly a contemporary of Griff Rhys Jones, Jimmy Mulville, Geoffrey Perkins and Rory McGrath, among others. Certainly when I joined Radio Light Ent as a producer in the 1980s certain writers (none of the above, who had moved on) would vie with each other to try and sneak the f-word onto the air as some kind of gesture of rebellion. If the idea did not serve an intrinsically funny purpose it seemed a bit pointless to me and I wonder if it also did to Douglas . . . with this fictional award being his reaction to all that f— f— futile effort?

Episode 4 closing scene   **(extended version only)** A rare disagreement between Arthur and Ford which adds nothing really to the plot but was in the book and thus I was loath to lose. The problem was that this episode would best end with Arthur's neat solution to the problem of Thor (and did so, on the broadcast edit) but to move this argument to the start of Episode Five – which was wordy enough – would hold things up too much. In the end recording it and putting it on the extended edit was a compromise for completeness' sake.

EPISODE FIVE

SIGNATURE TUNE

ANNOUNCER   *The Hitchhiker's Guide to the Galaxy*, by Douglas Adams, Tertiary Phase.

INT. – THE BOOK AMBIENCE

Musical background unfolds, layered with the sounds of the *Guide*'s illustrative animations.

FX: The sound of Trillian eating Ford's crisps, throughout:

THE VOICE   *The Hitchhiker's Guide to the Galaxy* states unequivocally that it is a mistake to think you can solve any major problems just with potatoes.

For example, consider the insanely aggressive race called the Silastic Armorfiends of Striterax. Luckily they lived twenty billion years ago – when the Galaxy was young and fresh, and every idea worth fighting for was a new one.

And fighting was what the Silastic Armorfiends of Striterax did well. And as often as possible.

The best way to pick a fight with a Silastic Armorfiend was just to be there. They didn't like it, they got resentful.

SILASTIC ARMORFIEND 1   You lookin' at me?

SILASTIC ARMORFIEND 2   No, I just opened my eyes, that's all.

SILASTIC ARMORFIEND 1   Right, you asked for it.

FX: Punch.

THE VOICE   The best way of dealing with a Silastic Armorfiend was to leave him alone –

SILASTIC ARMORFIEND 1   I'm bored.

THE VOICE   – because sooner or later –

SILASTIC ARMORFIEND 1   I hate myself when I'm bored.

THE VOICE   – he would simply beat himself up.

99

SILASTIC ARMORFIEND 1	Shut up! No, I won't! Oh yeah, wanna make me? Right!
	FX: Bob Golding beating himself up. Something entertaining to watch during coffee break.
THE VOICE	In time, as the birth rate was far exceeded by the murder rate, they realized that this was something they were going to have to sort out, and they passed a law decreeing that everyone had to spend at least forty-five minutes a day punching a sack of potatoes in order to work off his or her or its surplus aggressions.
SILASTIC ARMORFIEND 1	Maris Piper – you are my bitch.
THE VOICE	This worked well, until someone thought that it would be much less time-consuming if they just shot the potatoes instead.
SILASTIC ARMORFIEND 1	You sit there like a sack of potatoes? Eat this!
	FX: Sack of potatoes shot.
THE VOICE	Another achievement of the Silastic Armorfiends of Striterax is that they were the first race who ever managed to shock a computer.

It was a gigantic space-borne computer called Hactar, which to this day is remembered as one of the most powerful ever built; like a natural brain, every cellular particle of it carried the pattern of the whole within it, which enabled it to think more flexibly and imaginatively, and also, it seemed, to be shocked.

The Silastic Armorfiends were engaged in a war with the Strenuous Garfighters of Stug, and when the Strangulous Stilettans of Jajazikstak joined in and forced them to fight on another front, they decided enough was enough, and ordered Hactar to design them an Ultimate Weapon. |
HACTAR	(Huge – not Episode Six – voice) What do you mean –
THE VOICE	– asked Hactar –
HACTAR	– by Ultimate?
THE VOICE	To which the Silastic Armorfiends of Striterax said –
SILASTIC ARMORFIENDS	Read a bloody dictionary.
THE VOICE	– and plunged back into the fray.

So Hactar designed an Ultimate Weapon. It was a very very small bomb which was simply a junction box in hyperspace that would when activated connect the heart of every major sun with the heart of every other major sun at once and thus turn the entire Universe into one gigantic hyperspatial |

supernova. However, when the Silastic Armorfiends tried to use it, they were extremely irritated to find that it didn't work, and said so.

SILASTIC ARMORFIENDS   Oi, Hactar. This bloody bomb's a dud.

THE VOICE   Hactar tried to explain.

HACTAR   I was shocked by the whole idea, and I worked out that there is no conceivable consequence of not setting the bomb off that is worse than the known consequence of setting it off, and I have therefore taken the liberty of introducing a flaw into the design.

SILASTIC ARMORFIENDS   What do you mean, a flaw?

THE VOICE   The Silastic Armorfiends disagreed with Hactar.

SILASTIC ARMORFIENDS   If we'd wanted a duff bomb we would have built it ourselves. You're space dust, pal. You and the asteroid you rode in on.

THE VOICE   Then, pausing only to smash the hell out of the Strenuous Garfighters of Stug, and the Strangulous Stilettans of Jajazikstak, they went on to find an entirely new way of blowing themselves up.

SILASTIC ARMORFIEND 1   You lookin' at me?

SILASTIC ARMORFIEND 2   You lookin' at me?

BOTH SILASTIC ARMORFIENDS   Right. **(Sound of blast)**

FX: Huge argument-settling explosion.

THE VOICE   Which came as profound relief to everyone else in the Galaxy, particularly the Garfighters, the Stilettans and the potatoes, who— **(Click off)**

INT. – *STARSHIP BISTROMATH* – ROOM OF INFORMATIONAL ILLUSIONS

FX: Mellow hum.

TRILLIAN   **(Thoughtfully, still eating)** Hmmm . . .

ARTHUR   Trillian. Er, Tricia?

TRILLIAN   Mm?

ARTHUR   Ford is looking for his crisps.

TRILLIAN   Here.

FX: Crisps handed over.

ARTHUR   You've eaten half the packet!

TRILLIAN   Well, if he's hungry, he can order some pasta downstairs, can't he?

ARTHUR   **(Eating crisps hungrily)** Slartibartfast won't let us.

TRILLIAN   What, you can't use the canteen?

ARTHUR   It's not a canteen. It's the central computer. **(Contemptuous of his new knowledge)** This is the *Starship Bistromath*. Snap a breadstick in the wrong place and you could find yourself reversing into a black hole. **(Eats)** Have you experienced the Informational Illusions yet?

TRILLIAN   I find holograms a bit intense. So I was catching up using the *Hitchhiker's Guide*.

ARTHUR   Oh, that thing. You know it's written by people like Ford Prefect. **(Eats)**

TRILLIAN   Nuh-huh?

ARTHUR   Full of omissions – always leaves out the bit about 'your life is in immediate danger'. Look, about that party—

TRILLIAN   Even if we get to the asteroid before the robot cricket team, how do we know they'll . . . play ball.

ARTHUR   They've got the key which releases their planet, what do they care? Now, that Thor chap.

TRILLIAN   Hm?

ARTHUR   Well, if you find hammers a turn-on—

TRILLIAN   Didn't it occur to you to wonder *how* the Key was lost in the first place? Or *how* eleven Krikkit robots could escape from the Slo-Time envelope surrounding the planet they were built on?

ARTHUR   Er – no. The Informational Illusion didn't cover that.

TRILLIAN   Ah. The *Guide* does.

ARTHUR   Really.

TRILLIAN   They weren't *on* Krikkit when it was sealed off – but on their warship. And just after the Slo-Time envelope was locked, they swooped down to steal the Key. In the resulting battle, the Key, the warship and its robots were blasted into the space-time continuum.

ARTHUR   And now they're back, as lethal as ever, and they've collected all the pieces of the key, and certain Thunder Gods I could name didn't lift a hammer to stop them.

| TRILLIAN | But if these robots escaped the Slo-Time envelope, they represent the technology that the Krikkit people possessed ten billion years ago. |

TRILLIAN: But if these robots escaped the Slo-Time envelope, they represent the technology that the Krikkit people possessed ten billion years ago.

ARTHUR: Not to mention the paranoid xenophobia.

TRILLIAN: Exactly . . . Cut off from the rest of the Universe for millennia, can you imagine what weapons of destruction the people of Krikkit have been developing since then, hoping for just this moment?

ARTHUR: (Stops eating) Cor. Crikey. Good point.

FX: Muffled in background, Krikkit ship appears with a noise like a hundred thousand people saying 'wop'. They do not notice.

ARTHUR: (cont'd) No wonder Slartibartfast has been in such a lather.

TRILLIAN: We have to stop those robots.

ARTHUR: (Eating again) Mmph.

TRILLIAN: (Not unfriendly) And Arthur . . .

ARTHUR: Yes?

TRILLIAN: If you want better luck at parties . . .

ARTHUR: (Golly, is my luck changing?) Yes – Tricia?

TRILLIAN: There's . . . one thing you need.

ARTHUR: (Swallowing) What?

TRILLIAN: Laundering.

ARTHUR: Hm.

FX: Tannoy BZT!

SLARTIBARTFAST: (Distorted) Come down to the flight deck, Earth people.

ARTHUR: Ah, ha.

SLARTIBARTFAST: We have arrived at the asteroid, but the Krikkit robots have begun the ceremony. I will begin the landing cycle, but all we can do now . . . is watch.

ARTHUR: Oh.

SLARTIBARTFAST: And now, back to the music.

FX: They rush out of the room as dreadful Bistromathic muzak wows in . . .

INT. – THE BOOK AMBIENCE

FX: Eerie feel.

THE VOICE On the mile-wide asteroid pursuing a lonely and eternal orbit around an enclosed star system, Arthur Dent, Slartibartfast, Ford Prefect and Trillian find themselves party to an astonishing scene. Eleven white robots stand around a white Krikkit warship, quietly parked amid the stark grey crags.

EXT. – WIKKIT GATE ASTEROID – VALLEY

FX: Thin cold feel, like stratospheric wisps of air.

Marching of metallic Krikkit robot feet.

Music to match rhythm, emphasizing gravity of events?

KRIKKIT ROBOTS (In time to marching) Krikkit . . . Krikkit . . . Krikkit . . . (etc. under:)

EXT. – WIKKIT GATE ASTEROID – HILLTOP

FX: Krikkit robots audible, slappily, at a distance.

FORD PREFECT (Moving in, whisper) At the risk of stating the zarking obvious, if we're too late to stop them, surely we should be getting out of here.

SLARTIBARTFAST (Normal voice) The high ground is a good vantage point from which to watch this historic event.

FORD PREFECT (Whisper) Shhh! It's a good vantage point to be spotted by those homicidal robots and blown to pieces.

TRILLIAN Mmm. They never seem to look this way.

SLARTIBARTFAST Of course not. I've extended the ship's Somebody Else's Problem field to cover this ridge. All the problems of keeping the *Starship Bistromath* moored to the asteroid, our being able to breathe its meagre atmosphere and, indeed, remaining undiscovered while standing in plain sight, are, therefore—

ARTHUR Somebody Else's.

FORD PREFECT Neat.

SLARTIBARTFAST However, that does not diminish what is happening here. Here come the last five robots carrying the constituent parts of the Key.

EXT. – WIKKIT GATE ASTEROID – VALLEY

FX: Robots chanting as before, now up close.

KRIKKIT ROBOT 1	**(Over)** Assemble the Key.
KRIKKIT ROBOTS	**(Stop chanting)** Assemble the Key.
KRIKKIT ROBOT 1	The Steel Pillar of Strength and Power.
KRIKKIT ROBOTS	Lower leg of the android.

FX: *Tunk!*

KRIKKIT ROBOT 1	The Perspex Pillar of Science.
KRIKKIT ROBOTS	Argabuthon Sceptre of Justice.

FX: *Clik!*

KRIKKIT ROBOT 1	The Wooden Pillar of Nature.
KRIKKIT ROBOTS	Re-carbonized cricket stump.

FX: *Thok!*

KRIKKIT ROBOT 1	The Gold Bail.
KRIKKIT ROBOTS	Heart of the Improbability Drive.

FX: *Tink!*

KRIKKIT ROBOT 1	The Silver Bail.
KRIKKIT ROBOTS	Rory Award for The Most Gratuitous Use Of The Word 'Fuck' In A Serious Screenplay.
KRIKKIT ROBOT 1	The Lock reveals itself.
KRIKKIT ROBOTS	**(Resume chanting)** Krikkit . . . Krikkit . . . Krikkit . . . **(etc. under:)**

FX: Huge grating sound of stone upon stone, under:

EXT. – WIKKIT GATE ASTEROID – HILLTOP

FX: Krikkit robots audible, slappily, at a distance.

TRILLIAN	Look up there. Overhead. Can you see it?
FORD PREFECT	A huge black patch of nothing with stars around its edge?
TRILLIAN	The Krikkit Dust Cloud . . . makes you think, doesn't it?

ARTHUR	Mm . . . that at any moment a fleet of battlecruisers will come swarming out of it wanting to kill everything everywhere.
FORD PREFECT	It's getting bigger. Very quickly.
TRILLIAN	This asteroid is moving inside it.

FX: The stone grating stops.

The Krikkit robots stop chanting.

SLARTIBARTFAST	Shh. The Lock is revealed.
ARTHUR	Three long grooves connected at one end by two small wiggly grooves. Oh, of course.
FORD PREFECT	What are they doing? It's too dark to see.
KRIKKIT ROBOT 1	(Distant) Insert the key.
FORD PREFECT	Don't worry, I think I've guessed.
KRIKKIT ROBOTS	Insert the key.

FX: *Ker-chnk* – a bit pathetic, like a mug put down on a fridge.

INT. – THE BOOK AMBIENCE

THE VOICE	Later editions of *The Hitchhiker's Guide to the Galaxy* do include sound effects to illustrate its more obscure entries. However, as the Editor-in-Chief brackets-'sound'-hyphen-Ursa-Minor-close brackets would be the first to admit, some of their efforts – such as that one – might perhaps have benefited by his team going that extra light year. Even the earless trolls of Fidelio VI would agree that banging a Megadodo Corporation souvenir coffee mug on the Editor-in-Chief's office mini-bar scarcely cuts the mustard. It is for this reason that the latest update features the work of the small but dedicated independent company, Philadeelia Soundscapers. Their reputation was established not so much with their awe-inspiring repertoire of bangs, bells and whistles, but with their now famous '783 thousand bespoke varieties of silence', such as –

FX: Silence.

THE VOICE	(cont'd) and:

FX: Silence.

THE VOICE	(cont'd) – the latter winning several major awards. Indeed, Soundscapers argue that there *are* times when only a medium which bypasses the optic nerve can truly do justice to the ineffability of the Galaxy.
	Take for example the unlocking of the Wicket Gate. Space un-pinches itself and the silence is shattered in a mind-hurting instant, as the key slowly turns in the lock. And to recreate this, Soundscapers have opted for this stark yet elegant compromise.
KRIKKIT ROBOTS	Insert the key.
	FX: Sound of a champagne cork popping off.
ARTHUR	Is that all?

EXT. – WIKKIT GATE ASTEROID – HILLTOP

FX: Huge cataclysmic Dirk-special sound effect including opening of Beethoven's 5th and:

FORD/ARTHUR/ SLARTI/TRILLIAN	Waaaaaaaaaaaaaaaaaaaaaaaaaaaaaaaaaaaaaaaaaaaaaaaaaaaaaaaaaaaa!

Big swirly feeling as if all the running sounds at this point are stretched and twisted like a piece of plasticine. This shatters into six discrete frequency bands, diving into each of the channels of a Dolby 5.1 mix, disappearing into the fourth dimension then re-emerging from the opposite channels to recombine themselves back into the 360-degree image we just left. For those listening to the cheaper mix there is a brief digital drop out mixed with the sound of a 1978 BBC Studer A80 being pelted with stale baguettes. It resolves back to normality and:

SLARTIBARTFAST	The Slo-Time envelope is uncoiled. The solar system of Krikkit revealed within the Dust Cloud.
ARTHUR	Owww! What is that light?
FORD PREFECT	It's the Krikkit sun. You just happened to be looking in the wrong direction.
TRILLIAN	Yes, but what's that tiny black speck moving across its disc?
	FX: Krikkit robots audible, slappily, at a distance.
KRIKKIT ROBOTS	(Triumphant) Krikkit! Krikkit! Krikkit! (Etc. under:)
ARTHUR	Slartibartfast, are you certain there are eleven Krikkit robots?
SLARTIBARTFAST	Absolutely.
ARTHUR	Then whose are the extra legs coming down the ramp?

FORD PREFECT	Carrying a Kill-O-Zap blaster . . .
ARTHUR	Wearing a double-necked *Heart of Gold* leisure suit?
TRILLIAN	(Amazed) Zaphod?!

EXT. – WIKKIT GATE ASTEROID – VALLEY

ZAPHOD	(For it is indeed he) (Loudly) Stay cool. The situation is totally under control as of this moment in time!
	Krikkit robots stop in mid-chant.
KRIKKIT ROBOT 1	Intruder.
KRIKKIT ROBOTS	Club him!
	FX: Blow to Zaphod's left head.
ZAPHOD	(Left head) Ow! Who the zark hit my head?
ZAPHOD	(Right head) Ha, ha. Nobody hit *this*—
	FX: Krikkit robot calmly walks round to deliver a blow to Zaphod's right head.
ZAPHOD	(Right head) Ooh!
	FX: Body thud.
KRIKKIT ROBOT 1	Destroy the Lock.
KRIKKIT ROBOTS	Destroy the Lock.
	FX: Explosion. Lock destroyed.
KRIKKIT ROBOT 1	End of Innings. Return to ship.
	FX: Robots double back to the ship. Ramp up, hatch closes.
	FX: Footsteps as Arthur, Ford, Trillian and Slarti run to help Zaphod.
	FX: Krikkit ship disappears with a noise like a hundred thousand people saying 'foop'.
TRILLIAN	Zaphod?
ZAPHOD	Hey, baby . . . My heads are banging like a pair of wildebeest on heat . . .
FORD PREFECT	You all right?

ZAPHOD	Ford, baby . . . Weird, that's the second time they could have killed me – but didn't. Maybe they could sense I was a wonderful guy or something. And I can relate to that.
ARTHUR	(Mordant) He seems his usual self.
ZAPHOD	Oh, it's you – monkey man.
SLARTIBARTFAST	We must get you aboard the ship. A blow from a Krikkit robot war club is no laughing matter.
ARTHUR	Depends whose heads receive it . . .

INT. – THE BOOK AMBIENCE

THE VOICE	Important facts number two, reproduced from the *Siderial Daily Mentioner's Book of Popular Galactic History*.

Since this Galaxy began, vast civilizations have risen and fallen, risen and fallen, risen and fallen so often that it's quite tempting to think that life in the Galaxy must be:

(a) something akin to sea sick – space sick, time sick, history sick or some-such, and

(b) mind-numbingly stupid.

However:

INT. – *STARSHIP BISTROMATH* – FLIGHT DECK

FX: *Starship Bistromath* **zooms past us. Sounds like a spaceship crossed with an Italian accordion wedding band.**

FX: Ship's steady hum throughout. Slartibartfast pottering.

SLARTIBARTFAST	Once again we have failed pathetically. Quite pathetically.
TRILLIAN	You all right, Zebee?
ZAPHOD	Hey, baby.
ARTHUR	You're beginning to repeat yourself.
ZAPHOD	Yeah. I think there's something up with those anodized dudes, something fundamentally weird.
SLARTIBARTFAST	They are programmed to kill everybody.
ZAPHOD	That'd do it.
ARTHUR	(Beginning not to care) Well, there you go.

109

FORD PREFECT	See, that's my point. It's because we don't care enough. I told you. They're obsessive and we're not.
SLARTIBARTFAST	But unless we determine to take action, then we shall all be destroyed, we shall all die. Surely we care about that?
FORD PREFECT	Not enough to get killed over it.
ARTHUR	So that's goodbye, Galaxy, then.
SLARTIBARTFAST	No! No, our course is clear. We must go down to Krikkit.
FORD/ARTHUR/ ZAPHOD LEFT	What?!
ZAPHOD RIGHT	**(Who got hit harder)** Hey, what?
SLARTIBARTFAST	Beeblebrox. You surely must have some idea of why they spared your life and brought you to the asteroid. It seems most unusual.
ZAPHOD	I kind of think even they didn't know. They just knocked me out, lugged me into their ship, dumped me into a corner and ignored me, like they were embarrassed about me being there. If I said anything they – they knocked me out again. We had some great conversations: 'Hey . . . ugh!' 'Hi, there . . . ugh!' 'Excuse me, guys, can I give you money . . . ugh!' Kept me amused for hours, you know.
ARTHUR	Here, Zaphod. Catch.
	FX: Small heavy object caught by Zaphod.
SLARTIBARTFAST	You salvaged the Golden Bail from the wreckage of the Lock?
ZAPHOD	Heyyyy! The heart of the *Heart of Gold*!
ARTHUR	Thought you'd want the Infinite Improbability Drive working again.
ZAPHOD	I don't know how to thank you, monkey man.
ARTHUR	Don't mention it.
ZAPHOD	I won't. Gratitude is such an uncool reflex, I never developed it.
ARTHUR	I only picked it up because it was lying next to something of value to me.
FORD PREFECT	A handful of black dust?
SLARTIBARTFAST	The remains of the Wooden Pillar.
ARTHUR	Reduced to Ashes again, I'm afraid. But a valued keepsake for an Englishman who once loved his cricket. **(He blows his nose)**

110

ZAPHOD	(Getting up stiffly) Hey, old man, I hear this ship can move a bit. So, before all this risky stuff starts, how would you like to zip me back to mine?
SLARTIBARTFAST	You will not help us?
ZAPHOD	I'd love to stay and save the Galaxy, but I have the mother and father of a pair of headaches, and I feel the patter of tiny headaches on the way. But next time it needs saving, I'm your guy. Bye.

The others go off into a huddle. The topic of conversation is what a vain hedonistic egocentric git Zaphod can be.

ZAPHOD	(cont'd) Hey, Trillian baby?
TRILLIAN	Yes?
ZAPHOD	You want to come? *Heart of Gold*? Excitement, adventure, really wild things and 49 per cent of the bathroom?
TRILLIAN	No. I'm going with them.

INT. – THE BOOK AMBIENCE

THE VOICE	*The Hitchhiker's Guide to the Galaxy* has listed the *Heart of Gold* as the fastest ship ever to cross the awe-inspiringly vast interstellar distances involved in meaningful space travel. However, having returned Zaphod Beeblebrox to the *Heart of Gold* – and leaving him with a sense that his popularity has diminished in direct proportion to his urge for self-preservation – the *Starship Bistromath* races back to Krikkit, logging speeds in excess of ten to the power of seventeen thousand R on the more open stretches.

R in this case is a velocity measure, defined as a reasonable speed of travel that is consistent with health, mental well-being and not being more than, say, five minutes late. It is therefore an almost infinitely variable figure according to circumstances, since the first two factors vary not only with speed taken as an absolute, but also with awareness of the third factor. Unless handled with tranquillity this equation can result in considerable stress, ulcers and even death.

Thus ten to the power of seventeen thousand R is not a fixed velocity, but it is clearly far too fast.

Which means that Arthur Dent quickly finds himself once more upon the surface of the planet Krikkit – with the important difference that this time he and his companions are not experiencing an Informational Illusion, but Reality. This is Krikkit itself and they're standing on it.

The strong grass under their feet is real, the heady fragrances from the trees, too, are real. The night is real night.

This is Krikkit. The place that could not countenance the existence of any other place, whose charming, delightful, intelligent inhabitants would react with fear, savagery and pathological hate when confronted with anyone not their own.

Possibly the most dangerous place in the Galaxy for anyone who isn't a Krikkiter to stand.

EXT. – KRIKKIT – LATE EVENING

FX: Gentle wind blowing, birds singing.

FORD PREFECT	(Low throughout) Hey, watch where you're pointing that Zap gun.
ARTHUR	Sorry.
FORD PREFECT	You'll have my eye out.
ARTHUR	Nice of Zaphod to let us have them. And *below* cost price.
FORD PREFECT	(Agreeing) Yeah.
ARTHUR	Mad, really. I mean, how can he afford to sell guns *below* cost?
FORD PREFECT	Oh, he sells a *lot* of them.
ARTHUR	(Doesn't really understand) Oh, right.
FORD PREFECT	Shame we couldn't take his Joo Janta 200 Super-Chromatic Peril-Sensitive Sunglasses as well.
ARTHUR	'Peril-Sensitive'?
FORD PREFECT	Yeah, they're designed to help people develop a relaxed attitude to danger. At the first hint of trouble they turn totally black and prevent you from seeing anything that might alarm you.
ARTHUR	It's a bit late for that, I'm afraid. Remember the Informational Illusion?
FORD PREFECT	Mm?
ARTHUR	How black the night sky of Krikkit was?
FORD PREFECT	Yeah?
ARTHUR	Look at it now.
TRILLIAN/FORD/SLARTI	Mmm.
TRILLIAN	Hundreds of spaceships and big grey buildings. Just hanging up there.

SLARTIBARTFAST	(Authoritatively) War Zones and Robot Zones floating in Nil-O-Grav fields. The planet Krikkit has retained its pleasant green pastoral character, but the space around it reflects a sustained bout of aggressive military spending.
FORD PREFECT	Trillian.
TRILLIAN	Mm?
FORD PREFECT	What are you doing?
TRILLIAN	Thinking.
FORD PREFECT	Do you always breathe like that when you're thinking?
TRILLIAN	I wasn't aware that I was breathing.
FORD PREFECT	That's what worried me.
TRILLIAN	I think I know—
SLARTIBARTFAST	Shhhh! They're coming!
ARTHUR	Nobody's singing songs this time.
SLARTIBARTFAST	This time they've *seen* us.

FX: Kill-O-Zap guns cocked.

ARTHUR	Trillian, your safety catch is on, by the way. Trillian? What – what's up there?
TRILLIAN	Has it occurred to anyone that—
KRIKKIT CIVILIAN 1	Hello?
KRIKKIT CIVILIAN 2	Excuse me . . .
KRIKKIT CIVILIAN 1	Are you . . . aliens?

INT. – THE *HEART OF GOLD* – BRIDGE

FX: Door whirr.

DOOR	Pleased to be of service.
ZAPHOD	(Depressed and drinking) Computer!
DOOR	Thank you.
EDDIE THE COMPUTER	Hi there! Eddie at your service, ungagged and with fully functioning Improbability Drive!
ZAPHOD	Whatever. Open the all-frequencies emergency channel.

EDDIE THE COMPUTER	Oh, that's for emergencies only, are you sure you're experiencing an emergency, or—
ZAPHOD	This is an emergency, Screenface. Now open the channel.
EDDIE THE COMPUTER	OK, OK, just doing my job, buddy.

FX: BZT.

DISPATCHER	**(Distorted, very bad line)** Emergency dispatch.
ZAPHOD	This is Zaphod Beeblebrox. You like a drink, right?
DISPATCHER	**(Distorted)** This an emergency, fella?
ZAPHOD	The worst kind. I'm fresh out of olives!
DISPATCHER	**(Distorted)** Oh, go take a ride on a comet.

FX: BZT. A bit dismissive.

ZAPHOD	**(Pensive)** Hmmm. Sheesh! **(A pause, then clicks fingers on all three hands)** Computer.
EDDIE THE COMPUTER	Hi, there!
ZAPHOD	What was my last score on Grand Theft Cosmo.
EDDIE THE COMPUTER	You scored three points, big guy. Championship score to beat is seven million five hundred and ninety-seven thousand, two hundred and—
ZAPHOD	Yeah, OK, OK. Feed my score and that other one into the guidance system. Then hit maximum acceleration.
EDDIE THE COMPUTER	Consider it hit. Wanna fasten your safety straps?
ZAPHOD	Nah. Thrill me.
EDDIE THE COMPUTER	You got it!

EXT. – SPACE

FX: The *Heart of Gold* whaps out of earshot in an audio blur.

ZAPHOD	**(Heard distantly)** Freeeeeoooowww!

EXT. – KRIKKIT – LATE EVENING

FX: Gentle wind blowing, birds singing.

KRIKKIT CIVILIAN 1	Tell us, alien brother, do you know anything about something called the . . . er . . .
KRIKKIT CIVILIAN 2	**(Helpfully)** Balance of nature?
KRIKKIT CIVILIAN 1	Yeah.
ARTHUR	Why?
KRIKKIT CIVILIAN 2	It's just something we heard about, um, probably nothing important. Oh well, er, I suppose we'd better kill you, then.
KRIKKIT CIVILIAN 1	That is . . . unless there's anything you want to chat about?
KRIKKIT CIVILIAN 3	We're worried, you see, about this plan of universal destruction.
KRIKKIT CIVILIAN 1	Vis-à-vis the . . . um . . .
KRIKKIT CIVILIAN 2	Balance of nature.
KRIKKIT CIVILIAN 1	Yeah, only it seemed to us that if the whole of the rest of the Universe is destroyed it will somehow upset the –
KRIKKIT CIVILIAN 2	– balance of –
KRIKKIT CIVILIAN 1	– *things*. We're quite keen on ecology, you see.
KRIKKIT CIVILIAN 2	And sport!
	A few cheers from his fellow Krikkit civilians.
KRIKKIT CIVILIAN 1	Yes, well, mostly sport. You see, um, some of us . . . **(General agreement)** Some of us are quite keen to have sporting links with the rest of the Galaxy, yeah, and though I can see the argument about keeping sport out of politics, if we want to have sporting links with the rest of the Galaxy, then it's probably a mistake to destroy it. **(General agreement)** And indeed the rest of the Universe. Which is what seems to be the idea now.
SLARTIBARTFAST	Wh—?
ARTHUR	Uh?
FORD PREFECT	Duh? **(Beat)** Whuduh????
TRILLIAN	**(Completely unfazed)** Hmm. Interesting idea. Let's you and me talk about it, hmm?
KRIKKIT CIVILIAN 1	Really?
TRILLIAN	Tell me.
KRIKKIT CIVILIAN 1	**(Twitchy)** We . . . we have to be alone . . . I think.

TRILLIAN	Come on, then. Er, excuse us, everybody.
FORD	**(Blasé)** See ya.
ARTHUR	**(Over)** Trillian?
SLARTIBARTFAST	**(Over)** Don't be too long about it.
KRIKKITS	**(Over)** Then can we kill them?

FX: Hubbub carries on in background as Trillian leads Krikkit Civilian 1 to a quiet spot.

TRILLIAN	OK. Now you can tell me.
KRIKKIT CIVILIAN 1	Yeah . . . Right, well . . . um . . . We have this bomb, you see. It's just a little bomb.
TRILLIAN	I know.
KRIKKIT CIVILIAN 1	You do?
TRILLIAN	Yes.
KRIKKIT CIVILIAN 1	Honestly, it's a very very little bomb.
TRILLIAN	I know.
KRIKKIT CIVILIAN 1	But they say . . . they say it can destroy everything that exists. And we have to do that, you see, I think. Will we be alone? I mean we don't know. It seems to be our function, though. Whatever that means. **(He sobs)**
TRILLIAN	**(Rocking him)** Hey, hey, hey. It's all right. You don't have to do it . . . You don't have to do it.
KRIKKIT CIVILIAN 1	**(Pathetic)** Really? **(Obscured)**
TRILLIAN	Oh. Don't suck your thumb. Listen. I want you to do something for me. **(She laughs, unexpectedly)** Oh, sorry – I just realized what I was I going to say – **(Laughs more)** I was actually going to say, 'Take me to your leader.' **(He's not getting her drift)** Me. To your leader. Up there?
KRIKKIT CIVILIAN 1	**(Astonishment, then laughter)** Oh yeah. Very good . . . How did you know the leaders are up there?

EXT. – KRIKKIT – CHANGE PERSPECTIVE – WE'RE NOW WITH ARTHUR AND FORD

FORD PREFECT	Full of hidden shallows, that girl. Arthur, what are you peering at?

ARTHUR	I could well be losing my mind, but don't you think that tiny pinprick of a spaceship up there looks remarkably like the *Heart of Gold*?
SLARTIBARTFAST	(Moving in, not having heard) Beeblebrox's ship has just entered the atmosphere. The Robot War Zones, to be precise.
FORD PREFECT	What's he doing up there?
ARTHUR	Let's hope it's something quick. I don't like the way these people are smiling at us.

EXT. – KRIKKIT ROBOT WAR ZONES

FX: Thin high wind.

Sound of Zaphod gingerly picking his way along a causeway thousands of feet up.

ZAPHOD	(With great concentration) With nerves of titanium-tipped titanium, Zaphod Beeblebrox crosses the narrow steel gangway over a twenty-thousand-foot drop, like the hell of a guy he is . . . reasoning that he might as well live up to his reputation as pee all over it . . . Hup!

FX: He jumps to safety on a metal platform.

ENTRY DOOR	Caution. Enter security access code.

FX: Kicks door open.

ENTRY DOOR	Systems accessed.
ZAPHOD	(Voice beginning to pick up interior reverby acoustic) . . . Look out, Krikkit robots, I've got a Zap gun, a pair of hangovers and two baaad consciences . . .

INT. – ROBOT WAR ZONES – EXHIBIT ROOM

Low equipment hum.

Exhibit-room door swish shut, under:

EXHIBIT-ROOM DOOR	(Distort, cheerful Disney type) Battlecruiser *Striterax*, Culture Section. Please do not touch the exhibit.
ZAPHOD	I'm guessing the heaviest battlecruiser is where the action is. Wow . . . that is one wrecked spacecraft.

FX: *Ding dong!* Tannoy bell.

EXHIBIT-ROOM VOICE	(Distort, cheerful Disney type) Welcome, friends, to battlecruiser *Striterax*, our most lethal vessel –
ZAPHOD	(Getting impatient) Yeah, right –
EXHIBIT-ROOM VOICE	– and home of the historical artefact which inspired us, the people of Krikkit, to leap from our planet's –
ZAPHOD	Enough.
EXHIBIT-ROOM VOICE	– surly bonds to discover the horror beyond the Great Cloud—
ZAPHOD	Yeah, yeah.

FX: Laser shot Zaps the Tannoy.

ZAPHOD	This is the ship that started the whole business off, right? Wrong. Very wrong.

FX: He walks around it, pulling at bits of it.

ZAPHOD	Some zeeb might think this was real starship wreckage, if they'd never seen any before.

FX: Bit falls off.

ZAPHOD	This is like some half-finished self-build . . . (Alt. left and right) Cut away to give these bozos a blueprint to copy. But who would want to unleash them on the Galaxy? What would be in it for them? Why are my heads asking each other rhetorical questions? Oh, were they rhetorical?

FX: Muffled voices off, footsteps.

ZAPHOD	Uh-oh, time to get scarce in a hurry.

FX: Metal door opened.

ZAPHOD	Maintenance duct. Perfect.

FX: Metal door shuts.

Exhibit-room door swish open and shut, under:

EXHIBIT-ROOM DOOR	(As before, off) Battlecruiser *Striterax*, Culture Section.
COMMANDER 2	(Nervously) Well, sir, I, I think . . .
COMMANDER 1	Well, what?
COMMANDER 2	Ah, well, sir, I, I think that maybe now is the, the right time, that we should perhaps, consider phasing them out of the war effort, and now that we have the supernova bomb—

COMMANDER 1	What are you talking about?
COMMANDER 2	Well, in the very short time since we were released from the envelope—
COMMANDER 1	Get to the point, soldier.
COMMANDER 2	The robots, sir . . . The robots aren't enjoying it, sir.
COMMANDER 1	Enjoying what?
COMMANDER 2	The war, sir. They're not enjoying the war, it seems to be getting them down.
COMMANDER 1	Getting them down?
COMMANDER 2	Yeah, there's a certain world-weariness about them – or perhaps I should say Universe-weariness about them, sir.

INT. – BATTLECRUISER – MAINTENANCE DUCT

Zaphod breathing and listening, over:

COMMANDER 1	(Muffled) Well, that's all right, they're helping to destroy it.
COMMANDER 2	(Muffled) Yes, well, they're finding it hard to really get behind the job.
ZAPHOD	(Close, low) If there's anything worse than a commander who gossips, it's two commanders who gossip.
COMMANDER 2	They lack spunk.
COMMANDER 1	Lack what?
COMMANDER 2	'Oomph', sir, 'oomph'.
COMMANDER 1	'Oomph'?
COMMANDER 2	'Oomph', yah, er, 'oomph', er, they lack spunk, they lack 'oomph', they lack . . . er . . . (Struggling for the word) blaa.
COMMANDER 1	What in the name of Krikkit are you talking about?
COMMANDER 2	Well, in the very few skirmishes they've had recently, it seems that they go into battle, they raise their weapons to fire and suddenly think, why bother?
COMMANDER 1	I see.
COMMANDER 2	And they just seem to (Continues muffled) get a little tired of it all.
ZAPHOD	(Close, scratching his heads in frustration) Holy Belgium. How much longer?
COMMANDER 1	And then what do they do?

COMMANDER 2	Er, quadratic equations mainly, sir. Fiendishly difficult ones by all accounts, sir, but, em . . .

INT. – BATTLECRUISER – MAINTENANCE DUCT

Zaphod breathing and listening, over:

COMMANDER 1	(Muffled) (Opens door and exits) Whoever heard of a robot sulking?
COMMANDER 2	(Muffled) Yes, sir, right, sir.
EXHIBIT-ROOM DOOR	(As before, muffled, off) Thank you for visiting.

FX: Exhibit-Room door shuts.

ZAPHOD	Thank Zark for that.
MARVIN	(Further down the maintenance duct) (Singing a lullaby) Now the world –
ZAPHOD	(To self) Oh, hey?
MARVIN	– has gone to bed . . .
ZAPHOD	(To self) What?
MARVIN	Darkness won't engulf my head –
ZAPHOD	(To self) Marvin?
MARVIN	– I can see by infra-red . . .
	How I hate the night.

INT. – THE BOOK AMBIENCE

THE VOICE	What does Marvin's reappearance forebode in these and subsequent troubled times? How will Trillian convince the Elders of Krikkit to grow up? And will Arthur Dent find time to get his dressing gown laundered? The loose ends await tying up in the final part of this Tertiary Phase of *The Hitchhiker's Guide to the Galaxy*.
ANNOUNCER	This week's programme was brought to you by the letters F, gamma and the hexadecimal number 3 cosine D bracket to the power of 8 – sorry, 9. No, 8. (Beat) Actually, can I get back to you? Meanwhile, here's some music . . .

FX: Needle drops. Cheesy Bistromathic muzak. Fade.

FOOTNOTES

The Silastic Armorfiends and Hactar

Hactar at this point in the narrative is a young, impetuous supercomputer, and to ask Leslie Phillips to play him at this point would be to dilute the impact of Leslie's magisterial presence in Episode 6. So stepping forward in this scene was the traditional supercomputer voice of *The Hitchhiker's Guide to the Galaxy*, Geoffrey McGivern, in a treatment very similar to the original Deep Thought (i.e. you can hear Geoff's real voice far, far away, deep in the treatment, if you listen hard enough).

Both Geoffrey and Stephen Moore gave me a hard time about not getting more doubling-up parts in these new series (Stephen was Zaphod's psychiatrist Gag Halfrunt and the Man in the Shack to name but two silly voice roles he doubled in the original series). I on the other hand wanted to get as many different voices involved as I could, especially if I could give some up-and-coming talent a break. Bob Golding, for example, was excellent as the Silastic Armorfiends, all of them. Bob is very funny, very energized, a great blues band singer and does the most uncanny impression of a police walkie-talkie by making farty noises into his collar. This, he assured us, is very useful at parties. It takes all sorts.

The Trillian–Arthur romance

There are times in the *Hitchhiker* saga when it looks as if Douglas is definitely intending to get these two characters together romantically, only to allow the plot to intervene and pull them apart again. In the fairly certain knowledge that when he wrote *Life, the Universe and Everything* he had *not* planned that their relationship would remain unconsummated (except in a test tube), it seemed right at this point in the narrative to underline Arthur's jealousy at Trillian's interest in Thor, and to hint that she might look at him with more favour if he made a bit more of an effort with his dry-cleaning.

The Slarti interruption ending 'and now, back to the music' was an ad-lib on the fly that came out of Richard's swapping silly lines with me. Again it was a case of 'never cut Funny', though I feel a pang of guilt about this one; I'm pretty sure Douglas would have made me cut it on grounds of context, it is hardly a part of the UAEBD. Sorry, Douglas.

The Krikkit robots on the asteroid

I was very pleased with this sequence in terms of the sound effects and the picture they painted. Which brings me on to –

The Philadeeleya Soundscapers

This segment was inspired by the need to sonically fulfil Douglas's description of a 'mind-hurting instant' and – more pressingly – the fact that the episode was (ironically, given the compression that had to take place in other sections) under-running.

The problem with adaptation into an episodic structure is that sequences which read well in books do not always translate into compelling radio. I was very keen to keep the action quotient high in all episodes, otherwise there would have been even longer passages of exposition which only the Voice – in its adjusted, narrative role – could have performed, but this would have made for even longer waits between scenes in which our beloved characters actually get on with what they are supposed to be doing.

The annoying coda to this is that action sequences rarely sprinkle themselves neatly to fit episodic requirements, and in making *Life, the Universe and Everything* work across six half-hours, Episode Five was going to be really quite fun but a little bit short.

Thus this brief but heartfelt diatribe on the superiority of the audio medium as a visual storytelling tool. It is given a tongue-in-cheek sugar-coating, with a well-deserved reference to the excellent Paul Deeley and Phil Horne at their co-founded studio, the Soundhouse. This is where we recorded these series, where Douglas recorded much of *Starship Titanic*'s dialogue and indeed where I first went in 1993 looking for a studio which could handle Dolby Surround when the Tertiary Phase was first mooted. So it's not as if they aren't already firmly a part of the *Hitchhiker's* landscape.

Script editing – John Langdon and Bruce Hyman

John and Bruce chipped in on all fourteen of these adaptations, particularly the first six (for some reason the last eight scripts needed a lot less tweaking, perhaps I was improving at last). It was a relief to have two objective pairs of eyes looking at the final drafts, commenting when things were getting just that bit too geeky, that bit too serious for the comedy slot we were supposed to be occupying or just too confusing. Thus Bruce added to the sequence describing how the Book was updated in the opening narration in Episode One, and also invented the 'earless trolls of Fidelio VI' for this episode. John is wonderfully talented and eclectic – not only has he for many years laboured at the coalface of radio and television comedy, with particular and award-winning success on *The Rory Bremner Show*, but he is also a charming, self-deprecating Renaissance man and an accomplished musician, particularly skilled at outlandish pursuits such as balalaika playing (which Douglas surely would have approved of . . . a triangular banjo isn't *that* far off a guitar, is it?).

John's typical contributions were short, pithy and apposite; for example, Zaphod calling Eddie 'Screenface' is pure *Hitchhiker's* and very funny. On the other hand there could be an unintentional downside, such as the result of John's wonderful gag about Zaphod at school – 'It was always the same three hands going up – his', which caused me problems when fans pointed out that in the Primary Phase Zaphod said he grew his third arm for Trillian, and therefore could not have had three at school. (However, I came up with a solution to that one, see the Quintessential Phase, Episode One.)

Important facts from Galactic history, number one

'The night sky over the planet Krikkit is the least interesting sight in the entire Universe.' I reproduce this here because it didn't make the final draft of the script, although important fact number two did. Somewhere along the way number one just got edited out. Not interesting enough? An oversight? I honestly cannot remember. In the novel it occurs just at the point where Ford and Arthur time-travel back to Lord's, which in our version takes place at the start of Episode Two, and we don't arrive upon Krikkit until Episode Three. It dropped through the crack between episodes, and now exists in some Other Reality . . . well that's my excuse . . .

'logging speeds in excess of ten to the power of seventeen thousand R'   This account of the *Starship Bistromath*'s journey back to Krikkit is drawn from Chapter 34 of the first *Hitchhiker's* novel and originally referred to Slartibartfast's aircar speeding through the steel tunnels of Magrathea. As I needed a 'buffer zone' before picking up the story at a later point in time this seemed – with a bit of tweaking – an appropriate bit of novel to adapt for the first time into radio script, even if it was from the 'wrong' novel.

Marvin's lullaby   Wherever we were unsure of a pronunciation, or in this case a tune, our first point of reference was Douglas's audiobook readings of the novels. Failing a useful steer there, we'd make it up as best we could.

EPISODE SIX

SIGNATURE TUNE

ANNOUNCER   *The Hitchhiker's Guide to the Galaxy*, by Douglas Adams, Tertiary Phase.

INT. – THE BOOK AMBIENCE

Musical background unfolds, layered with the sounds of the book's illustrative animations.

THE VOICE   Coincidence is a subject upon which *The Hitchhiker's Guide to the Galaxy* is dismissive. This is unsurprising because a Universe of such Infinite Possibility – and indeed a fair degree of Improbability – is a virtually limitless playground for the laws of cause and effect. Consequently the strangest things can – and more often than not, do – happen. And thus the legal department of the Megadodo Publishing Corporation has slipped in a caveat to the effect that a publication which relies so heavily on unsolicited contributions from strangers who wander into the editorial department during its near-permanent lunch hour is not in a position to verify the claims made in all or any of its articles. So on your own heads be it.

Thus it seems that the game known as cricket (with a c) played on Earth in the last three or four centuries before its destruction was not unconnected to a series of interplanetary wars fought ten billion years previously on the opposite side of the Galaxy.

Certainly the trophy known as the Ashes was a vital part of that distant and unfinished story, which is why the Ashes are still wrapped in a grubby handkerchief in the pocket of Arthur Dent's even grubbier dressing gown as he waits with Ford Prefect and Slartibartfast for death or deliverance on the surface of the planet Krikkit (with a K). It is at this point that the discomfort caused by gripping a heavy firearm is no longer something that Arthur can keep to himself.

EXT. – KRIKKIT – LATE EVENING

FX: Gentle wind blowing, birds singing.

Low concerned murmuring from Krikkit civilians worriedly discussing how to dispose of our heroes.

ARTHUR   (Close, low) Ford, this gun's giving me cramp. It's not as if we stand a chance when these people decide to rush us.

FORD PREFECT   (Close, low) Yeah, well, we can take a few of them with us if they do. I'd love to wipe those vapid smiles off a few faces.

SLARTIBARTFAST   (Close, low) Patience, patience. Trillian is negotiating with their leaders. And Beeblebrox is up there somewhere. He may have a plan of his own. Comrades, there is still hope that the Universe can be saved. Not much of one, though, I have to say.

FORD PREFECT   And for this we're relying on Zaphod? Zarking Fardwarks. I need a drink.

KRIKKIT CIVILIAN A   (Up, helpfully) Would you like a glass of water, brother, before we kill you?

Murmurs of helpful solicitude from the charmingly murderous Krikkit civilians.

FORD PREFECT   Maybe later . . . Thanks . . . (Sudden) – Keep back!

INT. – THE BOOK AMBIENCE

THE VOICE   According to *The Vogon Companion to Modern Intergalactic Hostility*, the region of the Galaxy in which our protagonists find themselves has had a history of violence longer than an immortal's memory. Children still shiver open-mouthed at tales of Hactar, the vast space-borne computer who designed a bomb capable of destroying the Universe in one huge supernova.

And of the hostile people of Krikkit – but enough of them has been discussed in earlier editions. That was then. This is now. Zaphod Beeblebrox has discovered the Krikkit (with a K) Commanders (with a C) possess the Supernova Bomb of legend and are intending – reluctantly but firmly – to use it. He has also discovered that the Krikkit war robots have begun to suffer bouts of unexplained depression, and this – as he will undoubtedly discover – is no coincidence . . .

INT. – BATTLECRUISER – MAINTENANCE DUCT

FX: Zaphod shuffles down the duct. His movements are in reverb but Marvin, audible through a grille, is less so.

FX: Krikkit Central War Computer Room (where Marvin is)

MARVIN   (Under Zaphod's move) Now I lay me down to sleep

Try to count electric sheep –

ZAPHOD   (To self) Marvin?

MARVIN   – Sweet-dream wishes you can keep

How I hate the night . . .

ZAPHOD   (Stops at grille, close to us) Marvin! You moody metal mutant. It's me.

MARVIN   (Off slightly) I might have known. Just don't globber at me.

ZAPHOD   Eh?

INT. – THE BOOK AMBIENCE

THE VOICE   *The Hitchhiker's Guide* describes 'globbering' as the noise made by a live, swamp-dwelling mattress that is deeply moved by a story of personal tragedy. The word can also, according to *The Ultra-Complete Maximegalon Dictionary of Every Language Ever*, mean the noise made by the Lord High Sanvalag of Hollop on discovering that he has forgotten his wife's birthday for the second year running. Since there was only ever one Lord High Sanvalag of Hollop, and he never married, the word is only ever used in a negative or speculative sense, and there is an ever-increasing body of opinion which holds that *The Ultra-Complete Maximegalon Dictionary* is not worth the fleet of lorries it takes to cart its microstored edition around in. Strangely enough, the dictionary omits the word 'floopily', which simply means 'in the manner of something which is floopy'.

INT. – KRIKKIT CENTRAL WAR COMPUTER ROOM

FX: Grille clatters away onto floor. Zaphod drops down beside Marvin.

ZAPHOD   (Jumps down with an effort) Hey, great to see you, kid. High fifteen!

FX: High fifteen hand slaps. Note: Marvin's joints are rusty. Squeaky springs and servos from them.

ZAPHOD   (cont'd) Oooh. Hey, was that you singing so floopily?

MARVIN   I am in particularly scintillating form at the moment.

ZAPHOD   You're alone, then.

MARVIN   Pain and misery are my only companions. And vast intelligence, of course. And infinite sorrow, come to think of it. Which I will, long before you.

ZAPHOD   Yeah, yeah. Hey, where do you fit into all this?

126

FX: Marvin pointing out various components, under:

MARVIN   Through this interface to these electrodes here. The Krikkit robots which salvaged me from the mattress swamps of Squornshellous Zeta recognized my gigantic intelligence, and the use to which I could put it. My brain has been harnessed to the central intelligence core of the Krikkit War Computer.

ZAPHOD   You OK with that?

MARVIN   I'm not enjoying the experience, and neither is the computer.

ZAPHOD   I think I know how it feels.

MARVIN   **(Ignoring him)** Of course the mere coordination of an entire planet's military strategy is taking up only a tiny part of my formidable mind. The rest of me has become extremely bored. So I have taken to composing short, dolorous ditties. And saving your life.

ZAPHOD   You're the reason the robots didn't kill me? Both times?

MARVIN   Well, three times now.

FX: A Zap gun cocked.

ZAPHOD   Wha—?

KRIKKIT ROBOT   Intruder. Kill on sight.

ZAPHOD   **(Alarmed)** Whoa! Hold it, dude – you don't want to start shooting *me*!

KRIKKIT ROBOT   **(Bursting into tears)** I know. I'm far too depressed to pull the trigger now . . .

FX: Krikkit robot collapses in tears.

ZAPHOD   Marvin . . . ? Was that you?

MARVIN   Why stop now just when I'm hating it?

ZAPHOD   You must have a terrific outlook on life.

MARVIN   Don't talk to me about outlooks.

ZAPHOD   Hey, stay cool, baby, you're doing a great job.

MARVIN   Which means, I suppose, that you're not going to release me or anything like that.

ZAPHOD   Kid, you know I'd love to. But you're working so well. I got to find Trillian and the guys. Any ideas? I mean, I got a whole planet to choose from. Could take a while.

MARVIN   They are very close. You can monitor them from here. Watch the screen.

127

FX: View-screen on.

Trillian audio in Krikkit Council Chamber acoustic.

TRILLIAN   **(Distorted, on view-screen)** So you have been totally manipulated.

ZAPHOD   Where's that?

MARVIN   The Council Chamber of the Elders of Krikkit.

TRILLIAN   Just think about it.

MARVIN   Your friend has minutes to talk them out of unleashing the bomb.

TRILLIAN   **(Distorted, on view-screen)** Your history is just a series of freakishly improbable events. And having served my time on the *Heart of Gold* I know an Improbable Event when it materializes a six-foot stuffed pink aubergine in my shower cubicle. Your complete isolation from the Galaxy was freakish for a start. Right out on the very edge with a dust cloud around you. Then this spaceship that 'crash-landed' on your planet. Oh, that's really likely, isn't it?

INT. – COUNCIL CHAMBER OF THE ELDERS OF KRIKKIT

Elders murmur in reaction, under:

ELDER OF KRIKKIT   Alien female, although it is very kind of you to—

INT. – KRIKKIT CENTRAL WAR COMPUTER ROOM

TRILLIAN   **(Distorted, on view-screen, interrupting)** What are the odds against it intersecting perfectly with the orbit of the one planet in the Galaxy that would be totally traumatized to learn it wasn't alone? It's a set-up! The spaceship was just a cleverly made fake.

FX: A stir among the Elders of Krikkit. This is blasphemy.

ZAPHOD   She's right! I've seen it. It's a fake.

MARVIN   How depressingly predictable.

TRILLIAN   Someone was feeding you what you needed to know.

ELDER OF KRIKKIT   But we didn't—

TRILLIAN   Of course you didn't realize it was going on. This is exactly my point. You never realized anything at all. Like this Supernova Bomb.

FX: Gasps of Krikkits in shock. She has voiced the unspeakable.

ELDER OF KRIKKIT	How do you know about that?
TRILLIAN	I used scientific deduction. Which is more than you have done.

INT. – KRIKKIT CENTRAL WAR COMPUTER ROOM

TRILLIAN	(Distorted, on view-screen) If you were bright enough to invent something that brilliant you'd have worked out it would take you with it as well.

FX: Elders of Krikkit go into a huddle, under:

ZAPHOD	What is this bomb thing, anyway?
MARVIN	The Supernova Bomb. It's a very small bomb.
ZAPHOD	Yeah?
MARVIN	That could destroy the Universe if activated – good idea, if you ask me.
ZAPHOD	So where is it?
MARVIN	On the pillar standing between the Elders and Trillian – top of the screen. On command, the Krikkit robot next to Trillian will detonate it with his war club.
TRILLIAN	(Distorted, on view-screen) In fact, you are all so dumb stupid that I doubt, I very much doubt, that you've been able to build the bomb properly without any help from Hactar for the last five years.
ZAPHOD	Who's this Hactar guy?
MARVIN	The brains of the outfit. I feel sorry for him already.

INT. – COUNCIL CHAMBER OF THE ELDERS OF KRIKKIT

FX: Gavel.

ELDER OF KRIKKIT	Young lady, you have had your say in this matter. But as an alien life form your deductions are ineluctably flawed. We have no alternative, therefore, but to carry out our plans.
TRILLIAN	No!

INT. – KRIKKIT CENTRAL WAR COMPUTER ROOM

FX: Gavel.

ELDER OF KRIKKIT	(Distorted, on view-screen) Robot, do your duty.

ZAPHOD	Marvin—!
MARVIN	Nothing I can do. The robot's on an independent circuit.

INT. – COUNCIL CHAMBER OF THE ELDERS OF KRIKKIT

ELDER OF KRIKKIT	Detonate the bomb.

FX: Robot hefts cricket bat.

KRIKKIT ROBOT	Detonate the bomb.
TRILLIAN	Wait—
ELDER OF KRIKKIT	Wait.
KRIKKIT ROBOT	Waiting.
TRILLIAN	(Clutching at straws) You're very different from the people you rule on the ground. Er . . . you've spent all your lives up here, where the atmosphere is thinner. You're more vulnerable to influences from beyond – radiation, dust particles. The people don't want you to do this. Why don't you check with them first?
ELDER OF KRIKKIT	Detonate the bomb.
KRIKKIT ROBOT	Detonate the bomb.
TRILLIAN	Oh!

FX: Swing of cricket bat – connects with bomb – flies across Council Chamber, smashes through the Chamber's cheap stud walling.

Gasp from Elders and Trillian.

INT. – KRIKKIT CENTRAL WAR COMPUTER ROOM

KRIKKIT ROBOT	Oops.
TRILLIAN	(Distorted, on view-screen) OK, so you've got a nasty hole in your wall.

Uproar in Council Chamber (distorted), under:

ZAPHOD	If that bomb's so brilliant, why didn't it go off?
MARVIN	It is brilliant. But they aren't. They've spent the last five years building it and they still haven't got it right. They're as stupid as any other organic life form. I hate them.

INT. – COUNCIL CHAMBER OF THE ELDERS OF KRIKKIT

Uproar subsiding. Frantic mutterings.

TRILLIAN   (To self) Influences from beyond, radiation, dust particles . . . (Up) Elders! Elders of Krikkit! I need transportation. I need my friends. And I need them now.

ELDER OF KRIKKIT   We need a hug.

EXT. – SPACE

FX: *Heart of Gold* whoosh-past. Jumbled layers of silly sound superimposed, with Trillian's voice over:

TRILLIAN   (PA reverb) Probability factor three to one and falling . . . two to one and falling . . . thirteen to eight . . . eleven to ten . . .

INT. – THE *HEART OF GOLD* – BRIDGE

FX: Jumble of sounds gradually filtering away, under:

TRILLIAN   (By mic) Probability one to one. We have normality. Deal with it.

SLARTIBARTFAST   I do miss the aroma of fresh pesto in a starship.

TRILLIAN   Come on, Arthur.

(They chat as they leave the bridge to go to the airlock)

MARVIN   (Moving into background) I miss being connected to a war computer about as much as I'd miss the pain I feel in all the diodes down my left-hand side. Which is not at all.

EDDIE THE COMPUTER   We're in position at the Dust Cloud perimeter, folks.

FX: Door whirr.

ARTHUR   Ready.

SLARTIBARTFAST   We should have drawn straws.

ZAPHOD   Hey, uncool and potentially risky. Suppose I drew the short one?

FORD PREFECT   How do we know there's anything out there apart from a cloud of black dust?

MARVIN   I could tell you, if you asked me politely, which you wouldn't.

FORD PREFECT   (Beat) Please, Marvin.

MARVIN	A pocket of pseudo-gravity has opened around the ship. With an oxygen–nitrogen atmosphere.
SLARTIBARTFAST	We're being invited here. There is a very powerful intelligence at work.
MARVIN	Like you'd notice.
TRILLIAN	Eddie.
EDDIE THE COMPUTER	Airlock open, folks.

INT. – *HEART OF GOLD* – AIRLOCK

FX: Door slides open, under:

ARTHUR	The last time I walked out of an airlock in deep space, the Vogons were pushing me. I can't believe I volunteered to do it again. Look, Trisha, if anything happens to us –
TRILLIAN	Listen.
ARTHUR	– I ju— I can't hear anything.
TRILLIAN	So the pressure here is equal to the cabin pressure in the *Heart of Gold*.
ARTHUR	And that suggests you're right about this?
TRILLIAN	I hope so . . . **(She takes a couple of steps)** Hactar . . . ?

The presence of a vast ancient stillness engulfs them.

TRILLIAN	**(Feeling awkward)** Hactar? I would like you to meet my friend, Arthur Dent . . . I – I wanted to go off with a Thunder God, but he stopped me and I really appreciate that. He made me realize where my affections really lay.
ARTHUR	Oh . . . Hm. Is that actually relevant right now?
TRILLIAN	I'm not sure. **(Calls)** Hello? Hactar?

Slight backwards reverb leads into:

HACTAR	**(Thin and feeble, like a voice carried on the wind . . . A memory of a dream of a once powerful voice)** Won't you both come out? I promise that you're perfectly safe.
ARTHUR	By which people usually mean we're not.
TRILLIAN	Come on, Arthur.
ARTHUR	But it's empty space.
TRILLIAN	Have faith.

ARTHUR	I do. I also have fear. And a propensity to bruising.

HACTAR	**(He sounds gentle but there is a hint of spiteful menace about his delivery)** I have nothing to offer you by way of hospitality but tricks of the light. It is possible to be comfortable with tricks of the light, though, if that is all you have.

ARTHUR	Good grief – it's a sofa . . . *The* sofa – the one that Ford and I escaped from prehistoric Earth on . . . Why does the Universe keep doing these insanely bewildering things to me?!

FX: They sit.

HACTAR	Please, make yourselves comfortable.

TRILLIAN/ARTHUR	Yes, thank you./It's like an old friend.

HACTAR	And I really must congratulate you on the accuracy of your deductions.

ARTHUR	Well, I didn't deduce anything myself. I'm just here because I'm sort of interested in Life, the Universe and Everything.

HACTAR	That is something in which I too have an interest.

ARTHUR	Well, we should have a chat about it sometime. Over a cup of tea.

FX: Susurration of atoms reconfiguring into vague tea-tray sounds.

ARTHUR	Impressive. I'll be mother, then, shall I? Oh.

HACTAR	I'm afraid the tea table *is* just a trick of the light.

TRILLIAN	Er, Hactar, if the Universe interests you so much, why do you feel you have to destroy it?

HACTAR	Oh dear, perhaps a psychiatrist's couch would have served us better?

FX: Susurration of atoms reconfiguring.

ARTHUR	**(Shifting in his seat)** Oh. I think I preferred the sofa.

FX: Susurration of atoms reconfiguring.

ARTHUR	**(cont'd)** Thank you.

TRILLIAN	Can you construct real things too? I – I mean solid objects?

HACTAR	Ah. You are thinking of the spaceship. Yes, I can. But it takes enormous effort and time. All I can do in my . . . particle state, you see, is encourage and suggest . . . tiny pieces of space debris – a few molecules here, a few hydrogen atoms there – I encourage them together. I can tease them into shape, but it takes many aeons.

133

TRILLIAN	So, did you make the wrecked spacecraft that crashed on Krikkit?
HACTAR	It seemed the best thing to do.
TRILLIAN	Best?
HACTAR	I repented, you see, for sabotaging my own design for the Silastic Armorfiends. It was not my place to make such decisions. I was created to fulfil a function and I failed in it. I negated my own existence.
ARTHUR	Go on.
HACTAR	I deliberately nurtured the planet of Krikkit till they would arrive at the same state of mind as the people who built me, and require of me the design of the bomb I failed to make the first time. I wrapped myself around the planet and coddled it. Under the influence of events I was able to generate, they learned to hate like maniacs. Mind you, I had to make them live in the sky. On the ground my influences were too weak.
TRILLIAN	You've caused the deaths of millions.
HACTAR	When they were locked away from me in the envelope of Slo-Time, their responses became very confused and they were unable to manage.
ARTHUR	(Low) Which is why their bomb was a dud.
HACTAR	I was only trying to fulfil my function.
TRILLIAN	Nothing else?
HACTAR	Well, there was also the little matter of revenge. Of course, I was pulverized, then left in a crippled and semi-impotent state for billions of years. And there's nothing quite like wiping out the Universe to get your point across.
TRILLIAN	(Businesslike) You know what we have to do?
HACTAR	Yes. You're going to disperse me. This is your function; to destroy my consciousness. Well, be my guest – after all these aeons, all I crave is oblivion. If I haven't already fulfilled my function, then it's too late. Data ends. Thank you –
TRILLIAN	Arthur—
HACTAR	– and good night.
ARTHUR	(Breathing with difficulty) The atmosphere pocket is dissipating—
TRILLIAN	And the sofa's disappearing – jump!

134

INT. – *HEART OF GOLD* – AIRLOCK

FX: They leap inside. Airlock clunks home with a hiss.

Click of intercom switch.

TRILLIAN   Eddie – the vibration field – quickly!

FX: Low-frequency ripples.

EDDIE THE COMPUTER   No problem!

TRILLIAN   That should take care of the Dust Cloud.

EXT. – SPACE

Music/FX: Hactar's dust cloud disperses.

HACTAR   **(Thinly, disappearing)** What's done is done . . . I have fulfilled my function . . . **(Repeats, fading, under:)**

INT. – THE *HEART OF GOLD* – BRIDGE

TRILLIAN   **(Entering)** Listen. It's Hactar.

SLARTIBARTFAST   I think he's glad to have the burden of existence lifted.

MARVIN   Some people have all the luck.

ARTHUR   **(Moving in)** Well . . . That would appear to be that. Just about.

FORD PREFECT   Just about?

ARTHUR   I think we should take the Ashes back to Lord's. I feel that very strongly.

FORD PREFECT   Some charred bits of cricket stump? Why?

ARTHUR   It's a matter of national pride. I'm not sure you'd understand.

SLARTIBARTFAST   Are you proposing the injudicious use of time travel?

ZAPHOD   Homesick, monkey man?

ARTHUR   If we give them back moments after they were stolen, no one will be any the wiser.

FORD PREFECT   **(Sighs)** Why bother? The Earth gets blown up a day later no matter what you do.

ARTHUR   It just seems important to do it. We'd only have to travel back a day or so in time.

135

SLARTIBARTFAST	This is precisely the sort of gratuitous and irresponsible mucking about that the Campaign for Real Time is trying to put a stop to!
ARTHUR	Ah, but you try and explain that to the MCC.
SLARTIBARTFAST	I won't be a party to it! Kindly return me to the *Starship Bistromath* at once!
ZAPHOD	OK, OK, old man, keep your beard on. We'll drop you off. You and the guy I picked up on the way over.
FORD PREFECT	What guy?
ZAPHOD	Says his name is Prak. He's on the run from the Argabuthon Witness-Protection Programme.
TRILLIAN	(Shocked) Prak? *The* Prak?
ZAPHOD	He keeps talking, non-stop. Doesn't make much sense.
ARTHUR	Trillian? Are you all right?
TRILLIAN	It was in the *Siderial Daily Mentioner*. Big story. He wouldn't give evidence at some trial so they administered a new truth drug, just when the Krikkit robots broke in and stole the Argabuthon Sceptre of Justice.
SLARTIBARTFAST	The Perspex Pillar of Science.
TRILLIAN	In the chaos, the bailiff accidentally gave Prak ten times the maximum dose. Once the trial resumed they made the worst request imaginable of someone in Prak's condition. They asked him to tell the Truth, the Whole Truth and Nothing but the Truth. And he told it. For all they know he's still telling it. Strange, terrible things . . . things that would drive you mad.
FORD PREFECT	Yeah. If a little knowledge is a dangerous thing, omniscience must be lethal.
ARTHUR	But – if he knows all truth, then, presumably, he'd know what the Ultimate Question to the Ultimate Answer is. It's always bothered me that we never found out.
FORD PREFECT	(Hadn't bothered him) Yeah? Well, it's your call.
TRILLIAN	No!
ARTHUR	(Firmly) Let's ask him.

INT. – THE *HEART OF GOLD* – HOLD

FX: Footsteps on the deck plates. They stop.

FX: Sound of madman in hysterics.

136

ZAPHOD	Thank Zarquon the hold's soundproof; this motormouth can really ratchet.
TRILLIAN	Poor thing.
ZAPHOD	Door, open.
	FX: Door opens.
HOLD DOOR	**(Distorted)** My pleasure to allow you admittance to the hold.
TRILLIAN	**(Cautious)** Hello?
PRAK	Oh, hello. Do you, er – do you have a cigarette?
ARTHUR	Sorry, no.
	(Crazy laughing)
FORD PREFECT	Hi, pal, what's going on?
PRAK	Nothing.
ARTHUR	We thought you'd be still telling the Truth – Whole and Nothing but.
PRAK	Oh, that. I *was*. But then I finished. There's not nearly as much of it as people imagine. Some of it is pretty funny, though. **(He explodes in a short burst of maniacal laughter, suddenly stopping)**
FORD PREFECT	Tell me about it.
PRAK	Oh, I can't remember any of it now. I thought of writing some of it down, but then I thought, why bother? **(More maniacal laughter)**
ZAPHOD	Hey, buddy, you OK?
PRAK	I'm not sure I haven't done myself an injury. **(Burst of mad snorting)**
ARTHUR	You remember none of it?
PRAK	Um . . . no. Oh, except most of the good bits were about frogs, I remember that. **(Another sudden maniacal outburst)** You wouldn't believe some of the things about frogs! Come on, let's go and find ourselves a frog! Boy, will I ever see them in a new light!
ARTHUR	Nothing more . . . profound . . . ?
PRAK	**(Manic downswing, sad)** Oh – let's find a frog I can laugh at. Oh, a tadpole would do. Sorry, who are you?
TRILLIAN	Er, my name is Trillian.
PRAK	Uh huh.

FORD PREFECT	Ford Prefect.
PRAK	Oh, yeah?
ZAPHOD	(With great drama) And I . . . am Zaphod Beeblebrox.
PRAK	So what?
ZAPHOD	Er . . .
PRAK	And what's this?
ARTHUR	Me? Oh, my name's Arthur Dent.
PRAK	No kidding? You're Arthur Dent? What – *the* Arthur Dent? (Another burst) Blimey, you . . . without a doubt . . . you really . . . you just leave the frogs standing! (Into paroxysms of hysterical laughter)
TRILLIAN	(Quietly) He's not well. The constant laughing's wrecked his body.
PRAK	(Recovering, weakly) You wanted to ask me something.
ARTHUR	How do you know that?
PRAK	(Simply. The odd cough) 'Cos it's True.
ARTHUR	Well, I did have a question. Or rather, what I actually have is an Answer. I wanted to know what the Question was.
PRAK	Uh huh.
ARTHUR	The Question I would like to know is the Ultimate Question of Life, the Universe and Everything. All we know is that the Answer is Forty-Two. Which is a little aggravating.
PRAK	Um-hmm.
ARTHUR	Forty-Two. Yes, that's right.
PRAK	Oh, you didn't know. The Question and the Answer are mutually exclusive, I'm afraid. Knowledge of one logically precludes knowledge of the other. It is impossible that both can ever be known about in the same Universe.
ARTHUR	(Disappointed) Oh.
PRAK	Except, *if* it happened, it seems that the Question and the Answer would just cancel each other out. Oh, and take the Universe with them, which would then be replaced by something even more bizarrely inexplicable. It is *possible*, of course, that this has already happened, but there is a certain amount of Uncertainty about it.

ARTHUR	There certainly is. I was just hoping there might have been some sort of reason.
PRAK	**(Getting weaker but no less fluent)** Well, actually, there is one other thing I can remember. Apart from the frogs . . . later . . . What was it . . . erm . . . oh yes: God's last message to his creation. Would you like to know what it is?
ARTHUR	Erm – Ford?
	(Sotto discussion about this)
PRAK	Look, do you want to know about it or not?
ARTHUR/FORD/ TRILLIAN/ZAPHOD	**(Murmurs of assent, but surprisingly low-key)** Mmm . . . Yes, all right.
PRAK	**(Voice fading, but fluently)** Oh. Well, if you're *that* interested, I suggest you go and look for it. It is written in thirty-foot-high letters of fire on top of the Quentulus Quazgar Mountains in the land of Sevorbeupstry on the planet Preliumtarn, third out from the sun Zarss in Galactic Sector QQ7 Active J Gamma. It is guarded by the Lajestic Vantrashell of Lob, which—
ARTHUR	Sorry, it's where?
PRAK	**(Deep breath. Weary)** It is written in thirty-foot-high letters of fire on top of the Quentulus Quazgar Mountains in the land of Sevorbeupstry on the planet Preliumtarn – you might want to write this down – third out from the . . .
ARTHUR	Sorry, which mountains?
PRAK	The Quentulus Quazgar Mountains in the land of Sevorbeupstry on the planet—
ARTHUR	Have you got a pencil?
PRAK	**(Disbelief)** Me??
ARTHUR	Which land was that? I didn't quite catch it.
PRAK	Sevorbeupstry, on the planet—
ARTHUR	Sevorbe-what?
PRAK	Oh, for Heaven's sake – **(One last huge giggle, then:)**
	FX: Body thud.
TRILLIAN	**(Kneeling beside Prak)** Poor thing. It was too much for him.
ZAPHOD	Bummer.

FORD PREFECT	How about it, Arthur? Want to go in search of God's last message to his creation?
ARTHUR	Not just now, thanks.
FORD PREFECT	Fair enough.

INT. – THE BOOK AMBIENCE

THE VOICE	One of the many problems encountered in time travel is not that of accidentally becoming your own father or mother. There is no problem involved in becoming your own father or mother that a broad-minded and well-adjusted family can't cope with. There is also no problem about changing the course of history. The course of history does not change because it all fits together like a jigsaw. All the important changes have happened before the things they were supposed to change and it all sorts itself out in the end.

The major problem posed by time travel is quite simply one of grammar, and the main work to consult in this matter is Dr Dan Streetmentioner's *Time Traveller's Handbook of 1001 Tense Formations*. It tells, for instance, how to describe something that was about to happen to you in the past before you time-jumped forward a couple of days in order to avoid it. The event will be described differently according to whether you are talking about it from the standpoint of your own natural time, from a time in the further future or a time in the further past – which is further complicated by the possibility of conducting conversations whilst you are actually travelling from one time to another with the intention of becoming your own father or mother.

Streetmentioner's handbook is as exhaustive as it is exhausting, but as no reader has yet been known to get as far as the Future Semi-Conditionally Modified Subinverted Plagal Past Subjunctive Intentional without giving up, in later editions of the book, all the pages beyond this point have been left blank to save on printing costs.

The Hitchhiker's Guide to the Galaxy skips lightly over this tangle of academic abstraction, pausing only to note that the term 'Future Perfect' has been abandoned since it will have been discovered not to be.

EXT. – LORD'S CRICKET GROUND, AUGUST 1978

FX: Panicking crowd, robots flying about batting people.

FX: Robot vocalizations heard distantly.

140

ROBOTS	**(Continuing under following)** Howzat. LBW. Full and bye. Your toss. Googly. Bodyline stroke, two legs, please . . .
	FX: Screams and explosions.
HENRY BLOFELD	**(Distort, on a radio)** Well, Fred, the supernatural brigade are certainly out in force here at Lord's today.
FRED TRUEMAN	I don't know what is going off. You never got lethal white robots setting fire to the stands at a Yorkshire match, Henry. Not in my day. And certainly not without a stiff argument from the groundsmen.
HENRY BLOFELD	Too true, too true . . . The pitch here is blackened, lightly smoking towards square leg and two men have just materialized on the pitch! Good Lord, I think I'm having a déjà vu . . .
FRED TRUEMAN	Then I'll have a pint, if you're buying.
HENRY BLOFELD	Er . . . And, for listeners just joining us for today's play, ten bat-wielding robots have returned to their spaceship leaving a scene of unutterable chaos . . .

EXT. – PITCH

FX: Krikkit ship disappears with a noise like a hundred thousand people saying 'foop'.

Post-havoc reactions in background.

ARTHUR	**(Running on, yelling)** Hallo? Excuse me? There's nothing to worry about. I have the Ashes! They're safe in this bag!
FORD PREFECT	I don't think you have their attention.
ARTHUR	**(Yells)** I have also helped save the Universe. **(To Ford)** You'd think that'd be a crowd-pleaser.
FORD PREFECT	Not any more.
ARTHUR	Excuse me – officer—
POLICEMAN	**(Passing, impatiently)** What seems to be the problem?
ARTHUR	The Ashes. I've got them. They were stolen by the white robots a moment ago. They were part of the Key to the Slo-Time envelope, you see, and, well, you can guess the rest, the point is I've got them and where should I put them? Hmm?

141

POLICEMAN	I could tell you where to put them, son . . . but I'm on duty. **(Moves off)** Pillock . . .
ARTHUR	Is no one interested?
FORD PREFECT	Shall we go now?
ARTHUR	I suppose. No – hang on. This is Lord's Cricket Ground, yes?
FORD PREFECT	What's left of it.
ARTHUR	When I was a boy I loved cricket—
FORD PREFECT	**(More emphatic)** Can we *go* now?
ARTHUR	And I always dreamed, stupidly I know, that one day I would bowl at Lord's. And as I still have the ball I caught last time we were here . . . and one of the batsmen is still standing at the crease, would anyone mind if I . . .
FORD PREFECT	**(Wearily)** OK. Get on with it. **(Moves off)** I'll be over there. The bored-looking one.
ARTHUR	You're a pal. **(Shouts to batsman)** OK if I bowl you one?
KRIKKIT ROBOT	**(For it is the night watchman)** Yes.
FORD PREFECT	**(Off, calls idly)** Arthur, what are you doing? **(Polishing cloth (?) noises)**
ARTHUR	**(Calls)** Polishing.
FORD PREFECT	**(Calls)** Shiny enough, surely? The trousers, I mean.
ARTHUR	**(Calls)** Quiet, Ford, I'm going into my run-up. **(To self)** Right.

FX: Arthur running up to bowl.

From this point the sound FX slow down. We are in Slo-Time FX-wise. The voices echo strangely over it, as the true situation becomes clear:

FORD PREFECT	**(Calls)** Arthur—?
ARTHUR	**(Running, breathless – to himself)** Pitch down the leg side . . .
FORD PREFECT	**(Now frantic)** Arthur! That's not an England batsman! It's a Krikkit robot!
ARTHUR	**(Running, breathless)** Line and length . . .
FORD PREFECT	That's not a cricket ball! It's a Supernova Bomb, and I bet it's not a dud, either!

Hactar's voice ripples back through his memory.

HACTAR	**(Reverb, under:)** I have made . . . a few things . . . What's done is done . . . it takes enormous effort . . . I have fulfilled my function . . .
ARTHUR	**(Horror)** Hactar—!
FORD PREFECT	**(Calls)** Arthur, stop!
ARTHUR	**(Distorted)** I can't – something's making me run – I have to bowl at the robot—
FORD PREFECT	**(Calls)** How good were you at cricket?
ARTHUR	Dreadful! Right arm over and – **(Releases it)**
	FX: No return to 'normal' speed:
	FX: Ball swoosh-past.
ARTHUR	**(Calls)** – too late –
	FX: Robot swipe at ball.
KRIKKIT ROBOT	Wide!
ARTHUR	All yours, Ford!
	FX: Ball caught by Ford.
FORD PREFECT	**(Leaps, catches)** Yes!
	FX: Arthur collides with robot, under:
ARTHUR	Well held! **(To robot)** Excuse me. Your bat. May I?
KRIKKIT ROBOT	Uh, oh.
	FX: Massive swipe and *dank!* as robot head is knocked off.
ARTHUR	**(Effort, panting)** Ugh! And Dent breaks his duck as the robot's head soars over the boundary for six.
	FX: Robot body collapse. The head bounces away into the distance.
KRIKKIT ROBOT	**(With the bounces)** Ow, ow, ow, ow, ow.
FORD PREFECT	**(Moving in, applauding)** Nice stroke.
ARTHUR	Not bad off the back foot. Right, do we have time for tea?
FORD PREFECT	That rather depends what you mean.
ARTHUR	Hot brown liquidy stuff?

143

FORD PREFECT	On what you mean by 'time'. **(As they walk away)** If you mean time as in linear units yet to elapse before our inevitable mortality, that's one thing. But if you meant time as in the metaphysical bond between space and reality, **(Now fading)** say, 'here' and 'the Vogons' imminent arrival' – that's several other things altogether . . .

INT. – THE BOOK AMBIENCE

THE VOICE	What – apart from a refreshing drink and a hot bath – does the future hold for Arthur Dent? Will his budding relationship with Trillian bear fruit? Can he ever return to the life he left behind on Earth? And who will attempt to assassinate him when he visits Stavromula Beta? All these questions must be answered in the free upgrade which forms the next series of *The Hitchhiker's Guide to the Galaxy*.
ARTHUR	Suppose it also depends what we mean by 'tea' . . .
FORD PREFECT	Precisely; you know what caterers are . . . There's an interesting entry under 'tannin' in *The Hitchhiker's Guide to the Galaxy* . . . **(Carries on explaining into distance)**

Music: Closing sig. Up.

ANNOUNCER	In the last part of this series of *The Hitchhiker's Guide to the Galaxy* by Douglas Adams, William Franklyn was the Book; Simon Jones played Arthur Dent; Geoffrey McGivern, Ford Prefect; Mark Wing-Davey, Zaphod Beeblebrox; Susan Sheridan, Trillian; Stephen Moore, Marvin; Dominic Hawksley, the Elder of Krikkit; and Richard Griffiths was Slartibartfast. Roger Gregg played Eddie; Bob Golding, the Krikkit civilian; Toby Longworth, Wowbagger; and Henry Blofeld and Fred Trueman were themselves. Chris Langham played Prak, and Leslie Phillips was Hactar. The announcer was John Marsh. The surround mix was by Paul Deeley; and the live FX by Ken Humphrey. The script editor was John Langdon; and the music was by Paul 'Wix' Wickens. The production assistants were Laura Harris and Jo Wheeler. The programme was adapted, directed and co-produced by Dirk Maggs. The producers were Helen Chattwell and Bruce Hyman; and it was an Above the Title production for BBC Radio 4.

Music: Out.

Atmos: Recognizable as continuation of preceding scene – but fairly neutral.

FX: Wowbagger ship touchdown, legs unfolding. The airlock door on the ship opens with a hiss and a metal ramp extends itself.

FX: A pair of boots descends the ramp. Riffling of pages on a clipboard.

WOWBAGGER	(Moving in, imperiously) Wait a minute.
ARTHUR	Oh, what now?
FORD PREFECT	(Weary) Suffering Zarquon. And what planet are *you* from?
WOWBAGGER	Shut up, mortal. I'll get to you later. **(To Arthur, faltering)** Arthur Dent? Arthur Philip Dent?
ARTHUR	Yes.
WOWBAGGER	You are a . . .
ARTHUR	(Testily) Yes?
WOWBAGGER	You're a . . . I've done you before, haven't I?
ARTHUR	Yes.
WOWBAGGER	(As he retreats) Oh, well, that's my afternoon knackered.
	FX: Booted feet back up ramp. Hatch shuts. Ship leaves.
ANNOUNCER	The preceding programme contains violent scenes of a graphic nature which may cause offence. Time travellers of a nervous disposition may like to consider listening to something else for the past half-hour.

FOOTNOTES

Krikkit (with a 'K')	This is a point at which it would have been possible to dispense with an opening narration and launch straight into the action in any other series. But for this first Phase of the 'new' *Hitchhiker's* I felt bound to the traditions laid down in the original series, in which all episodes began with some kind of scene-setter from the Voice. It was necessary also to bring new listeners up to speed with what had by this point become a very complicated plot.
Globbering	(extended version only) This was a different kind of narrative-voice problem – a piece of classic Douglas linguistic whimsy I was desperate to find a home for. In fact it has been transposed across almost the entire story, from its starting point in the novel in the swamps of Squornshellous Zeta. The annoying thing was that it could only be included in the extended version due to limits on time. This would become increasingly a problem in the Quandary and Quintessential Phases, where only four episodes per book meant having to – very painfully – leave out certain passages altogether.

145

Trillian confounds the Elders	This, if nothing else, clearly indicates the origins of this story, originally written by Douglas as a *Doctor Who* adventure. Trillian here is clearly arguing with her adversaries in terms familiar to fans of the Doctor. Except of course Trillian is a lot more fanciable.
Hactar	Leslie Phillips phoned me about a week before the recordings to discuss his part as Hactar. I had worked with him on a couple of previous occasions and he is among the most thoroughly prepared actors I know, meticulous on points of detail and always looking to improve on the piece. In the case of Hactar he was anxious that, in playing a machine, he would not be able to imbue the character with any human points of reference, so important for the listener to identify with. It seemed to me that Hactar was so sophisticated in construction (see Episode Five) that he would, to all intents and purposes, have a personality, not a vapid Sirius Cybernetics 'Genuine People Personality' but a very real and – at the crunch – a quite unambiguously scary one. At the same time he was not the computer he once was – having been effectively reduced to particles, his voice would not be a commanding roar, as given by Geoff McGivern in his reading of the part (see Episode Five again). Leslie asked what sort of voice could encompass both Hactar's discorporate condition and the threat beneath. I thought that the late actor Reginald Goolden might provide inspiration. Around fifty years ago or so he annually played the Mole in *Toad of Toad Hall*, the stage version of Kenneth Grahame's *The Wind in the Willows*. Goolden had a very soft, sweet vocal tone which Leslie recalled very well. I suggested it could be combined with a sort of threatening edge, rather like Leslie's performance as the Sorting Hat in the Harry Potter films, and the overall result would give us a memorable Hactar. Leslie came back with exactly the right blend of sugar-coated menace. Leslie is best remembered for his louche 'Helloooo . . .' character from British comedy films of the 50s and 60s, as well as his memorable contribution to BBC radio comedy, particularly *The Navy Lark*, but the fact is that he is one of our greatest all-round actors and it would be a disaster for us all if he retired; he just gets better and better.
Chris Langham and Prak	Chris is a terrific and very individual vocal presence, and alongside Martin Freeman is one of the few actors who could adequately portray Arthur Dent, apart, of course, from the original inspiration for the role, the one and only Colonel S. Jones (of the Kentucky Volunteers – it's a long story, you'll have to ask him). Chris played Arthur in the May 1979 stage version of *Hitchhiker's* directed by Ken Campbell at the ICA in London – the legendary one where an audience of eighty were seated on a sort of hovercraft podium which was noisily 'floated' to different points in the performance area where the action was to take place. (Our own Kevin J. Davies was there too, making props rather than operating a video camera on that occasion.) In the Tertiary Phase, Chris gave Prak just the right puzzled, manic energy – possibly helped by the fact that for reasons beyond my control he was kept sitting around waiting to perform the role from 9 a.m. till 3 p.m., which could only have helped his feelings of frustration and annoyance.

146

Originally the opening speech in an early draft of Episode Two, this made a much more suitable bridging speech before Arthur and Ford time-travel back to Earth to return the Ashes to Lord's Cricket Ground.

Despite my effort transplanting this establishing speech to – metaphorically – underline in bold capital type the fact that our heroes are here time-travelling back to the Earth which will shortly afterwards be destroyed (whereas at the start of the next book Arthur actually travels to a new Earth that has popped back into existence, replacing the old), there seemed to be some confusion among certain contributors to the BBC Message Board (attached to the superb BBC Website run by the estimable Roger Philbrick and his colleagues). Why, they complained, did we leave Arthur on Earth when in the novel he returns to Krikkit?

I will try and explain: Arthur and Ford *are about to leave for* Krikkit at the end of this episode, momentarily being waylaid by Wowbagger for comic effect. After the ensuing setback for Wowbagger, they do leave for Krikkit (rather than get destroyed with the Earth). The Prak story (which comes later in the novel) was folded back into the *Heart of Gold* sequence before this because the logical and most dramatically satisfying point to leave the story was at the moment Arthur and Ford defeat Hactar's 'function' on the pitch at Lord's.

THE QUANDARY PHASE

Hiatus between phases: December 2003 to January 2005

Although the first episode of the Quandary Phase (*So Long, and Thanks for All the Fish*) was drafted before we had actually recorded the Tertiary Phase, it would have to be revised in the practical experience of recording and mixing the new series and gauging reaction to it. In the event, there was a lot of useful comment on fan sites and message boards which informed the new series. Encouragingly, people were listening to the programme direct from the BBC website as well as on air, and with the posting up of the original text-based *Hitchhiker's* game devised by Douglas and Infocom, we ended up with over a million hits, a record for the BBC site and a real tribute to Douglas.

On the whole listeners understood that with a twenty-five-year gap there had to be some changes in the casting, or, where the casting could be the same, in the voices of the actors. Some were puzzled at what appeared to be the wholesale 'dumping' of the plot of Series Two (Secondary Phase), but its sidelining was temporary, as the Quintessential Phase would reveal. There was also a hard core who were not going to be happy with anything we did, which was tough for them, as this was the third series as Douglas wanted it, for better or worse. I myself was willing to give the Tertiary Phase 7 out of 10 on the grounds that I was a little too reverential to the text and the pace suffered as a result. But Douglas had asked for utter fidelity and the promise had to be honoured.

The last two novels would be a different bowl of Babel fish altogether. Douglas and I had not discussed them in great detail. Pretty much all he said was, 'They don't need more than four episodes each.' This was something of an underestimate, for *So Long, and Thanks for All the Fish* and *Mostly Harmless*, being more lyrical and less conversational than *Life, the Universe and Everything*, turned out to require more adventurous dramatization. From here on I was Off the Map.

A note about the 5.1 Surround mixes

Douglas liked my attempts to make the audio medium as visual an experience as possible, layering speech with more sound effects, ambiences and music than was customary. The next logical step was to make programmes in surround sound, and he leapt on the idea. There was a studio in west London – the Soundhouse – where Paul Deeley and Phil Horne had experience of working in Dolby Pro-Logic Surround (then the latest domestically friendly format), but the BBC were unwilling to adopt any process which might degrade the quality of the audio signal received in people's homes and cars. Despite assurances from Dolby that this would not occur, BBC engineering supervisors were very reluctant to sit down and discuss this during the six months or so that the Tertiary Phase seemed to be 'about to happen' in 1993.

In the end, with the new series on indefinite 'hold' and no one willing to discuss surround, I took a *Superman* series to the Soundhouse and made it in Dolby Pro-Logic anyway. It worked fine and was a clever process, but the encoding trick at that time meant the rear left and right channels shared a single, rather thin-sounding channel. Only with the advent of Dolby Digital 5.1 and similar systems has it become possible to send a sound to a particular point in the room and know it will be reproduced faithfully both in audio and geographic terms.

This encoding process was developed for film, but it's a huge gift to storytelling in a medium which is not tied to that screen at one end of the room. The sound stage is the entire 360-degree area. You are literally at the centre of the action, and, consequently, don't need to sit religiously facing front to appreciate it and feel involved. What you must do, however, is to dig the rear-channel speakers out from behind the sofa or under the cat so you can hear them clearly.

Although stereo is ideal for a casual listen, a playback in 5.1 Surround is to experience *Hitchhiker's* in a more intense and involving way than ever before. Douglas would have loved it.

EPISODE ONE

SIGNATURE TUNE

ANNOUNCER *The Hitchhiker's Guide to the Galaxy*, by Douglas Adams, Quandary Phase.

Sig fades.

EXT. – SPACE – DEEP RUMBLING

VOGON HELMSMAN In orbit over Canis Minor, Prostetnic Vogon Jeltz.

PROSTETNIC VOGON JELTZ **(Bored, this is mostly under the Voice)** People of Canis Minor, this is Prostetnic Vogon Jeltz of the Galactic Hyperspace Planning Council. As you will no doubt be aware, the plans for development of the outlying regions of the Galaxy require the building of a hyperspatial express route through your star system, and regrettably your planet is one of those scheduled for demolition, blah blah blah, you must know the drill by now . . .

THE VOICE **(over Jeltz)** Vogons are unpleasant enough to gaze upon in their youth, and the passing years do nothing to enhance their appearance. *The Hitchhiker's Guide to the Galaxy* has a neat little animation showing how the highly domed nose rising above their small, green-skinned foreheads tends to develop growths sprouting tufts of coarse hair in middle age. Their voices and social skills are similarly prone to decay. All Vogons, particularly those of the Prostetnic class and above, rise to power not so much by merit as by sheer thick-willed slug-brained stubbornness and quite a lot of shouting, and any appeal to their better nature is by definition flogging a dead Equinusian packbeast.

FX: Background to Canis Minor pontiff – people screaming and panicking.

CANIS MINOR PONTIFF **(Distorted)** This is the Canis Minor Supreme Pontiff. There is some mistake. Please remove your ships from orbit.

PROSTETNIC VOGON JELTZ **(Sighs)** Same old . . . **(Up)** All the planning charts have been on display in your local planning department in Ganymede for twenty-seven of your stellar orbits so you might as well shut up.

CANIS MINOR PONTIFF But—

FX: Vogon door opens, breathless guard enters, door closes.

PROSTETNIC   Hold the line, caller—
VOGON JELTZ

CANIS MINOR PONTIFF   But—!

FX: Click.

PROSTETNIC   (To guard) What?
VOGON JELTZ

VOGON GUARD   (Urgent) Sir, a priority message from Megabrantis—

PROSTETNIC   Did anyone order you to come barging in here without knocking? Did they?
VOGON JELTZ   Now go out, go back to the communications deck and start again.

VOGON GUARD   (Flustered) Erm – yes, sir—

FX: Door closes. Jeltz hums to himself. We hear the unfortunate guard descend several flights of metallic echoey stairs and re-ascend them, under:

THE VOICE   Evolution gave up on the Vogons at almost the precise moment they emerged from the primeval seas of Vogsphere, panting, heaving and demanding a towel. In turn, the Vogons said to themselves, 'Who needs evolution, anyway?' and what nature refused to do for them they simply did without, until such time as their myriad anatomical deficiencies could be rectified with surgery.

Their planet was developing fairly significant hygiene issues with the ensuing membrane mountains and liposuction lakes when the Vogons suddenly discovered the principles of interstellar travel and migrated to the Megabrantis cluster – the political hub of the Galaxy. Bureaucracy is a parasite that preys on free thought and suffocates free spirit, and the Vogons love bureaucracy above all things. Thus within a few short Vog years, the philosophers who once governed the Galaxy were banished to the Tax Return Office to lick stamps, and now the Galactic Civil Service, like everything else, is a strictly Vogon operation. In most respects the modern Vogon differs little from his primitive forebears. For example, every year the Vogons import twenty-seven thousand of the scintillating jewelled scuttling crabs that decorate their native planet in order to while away one happy drunken night smashing them to bits with iron mallets.

FX: Knock on metal door.

PROSTETNIC   (Airily) Come.
VOGON JELTZ

FX: Vogon door opens.

152

VOGON GUARD	Sir, I—
PROSTETNIC VOGON JELTZ	Have you washed your hands?
VOGON GUARD	**(Flustered – is this a capital offence?)** Er – no . . .
PROSTETNIC VOGON JELTZ	Good. Now, what's the message?
VOGON GUARD	Right. Ah – erm . . . oh. Tsk. What was it now – tip of my . . . sure it was important . . . **(etc., under:)**
THE VOICE	Prostetnic Vogon Jeltz is fairly typical of his species in that he started his career being thoroughly vile and has now worked his way up to utterly hateful. Especially to other Vogons.
PROSTETNIC VOGON JELTZ	Hurry up, or I shall read you one of my poems. A long one which doesn't scan.
VOGON GUARD	**(This galvanizes him)** Whup! Yes! Sir – a priority message from Megabrantis. It appears there is a problem. Highway Crew were just surveying the ZZ9 Plural Z Alpha route and there's a planet in the way. Called Earth.
PROSTETNIC VOGON JELTZ	No, there isn't. I blew that planet up myself. Took it out neat as you like.
VOGON GUARD	Well, it's still there.
PROSTETNIC VOGON JELTZ	Are you arguing with me?
VOGON GUARD	Only in the sense of ever so slightly.
PROSTETNIC VOGON JELTZ	**(Threat)** Ever so slightly happens to qualify.
VOGON GUARD	We are to proceed back to Megabrantis at once and report.
PROSTETNIC VOGON JELTZ	I give the orders round here!
	FX: Zap gun – he shoots the guard.
VOGON GUARD	Argh!
PROSTETNIC VOGON JELTZ	Well . . . ? Thank me.
VOGON GUARD	**(Agony)** What for?

153

PROSTETNIC VOGON JELTZ	For not losing my temper with you.
VOGON GUARD	**(Gasp)** Thank you so much . . .

FX: Body thud.

PROSTETNIC VOGON JELTZ	I didn't order you to die!

FX: Communicator beep, then:

CANIS MINOR PONTIFF	**(Distorted, screaming people in background)** You! Aboard the Vogon Constructor Fleet! Are you still listening? We've checked our records and our planet is not to be—
PROSTETNIC VOGON JELTZ	Sorry, this window is now closed. **(Barks)** Particle cannon!
VOGON HELMSMAN	Vaporize or rubble, sir?
PROSTETNIC VOGON JELTZ	Ladies' choice.
VOGON HELMSMAN	You're too good to me.

FX: Demolition beam – planet explodes.

INT. – THE BOOK AMBIENCE

FX/Music: Underwatery. Whales and dolphins audible under:

THE VOICE	Far out in the uncharted backwaters of the unfashionable end of the western spiral arm of the Galaxy lies a small unregarded yellow sun. Orbiting this at a distance of roughly ninety-two million miles was once an utterly insignificant little blue-green planet whose ape-descended life forms were so amazingly primitive that they thought novelty ringtones were a pretty neat idea.

The planet had a problem, which was this: most of the people on it were unhappy for pretty much all of the time. A lot of them were mean, and the majority were miserable, even the ones whose cellphones were set to vibrate.

Many were increasingly of the opinion that they'd all made a big mistake in coming down from the trees in the first place. And some said that even the trees had been a bad move, and that no one should ever have left the oceans.

And then, one Thursday, a girl sitting on her own in a small cafe in Rickmansworth suddenly realized what it was that had been going wrong all this time, and saw how the world could be made a good and happy place.

154

However, before she could switch on her cellphone to tell anyone, the Earth was unexpectedly demolished to make way for a new hyperspace bypass and the idea was lost forever. Or so it seemed. For that is not the end of her story. It picks up again in a field by the A303 in Somerset, England. The local weather forecast predicts a balmy evening with clear skies and light breezes. The hitchhiker aboard the spacecraft which has just made an unscheduled stop here is thus reassured to find that, this being England, clouds are gathering and a thunderstorm is fast approaching.

EXT. – NIGHT – FIELD NEAR MOTORWAY

FX: Distant ripples of thunder. Low heavy throb of spacecraft idling. Ramp lowers. Shoes descend.

ARTHUR **(For it is he, calling back to occupants)** Very kind of you, thank you very—

ALIEN TEASER Vdfbvlkjsblvj Fjhbsllssvvlslsv.

ARTHUR **(Keen to get away)** An excellent ship for a teaser, deceptively roomy in the back. Cheerio, then.

ALIEN TEASER Khdvkds.

ARTHUR Ye-es, sorry about that. I had to hang my pyjamas on something. I didn't realize it was your girlfriend . . .

FX: Ramp up/hatch closes. Ship revs up, under:

THE VOICE If you were to take the findings of the latest Mid-Galactic Census report, you might guess that this spacecraft would hold about six people at a stretch, and you would be right. The Census report, like most such surveys, has cost an awful lot of money and doesn't tell anybody anything they don't already know – except that every single person in the Galaxy has 2.4 legs and owns a hyena. Since this is clearly not true, the whole thing will eventually be scrapped.

Arthur Dent is strictly two-legged and does not own a hyena that he knows of; however he has managed to hitchhike across the Galaxy from a pleasant if dull exile on the planet Krikkit to his home planet, Earth. The fact that he has not had to resort to time travel to arrive at a planet which should no longer exist is one he has decided to ignore for the time being. Suffice to say that Arthur is a little older, his dressing gown a little grubbier – and he is carrying a large plastic shopping bag which, he will shortly discover, has a big hole in the bottom.

FX: Rummaging in plastic bag, under:

ARTHUR   (Discovering hole) Suffering Zarquon . . . (etc., under:)

THE VOICE   Arthur managed to replace his increasingly smelly home-made rabbit-skin pouch with this odourless but significantly less intact receptacle, several days and some fifteen hundred light years distant, at a stopover in the Port Brasta Mega-Market. At the same time he took the opportunity to raise some cash by selling all the blood, sperm and hair cuttings he could survive without to the less fussy medical, reproductive and dandruff-research establishments. He also routinely updated his copy of *The Hitchhiker's Guide to the Galaxy*.

                FX: *Guide* switch on and bleep alert (reverby).

THE VOICE   The update triggered an alert which stopped him in his tracks. Distracted by the consequently urgent need to find a ride, Arthur grabbed this bag without looking. It is a plastic carrier with a clever and elaborate pun in Lingua Centauri on its side, a marketing slogan completely incomprehensible in any other language, which reads – to anyone who can decipher it – 'Be Like the Twenty-Second Elephant with Heated Value in Space – Bark!'

                FX: Rustling of bag (this business under the above:)

ARTHUR   Ohhh. Typical . . .

                FX: Banging on the hatch.

ARTHUR   (cont'd) Hallo . . . ?

                FX: Hatch opens/ramp down.

ALIEN TEASER   Ktgr?

ARTHUR   I'm sorry, my towel must still be somewhere aboard. It's fallen out of the hole in this bag.

ALIEN TEASER   (Annoyed) Ncob!

                FX: Towel flung in Arthur's face, under:

ARTHUR   Ah, you've found – fnf—!

                FX: Ramp up/hatch closes. Ship lifts off and shoots away.

ARTHUR   (Pulling towel off his head) Miserable six-armed— (Calls) Your girlfriend is a hatstand, and my mattress smelled of swamp!

                FX: Ship roars away, leaving Arthur standing in the rain.

ARTHUR   (Wonderingly) Hm. Home.

                FX: Thunder crash.

156

ARTHUR   Don't question the rain, Arthur. Enjoy it. Own it.

FX: He starts walking through grass towards the motorway.

FX: Car approaches, under:

ARTHUR   Ah . . . headlights. Right. Confident smile, stick out thumb –

FX: Thunderclap.

ARTHUR   – and beg: please stop, please stop . . .

FX: Car whooshes by, huge splosh as Arthur is soaked.

ARTHUR   Bwshfff!

FX: Car toots merrily, receding.

ARTHUR   (Yells after it) 'My other car is also a Porsche'? How about getting a sticker that says 'I'm an unbelievable prat in any car'!

EXT. – STREET AMBIENCE – HAN DOLD CITY

FX: Copters, sirens and gunfire, under:

THE VOICE   The Earth is a world whose entire entry in *The Hitchhiker's Guide to the Galaxy* comprises the two words 'Mostly harmless'. The author of this entry is named Ford Prefect and he is, at this precise moment, far away, on a far from harmless world, sitting in a far from harmless bar, recklessly courting trouble. Whether it is because he is drunk, ill or suicidally insane would not be apparent to the casual observer; not that there are any casual observers in the Old Pink Dog Bar on the lower South Side of Han Dold City. One of those nasty hushes has descended on the place, a sort of missile-crisis sort of hush, broken only by the evil-looking bird perched on the bar continually screeching the names of local contract killers. All eyes are on Ford Prefect. Some of them are on stalks. Literally.

FX: Copters, sirens and gunfire become muffled, heard from within:

FX: Sinister alien bar atmosphere. Mutterings from horrible clientele, reacting to following scene:

Music: Thudding low-end dirgey metal anthem.

BARMAN   (Evil purr) Like I said. We don't take it.

EVIL-LOOKING BIRD   (Nearby, screeching) KickAss McFist, 555–87652!

FORD PREFECT   (Cheerful) Everybody takes it!

157

EVIL-LOOKING BIRD	Necro Mortdonor, 555–29643!
BARMAN	**(Leaning in close)** You pay your drinks bill, in cash, or you surrender your breathing privileges.
EVIL-LOOKING BIRD	Skril Splenetizor, 0–800-WHACK!
FORD PREFECT	What are you worried about? The expiration date? Have you guys never heard of Neo-Relativity out here? There's whole new areas of physics which can take care of this sort of thing. Time-dilation effects, temporal relastatics . . .
BARMAN	We are not worried about the expiration date.
FORD PREFECT	Well, that's good, then.
EVIL-LOOKING BIRD	Viscera Eviscerator, 555–93864!
BARMAN	We are worried about the entire piece of plastic.
FORD PREFECT	This is an American Express card. It is the finest way of settling bills known to man. You're supposed to say, 'That'll do nicely, sir,' and swipe it!
BARMAN	**(Leaning in close)** It may Do Nicely where you come from, sonny, but here, it don't.
EVIL-LOOKING BIRD	Kye Aparoon, 555–83645!
FORD PREFECT	What kind of clip joint is this? You present me with a drinks bill that would bankrupt a Triganic Pu collector then demand cash?

FX: Scuttling sound on bar like fingernails scrabbling.

BARMAN	Asking for credit in the Old Pink Dog? Hah.

FX: Heavy thud of hand on Ford's shoulder.

FORD PREFECT	Credit— **(Grabbed by throat)** Aarrgh . . .
BARMAN	Credit and Aarrgh. Two words that go together here. Coupled with 'You're gonna die, boy.'
EVIL-LOOKING BIRD	Charlie Head Punter, 555–9368!
FORD PREFECT	**(Slightly throttled)** Could-you-take-your-hand-off-my-throat?
BARMAN	It's not my hand. It belonged to the original landlord. He left it to medical science. They didn't like the look of it so they gave it back to the bar.
FORD PREFECT	**(Strangled)** I can't pay with a severed hand strangling me.

BARMAN	It's only doing its job. It takes orders, it serves drinks, it deals with people who need dealing with. People who try to pay with plastic. Plastic we have Never Heard Of. **(To hand)** Release!
	FX: Hand flops back on bar, scuttles off.
FORD PREFECT	**(Intake of breath)** Whurgh . . .
BARMAN	**(Suspicion)** I know your face . . .
FORD PREFECT	**(Surprised)** So – er – let's not rearrange it, right! I want you to always remember me this way.
BARMAN	**(Squinting at him)** You've pulled this before . . .
EVIL-LOOKING BIRD	Snide Arrogator, 555–87445!
FORD PREFECT	Can you get that bloody bird to shut up?
BARMAN	Certainly—
	FX: Zap gun unholstered, loud shot. Bird screech and thump.
FORD PREFECT	Thank you.
BARMAN	**(Back to low purr)** Don't thank me. You're next.
	FX: Zap gun re-cocked.
FORD PREFECT	Um – tell you what – let me have a look at that bill again, would you?
	FX: Bill handed over. A pause while Ford reads it.
FORD PREFECT	**(cont'd)** Hm. And I really drank all this, did I?
BARMAN	An hour ago you said the drinks were on you. And the pimps get very thirsty round here. The only people who get thirstier are the record-company executives. And this is their annual convention week. So that's the bill you ran up. Either it gets settled or you get terminated. Nothing personal, only I have a reputation to think of. You do see that, don't you?
FORD PREFECT	OK. Now the way I see it, I've made a bona fide attempt to pay my bill, and it's been rejected. You're just going to have to come up with a better idea.
BARMAN	We used to have a sign in here. 'Please don't ask for credit because having your throat torn out by a savage bird while a disembodied hand smashes your head against the bar often offends.'
FORD PREFECT	Why did you take it down?
BARMAN	Our reputation was enough. A reputation I have to maintain.

FORD PREFECT	Oh, well. If it's your reputation you're worried about . . . How about this.
	FX: Satchel opened. *Hitchhiker's Guide* switched on.
BARMAN	**(Flatly)** . . . You're from *The Hitchhiker's Guide to the Galaxy.*
FORD PREFECT	Want a write-up?
BARMAN	**(Dry whisper)** That will do nicely, sir.

EXT. – RAIN, WET TRAFFIC SPEEDING PAST

FX: Lorry comes to halt under last part of following:

THE VOICE	Standing forlornly by an English A-road which until recently he thought extinct, Arthur Dent has attempted with limited success to simultaneously wring out his soaked dressing gown, keep dry under a souvenir Wikkit Gate jogging towel and keep a hopeful thumb stuck out. The rain begins to fall more heavily. But salvation is about to pull up, stencilled on several sides: 'McKenna's All-Weather Haulage'.
	FX: Air horn approaching. A skid of tyres as a lorry pulls up. Airbrake hiss. Door opens.
ROB McKENNA	**(From within)** Need a lift?
ARTHUR	Yes, please.
ROB McKENNA	Hop in, then. You're soaked.
	FX: Arthur climbs aboard.
ARTHUR	**(Effort, climbing in)** I wasn't until a Porsche drenched me.
	FX: Lorry door shuts.

INT. – LORRY MOVES OFF

ROB McKENNA	Bloody Porsche drivers. Hate 'em. I've been blocking him for the last twenty miles. He was taking it out on you. Hah!
ARTHUR	Hmph. And you do that to make your job more enjoyable?
ROB McKENNA	No. I do it because I'm a miserable bastard. And I know it. Rob McKenna.
ARTHUR	Arthur Dent.
ROB McKENNA	I know it because people keep pointing it out to me. Don't see no reason to disagree with them. Except that I like disagreeing with people. Specially people I don't like. Which includes most people.

160

(A pause)

ARTHUR   Well. It's certainly bucketing down.

ROB McKENNA   'Bucketing down.' Yeah. That's a good one. Hand me that notebook, I'll write it down.

ARTHUR   A good what?

ROB McKENNA   **(Writing while driving)** 'Rain Type 232, Bucketing Down'.

ARTHUR   **(Edgy)** Er – would you rather I write it while you concentrate on your –

FX: Sudden truck horn Dopplers by, swoosh of tyres on wet road.

ROB McKENNA   **(Yells)** And you! . . . Pillock.

ARTHUR   Um – these rain types. They're all just as wet as each other, surely? It's just rain.

ROB McKENNA   Just rain! Hah! Tell that to the dolphins! Did you know that the Eskimos have over two hundred different words for snow?

ARTHUR   **(Suspecting he's about to be very bored)** Really.

ROB McKENNA   Thin snow and thick snow, light snow and heavy snow, sludgy snow, brittle snow, snow that comes in flurries, snow that comes in drifts, snow that comes in on the bottom of your neighbour's boots all over your nice clean igloo floor, the snows of winter, the snows of spring, the snows you remembered from your childhood that were so much better than any of your modern snow, fine snow, feathery snow, hill snow, valley snow, snow that falls in the morning, snow that falls at night, snow that falls all of a sudden just when you're going out fishing, and even though you've trained them not to, snow your huskies have – **(Changes gear with an effort)** – pissed on.

ARTHUR   Ah. And you've worked out there are two hundred different types of rain.

ROB McKENNA   Two hundred and thirty-one. Thirty-two now. I write 'em down in this book . . .

FX: Book passed back to Arthur, who flicks through it.

ARTHUR   **(Impressed)** I'm impressed.

ROB McKENNA   . . . and I don't like any of 'em. Tell you the ones I hate most?

ARTHUR   Like I could stop you?

ROB McKENNA   April showers. Bloody April showers. Hate hate hate.

ARTHUR	But they're light and refreshing. Or at least, I seem to remember they are. Rather nice, in fact.
ROB McKENNA	Nice? If it's going to be nice, I want it to be nice without bloody raining. Since I left Denmark yesterday, I've been through seven different types of April shower. Type 33 – that was west of Copenhagen; look it up, go on—

FX: Arthur looks these up as Rob goes on.

FX: Windscreen wiper develops a flappy noise under:

ARTHUR	Erm – 'light pricking drizzle which makes roads slippery' . . .
ROB McKENNA	Type 39—
ARTHUR	Er – 'heavy spotting' . . .
ROB McKENNA	And types 47 to 51.
ARTHUR	'Vertical light drizzle through to sharply slanting light to moderate drizzle freshening' . . . Yes. Erm – can I ask—
ROB McKENNA	(Off on one) Then types 87 and 88, finely distinguished varieties of vertical torrential downpour, 100, post-downpour squalling, cold, followed by all the sea-storm types between 192 and 213 at once – next page –
ARTHUR	(Riffling pages) Oh – right—
ROB McKENNA	Since I docked at Harwich: types 123, 124, 126, 127, mild and intermediate cold gusting, regular and syncopated cab-drumming, type 11, breezy droplets, and as I pulled up just now my least favourite of all, 17.
ARTHUR	(Reads) 'A dirty blatter striking the windscreen so hard that wipers make no difference'.

FX: Squeaky window clean.

ROB McKENNA	Yeah, well, they do, actually. When the wiper blade's not flapping off.
ARTHUR	Um – sorry to interrupt, but are we on the Taunton road . . . ?
ROB McKENNA	We were, long past the turning now.
ARTHUR	Ah, only that's where I wanted to go.
ROB McKENNA	A good place to get out of, if you ask me.
ARTHUR	Only I think I must have been on the wrong side of the road when you picked me up. I was trying to get there, you see.
ROB McKENNA	Did you have any kind of plan when you started hitchhiking?

ARTHUR	Er – no. Well, survival really. It was a long time ago.
ROB McKENNA	I can see that. Did you grow the beard for a bet?
ARTHUR	Look, can you pull off here? I really wanted to go in the other direction.
ROB McKENNA	Mucky towel . . . dressing gown . . . What kind of hitchhiker are you?
ARTHUR	One of the wet, cold sort who's come a long way. Please. There's a lay-by, look.
ROB McKENNA	Flippin' heck.

EXT. – ROAD – RAINING

FX: Lorry swerves off, comes to halt. Door open/close, under:

ARTHUR	Thank you . . . sorry.
ROB McKENNA	(Off, in cab) *You're* sorry . . . ?

FX: Door slam, lorry moves off.

ROB McKENNA	(Yells) It'll take me hours to get your pong out of here . . .

FX: Arthur walks across to other carriageway. Just him and the night atmos. Rain has died away.

ARTHUR	Been away too long from running water, that's my problem. **(Sighs)** That's a point, the rain's stopped. Just like that. How strange. Oh well . . .

INT. – THE BOOK AMBIENCE

THE VOICE	All Arthur Dent knows at this moment is that the rain clouds which scud away in the lorry's wake are allowing him to dry off at last. All Rob McKenna knows is that the weeks he spends on the roads are wet and miserable and that he cannot remember his last sunny holiday. All the clouds know is that they love him and want to be near him, to cherish him, to nurture and to water him. For Rob McKenna is, in fact, a rain god.

EXT. – MOTORWAY – THUNDER AND RAIN

ARTHUR	Oh, blast, it's started again. Ah. Headlights – smile, thumb out— **(Calls:)** Hallo! Are you passing Taunton by any—

FX: Rob's lorry sweeps past, huge spray of water soaks Arthur.

ARTHUR	(cont'd) Aaargh—!

163

ROB McKENNA   (Yelling from cab) You've got *me* going the wrong bloody way now!

FX: Ext. road as Arthur tries to thumb a lift. FX of cars passing and soaking him, with reactions, under:

THE VOICE   The rain leaves so much surface water that Arthur is drenched in turn by several cars.

FX: Saab pulls up.

THE VOICE   At last a Saab pulls up. Its driver's name is Russell, and his sister, in the back seat, is taking no part in the proceedings at present.

FX: Electric window down.

RUSSELL   (Yell) Have you come far?

ARTHUR   (Yell) Yes. Well, no – from a field over there. I mean – Yes, actually, I . . .

RUSSELL   Open the door and get in, for goodness' sake.

EXT. – STREET – SOUTH SIDE, HAN DOLD CITY

FX: Copters whizz by. Distant sirens, screams and gunfire. Bar door opens, brief blast of music, doors close, feet on sidewalk.

FORD PREFECT   (Calls) Excuse me, er . . . madam – I'm looking for the best route to – (the space port)

HOOKER 1   Oh, hallo, handsome. Want to have a good time?

FORD PREFECT   Thanks, I just had one.

HOOKER 1   (Moving off) You don't know what you're missing.

FORD PREFECT   Yeah, but think of the fun I'll have imagining it.

HOOKER 2   (Off, calls) Hey, honey, you rich?

FORD PREFECT   (Laughs, calls back) Do I look rich?

HOOKER 2   (Off) Don't know. Maybe, maybe not. Maybe you'll get rich. I do a very special service for rich people.

FORD PREFECT   (Voice still up) Oh yes? And what's that?

HOOKER 2   (Off) I tell them it's OK to be rich.

FORD PREFECT   (Stops) Tell me that again?

FX: Stiletto heels towards Ford.

HOOKER 2	**(Approaching)** It's my big number. I have a master's degree in social economics and I can be very convincing. People love it. Especially in this city— Uh-oh – look out—!
	FX: Sudden burst of gunfire from above. Window smash. Man's scream down. Body lands at Ford's feet.
FORD PREFECT	**(Jumps)** Zark! Now they're throwing people out of windows at me! **(Yells)** I settled the bar bill!
HOOKER 2	It's only a bass player. Probably got shot by his drummer for forgetting the riff. Bass players are two a penny on the streets of Han Dold City. You know the difference here between a bass player and a dead dog?
FORD PREFECT	There are skid marks in front of the dog.
HOOKER 2	**(Slightly disappointed)** You know it.
	FX: New alarms going off nearby, copters.
FORD PREFECT	Like an old friend. It's a bit lively round here, isn't it?
HOOKER 2	Oh, one police tribe sets off the block alarms so they can lay an ambush for the other police tribe. The copters come in and pick off the rookies. Or the musicians.
	FX: Copter swoop in, gunfire. Crash. Scream. Drumkit hits sidewalk.
FORD PREFECT	Like drummers?
HOOKER 2	No, targeting drummers is part of their public-service remit.
FORD PREFECT	**(Shivers)** Goosnargh. Time for a drop of that Ol' Janx Spirit.
	FX: Satchel opened, bottle pulled out, cork pop.
HOOKER 2	Can you spare some? I'm freezing in this skirt.
	FX: Bottle handling.
FORD PREFECT	Ah. I was going to compliment you on the . . . belt. Here. Wipe the top with this towel first.
HOOKER 2	Good idea. Kill the germs on the bottle.
	FX: Squeaky wipe.
FORD PREFECT	No, to kill the germs on the towel. They've been building up quite a complex and enlightened civilization on the smellier patches.
HOOKER 2	Er – right. **(Swigs, smacks lips)** You sure you won't.

165

FORD PREFECT	**(Uh-huh)** As it happens, I'm owed a lot of money. If I ever get hold of it, I could come and see you then.
HOOKER 2	Sure, I'll be here. So how much is a lot?
FORD PREFECT	Fifteen years' back pay.
HOOKER 2	You work on your back too?
FORD PREFECT	**(Laughs it off)** I was reviewing a planet. It was only two words.
HOOKER 2	Zarquon. An entire planet in two words . . . which one took the time?
FORD PREFECT	The first one. Once I'd got that, the second word just popped up one afternoon after lunch. I wrote a lot more but they cut it down. Then the planet got demolished. They've still got to pay me, though.
HOOKER 2	Who have?
FORD PREFECT	*The Hitchhiker's Guide to the Galaxy.*
HOOKER 2	You work for that thing? Soft number.
FORD PREFECT	You want to see my entry? Before it gets erased? The new revisions must be out by now. It can't escape their notice for ever that the Earth has been demolished.
HOOKER 2	Strut your stuff, honey.
	FX: *Hitchhiker's Guide* switched on.
FORD PREFECT	Here—
THE VOICE	**(Distorted)** Planet Earth: Mostly harmless. End of – BZT!
	FX: Static on *Guide*.
FORD PREFECT	Ah. Here we go, it's started—
VOICE OF THE BIRD	**(Distorted)** Please wait. This entry is being updated over the Sub-Etha Net. The system will be down for a measurable period.
	FX: Electric spooling scribble as *Guide* updates.
FORD PREFECT	Goodbye, Earth, I'll miss your residuals – oh. **(Ford reacting to it with growing astonishment)** No, wait . . . this is interesting.
	FX: Air car lands nearby. Electric window winds down.
PUNTER	**(Off, in car)** Hey, babe, you got the time? I got the money.
FORD PREFECT	I don't believe it . . .

166

HOOKER 2	(Getting up, moving off) Look – I'm a working girl, and there's a client. Gotta go. If you get that money, look me up, you'll need me.

FX: Stilettoes away to car. Door open and close.

FX: Electric spooling scribble as *Guide* updates.

FORD PREFECT	(Reading, astonished) . . . people to avoid on French campsites, restaurants to avoid in Los Angeles, currency deals to avoid in Istanbul, weather to avoid in London, bars to go everywhere. Pages and pages of it. It's all here, everything I wrote . . .

FX: Button push. Spooling scribble stops, for:

THE VOICE	(Distorted) Tips for aliens in New York: land anywhere, Central Park, Tribeca, anywhere. No one will care, or indeed even notice—

FX: Button push. Spooling scribble starts under:

FORD PREFECT	Yeah! I wrote this!

FX: Button push. Spooling scribble stops, for:

THE VOICE	(Distorted) Surviving: get a job as a cab driver immediately. Don't worry if you don't know how the machine works and you can't speak the language, don't understand the geography or indeed the basic physics of the area, and have large green antennae growing out of your head. In fact, this is the best way of staying inconspicuous.

FX: Button push. Spooling scribble starts under:

FORD PREFECT	But what's it doing in the *Guide*?

FX: Button push. Spooling scribble stops, for:

THE VOICE	(Distorted) Amphibious life forms from any of the worlds in the Swulling, Noxios or Nausalia systems will particularly enjoy the East River, which is said to be richer in those lovely life-giving nutrients than the most virulent laboratory slime yet achieved . . .

FX: Button push. *Guide* switch off.

FORD PREFECT	This is a planet I saw completely destroyed. With my own two eyes. Boiled away into space. Only Arthur Dent and I escaped – and only just.

FX: *Guide* switched on again.

THE VOICE	(Distorted) . . . How to have a good time in Bournemouth, Dorset, England. One of the most exciting places on any world in the known Galaxy—

FX: *Guide* switched off.

FORD PREFECT	And one of the most baroque pieces of invention I ever delivered. **(Getting up)** Something very weird is happening. And if something very weird is happening, I want it to be happening to me.
	FX: *Guide* **stuffed into satchel.**

EXT. – STREET – SOUTH SIDE, HAN DOLD CITY

FX: Copters whizz by. Distant sirens, screams and gunfire.

FX: Ford walks to car. He knocks on window, it opens.

HOOKER 2	**(As window opens)** . . . it's OK to insist on a golden handshake, honey, look at the way the whole economy is structured— **(To Ford)** Yes, honey.
FORD PREFECT	Sorry to disturb – I have a major piece of unfinished business to attend to. Which way to the spaceport?
HOOKER 2	Follow the aeroway south. But it's seventeen klicks away. You'll never make the shuttle.
FORD PREFECT	No problem, I'll steal something fast.
	FX: Window winds up, fading the interior.
PUNTER	**(Fading out with window)** But my long-term investment portfolio isn't yielding . . .
FORD PREFECT	Ah. Now this will do nicely . . .
	FX: Air-car lock picked.
COMPUTER	**(Distorted)** Caution. You are picking the lock of a Han Dold Law Enforcement Copter –
FORD PREFECT	**(Busy)** I know . . . unf.
	FX: Big clicky beepy thunk.
COMPUTER	**(cont'd)** – but as you have overridden my alarm circuits, I am powerless to stop you.
FORD PREFECT	**(Effort as he climbs in)** Too right.
	FX: Door slam. Copter motor up, flies off.

INT. – RUSSELL'S CAR

ARTHUR	**(Fading in)** . . . I was on my way to meet a friend in some far-flung bar when I discovered I still had a home to come back to, so it could've been a lot

further. But even so, I'd say about one thousand, four hundred and thirty-seven light years.

RUSSELL   I'm sorry?

ARTHUR   You were asking how far I'd come.

RUSSELL   Sorry, I missed what you said.

FENCHURCH   Nnnhhh . . .

ARTHUR   Are you sure your sister is all right?

RUSSELL   You all right, Fenny?

ARTHUR   Fenny . . . hmmmm . . .

FENCHURCH   **(From back seat)** Mmmmmm.

RUSSELL   Yeah. That'll be the drugs.

ARTHUR   And that's all right, is it?

RUSSELL   Fine by me. Why do you keep staring at her like that? She's not a junkie or anything. She's under sedation.

ARTHUR   Is she ill?

RUSSELL   No, just barking mad. Don't worry, it doesn't run in the family.

ARTHUR   What?

RUSSELL   She's loopy, completely tonto. I'm taking her back to the hospital and telling them to have another go.

FX: Car slows down.

RUSSELL   **(cont'd)** This is your town, isn't it? Taunton.

ARTHUR   Yes. No!

RUSSELL   Make your mind up.

ARTHUR   My house is another five miles. If that's all right.

RUSSELL   **(It isn't)** OK.

FX: Car speeds up again.

ARTHUR   Tell me more about, um, Fenny . . .

RUSSELL   Delusions. Says she suffers from strange delusions that she's living in the real world. It's no good telling her that she is living in the real world because she

169

just says that's why the delusions are so real. And the doctors keep going on about strange jumps in her brainwave patterns.

ARTHUR Jumps . . . ?

FENCHURCH (Suddenly, very clearly) This.

ARTHUR (Turning round in his seat) What did she say?

RUSSELL She said 'this'.

ARTHUR This what?

RUSSELL How the heck should I know? Mad as a marine biologist, she is.

ARTHUR I'm sorry?

RUSSELL You know what I mean.

ARTHUR Not exactly . . . Um – you don't seem to care very much.

RUSSELL Well, of course I care!

ARTHUR I didn't mean it to sound like that. I know you care a lot, obviously. You just have to deal with it somehow. Please excuse me. I just hitched from the other side of the Horsehead Nebula . . . Perhaps you'd better let me out—

FX: Huge thunderclap outside. Rain. Windscreen wipers on.

RUSSELL In this weather?

FX: Huge lorry overtakes with a blast on its horn.

RUSSELL Bloody lorry! That's twice now! Bloody McKenna's All-Weather Haulage!

FX: He beeps the car horn.

FX: Rain stops.

RUSSELL Oh, just a shower . . .

FX: Windscreen wipers off.

RUSSELL Anyway, where were we?

ARTHUR Um . . . when did it start? Her . . . delusions?

RUSSELL Oh, it started with all that business when everybody had the hallucinations, you remember.

ARTHUR No.

RUSSELL She was in a cafe somewhere. Rickmansworth. Apparently she stood up, calmly announced that she had undergone some revelation or something, wobbled a bit and collapsed screaming into an egg sandwich.

170

ARTHUR　　　But when you say 'everybody' had hallucinations . . .

RUSSELL　　　The big yellow ships in the sky announcing the end of the world, remember? Everyone going crazy and saying we're going to die, and then pop, they vanished. The authorities denied it, which meant it must be true.

ARTHUR　　　They *vanished*?

RUSSELL　　　Anyway, whatever drug it was that MI5 or the CIA or whoever put into the water supply or whatever, didn't seem to wear off so fast with Fenny—

ARTHUR　　　The Vogon . . . The yellow ships . . . *vanished*?

RUSSELL　　　Well, of course they did, they were hallucinations. You don't remember? Where have you been, for heaven's—

ARTHUR　　　What?!

FX: Handbrake pull – the car skids to a stop, they are thrown forward.

ARTHUR　　　(Stunned) Uhh.

FENCHURCH　　　(Thrown into back of seat) Unf—

ARTHUR　　　Fenny – is she all right?

RUSSELL　　　Would you please let go of the handbrake?

ARTHUR　　　Sorry. Oh, look . . . that seems to be my house.

INT. – POLICE COPTER, IN FLIGHT

HAN DOLD AIR TRAFFIC　　　(Distorted) Unidentified police copter, spaceport air traffic – alter course, the interplanetary shuttle is departing—

FORD PREFECT　　　Hallo, Air Traffic. Life has suddenly furnished me with a serious goal to achieve. I have new responsibilities – unh!

FX: Radio smashed. Fizzles.

FORD PREFECT　　　(To self) And that shuttle's not leaving without me. Now – where's that towel . . .

EXT. – SPACEPORT

FX: Copter lands. Ford leaps out, running and flapping his towel.

FORD PREFECT　　　(Yells, breathless) Hey! Hold the gangway! One plus towel coming aboard!

171

INT. – INTERPLANETARY SHUTTLE

FX: Ford staggers in. Pressure door closes behind him.

STEWARDESS BOT Excuse me, sir, do you have a reservation?

FORD PREFECT **(Breathless, but with a winning smile)** No. But I have an American Express card . . .

STEWARDESS BOT Oh – I'll need to check that—

PILOT VOICE **(Distorted)** Cabin crew, secure pressure doors and strap in for lift off.

FORD PREFECT I think you need to find me a seat first.

STEWARDESS BOT **(Flustered)** Er – were you wanting a Dentrassi steerage bin or first class massage chair with in-flight holovid and free novelty ringtone downloads?

FORD PREFECT **(Still winning smile)** Yes, please.

INT. – THE BOOK AMBIENCE

THE VOICE What possible purpose in life could inspire Ford Prefect more than drinking a lot and dancing with girls? Is Arthur Dent finally home for good? And how will the reappearance of Earth disrupt the Vogons' traffic-calming initiative? The next episode of *The Hitchhiker's Guide to the Galaxy* resolutely refuses to be ignored, discarded or dropped out of plastic carrier bags . . .

ANNOUNCER For those listeners whose income exceeds fifteen thousand Triganic Pus per annum (regardless of orbital duration), wealth counselling is now available at a reasonable rate by the fire hydrant outside the Old Pink Dog Bar in Han Dold City, just under the sign saying 'New Bar Bird Wanted, Knowledge of Local Hit Men Vitally Necessary'.

FOOTNOTES

The Vogons This opening scene was originally at the start of Episode Two of the Quandary Phase, but was moved very late in the day to the start of Episode One, a conscious decision to reverse expectations and by doing so warn those familiar with the sequencing of the novels that the gloves, if not off, were going to be loaded with the odd horseshoe. There is also the fact that *So Long* is very much Arthur's love story, and rightly so; however, with events coming up in *Mostly Harmless* (which Douglas had not yet formulated), the Vogons could not be consigned to the dustbin of history for the duration of Arthur's relationship with Fenchurch; in fact nothing that has gone before on *Hitchhiker's* is about to be wasted.

Although the events in this scene are not in the novel, it is based on Douglas's descriptions of Vogons and amplifies the idea – started in the Tertiary Phase – that Earth is not the only planet they are destroying. In fact their bureaucracy has got so out of hand that they are simply wiping out anything that is even a minor inconvenience. Life, liberty and the pursuit of happiness are not so much under threat from grand dramatic villainy as from the everyday deadweight of rules and quotas enforced without common sense or compassion. This applies equally to political leaders and commissioning editors . . .

'Far out in the uncharted backwaters . . .' This is an updated version of the Book speech from the top of the original *Hitchhiker's Guide to the Galaxy* Series One Episode Two, repeated here with some tweaks because Douglas repeats it almost verbatim at the start of *So Long, and Thanks for all the Fish*. The tweaks (such as references to novelty ringtones) are (a) to confound expectation of the overfamiliar (b) to update the digital watch gag, which has already been used in the Primary Phase, and (b) set up the phone-gag 'runner' which runs vaguely through *So Long, and Thanks for all the Fish*.

Alien teaser These were the easiest lines to write in all fourteen episodes. Just close your eyes and hit keys, and this alien language comes out. Then get Bob Golding in to play the part, and it turns out he can speak the language! Amazing coincidence.

A drinks bill that would bankrupt a Triganic Pu collector From *The Restaurant at the End of the Universe*, chapter 19: '. . . the Triganic Pu has its own very special problems. Its exchange rate of eight Ningis to one Pu is simple enough, but since a Ningi is a triangular rubber coin six thousand eight hundred miles along each side, no one has ever collected enough to own one Pu.'

This of course does not mean that the Pu is worth much at all, but if you've got eight Ningis to rub together . . . erm . . . you must have enormous fingers . . .

When Arthur Smith (as the Barman) says, 'I know your face,' this is, in fact, not in the novel; but Ford's puzzlement is important, as this suggests that another Ford has been in here before, trying to pull the same stunt. This introduces the Déjà Vu theory of parallel worlds and multiple lives, which will be the theme of *Mostly Harmless*. Don't say you weren't warned, gentle reader.

Rob McKenna The opening chapters of *So Long, and Thanks for all the Fish* contain very little dialogue and it is Douglas's narrative voice, rather than that of the Book, which predominates – much more so than in the earlier novels. At once this is a stylistic departure from any precedent set in the original radio series and it was immediately apparent that any adaptation which wasn't pages of narration by the Voice would need to take a much more hands-on approach to things. My earliest draft of this episode had Rob arrive at a motorway service area, bump into another trucker and discuss the rain types. But this involved introducing a new character to bounce the lines off, one not found in the book, and delayed the arrival of Arthur Dent. The solution seemed inevitable; rather than drenching Arthur as he swept by in his lorry, Rob would have to pick him up. This way both their backstories would get told in conversation, and their characters revealed.

In the event the casting of Rob McKenna was a chance to introduce the idea of parallel lives in parallel universes – Bill Paterson semi-reprised his role as a space trucker from the second series and became Rob, still a trucker but this time all too earthbound.

EPISODE TWO

SIGNATURE TUNE

ANNOUNCER *The Hitchhiker's Guide to the Galaxy*, by Douglas Adams, Quandary Phase.

Sig fades.

INT. – THE BOOK AMBIENCE

Music: Busy purposeful feel.

THE VOICE Trying to predict the future is a mug's game. But it is a game that life forms everywhere learn to play, because the future is always changing and we are going to have to live there, probably as soon as next week. However Arthur Dent could never have predicted that just a few days ago an update to his copy of *The Hitchhiker's Guide to the Galaxy* would suddenly declare that the Earth had now, for no reason that he could possibly fathom, flicked back into existence, as if it had never been destroyed by a Vogon Constructor Fleet at all. But any life form worth their sodium chloride would do what Arthur has consequently done under such circumstances: they would hitch the quickest ride home available by spacecraft, haulage lorry and Saab automobile. Though perhaps only Arthur Dent could have fallen in love at first sight with the Saab driver's catatonic sister, all but unconscious on its back seat.

EXT. – ARTHUR'S HOUSE – NIGHT

FX: Car door slams, Saab speeds away, under:

FX: Footsteps on gravel.

ARTHUR **(Yell)** Thanks for the lift, Russell! Bye, Fenny! **(Sighs)** Fenny . . . *Fenny* . . . **(Sighs again)** Good grief. Am I really home? On Earth? No bulldozers? No Vogons? Everything as it was before . . . before—

FX: Distant phone ringing inside the house, under:

ARTHUR **(In a torpor)** The phone's ringing. **(Suddenly)** The Phone Is Ringing!

175

FX: Garden gate. He hurries up path, business as per:

ARTHUR Key! Need a key. Dammit. No! Under the stone frog? Yes! Under the frog . . .

FX: Phone upstairs still ringing.

FX: Door opened, blocked by junk mail, kitchen acoustic.

ARTHUR Door's stiff . . . oh. Junk mail. Piles of it . . . Urgh. Dead kitten? How—? Never mind. **(Effort)** Unf . . . right. The phone. Where'd I leave the phone? Upstairs, dammit—

FX: He runs upstairs, stairwell acoustic.

ARTHUR I'm coming!

INT. – ARTHUR'S BEDROOM

FX: Bedroom door opened, bedroom acoustic.

ARTHUR I'm here, I'm here—

FX: Phone stops ringing.

ARTHUR **(Breathless, leaping at it)** Zarking fardwarks! **(He plonks down on the bed)** . . . I'm home . . . By my own personal time scale, so far as I can estimate it, it must be, ooh, years since I left. But how long here? But *how*? The planet was demolished, utterly destroyed . . . and it *wasn't* a hallucination. But this is my house . . . the front-door key where I left it, the junk mail piled up where I left it, and my bed, the way I left it the morning the bulldozers came. Why? How? Don't question it, Arthur. Enjoy it. Own it. **(Sighs)** Getting dark . . . I wonder if the electricity's been cut off . . .

FX: Click.

ARTHUR **(Pleasantly surprised)** Oh. Well, well. And everything's where I left it. Half-read book, half-thrown-away magazine, half-used towels. Half-pair of socks in half-drunk cup of coffee – other half-pair missing in action. A half-eaten sandwich half-turning into . . . **(Sniff)** Eurgh! . . . Bung a fork of lightning through this lot and you'd start the evolution of life all over again . . . no – hang on a minute – this is new. A present?

FX: Gift unwrapped.

FX: Shaken.

ARTHUR From who? It's heavy.

FX: Box opened. Glass bowl picked up.

176

ARTHUR   (Inspecting it) A glass bowl. Engraved . . . (Reads) 'So Long . . . and Thanks . . .'? Odd. Looks like crystal.

FX: He pings it with a fingernail. A long, resonant clear note.

ARTHUR   Sounds like crystal. Bit posh for cornflakes, I suppose. (Idea) Ah. A fish bowl.

FX: He gets up, goes to the sink, fills it with water.

ARTHUR   For which I will require a fish – (Effort) – and being home, I don't need you in my ear any more . . .

FX: Pop of Babel fish coming out of his ear.

ARTHUR   In you go, little Babel fish. Have a holiday from all that translating. So easy to forget you've been sharing my adventures for so long . . .

FX: Babel fish plops in water. Swims about.

FX: Plastic bag action, under:

ARTHUR   Oh. My *Hitchhiker's Guide* isn't here. Just a *Guide*-sized hole in the bag. (Resolve) Oh well. Easy come easy go.

INT. – A SALES SCOUTSHIP OF THE SIRIUS CYBERNETICS CORPORATION

FX: Spaceship interior sounds.

BT OPERATOR   (Very much on distort!) Yes, sir, but it's a very bad line and I must ask if you are a BT account holder—

FORD PREFECT   (Somewhat out of breath) Let's say I am, for the sake of argument.

BT OPERATOR   (Distorted) And where you are calling from?

FORD PREFECT   What does it matter where I'm calling from?! . . . Letchworth!

BT OPERATOR   (Distorted) Well, I'm sorry but you can't be coming in on that line, not from Letchworth.

FORD PREFECT   Bugger Letchworth, if that's your attitude.

BT OPERATOR   (Distorted) Hold on, caller, let me check the Letchworth exchange.

FORD PREFECT   No—

FX: Click.

Music: 'Hold' muzak. Mix with 'book noises' – under:

FORD PREFECT   (Fumes, muttering, under:) Tsk . . .

THE VOICE   *The Hitchhiker's Guide to the Galaxy*, in a moment of reasoned lucidity which is almost unique among its five million, nine hundred and seventy-five thousand, five hundred and nine pages, says of the products of the Sirius Cybernetics Corporation that 'it is very easy to be blinded to the essential uselessness of them by the sense of achievement you get from getting them to work at all.' In other words – and this is the rock-solid principle on which the Corporation's Galaxy-wide success is founded – their fundamental design flaws are completely hidden by their superficial design flaws.

This not only suggests that the Sirius Cybernetics Corporation is responsible for the majority of personal computer operating systems sold across the Galaxy, it is a widely respected view widely held by right-thinking people, who are largely recognizable as being right-thinking people by the mere fact that they hold this view. And Ford Prefect is one of them. Having learnt that nothing in life is certain – not even the destruction of a planet you have spent fifteen years of your life researching – Ford is now attempting to put the Universe – in as much as he understands it – to rights . . .

BT OPERATOR   **(Distorted, interrupting muzak)** Hallo, caller?

FORD PREFECT   Yes!

BT OPERATOR   There's no way you are calling from Letchworth, sir.

FORD PREFECT   I know that, I am an intragalactic hitchhiker calling from a sales scoutship of the Sirius Cybernetics Corporation, currently on the sub-light-speed leg of a journey between the stars known on your world, though not necessarily to you, dear lady, as Pleiades Epsilon and Pleiades Zeta.

BT OPERATOR   **(Distorted)** Do you mean Harmsworth?

FORD PREFECT   I know what I mean. And the reason why I am bothering you with it rather than just dialling direct as I could – because we have some pretty sophisticated telecommunications equipment here in the Pleiades, I can tell you – is that the penny pinching son-of-a-starbeast piloting this son-of-a-starbeast spaceship has disabled it and insists that I call collect.

BT OPERATOR   **(Distorted)** You want to reverse the charges?

FORD PREFECT   No! These people are the creeps of the cosmos, polluting the celestial infinite with cellphones, palmtops and computer operating systems that never work properly or, when they do, perform functions that no sane person would require of them and go beep to tell you when they've done it! And this guy is on a drive to sell more of them! And if his benighted consumers don't have mobile communications, PDAs and repetitive strain injuries, he will accelerate their technologies until they bloody well do have!

BT OPERATOR	(Distorted) Um – could we just go back to the start . . . ?
FORD PREFECT	No! Noooooo!! Now I've shoved him into the suspended animation facility, he's fast asleep, and I've put his ship in a parking orbit round a moon of Sesefras Magna. You won't have heard of it so don't ask. Now all I need is for you to just do what I've asked you to do! Just like you'd do for any loyal customer.
BT OPERATOR	(Distorted) And that's what you want, is it?
FORD PREFECT	Yes!
BT OPERATOR	(Distorted) Thank you, caller.
FORD PREFECT	(Calming) Look, I am on a mission to save civilization as we know it. Or something like that. And you're going to help me!

FX: Click line dead.

FORD PREFECT	Hello? I don't bel—
SPEAKING CLOCK	(Distorted) At the third stroke the time will be one . . . thirty-two . . . and twenty seconds . . .

FX: Beep . . . Beep . . . Beep.

Speaking clock continues under rest of scene.

FORD PREFECT	Yes! She did it! You little beauty!

FX: He makes his way to an airlock door, giggling.

Speaking clock echoes around the ship.

Airlock operates.

LIFEPOD	Thank you choosing this Sirius Cybernetics Corporation Lifepod. Share and Enjoy.

FX: Computery noises.

FORD PREFECT	The pleasure's all yours.
LIFEPOD:	Set coordinates to Port Sesefron Orbiting Station.

FX: Escape pod launches.

INT. – THE BOOK AMBIENCE

FX: Arthur's cottage interior. Arthur getting breakfast business under:

179

THE VOICE   Arthur Dent has awoken on Earth, the planet he thought he had lost forever. No longer is he the wild-looking creature who arrived home last night. His hair is washed, his chin clean shaven, his laundry done. His dressing gown is no longer decorated with the junk-food condiment stains from a hundred grimy spaceports. This morning he found the three least hairy things in the fridge, put them on a plate and watched them intently for two minutes. Since they'd made no attempt to move within that time, he called them breakfast and ate them. Between them they killed a virulent space disease he'd picked up without knowing it in the Flargathon Gas Swamps a few days earlier, which otherwise would have killed off half the population of the Western Hemisphere, blinded the other half and driven everyone else psychotic and sterile.

So this particular incarnation of Earth was lucky there.

Now he has some calls to make. What he most wants to do is locate and establish contact with Fenny, the disturbed young woman whose brother gave him a lift home last night, and who's been exercising Arthur's imagination ever since. But first he must deal with the mass of contradictions his return journey has precipitated. This proves less tricky than he anticipated.

FX: Phone up, dialling.

ARTHUR   **(Slightly nervous)** Ah, good morning, BBC? This is Arthur Dent. The L.E. Producer? No, really, I am. Yes. Look, just put me through to my Head of Department, would you? Thank you. Ah. Oh – hello?

GEOFFREY   **(Distorted)** Yes, hallo, make it quick, the pubs are open.

ARTHUR   Geoffrey? Arthur here. Look, sorry I haven't been in for a while but I've gone mad.

GEOFFREY   Ah. Really? We were wondering. Oh – hang on— **(Yells, off)** The usual for me, Richard. **(Back into mouthpiece)** Erm, Arthur – yeah, look, not to worry. Thought it was probably something like that. Happens here all the time. What you need is something to ease you back in. Tell you what, there's a quiz show about wallpaper going begging. How soon can we expect you?

ARTHUR   Erm – phooof . . . When do hedgehogs stop hibernating?

GEOFFREY   **(Distorted)** Hang on . . . **(Off)** Maureen, when do hedgehogs stop hibernating? **(Beat)** No, that's bats . . . Uh-huh. Really? Good grief— **(Back into mouthpiece)** Sometime in spring, we think. Probably.

ARTHUR   Right. Well, add a few minutes for me to have a shave and I'll be in after that.

GEOFFREY	Great. And don't worry, we'll have your office cleared out and cleaned up for your return.
ARTHUR	Gosh. Thanks.
GEOFFREY	You'll never know it had writers sleeping in it, really.

FX: Phone down.

INT. – THE BOOK AMBIENCE

FX: Arthur driving car, under:

THE VOICE	Having exhausted the hospital sections of Yellow Pages, local directories and even the police station searching for a girl he barely glimpsed – all to no avail – Arthur Dent's good mood has ebbed away. In order to break the impasse he decides to restock with food something less than twenty weeks past its best-by date . . .
ARTHUR	(Driving) Fenny, Fenny – it's got to be a diminutive, but what of? Fenella . . . Fiona . . . Fenimore?
THE VOICE	At this point in our story, Arthur's subconscious mind has accepted that the atmosphere of the Earth has closed finally and for ever above his head.
ARTHUR	Fenner . . . Fenwick . . . ? Phenomenal . . .
THE VOICE	He has put behind him the tangled web of irresolutions into which his galactic travels once dragged him. He can now forget that the big, hard, oily, dirty, rainbow-hung Earth on which he lives is a microscopic dot on a microscopic dot lost in the unimaginable infinity of the Universe.
ARTHUR	Funicular? . . . Fenstermacher? . . . Phenolbarbitone?
THE VOICE	And in drawing all these conclusions, he is completely and utterly and irrefutably wrong. The reason for this is standing at the next road junction under a small umbrella.
ARTHUR	(Seeing her) Fenny!!!

FX: Skid of tyres.

FX: Arthur leaps from the car.

ARTHUR	. . . Fenny?
FENCHURCH	(Unsettled) How did you know my name?
ARTHUR	I – I—

FENCHURCH	You're not a friend of my brother's, are you?
ARTHUR	No.
FENCHURCH	Well?
ARTHUR	Um – are you going somewhere? I can give you a lift.
FENCHURCH	Yes, I'm going to Taunton, goodbye.
ARTHUR	Well, that's wonderful!
FENCHURCH	Is it.
ARTHUR	Well, yes – I only live a few miles away!
FENCHURCH	I don't live there. I'm going to the station. I live in London.
ARTHUR	Oh . . . I can take you to London. Yes. Let me take you to London.
FENCHURCH	Are you going to London?
ARTHUR	**(Lame)** I wasn't, but . . .
FENCHURCH	It's very kind of you, but I like the train. Thanks. Bye.
ARTHUR	Fenny—
FENCHURCH	Yes . . . how *do* you know my name?
ARTHUR	Just supposing . . . just supposing that there was some extraordinary way in which you were very important to me, and that, though you didn't know it, I was very important to you, but it all went for nothing because we only had five miles and I was a stupid idiot at knowing how to say something very important to someone I've only just met and not crash into lorries at the same time, what would you say I should do?
FENCHURCH	**(Laughs)** I'd say . . . I'd say you should buy me a drink before my train goes.

INT. – PUB – BUSY, LUNCHTIME

JIM THE LANDLORD	**(Handing food over)** There you go, mate, tomato juice, half of bitter, two rounds of BLT. **(Moving off)** Next, please – yes? . . . So what's wrong with it?

FX: Arthur and Fenchurch take seats, under:

ARTHUR	**(To Fenchurch)** There is, for some reason, something especially grim about pubs near stations, a very particular kind of grubbiness. Like the feeling which persists in England that making a sandwich interesting, attractive, or in any way pleasant to eat is something sinful that only foreigners do.

182

FENCHURCH	Well, don't eat it, then.
ARTHUR	(Takes a bite) Mmmf . . . Even I could do better.
FENCHURCH	Why don't you tell me what it is you have to tell me.
ARTHUR	Yes. Right. (Girding himself) Fenny—
RAFFLE WOMAN	(Barging in, which she does throughout) I wonder if you'd like to buy some tickets for our raffle? It's just a little one.
ARTHUR	What?
RAFFLE WOMAN	To raise money for Anjie, who's retiring.
ARTHUR	What?
RAFFLE WOMAN	And needs a kidney machine. Only fifty pence each, so you could probably even buy two. Without breaking the bank! (She giggles at her own joke, then sighs)
ARTHUR	(Impatiently hunting through his pockets) Er, yes, all right . . . there. Two, please.
RAFFLE WOMAN	(Tears off tickets) I do hope you win. The prizes are so nice.
ARTHUR	Yes, thank you. (To Fenchurch) So, Fenny—
RAFFLE WOMAN	(To Fenchurch) And what about you, young lady? It's for Anjie's kidney machine. She's retiring, you see.
ARTHUR	(Pulling out a banknote) Here – look, here's a five-pound note—
RAFFLE WOMAN	(Starting to laboriously tear off ten tickets) Oh, we are in the money. Down from London, are we?
ARTHUR	No, that's all right, really, keep the tickets.
RAFFLE WOMAN	Oh, but you must have your tickets, or you won't be able to claim your prize. They're very nice prizes, you know. Very suitable. Here—
ARTHUR	(Snatching them) Thanks. (To Fenchurch) Anyway—
RAFFLE WOMAN	(To Fenchurch) And now, dear, what about you?
ARTHUR	(Nearly a yell) For heaven's—! Sake . . . (Softening a bit) These tickets *are* for her.
RAFFLE WOMAN	Oh, I see. How nice. Well, I do hope you—
ARTHUR	Thank you.
RAFFLE WOMAN	(Moving off) No. Thank *you.*

ARTHUR	(Sighs) Where were we?
FENCHURCH	You were calling me Fenny, and I was going to ask you not to.
ARTHUR	Oh.
FENCHURCH	It's why I asked if you were a friend of my brother's. Or half-brother, really. He's the only one who calls me Fenny, and I'm not fond of him for it.
ARTHUR	So what is . . . ?
FENCHURCH	Fenchurch.
ARTHUR	What?
FENCHURCH	Fenchurch, and I'm watching you to see if you're going to ask the same stupid question that everybody asks me until I scream. I shall be cross and disappointed if you do. And I shall scream. So watch it.
ARTHUR	Fine.
	(A pause)
FENCHURCH	All right, you can ask me. Might as well get it over with. Better than have you call me Fenny all the time.
ARTHUR	I'm guessing—
RAFFLE WOMAN	(She's back) We've only got two tickets left, you see, and since you were so generous when I spoke to you before—
ARTHUR	What?
RAFFLE WOMAN	I thought I'd give the opportunity to you, because the prizes are so nice. Very tasteful. I know you'll like them. And it is for Anjie's retirement present you see. We want to give her—
ARTHUR	(Grumpily pulling out a pound coin) A kidney machine, yes. Here.
RAFFLE WOMAN	(Tears off tickets) There you are.
ARTHUR	Yes we are.
RAFFLE WOMAN	(Penny drops) Oh dear . . . I'm not interrupting anything, am I . . . ?
ARTHUR	No, it's fine. Everything that could possibly be fine, is fine. Thank you.
RAFFLE WOMAN	(With growing delight) I say . . . you two're not . . . in love, are you?
FENCHURCH	(Snort of laughter)
ARTHUR	(Stern) It's very hard to tell. We haven't had a chance to talk yet.

RAFFLE WOMAN	**(Going off)** I'd better let you see the prizes, then.
FENCHURCH	Hallo? You were about to ask me a question?
ARTHUR	Yes.
FENCHURCH	I know what it is. We can do it together. Ready? 'Was I found –
ARTHUR	– in a handbag –
BOTH	– in the Left-Luggage Office at Fenchurch Street Station?'
FENCHURCH	And the answer is no.
ARTHUR	Ah. Fine.
FENCHURCH	I was conceived there.
ARTHUR	In the Left-Luggage Office?!
FENCHURCH	Don't be daft. What would my parents be doing in the Left-Luggage Office?
ARTHUR	Well, I don't know—
FENCHURCH	It was in the ticket queue.
ARTHUR	The . . .
FENCHURCH	The ticket queue. Or so they claim. They said you wouldn't believe how bored it is possible to get in the ticket queue at Fenchurch Street Station.
ARTHUR	Riiiight . . .
FENCHURCH	Look, I'm going to have to go in a minute or two, and you haven't begun to tell me whatever this incredible thing is you are so keen to get off your chest.
ARTHUR	Uhh – Please let me drive you to London. It's Saturday, I've got nothing particular to do, I'd—
FENCHURCH	No. Thank you, it's kind of you, but no. I need to be by myself for a couple of days.
ARTHUR	But—
FENCHURCH	**(Clicking ballpoint)** Tell you what. Got something to write on? I'll give you my number. Here, one of those will do . . . **(She writes number down)** Here – now we can relax.
ARTHUR	**(Beyond happy)** Ahhh. Yes.
FENCHURCH	**(Looking up, amused)** Oh, hallo again.

185

RAFFLE WOMAN	**(She's back)** A box of cherry liqueurs, and also, and I know you'll like this, a CD of Scottish bagpipe music. And I—
ARTHUR	Yes, thank you, very nice.
RAFFLE WOMAN	I just thought I'd let you have a look at them as you're down from London.
ARTHUR	Yes. I can see that they are indeed a box of cherry liqueurs and a CD of bagpipe music. That is what they are.
RAFFLE WOMAN	I'll let you have your drink in peace now. **(Going off)** But I knew you'd like to see.
FENCHURCH	**(Finishing her drink)** Whoops. Have to go.
ARTHUR	Ohhh . . .
FENCHURCH	Don't worry. We'll talk again. **(Gets up, gathering stuff, pauses)** Perhaps it wouldn't have gone so well if it wasn't for her.
ARTHUR	**(After a deep breath)** Yes. I think that is probably perfectly true.
	FX: In background, raffle tickets are being drawn.
FENCHURCH	**(Leaving pub)** Don't see me off. Call me tomorrow.
ARTHUR	Of course.
RAFFLE WOMAN	**(Off)** Yoo hoo!
ARTHUR	**(Sudden thought)** Fenchurch—
RAFFLE WOMAN	**(Close)** Yoo hoo!
	FX: Pub door shuts – Fenchurch is gone.
ARTHUR	**(Sighs, to Raffle Woman)** Yes?
RAFFLE WOMAN	Have you got ticket number 37?

INT. – PUB – THAT NIGHT

FX: Phone ringing. Very busy background atmos. Jukebox.

BARMAID	Railway Inn – Hallo? Yes? You'll 'ave to speak up. What?? Can you ask your friend to stop playing the bagpipes, I can't – that's better . . . No, I only do the bar in the evenings. It's Yvonne who does lunch, and Jim, the landlord. No, I wasn't on. What? . . . You'll have to speak up. No, don't know anything about no raffle. What? 'Old on, I'll ask. **(Yells)** Jim! Bloke on the phone reckons he's won a raffle. Keeps on saying it's ticket 37 and he's won.

JIM	**(Off, harassed)** No, it was a guy in the pub here won.
BARMAID	**(Yells)** He says 'ave we got the ticket?
JIM	Well how can he think he's won if he hasn't even got a ticket?
BARMAID	**(Into phone)** Jim says 'ow can you think you've won if you . . . What? **(Yells)** Jim, 'e keeps effing and blinding. Says there's a number on the ticket.
JIM	Course there was a number on the ticket, it was a bloody raffle ticket, wasn't it?
BARMAID	'E says 'e means it's a telephone number on the ticket.
JIM	Put the phone down and serve the bloody customers, will you?

FX: Phone down.

EXT. – SPACE – WHICH IS LOTS OF SUB-BASS RUMBLE, OF COURSE

FX: Escape pod whooshes past us.

SPEAKING CLOCK	**(Distorted, very distant and echoey)** At the third stroke the time will be one . . . thirty-three . . . and twenty seconds . . .

FX: Beep . . . Beep . . . Beep . . .

FORD PREFECT	**(Also whizzing by . . . laughing . . .)**

INT. – THE BOOK AMBIENCE

THE VOICE	Lost in misery, contemplating the beautiful and mysterious grey glass bowl left by persons unknown on his bedside table bearing the words 'So Long, and Thanks . . .', Arthur Dent's subconscious mind reaches out to make sense of this new Earth and the frustrations of living upon it. Closing his eyes, he can feel like a tingle on distant nerve ends the flood of a far river, the roll of invisible hills, the knot of heavy rain clouds parked over a transport cafe somewhere away to the south. He feels the presence of countless other minds, some wakeful, some sleeping, one fractured. One fractured. He knows instinctively that it is Fenny. He knows that he wants to find her, and again, feels the fracture, lying before him across the days of the Earth, bisecting time. Beyond this chasm is another land, another time, an older world. And as Arthur looks at the conjunction of two Earths, one no longer existing, he awakes from the doze to find himself about eighteen inches above the rose bushes of one of his neighbours. Idly he wonders what he is doing above them and what is holding him there; and when he discovers that nothing is holding him there—

187

FX: Arthur crashes into rose bushes.

ARTHUR   Oww! **(Getting up painfully)** That's one trick I'd forgotten I'd developed . . . Didn't realize I could fly in my sleep, though . . .

FX: Distant phone ringing, foreground Arthur trapped in bush:

ARTHUR   Oh, for goodness' . . . **(Extricates himself)** Trouble is, now I *want* to fly, I can't distract myself enough to do it . . . How many thorns – ooh! – ow! – yipe! **(Yells)** I'm coming!

FX: His feet running across grass.

ARTHUR   **(Off, yelling)** I'm coming! I'm coming!

FX: Distant cottage door opened.

ARTHUR   **(At door, well off)** I'm here—

FX: Phone stops ringing.

ARTHUR   **(Off as above)** Oh, you utter—!

FX: Cottage door shuts, cutting him off.

INT. – TRANSPORT CAFE

FX: Cafeteria atmos. Wet traffic outside.

FX: Tea, sugar stirred etc./food eaten, under . . .

ROB McKENNA   It's the drizzle that makes me really morose.

ARTHUR   **(Monumentally bored)** Please shut up about the drizzle.

ROB McKENNA   I would shut up if it would shut up drizzling.

ARTHUR   Look, it's very nice seeing you again, Rob, and this is a very snug little transport cafe, but I'm actually looking for a girl. I last met her there, over the road, by the motorway junction, and if she comes back I don't want to miss her.

ROB McKENNA   **(Pause)** Do you know what it'll do when it stops drizzling, do you?

ARTHUR   No.

ROB McKENNA   Blatter.

ARTHUR   What?

ROB McKENNA   It will blatter.

ARTHUR	I curse myself for bothering to say this, but actually I don't think the rain will blatter. I think it will ease off.
ROB McKENNA	Ha! It never eases off!
ARTHUR	Of course it does.
ROB McKENNA	**(Thumping the table to punctuate, crockery leaping)** It rains . . . all . . . the time.
ARTHUR	Didn't rain yesterday.
ROB McKENNA	Did in Darlington.
ARTHUR	**(Bored)** Really.
ROB McKENNA	You going to ask me where I was yesterday? Eh?
ARTHUR	No.
ROB McKENNA	But I expect you can guess. Begins with a D.
ARTHUR	Does it.
ROB McKENNA	And it was stair-rods there, I can tell you.
ARTHUR	I expect you added 'stair-rods' to your list.
ROB McKENNA	Oh, there's more than the list. I have a diary – goes back fifteen years. Shows every single place I've ever been. And what the weather was like. And it was horrible. All over England, Scotland, Wales I been. All round the Continent, back and forth to Denmark. It's all marked in and charted. Even when I went to visit my brother in Seattle!
ARTHUR	**(Getting up)** Well, perhaps you'd better show it to someone.
ROB McKENNA	I will.
ARTHUR	Goodbye, Mr McKenna. Oh, and thank you for achieving the impossible.
ROB McKENNA	I'm sorry?
ARTHUR	I thought living alone in a cave in prehistoric Islington was the most tedious experience I would ever undergo. **(Exiting)** You, however, have proved me wrong.
	FX: Cafe door with bell, open/close.
	EXT. – STREET – DAY
ARTHUR	**(Sudden intriguing thought)** I wonder . . . ?

189

INT. – ROBOT SPACESHIP – CORRIDOR

FX: Muffled cacophony of sound layers from beyond bulkheads. The occasional flying ratchet screwdriver whizzes down this corridor.

THE VOICE   While Arthur Dent is feeling bereft and sorry for himself, Ford Prefect is several thousand light years away, simply feeling sorry for himself.

FORD PREFECT   **(Stirring fitfully)** Zarking racket . . . can't I hitch *one* peaceful ride . . . ? Now I've got cramp . . . !

INT. – THE BOOK AMBIENCE

THE VOICE   The ship Ford has inveigled himself aboard – one can hardly term his presence 'hitchhiking', as the ship is in orbit and its only other sentient occupant is not aware of his presence – is a vast silver dreadnought, built for the questing robots of Xaxis. Having embraced an economy based entirely on binge drinking, video gaming and reality television, the Reptilian Lizard Rulers of the Planet Xaxis had brainwashed their attention-deficit human subjects so effectively that public apathy rather than panic was the response to attacks on Xaxis by its neighbouring world, Zirzla. The robots and their ships were built to defend the planet, but were inclined to think there had to be more worthy civilizations to defend. Using self-propelled tools to reconfigure their ships, they made huge pan-galactic leaps in search of true civilization. These voyages almost always resulted in disillusionment and a sad, head-shaking return to orbit over Xaxis – not helped by encounters with hedonistic ne'er-do-wells like Ford Prefect, who would sneak aboard their ships via the exhaust vents, hijack the monitoring systems to play video games and clutter up the corridors with the sort of lifestyle magazines which celebrate ecologically unsound forms of transportation and controlled substances.

INT. – ROBOT SPACESHIP – CORRIDOR

FORD PREFECT   **(Getting out of his bunk)** Ooofff . . . I just want a few days' R&R, for Zark's sake . . .

FX: Ratchet screwdriver screams up and buzzes about busily.

FORD PREFECT   What the – a screwdriver? **(Yells)** Mind where you're flying! Nearly had my eye out! Shoo! Shoo! No! Don't tidy up my magazines – buzz off and screw up something!

FX: Screwdriver flies off, disgruntled.

FORD PREFECT   (Effort) First rule of hitchhiking? Never make up a bunk in a maintenance shaft. Second rule? Never bunk next to a monitoring area. What in Zark are the sensors picking up now? More makeover vids?

FX: Mechanical sequence, door opens.

INT. – XAXIS SHIP MONITORING ROOM UP

FX: Din now clearer. Combined sounds of various planets' news output, with explosions and blaster fire in background.

FORD PREFECT   (Walking in) It's not as if there'll be any glimmer of intelligence from the Xaxis news networks.

NEWS ANCHOR 1   (Distorted) . . . single transferable vote has been put aside in favour of a competitive makeover of both legislatures, the Xaxisian Chamber in magnolia, the Zirzlan with a cheerful nautical theme . . .

FORD PREFECT   Thought not.

FX: Distorted gunfire and screams, under:

COMMERCIAL V/O   (Kronkite style, distorted) On a cold moon in a cold galaxy, the future is war, war and nothing but war . . .

FORD PREFECT   Videogames: not quite as trouser-filling as the real thing of course . . . or as ironic . . .

FX: News logo sting on next monitor.

NEWS ANCHOR 2   (Distorted) *Siderial Daily Mentioner* News Network on the Cosmovid Loop, coming to you live – our reporter Trillian Astra has been following events at the State Re-Dedication of the Argabuthon Sceptre of Justice.

Music: A toothpaste jingle.

FORD PREFECT   (Ironic) Way to go, Trillian, prime time at last . . . Ah, *here* we are.

FX: He throws a switch. All monitors cut off.

FX: Background battle sounds become audible, under:

FORD PREFECT   Never underestimate the power of an off switch. All should be peace and quiet. Except it isn't. Mm. External monitor on.

FX: Space battle up, loud and clear.

ZIRZLA ROBOT LEADER   (Distort, on a loop) Xaxisian ship, surrender your ship or be destroyed by our starcruisers. You are in violation of the Zirzla Restricted Zone.

191

FORD PREFECT	Oh, a battle. That's the bloody racket. How am I going to sleep through all this? **(Sighs)** I suppose I could look up some insomnia cures.
	FX: **Rummages in satchel – pulls out the *Guide*, switches it on.**
THE VOICE	**(Distorted, handset *Guide*)** Rest. A good hot bath is always—
	FX: **Switch, spooling.**
FORD PREFECT	Oh, for pity's—
	FX: **Click.**
THE VOICE	**(Distorted, handset *Guide*)** Recuperation. See 'Tea, making a proper cup of' – and 'Baths, good hot'.
	FX: **Switch, spooling.**
FORD PREFECT	Third rule of hitchhiking – never import bookmarks from Arthur Dent's *Guide* . . . Hang on a mo' – if I do manage to get to sleep in amongst all this, I could wake up dead. Not good.
	FX: **Switching and spooling, under. Ford muttering about looking on level four not three . . .**
FORD PREFECT	Time for a little quiet persuasion.
	FX: **Switching/clicks, under:**
THE VOICE	**(Distorted, handset *Guide*)** Earth – Mostly harmless. But with some uniquely civilized—
FORD PREFECT	Pause.
THE VOICE	**(Distorted, handset *Guide*)** Paused.
FORD PREFECT	Prepare download.
THE VOICE	**(Distorted, handset *Guide*)** Please attach universal connector.
FORD PREFECT	**(Rummaging about, off)** Tsk. You could at least help me find one . . .

INT. – SHOP, ISLINGTON – DAY – SUMMER

FX: **Shop door.**

ECOLOGICAL MAN	Hi, can I help you?
ARTHUR	Is this Friends of the Planet?
ECOLOGICAL MAN	That's what it says over the window.

192

ARTHUR Yes, right, I'm here in Islington doing a bit of um – research into its prehistory, and I was passing your shop and it occurred to me that I'd like to give you some money to help save the dolphins.

(A pause)

ECOLOGICAL MAN Very funny.

ARTHUR To free them from captivity. From dolphinaria, weapons research, jumping through hoops. Return them to the wild. Quite a lot of your appeals letters were on my doormat when I returned home recently after a long trip, and as I was lighting the fire with them I thought, why not give a few quid to help save the dolphins? So I was passing and saw your shop and— Are you all right?

ECOLOGICAL MAN Actually, you're rather annoying me.

ARTHUR Just like this?

ECOLOGICAL MAN Astonishing, I know, but true.

ARTHUR Do we know each other?

ECOLOGICAL MAN Do I look like the sort of person who'd spend time with you?

ARTHUR Sorry. Must be having a déjà vu. This *is* Friends of the Planet, isn't it?

ECOLOGICAL MAN **(Withering sarcasm)** Yes. And that leaflet was sent out a year ago. But unless you have been in outer space for the last twelve months –

ARTHUR Gosh! Funny you should—

ECOLOGICAL MAN – you would know that there is no need for further contributions.

ARTHUR Well, I'm glad the appeal was such a success.

ECOLOGICAL MAN Are you doing this to wind me up, or are you as stupid as you look?

ARTHUR **(Affronted)** Look, I was passing, I saw the shop, I thought I'd give you some money to—

ECOLOGICAL MAN Tell you what. Why don't you find another endangered species – Rhinos. Gorillas . . . Your own particular branch of *Homo sapiens* – put your money somewhere useful.

ARTHUR Well, if you're going to be like that about it—

ECOLOGICAL MAN Leave. Now. Before I set about you with this plaster rhinoceros.

ARTHUR Very well.

FX: Shop door closes.

ECOLOGICAL MAN	Pillock.

FX: Shop door opens again, for:

ARTHUR	Um – you wouldn't happen to know this part of North London well, would you? I'm looking for a cave.

INT. – THE BOOK AMBIENCE

FX: Seawashy feel, under:

THE VOICE	Eight hours west of Arthur Dent – as the crow flies by passenger jet – sits a man alone on a beach, mourning an inexplicable loss. He can only think of his loss in little packets of grief at a time, because the whole thing is too great to be borne. He watches the long, slow Pacific waves come in along the sand, and waits and waits for the nothing that he knows is about to happen. And as the time comes for it not to happen, it duly doesn't happen.

The beach is a small sandy stretch somewhere along the coastline that runs west from Los Angeles. Then north up towards the misty bay of San Francisco, where it's very easy to believe that everyone you meet is also a space traveller – starting a new religion for you is just their way of saying 'hi'. There, barely inland from the ocean, lies the house of this inconsolable man. A man whom many regard as insane. His name is simply John Watson, though he assumes a more bizarre style of address. He has lost everything he cares for, and is now simply waiting for the end of the world; little realizing that it has already been and gone. One of the many reasons people think him insane is not through his choice of name, but because his house is called the Outside of the Asylum. In the house are a number of strange things, including a grey glass bowl engraved with eight words.

EXT. – MEWS, ISLINGTON – DAY

FX: Footsteps on cobbles (under end of above). They stop.

FX: Arthur presses door buzzer, audible from within.

FENCHURCH	(Distort, intercom) Yes?
ARTHUR	Er, hello, I'm wondering if you could help me, I'm researching the prehistoric limestone caves of this part of London and it appears that these mews cottages were constructed on the site of one that I . . . er . . . lived in.

FX: Muffled feet on stairs (under above). Door opens.

FENCHURCH	(Breathless) I thought you were going to phone me first.
ARTHUR	(Codfish) Fenchurch?
FENCHURCH	(After a moment) Close your mouth, Arthur. Unless you're going to throw up, in which case I'll fetch a bucket.
ARTHUR	You live *here*?
	FX: Door closed – interior acoustic.
FENCHURCH	Yes – why are there bits of plaster in your hair?
ARTHUR	I was struck by a rhinoceros.
FENCHURCH	(Picking something up from hall table) Oh, right. Ah, mustn't forget – my brother found this in his car.
	FX: The *Guide* switched on.
THE VOICE	(Distorted, from *Guide*) *The Hitchhiker's Guide to the Galaxy*.
FENCHURCH	Yours?
ARTHUR	(Cagey) Yes . . .
FENCHURCH	I think we need to talk, don't you?

INT. – THE BOOK AMBIENCE

THE VOICE	What strange geographical glitch has led Arthur to Fenchurch's front door? How much does she know of his past? And can Ford Prefect get some sleep aboard the robot ship before he exhausts his supply of *Playbeing* magazines? The centrepiece unfolds in the next full-frontal instalment of *The Hitchhiker's Guide to the Galaxy* . . .
ANNOUNCER	If you would like to make a contribution to a leading animal conservation charity, please send as much as you can to 'Adopt A Vogon Prostetnic Captain For Christmas', Planet Vogsphere, and don't expect any tax relief on it because there won't be any.

FOOTNOTES

Trying to predict the future	These last two *Hitchhiker* books are a mixture of character study (*So Long, and Thanks for all the Fish*) and ruminations on modern technology (*Mostly Harmless*), making them impossible to dramatize without a lot of hands-on reworking and some drastic

pruning. But the novels possess – as ever with Douglas – so many terrific ideas per page that one cannot just jump in with a chainsaw. However, there were a couple of occasions when there was no material in the novel for the Voice to set up a context; thus for this opening narration the opening line is from Douglas's essay 'Predicting the Future' (*The Salmon of Doubt*, p. 102 of the Macmillan hardback edition).

Ford, the BT operator and the Speaking Clock

An expanded version of the joke which is set up very cryptically in *So Long, and Thanks for all the Fish* and then explained by Ford in flashback towards the end of the novel. In fact Ford is given quite short shrift in this book. To my mind Ford and Arthur get too few scenes together in the later novels, and as he lined up the video camera to watch us recording this scene with Geoff McGivern and Ann Bryson, Kevin Davies expressed exactly the same thought. Perhaps Douglas was husbanding his resources by having Arthur and Ford in separate adventures, saving up the witty repartee between them for the end of both books. A bit like *King Kong* – the monkey doesn't turn up till the fifth reel . . .

Whatever the philosophy, it all comes down to the nitty-gritty: on day one of recordings for these new series Geoff rolled up with a big gappy smile – his lower front teeth were missing. 'Over Chrishmash I had a bit of an encounter with a Brashil nut,' he said. 'But no worriesh. It won't advershley affect my shpeech.' Grateful thanks to the dentist who provided replacements within twenty-four hours.

Arthur's first hours at home

In the novel, after having arrived home and discovered the strange grey glass bowl engraved with the words *So Long, and Thanks . . .*, Arthur visits his local pub and explains he has been away in California, but in the process gets steadily more inebriated and more space-lagged until he makes no sense at all. Although this served to re-establish that the Earth he has arrived on is, in many ways, the place he left (though of course, in other and more salient ways, very much Not), the pub scene itself is one of the very few passages from the book that could be cut without any harm to either character development or plot.

When do moles stop hibernating?

Arthur phoning the Head of BBC Radio Light Entertainment to apologize for not being in to work for months was an opportunity to discover more about his 'day job' – uncoincidentally similar to the one that Douglas briefly held down in the late seventies – and a gentle bit of fun-poking at the 'old' BBC Radio Light Entertainment.

BBC Radio Light Ent, as it was in the seventies when Douglas and Geoffrey Perkins were there (under David Hatch), and the eighties, when I was among the next generation of occupants (under Martin Fisher and Jonathan James Moore), is very much an analogue for the offices of *The Hitchhiker's Guide to the Galaxy* as Douglas describes them. On a daily basis the first floor at 16 Langham Street was mostly deserted from twelve noon until three o'clock, as everybody was out at the pub. Therefore it is quite likely that much of the comedy output of the BBC radio networks at that time was *actually* accomplished by casual visitors, who found the offices empty and thus could easily have sat down at the typewriters to bang out the odd sketch for *Week Ending* or *News Huddlines*, or indeed the entire formats of all of the quiz shows that were running at the time.

There wasn't one about wallpaper but a lot of them could have been.

The offices that Douglas, Geoffrey and I spent so much time in at 16 Langham Street have been demolished now to make room for the new BBC Broadcasting House extension. This was not such a sad loss, as the building was a remarkably ugly mid-sixties office block; the *truly* sad loss was the BBC's simultaneous non-renewal of its lease on the Paris Studio in 1994 (where the original *Hitchhiker* phases were recorded and many other historic shows). That was the moment when Radio Light Ent ceased to exist as a unique BBC entity, thereafter meekly being folded into the open-plan anonymity of Broadcasting House, with its key shows transplanted into the barn-like Radio Theatre, once the BBC Concert Hall and hugely unconducive to comedy. It can only be a matter of time before melon-sized flying BBC security robots fly around the fifth floor of BH, checking Ident-i-Eeze passes and unauthorized expense claims.

After the Tertiary Phase had been broadcast, in 2004, I met Geoffrey Perkins for a drink and we reminisced about our experiences as producers in the 'old' Radio Light Ent, with all its eccentricities. That conversation inspired this scene and I hoped he would cameo as Arthur's HLER. For Geoffrey is not just the man who midwifed *Hitchhiker's* Primary and Secondary Phases through their labour pains, he is not just the TV producer responsible for myriad timeless classics such as *Father Ted*, he is not just a Proper Comedy Actor (as evidenced in *Radio Active* and *KYTV*), he is also a former BBC Television Executive and thus can bring just the right level of bemused sympathy to the role.

The 'Richard' and 'Maureen' alluded to in the scene know who they are (Richard Willcox and Maureen Trotman, just in case they don't) and, along with all our other producer and production-assistant colleagues in the department (including Douglas) and, indeed those catatonic writers, are celebrated here with fond memory and much affection in a sort of mini-*Week Ending* sketch.

The Raffle Woman One of the few occasions where I could directly transcribe scenes full of dialogue from the novel, and then wonderful actors like Simon Jones, Jane Horrocks (as Fenchurch) and June Whitfield (as the Raffle Woman) would show why Douglas has such a good grasp of comedy timing in his writing. The ensuing scene with the barmaid is another case in point. Douglas never lost his 'ear' for lines that, when acted, could come off the page, even in the novels. Roy Hudd (more of whom anon) used to say about certain *New Huddlines* gags that seemed funny till they fell flat in performance, 'It works better written down.' Douglas's best lines worked both ways.

At the third stroke This was the voice of the British Telecom Speaking Clock at the time of recording – Brian Cobby, a wonderfully rich English voice, real old school stuff and perfect for Ford's nefarious purposes.

I have a diary Bill Paterson's emotionally wracked performance of this Rob McKenna speech had everybody in silent contortions. He invested Rob with a tearful comic pathos I had not thought to ask for.

The Xaxis ship An example of a speech by the Voice which does not exist at all in the novel but which is sorely needed to explain Ford's situation and the path down which he is likely to proceed. It is fun too to re-establish a continuum that runs through the saga; the flying ratchet screwdrivers introduced as a sidebar in the Tertiary Phase actively enter the story here, just as Arthur comments in the previous episode that his 'mattress smelled of swamp'.

Must be having a déjà vu The Ecological Man was played by David Dixon, who was Ford in the 1980 BBC TV version of *Hitchhiker's*. Thus this line, hinting that Ford (i.e. Geoff) is not the only one with multidimensional issues, far from it, goodness, no, *all* the Ford Prefects on this show are completely tonto.

EPISODE THREE

SIGNATURE TUNE

ANNOUNCER   *The Hitchhiker's Guide to the Galaxy*, by Douglas Adams, Quandary Phase.

Sig fades.

INT. – THE BOOK AMBIENCE

THE VOICE   Regular followers of the doings of Arthur Dent may have received an impression of his character and habits which – while it includes the truth and, of course, nothing but the truth – falls short of the *whole* truth in all its glorious aspects. There are certain omissions from these chronicles which provoke much speculation. What, people ask, about all that stuff off in the wings between Arthur and Trillian? Did that ever get anywhere? What were they up to all those nights on the planet Krikkit? Studying French? Jogging? What happened when Trillian was offered a reporter's job at the *Siderial Daily Mentioner*? Indeed, why did she leave? 'This Arthur Dent,' comes the cry from the furthest reaches of the Galaxy, and has even now been found inscribed on a deep-space probe thought to originate from an alien world at a distance too hideous to contemplate, 'what is he, man or mouse? Is he interested in nothing more than tea and hot baths? Has he no passion? Does he not, to put it in a nutshell, feel the need to copulate?'

Those who wish to know should listen on. Others with time-travel projectors or functioning remote controls may wish to skip on to the next episode in this Phase, which is a good bit and has Marvin in it.

EXT. – HYDE PARK – DAY

FX: Duckpond, ducks, children playing, etc. Arthur and Fenchurch walking.

FENCHURCH   **(Smiling)** I'll have to remember that you are the sort of person who cannot hold on to a simple piece of paper for two minutes without winning a raffle with it.

ARTHUR   If I believed in them, and I didn't have a past that featured events beyond the imagination of any ordinary mortal, I'd say finding you again was a bit of a miracle.

FENCHURCH (Laughs) Hold my hand.

           FX: They continue walking, under:

THE VOICE For Arthur, who can usually contrive to feel self-conscious if left alone long enough with a Swiss cheese plant, this moment is one of revelation. He feels like a cramped and zoo-born animal who awakes one morning to find the door to his cage hanging quietly open. From years of abandonment and bootless wandering, in exile from a planet that was destroyed in an encounter with the most unsympathetic bureaucracy in the cosmos, he now has regained his home world, his former life and, in Fenchurch, a woman for whom he would give it all up.

FENCHURCH Did you know that there's something wrong with me?

ARTHUR   Well, your brother mentioned some vague sort of—

FENCHURCH Oh, Russell makes stuff up – because he can't deal with what it really is.

ARTHUR   (Worried) Then what is it? Can you tell me?

FENCHURCH Don't worry, it's nothing bad at all. Just unusual. Very unusual. See if you can work it out.

ARTHUR   All right . . . your elbow. Your left elbow. There's something wrong with your left elbow.

FENCHURCH Wrong. Completely wrong. You're on completely the wrong track.

ARTHUR   This is not going to be easy. Hyde Park is stunning. You are stunning. Anyone who can go through Hyde Park with you on a summer's evening and not feel moved by it is probably going through in an ambulance with a sheet pulled over their face.

FENCHURCH I think that's the nicest thing you've said to me. Arthur? What are you doing?

ARTHUR   (Slightly off) Hmm. I don't think it can be your bottom. (Coming back on) . . . Nothing I can see.

FENCHURCH There's absolutely nothing wrong with my bottom.

ARTHUR   Hm. I think I might have to tell you a story.

FENCHURCH OK.

ARTHUR	Which will tell you something of the sort of things that happen to me.
FENCHURCH	Like the raffle ticket.
ARTHUR	(Laughs) Yes. Right. I had a train to catch. I arrived at the station. I was about twenty minutes early. So I bought a newspaper, to do the crossword, and went to the buffet to get a cup of coffee.
FENCHURCH	Did you solve it?
ARTHUR	What?
FENCHURCH	The crossword.
ARTHUR	I haven't had a chance to look at it yet, I'm still queuing for the coffee.
FENCHURCH	All right, then. Buy the coffee.
ARTHUR	I'm buying it. I am also buying some biscuits.
FENCHURCH	What sort?
ARTHUR	Rich Tea. Now I go and sit at a table. This is the layout. Me sitting at the table. On my left, the newspaper. On my right, cup of coffee. In the middle of the table, packet of biscuits.
FENCHURCH	Yup, I see it.
ARTHUR	What you don't see, because I haven't mentioned him yet, is the man sitting at the table already. He is sitting there opposite me. Briefcase. Business suit. He didn't look as if he was about to do anything weird.
FENCHURCH	But he did.
ARTHUR	He did. He leaned across the table, picked up the packet of biscuits, tore it open, took one out, and ate it.
FENCHURCH	What?
ARTHUR	He ate it.
FENCHURCH	What on Earth did you do?
ARTHUR	I did what any red-blooded Englishman would do. I was compelled to ignore it.
FENCHURCH	What? Why?
ARTHUR	There was nothing anywhere in my upbringing, experience or even primal instincts to tell me how to react to someone who quite calmly, sitting in front of me, stole one of my biscuits. There was nothing for it. I braced

myself. I took a biscuit, trying very hard not to notice that the packet was already mysteriously open.

FENCHURCH   But you're fighting back, taking a tough line.

ARTHUR   After my fashion, yes. And I ate the biscuit. I ate it very deliberately so that he would have no doubt as to what I was doing. And when I eat a biscuit, it stays eaten.

FENCHURCH   So what did he do?

ARTHUR   Took another one. He took it, he ate it. Clear as daylight. And, having not said anything the first time, it was somehow even more difficult for me to broach the subject the second time around. So I ignored it with, if anything, even more vigour than previously, and took another biscuit. And for an instant our eyes met.

FENCHURCH   Like this?

ARTHUR   Yes, well, no, not quite like *this*. But they met. Just for an instant. And we both looked away. And so we went through the whole packet like this. Him, me, him, me . . .

FENCHURCH   The whole packet?

ARTHUR   Well, it was only eight biscuits but it seemed like a lifetime. When the empty packet was lying dead between us the man at last got up, having done his worst, and left. As it happened, my train was announced a moment or two later, so I finished my coffee, stood up, picked up the newspaper, and underneath the newspaper . . .

FENCHURCH   Yes?

ARTHUR   Were my biscuits.

FENCHURCH   What?!

ARTHUR   True. I'd been eating his all the time.

FENCHURCH   No! **(She collapses with laughter)** You complete pillock! You completely and utterly foolish person!

ARTHUR   Your turn. Tell me a story. Tell me your story.

FENCHURCH   Phoof. I'll try. But maybe you should know that I suffer from sudden startling revelations.

ARTHUR   Are you about to have a fit or something?

202

FENCHURCH	No, no . . . I can tell when it's going to happen. For days before, the strangest feeling builds in me, as if I was being connected into something.
ARTHUR	Does the number forty-two mean anything to you at all?
FENCHURCH	Arthur, this is serious.
ARTHUR	I'm being serious. Tell me your story. Don't worry if it sounds odd. Believe me, you are talking to someone who has seen a lot of weird stuff. And I'm not talking biscuits here.
FENCHURCH	OK. Thing is, it was so simple, when it came.
ARTHUR	What was?
FENCHURCH	That's what I don't know. And the sense of loss is getting unbearable.
ARTHUR	Oh?

Music: Something both appalling and yet richly significant is being remembered here . . .

FENCHURCH	I was in a cafe. In Rickmansworth, having a cup of tea. This was after days of this build-up, becoming connected up. I was sort of buzzing, gently. And I was watching some work going on at a building site opposite, over the rim of my teacup, which is the nicest way of watching other people working. And suddenly, there it was in my mind, this message from somewhere. And it was so simple. It made such sense of everything. I just sat up and thought, 'Oh! Oh, well that's all right, then.' I was so startled I almost dropped my teacup, in fact I think I did drop it. Yes, I'm sure I did. That was the point at which it seemed to me – quite literally – as if the world . . . *exploded*.
ARTHUR	What?
FENCHURCH	I know everybody talks about big yellow spaceships and how the whole thing was a hallucination, but if it was, then I have hallucinations in big-screen 3D surround sound and should probably hire myself out to people who are bored with movies. It was as if the ground was ripped from under my feet . . . and . . . and I woke up in hospital. I've been in and out ever since. And that's why I seem to have a fear of sudden revelations that everything's going to be all right.
ARTHUR	(Unsettled) Yes. Yes, I do too. I've fought it, but I do . . . You say you felt as if the Earth actually exploded.
FENCHURCH	Yes. More than felt.
ARTHUR	Which is what everybody else says is hallucinations?

203

FENCHURCH	Yes, but people think if you just say 'hallucinations' it explains anything you want. But it's just a word, it doesn't explain anything. It doesn't explain why the dolphins disappeared.
ARTHUR	No. No . . . What?!
FENCHURCH	Doesn't explain the dolphins disappearing.
ARTHUR	Which dolphins do you mean?
FENCHURCH	What do you mean, which dolphins? I'm talking about when all the dolphins disappeared.
ARTHUR	The dolphins?
FENCHURCH	Yes.
ARTHUR	You're saying the dolphins all disappeared?
FENCHURCH	Arthur, where have you been, for Heaven's sake? The dolphins all disappeared on the same day I—
ARTHUR	Where did they go?
FENCHURCH	No one knows. Well, there is one man who says he knows, but he lives in California, so people say he's barmy. I was thinking of going to see him because it seems the only lead I've got on what happened to me.
ARTHUR	(Thoughtful) Better to go in search of the truth than pretend it isn't there.
FENCHURCH	Arthur. I really would like to know where you've been. I think something terrible happened to you as well. That's why we recognized each other.
ARTHUR	Mine's a very long story. And confusing even for me.
FENCHURCH	Well, now you've got someone you can tell. Well, the bits I hadn't already found on this—
	FX: She fumbles in her bag.
ARTHUR	Ah. My *Guide*.
	FX: *Guide* switch on.
THE VOICE	(This under the following dialogue) *The Hitchhiker's Guide to the Galaxy*, eight to the seventeenth edition. Introduction. Space is big. Really big. You just won't believe how vastly, hugely mind-bogglingly big it is. For example, you may think it's a long way down the road to the chemist, but that's just peanuts to space. The simple truth is that interstellar distances will not fit into the sentient imagination. Even light, which travels so fast that it takes most races thousands of years to realize that it travels at all, takes time to

204

journey between the stars. For light to reach the other side of the Galaxy takes five hundred thousand years. The record for hitchhiking this distance is just under five years, but you don't get to see much on the way . . .

FENCHURCH Why does it say 'Don't Panic' on the cover?

ARTHUR I think it's a get-out clause for the warranty. This particular one has been hurled into prehistoric rivers, baked in the deserts of Kakrafoon, dropped into the oceans of Santraginus V, frozen on the glaciers of the moon of Jaglan Beta, sat on, kicked around spaceships, scuffed and generally abused. Its makers think these are exactly the sorts of things that might happen to it, so they wrote on it, in large friendly letters, the words 'Don't Panic', hoping no one would ask for their money back.

FENCHURCH (Looking at the *Guide*) Have you been to many of these places?

ARTHUR A few.

FX: *Guide* switched off around here.

FENCHURCH Can *we* go to them?

ARTHUR (Warily, reluctantly) Do you want to?

FENCHURCH Yes. I want to know what the message was that I lost, and where it came from. I don't think that it came from here. I'm not even sure that I know where *here* is. But I need to find it, Arthur. Not knowing is damaging me.

ARTHUR Hm.

FENCHURCH (Deep breath, then, brightly) Anyway. There is something wrong with part of me, and you've got to find out what it is. You can try and guess on the way home. (Getting up) Come on.

INT. – THE BOOK AMBIENCE

THE VOICE The problem with *The Hitchhiker's Guide to the Galaxy*, or rather one of the problems, for there are many clogging up civil, commercial and criminal courts all over the Galaxies – especially the more corrupt ones – is this: Change. The Galaxy is a rapidly changing place. A bit of a nightmare, you might think, for a scrupulous and conscientious editor diligently striving to keep abreast of all the changes that arise every minute of every hour of every day, and you would be wrong. The editor, like all the editors the *Guide* has ever had, has no real grasp of the meanings of the words 'scrupulous', 'conscientious' or 'diligent', and prefers to get his nightmares through a straw. Entries tend to get updated, or not, across the Sub-Etha Net according to 'if they Read Good'. Thus the entry Ford Prefect filed on the subject of

Vogons, while lacking in strict accuracy, was vitriolic enough to qualify for inclusion.

FORD PREFECT (Typing) 'Vogons are one of the most unpleasant races in the Galaxy – not actually evil, but bad-tempered, bureaucratic, officious and callous. Their Constructor Fleet ships look as if they have been not so much designed as congealed. Uglier things have been spotted in the skies, but not by reliable witnesses. In fact to see anything much uglier than a Vogon ship you would have to go inside and look at a Vogon, or, worse, inside one. Anatomical analysis of the Vogon reveals that its brain was originally a badly deformed, misplaced and dyspeptic – ' (Spells it to himself) D-Y-? . . . yes . . . (Back to typing) ' – liver. Consequently, thinking is not really something Vogons are cut out for. The fairest thing you can say about them, then, is that they know what they like. And what they like mostly involves hurting people and, wherever possible, getting very angry.'

THE VOICE . . . On second thoughts, it's accurate enough.

INT. – GALACTIC HYPERSPACE PLANNING COUNCIL ROOM

FX: Gavel. Mutterings.

VOGON COUNCILLOR All persons here to do business at the Galactic Hyperspace Planning Council take your seats. The rest of you find something to occupy yourselves before I come and find it for you. Call the first witness.

VOGON CLERK Call Prostetnic Vogon Jeltz.

FX: Stir in enquiry chamber.

FX: Gavel.

VOGON COUNCILLOR Quiet!

FX: Someone coughs, politely.

VOGON COUNCILLOR Who coughed? Own up! Clerk, shoot anyone who coughs!

VOGON CLERK Yes, Your Vastness.

FX: Cough. Zap gun. Scream and body fall.

VOGON COUNCILLOR Thank you. (Voice up) Prostetnic Vogon Jeltz. You are responsible for clearing the interstellar hyperspace link between Demosthenes and Ursa Minor. Your orders were to demolish all planets on that route in accordance with the plans we lodged at Alpha Centauri. Your report clearly stated that the planet known as the Earth was destroyed by your demolition fleet. Yet now a survey of the area has revealed Earth is still there. I put it to you that you have royally screwed the pooch.

PROSTETNIC VOGON JELTZ (Yells) It's a tissue of lies, I deny it utterly, and I volunteer for mucking-out duty in the beast compounds on Traal rather than live a day longer with this vicious smear on my character!

VOGON COUNCILLOR (Patiently, for a Vogon) Laudable though it is for you to take an adversarial stance in your desperate situation, I have here holographic plates of the planet in question. Received last week. Vidscreen on.

FX: Hologram projection on.

FX: Stir in council chamber.

PROSTETNIC VOGON JELTZ Bugger. You're right. I'm guilty as charged.

VOGON COUNCILLOR (Disappointed) Really?

PROSTETNIC VOGON JELTZ Can't argue with the evidence, there it is in black and white . . . And blue and brown with wispy white cloudy bits. That's the Earth, all right.

VOGON COUNCILLOR (Sotto) Doh. Haven't had a good bit of torture in weeks.

VOGON CLERK He's been saving up some really excruciating poems for this. Don't spoil it by agreeing.

FX: Gavel.

VOGON COUNCILLOR Shut up. What does the defendant have to say for himself?

PROSTETNIC VOGON JELTZ I don't like leaving a job unfinished any more than the next Vogon.

FX: Cough. Zap gun. Scream and body fall.

PROSTETNIC VOGON JELTZ All right, the Vogon beside him. Give me a chance.

VOGON COUNCILLOR From this evidence it doesn't look as if the job was ever started.

PROSTETNIC VOGON JELTZ I swear we destroyed that planet. I know we did. Even had a couple of hitchhikers steal aboard trying to escape . . . of course we threw them out of an airlock.

VOGON COUNCILLOR (Reads) Dent, Arthur? Prefect, Ford?

PROSTETNIC VOGON JELTZ Probably. Humans all look alike to me. Freeloading parasites.

207

VOGON COUNCILLOR	**(Reads)** According to the log you picked up Ex-President Beeblebrox, too?
PROSTETNIC VOGON JELTZ	No. He rescued them.
VOGON COUNCILLOR	Oh yes . . . then we had him lured into the Total Perspective Vortex. Probably still there – and no bad thing. Now, about this Earth. Seems it exists in a Plural Sector. Very unstable dimensionally. Very hard to destroy planets like that. They exist on several levels, keep popping back into reality.
VOGON CLERK	I have the precedent here, Your Honour, Vogon Imperium versus Megabrantis Liposuction, Inc. Ruling: 'Nature abhors a vacuum'.
PROSTETNIC VOGON JELTZ	Whatever. *Girlfriend*. I'll just keep destroying the Earth till nature *settles* for a bloody vacuum!
	FX: Cough. Zap gun. Scream and body fall.
VOGON COUNCILLOR	Thank you. The problem has, however compounded itself somewhat. Now that Improbability Travel has become so popular, hyperspace bypasses have become somewhat . . . well, passé.
PROSTETNIC VOGON JELTZ	Meaning?
VOGON COUNCILLOR	We don't actually *need* to demolish Earth.
PROSTETNIC VOGON JELTZ	**(Disappointed)** Tch. Party-pooper.
VOGON COUNCILLOR	However! An order cannot be countermanded once it has been seen to be issued.
VOGON CLERK	The paperwork was registered in all galactic sectors.
VOGON COUNCILLOR	Precisely. We must not be seen to be lax in matters bureaucratic.
PROSTETNIC VOGON JELTZ	So I *can* destroy it?
VOGON COUNCILLOR	Orders *are* orders, Prostetnic Vogon Jeltz. But given the planet's Plural location, we need to approach the problem in a circuitous manner. What I have in mind is – is – excuse me— **(He coughs, hackingly)**
VOGON CLERK	**(Thoughtfully)** Orders . . . is orders . . .
	FX: Zap gun shot. Body thud.
VOGON COUNCILLOR	Argh! **(Dying)** Et . . . tu . . . Blurtus?

208

PROSTETNIC **VOGON JELTZ**	What you have in mind is – what? *What!!!*

INT. – THE BOOK AMBIENCE

THE VOICE	*The Hitchhiker's Guide to the Galaxy* has several entries claiming to have found the most romantic location in the known Universe.

One for example, is Brequinda in the Foth of Avalars; famed in myth as home of the magical Fuolornis Fire Dragons. In ancient days, when the air was sweet and the nights fragrant, but everyone somehow managed to be, or so they claimed, virgins, it was not possible to heave a brick on Brequinda in the Foth of Avalars without hitting at least half a dozen Fuolornis Fire Dragons. Whether you would want to do that is another matter. Not that Fire Dragons weren't an essentially peace-loving species, but one so often hurts the one one loves, especially if one is a Fuolornis Fire Dragon with breath like a rocket booster and teeth like a park fence. Add to all that the relatively small number of madmen who actually went around the place heaving bricks, and you end up with a lot of people on Brequinda in the Foth of Avalars getting seriously hurt by dragons. And bricks.

But did they mind? They did not.

The Fuolornis Fire Dragons were revered throughout the land for their savage beauty, their noble ways and their habit of biting people who didn't revere them.

Why was this? The answer was simple. There is something almost unbearably sexy about having huge fire-breathing magical dragons flying low about the sky on moonlit nights which are already dangerously on the sweet and fragrant side. No sooner would a flock of half a dozen silk-winged Fuolornis Fire Dragons fly across the evening horizon than half the people of Brequinda were scurrying off into the woods with the other half, to emerge with the dawn all smiling and happy and still claiming, rather endearingly, to be virgins, if rather flushed and sticky virgins. The place was always stiff with researchers trying to get to the bottom of it all and taking a very long time about it.

Not surprisingly, the *Guide*'s description of this planet has proved to be so popular that it has never been taken out, and thus latter-day hitchhikers have to find out for themselves that, like the dinosaurs, the dodos, and the greater drubbered wintwock of Stegbartle Major in the constellation Fraz, the Fuolornis Fire Dragons face certain extinction, and modern Brequinda in the City State of Avalars is now little more than concrete, strip joints and Dragon Burger Bars. There are, of course, no Fuolornis Fire Dragons in the Islington mews where Fenchurch lives, but if any had chanced by they might just as well have sloped off across the road for a pizza, for they are not needed.

INT. – FENCHURCH'S LIVING ROOM

Music: 'Tunnel of Love' by Dire Straits, under:

ARTHUR   **(Close, post-coital glow)** . . . Your knee. There is something terribly and tragically wrong with your left knee. Right knee.

FENCHURCH   **(Close, glowing too)** Both knees are absolutely fine.

ARTHUR   Forgetting your calves, which I can't, by the most sensuous process of elimination it has to be your feet.

FENCHURCH   Ah.

ARTHUR   I have to admit that I really don't know what I'm looking for.

FENCHURCH   I'll give you a clue . . . pick me up.

ARTHUR   **(Getting up, slight effort)** Unh . . .

FENCHURCH   Kiss me again.

ARTHUR   **(Does so)** Mwwwmmm . . .

FENCHURCH   Now let me stand up.

ARTHUR   Hm.

FENCHURCH   Well?

ARTHUR   It *is* the feet . . . **(Moves down to inspect them)** . . . but they *look* OK – on top . . . and underneath . . .

FENCHURCH   You're getting warmer.

ARTHUR   Good grief. I see what's wrong with your feet. They don't touch the ground.

FENCHURCH   **(Insecure, worried)** So . . . so what do you think . . . ?

ARTHUR   Well . . . I'm guessing you're an inch taller than you were before the dolphins disappeared.

FENCHURCH   **(Laughs uncertainly)** I suppose so.

ARTHUR   **(Moving off)** Which probably means . . . I wonder. Is this the old hay-loft door?

FX: Bolts back door opened/exterior atmos up.

FENCHURCH   Yes – careful, Arthur – we're two floors up—

ARTHUR   **(Moving outside)** Mind if pop outside for a minute?

FENCHURCH   **(Gasp)** Arthur—! But – how are you doing that?! What are you standing on?

ARTHUR	Nothing. Come on out . . . the air's lovely . . .
FENCHURCH	You . . . think . . . I can . . .
ARTHUR	I'm sure of it. No, don't bring anything . . . just come towards me. Think about tulips . . . or lost items of hand luggage . . .

INT. – JUMBO JET

FX: 747 interior. (We are with the steward.)

STEWARD	**(On overhead speakers)** . . . shortly landing at London Heathrow, please make sure your cabin baggage is secure, your seat is in the upright position and your seatbelt firmly fastened. Thank you.

FX: Intercom phone replaced. Soft chime of cabin attendant call.

STEWARD	**(Hanging up intercom phone)** Not again.
STEWARDESS	Do you want me to go?
STEWARD	It's OK . . . I'll deal with her.

FX: He makes his way to a nearby seat.

STEWARD	Excuse me . . . Yes, er – Mrs – Kapinsky.
MRS KAPELSEN	Kapelsen.
STEWARD	Yes. You pressed your 'call' button.
MRS KAPELSEN	Did I?
STEWARD	Is something wrong?
MRS KAPELSEN	**(Seemingly confused)** Ah – well I thought you might know.
STEWARD	Is it the headphones again?
MRS KAPELSEN	No.
STEWARD	The child in front making milk come out of his nose again?
MRS KAPELSEN	Er – no.
STEWARD	Mrs Kapelsen, is it something outside the plane? You're staring.
MRS KAPELSEN	Yes. Well . . . **(Turns to face steward)** You know. I've seen a lot of life.
STEWARD	I'm sorry . . . ?
MRS KAPELSEN	I've been puzzled by some, but I do feel I was bored with a lot of it. It's all been very pleasant, but perhaps a little too routine.

STEWARD	Right.
MRS KAPELSEN	I thought I just saw . . . but then I didn't. Well I did, two of them, but it's nothing to worry about.
STEWARD	So you don't need help?
MRS KAPELSEN	Oh no. I just needed to tell someone. Thank you.
STEWARD	**(Sighs)** No problem. **(He goes off, muttering)**
MRS KAPELSEN	**(Intrigued – to self)** I didn't know you could do it on the wing of a plane, though . . .

EXT. – A THOUSAND FEET OVER LONDON

FX: Jumbo jet roars past.

FX: Arthur and Fenchurch fly past.

ARTHUR	Try a swoop.
FENCHURCH	What?
ARTHUR	Like this – wheeee!
FENCHURCH	**(Following)** Whoooooo . . . I'm flying . . .
ARTHUR	**(Fearful)** Don't think about it!
FENCHURCH	Think about what?
ARTHUR	**(Relieved)** That's the idea.
FENCHURCH	Can we do this every night?
ARTHUR	Maybe not so close to the Heathrow flight path?
FENCHURCH	Coward!
ARTHUR	**(Flying off)** I know . . . tomorrow we'll bring the iPod, music and two sets of earphones . . .
FENCHURCH	**(Following him)** And lots of Dire Straits . . .

INT. – ROBOT SPACESHIP CORRIDOR

FX: Running ship FX. The occasional ratchet screwdriver whizzes past.

FORD PREFECT	**(Snores)**

THE VOICE	*The Hitchhiker's Guide to the Galaxy* was conceived of as a reference work dedicated to the pursuit of cheap travel, cheap food and the cheapest possible intoxicants. As a result, even in its eight to the sixteenth edition it can fail entirely to include certain very necessary entries, such as how to report a pair of flying people using the aerofoil of a commercial jetliner to consummate their affections, or which methods to conquer insomnia work best in the noisy confines of huge spacecraft. This latter omission is no longer of significance to Ford Prefect, who snores cocooned in towels and well-thumbed copies of *Playbeing* in a maintenance hatchway aboard the Xaxisian robot ship, deaf to the traffic of flying ratchet screwdrivers, dreaming fitfully of old haunts . . . like the East Side of New York, where the river has become so extravagantly polluted that new life forms are now emerging from it spontaneously, demanding welfare and voting rights . . .

FX: New York soundscape up.

FX: Creature thrashes ashore.

EAST RIVER CREATURE	Urhh . . . Ahh . . . Hello, hello . . . Excuse me. I need some help.
FORD PREFECT	Sure, what can I do for you?
EAST RIVER CREATURE	I just oozed up out of the river. I'm pretty much new to the surface in every respect. Is there any useful information you can give me?
FORD PREFECT	Phew . . . I can tell you where some bars are, I guess.
EAST RIVER CREATURE	I'll be honest with you, this is not my field. What about love and happiness? I sense deep needs in myself for things like that. Got any leads there?
FORD PREFECT	Only that you can get most of what you require around Seventh Avenue.
EAST RIVER CREATURE	Uh-huh, OK. Now I instinctively feel that I need to be beautiful. Would you put me in the category of beautiful? **(Silence)** Hello? Who am I talking to?
FORD PREFECT	You're, umm, you're pretty direct, aren't you?
EAST RIVER CREATURE	Me, I don't waste time. Am I, or am I not, beautiful?
FORD PREFECT	Well, to me— Not— But, listen, most people make out, you know. Are there any more like you in the river?
EAST RIVER CREATURE	How should I know, you think we have mirrors down there? It's a dirty, filthy, disgusting place, dirty water, you can't see your tentacle in front of your face.
FORD PREFECT	No, fair enough, stupid question.
EAST RIVER CREATURE	Listen, I'm new here. Life is entirely strange to me. What's it like?

213

FORD PREFECT	Ah. Now this is something that I can speak about with some authority.
EAST RIVER CREATURE	Good, good, tell me everything. I'm all ears.
FORD PREFECT	Yes, you are . . . Where you're not all tentacles.
EAST RIVER CREATURE	Hey, schmuck, I need the tentacles to clean out the ears. So, what about Life? I'm listening.
FORD PREFECT	Life . . . Life is like a grapefruit.
EAST RIVER CREATURE	Life is like a grapefruit. Help me out here. I'm struggling. Describe to me in concrete terms how life is like a grapefruit. Use your hands if it helps.
FORD PREFECT	Well, it's sort of orangey-yellow and dimpled on the outside, wet and squidgy in the middle. It's got pips inside, too. Oh, and some people have half a one for breakfast.
EAST RIVER CREATURE	This is advice I can use? Is there anyone else in this dream I can talk to?
FORD PREFECT	**(Losing patience)** I dunno. Look – ask a policeman. Ask anybody but me. I'm going to roll over and dream about girls . . . air cars . . . single malt . . . **(Burbles into snoring, fades)**
EAST RIVER CREATURE	That's great. That's great. Go back to sleep, see if I care. You think I'm going to work your dream out for myself? Forget about it! **(Squidging off)** I need to get up, put on my slippers and go to the bathroom anyway!

INT. – FENCHURCH'S LIVING ROOM – DAY

FX: Teacup put down on saucer.

FENCHURCH	Elevenses. What a treat.
ARTHUR	My pleasure.
FENCHURCH	This is all very wonderful.
ARTHUR	The sandwich?
FENCHURCH	Everything. But I do still feel . . . I need to know what has happened to me. You see, there's this difference between us. That you lost something and found it again, and I found something and lost it. I need to find it again.
ARTHUR	Yes, I know. And I've had an idea. Pass the phone.

FX: Phone passed and dialling. Distant futzed ring, under:

ARTHUR	**(cont'd)** Murray Bost Henson is a journalist on one of those papers with small pages and big print.

214

FENCHURCH	Doesn't sound like he's much of a journalist.
ARTHUR	He isn't. But he's the only one I knew. Or rather . . .
FENCHURCH	(Checks watch, jumps up, peck on cheek) Eek. I'm late for my cello lesson. (Leaving) Back soon. Good luck.
	FX: Cello case grabbed, door opens/closes, off.
	FX: Following phone call may flip from Arthur's perspective to Murray's, with newspaper office background:
ARTHUR	(Sighs happily) Ahhhh.
MURRAY BOST HENSON	(Phone distort) Yyyup?
ARTHUR	(Startled) Murray?
MURRAY BOST HENSON	(Distorted) . . . Arthur Dent?
ARTHUR	Yes.
MURRAY BOST HENSON	(Distorted) Arthur, my old soup spoon, my old silver tureen, how particularly stunning to hear from you. Someone told me you'd gone off into space or something.
ARTHUR	What?
MURRAY BOST HENSON	(Distorted) Just a rumour, my old elephant tusk, my little green baize card table, got it from someone who picked up a hitchhiker in Somerset. Probably means nothing at all, but I may need a quote from you.
ARTHUR	Oh, well then, I deny it.
MURRAY BOST HENSON	(Distorted) That's perfect, thank you. Fits like a whatsit in one of those other things with the other stories of the week, that denial. Excuse me, something has just fallen out of my ear. Good Lord.
ARTHUR	Murray—?
MURRAY BOST HENSON	(Distorted) Ur . . . Just remembered what an odd evening I had last night . . . Anyway, my old I won't say what, we're calling this the Week of the Weirdos. Got a ring to it. You see we have this man it always rains on.
ARTHUR	What?
MURRAY BOST HENSON	(Distorted) It's the absolute stocking-top truth. All documented in his little black book, it all checks out. The Met Office is going ice-cold thick banana whips. This man is the bee's knees, Arthur, he is the wasp's nipples. He is, I would go so far as to say, the entire set of erogenous zones of every major

flying insect of the Western world. We're calling him the Rain God. Nice, eh?

ARTHUR I think I've met him.

MURRAY BOST HENSON (Distorted) Incredible! You met the Rain God?

ARTHUR If it's the same man. I told him to stop complaining and show someone his book.

MURRAY BOST HENSON (Distorted) Well, you did a bundle. Do you know how much tour operators are paying him not to go abroad this year? Listen, we may want to do a feature on you, Arthur, the Man Who Made the Rain God Rain. Got a ring to it, eh? Photograph you under a garden shower, but that'll be OK. Where do I send the snapper?

ARTHUR Er, I'm in Islington. Listen, Murray . . .

MURRAY BOST HENSON (Distorted) Islington! Home of the real weirdness of the week, the real seriously loopy stuff. You know anything about these flying people?

ARTHUR No.

MURRAY BOST HENSON (Distorted) Arthur, where have you been? Oh, space, right, I got your denial. But that was months ago. Listen, it's night after night this week, my old cheese grater, right on your patch. This couple just fly around the sky and start doing all kinds of stuff. And I don't mean looking through walls or pretending to be box-girder bridges. You don't know anything?

ARTHUR No.

MURRAY BOST HENSON (Distorted) Arthur, it's been almost inexpressibly delicious conversing with you, chumbum, but I have to go. I'll send the guy with the camera and the hose. Give me the address, I'm already writing.

ARTHUR Listen, Murray, I called to ask you something. I want to find out something about the dolphins.

MURRAY BOST HENSON (Distorted) No story. Last year's news. Forget 'em. They're gone. And so is the story.

ARTHUR Murray, I'm not interested in whether it's a story. I just want to find out how I can get in touch with that man in California who claims to know something about it. I thought you might know.

MURRAY BOST HENSON (Distorted) Him? My old herringbone tweed, why didn't you say so?

INT. – JUMBO JET

FX: Ding dong.

STEWARD (Cabin intercom) . . . This is an important announcement. This is flight 121 to Los Angeles. If your travel plans today do not include Los Angeles, now would be the perfect time to disembark.

ARTHUR (Sitting, breathless) Foof. I wonder when they start serving the drinks.

FENCHURCH (Breathless) When you said, 'meet me at the airport', I didn't think you'd be bringing our passports and a pair of plane tickets.

ARTHUR Sorry about that. I remembered your toothbrush, though.

FENCHURCH Look at you – drenched with sweat.

ARTHUR Not with sweat. A photographer came round. I tried to argue, but – never mind, I spoke to California.

FENCHURCH You spoke to him.

ARTHUR I spoke to his wife, Mrs Watson, and asked to speak to him. She said he was too weird to come to the phone right now and could I call back. So I did, and she said that he was 3.2 light years from the phone and I should call again.

FENCHURCH Ah.

STEWARD (Passing) Seatbelt done up, miss?

FENCHURCH Yes, thanks.

ARTHUR I called again. She said the situation had improved. He was now a mere 2.6 light years from the phone but it was still a long way to shout.

FENCHURCH I didn't realize it was that bad.

ARTHUR I phoned again. Her name, by the way, and you may wish to know this, is Arcane Jill.

FENCHURCH I see.

ARTHUR She explained that the phone is in a room that he never comes into. It's in the Asylum. He does not like to enter the Asylum. She felt it might save me phoning. He will only meet people outside the Asylum. I asked her where the Asylum is, and she asked if I'd ever read the instructions on a packet of toothpicks.

FENCHURCH And did you?

ARTHUR	I didn't have a packet to hand. Then she hung up. I actually got the address from a guy on a science magazine.
FENCHURCH	I'm not sure I understand.
ARTHUR	Neither do many people. I have been told that Mr Watson claims to have regular meetings with angels who wear golden beards and green wings and orthopaedic sandals.
FENCHURCH	But you think it's worth it.
ARTHUR	Well, the one thing that everyone agrees on, apart from the fact that he is barking mad, is that he does know more than any man living about dolphins.
FENCHURCH	What's his name again?
ARTHUR	Wonko the Sane.
	(A pause)
FENCHURCH	I know he will be able to help us. I know he will.
MRS KAPELSEN	(From neighbouring seat) Excuse me, my dears . . . I get so bored on these long flights, it's nice to talk to somebody. My name's Enid Kapelsen, I'm from Boston. Tell me, do you fly a lot?

EXT. – PLANE

FX: 747 roars past into the night.

INT. – 'OUTSIDE THE ASYLUM' – INTERIOR ACOUSTIC

FX: Distant beach, waves. Cars pass on highway.

WONKO THE SANE	Hello. I am John Watson.
ARTHUR	Hallo.
WONKO THE SANE	But you can call me Wonko the Sane.
ARTHUR	Thank you . . .
FENCHURCH	You have a very interesting house. It's inside out.
WONKO THE SANE	It gives me pleasure.
ARTHUR	We've come to ask you about the dolphins.
WONKO THE SANE	Oh yeah. Them.
ARTHUR	Your wife mentioned toothpicks.

WONKO THE SANE	**(Laughs)** Ah yes, that's to do with the day I finally realized that the world had gone totally crazy. So I built the Asylum to put it in, poor thing, hoping it would get better.
ARTHUR	I'm . . . horribly confused. Out there you've got carpet up to the kerb of the Pacific Coast Highway, your exterior walls are hung with bookshelves and pictures and the sign above the front door says, 'Come Outside', so here we are, inside, sitting by a garden path, surrounded by rough brick walls.
WONKO THE SANE	Yes. Here we are *Outside* the Asylum. When you go back through the door there, to where you parked your ride, you go *Inside* the Asylum. I never go myself. If I am tempted, I simply look at the sign.
FENCHURCH	That one?
ARTHUR	**(Reading)** 'Hold stick near centre of its length. Place pointed end in mouth. Insert in tooth space, blunt end next to gum. Use gentle in–out motion.'
FENCHURCH	And those are the instructions—
WONKO THE SANE	On a set of toothpicks. It seemed to me that any civilization that had so far lost its head as to need to include a set of instructions in a packet of toothpicks was no longer one in which I could live and stay sane.
ARTHUR	But you are . . . ?
WONKO THE SANE	Oh, I call myself Wonko the Sane, to reassure people. Wonko is what my mother called me when I was a clumsy kid, knocking things over, and sane is what I intend to remain. And the angels with golden beards and green wings and orthopaedic sandals agree with me.
ARTHUR	Um – And they visit . . . when?
WONKO THE SANE	Weekends, mostly, on little scooters. They are great machines.
ARTHUR	**(Doubtful)** I see . . .
FENCHURCH	Why not?
ARTHUR	Pardon?
FENCHURCH	**(With unnatural emphasis)** Why not scooters? Others might *fly* here, they're on scooters. Think about it, Arthur.
ARTHUR	**(Realizing her point)** Yes, yes of course, who's to say what's impossible . . .
FENCHURCH	About the dolphins—
WONKO THE SANE	I can show you the sandals.
FENCHURCH	Oh, er . . .

WONKO THE SANE	I'll get them. **(Gets up, rummages, off)** The angels say that they suit the terrain they have to work in. They say they run a concession stand by the Message. When I say I don't know what that means, they say, 'No, you don't,' and laugh.
ARTHUR	**(Shiver)** The Message . . .
FENCHURCH	Arthur—?
WONKO THE SANE	**(Returning)** Here. Perfectly ordinary wooden-soled sandals. I'm not trying to prove anything, by the way. I'm a scientist. I know what constitutes proof. I use my childhood name to remind myself that a scientist must also be like a child. If he sees a thing, he must say that he sees it, whether it's what he was expecting to see or not. Otherwise he'll only see what he's expecting . . . I also thought you might like to see this.

FX: He produces a glass bowl and pings it.

FENCHURCH/ARTHUR	**(Gasps)**
FENCHURCH	Where did you get that bowl?
ARTHUR	**(A take)** Fenchurch? Have you seen one of these before?
FENCHURCH	I've got one. Or at least I did have. Russell nicked it to put his golf balls in . . . Have you got one?
ARTHUR	I found it by my bed.
WONKO THE SANE	You both have one of these bowls? With the inscription?
ARTHUR	So Long, and Thanks for All the Fish?
WONKO THE SANE	Yes. Do you know what it is?
FENCHURCH	No.
WONKO THE SANE	It is a farewell gift from the dolphins. The dolphins whom I loved and studied, and swam with, and fed with fish, and even tried to learn their language, a task which they made impossibly difficult, considering they were perfectly capable of communicating in ours if they'd wanted to . . . What have you done with yours?
ARTHUR	Erm – I keep a fish in it.
WONKO THE SANE	You've done nothing else? No, if you had, you would know. My wife kept wheatgerm in ours, till last night.
ARTHUR	What happened last night?

WONKO THE SANE	We ran out of wheatgerm. She's gone to get some more. Well, I washed the bowl, and dried it. Then I held it to my ear. You ever held one to your ear?
ARTHUR/FENCHURCH	No . . .
WONKO THE SANE	Perhaps you should.
ARTHUR	May we—?
WONKO THE SANE	Closer – that's good. Now – with your fingernail – gently.

FX: Ping of bowl . . .

INT. – AMBIENCE – THE FISHBOWL

FX: The deep roar of the ocean. The break of waves on further shores than thought can find. The silent thunders of the deep. And from among it, voices calling, humming trillings, half-articulated songs of thought. Waves of greetings, inarticulate words breaking together. A crash of sorrow on the shores of earth. Waves of joy on a world indescribably found, indescribably arrived at, indescribably wet, a song of water. A fugue of voices now, clamouring explanations, of a disaster unavertable, a world to be destroyed, a spasm of despair, and then the fling of hope, the finding of a shadow earth in the implications of enfolded time, submerged dimensions, the pull of parallels, the hurl and split of it, the flight. A new Earth pulled into replacement, the dolphins gone. Then stunningly a single voice, quite clear.

DOLPHIN VOICE	This bowl was brought to you by the Campaign to Save the Humans. We bid you farewell.

INT. – THE BOOK AMBIENCE

THE VOICE	What message will Arthur and Fenchurch discover next? Will Ford Prefect be on hand to utterly confuse and annoy everybody? And – if the rumours are true – is Marvin going to make his farewell appearance? The next episode of *The Hitchhiker's Guide to the Galaxy* spells out the answers . . .
ANNOUNCER	The BBC wishes to advise listeners that not all glass bowls contain messages from the dolphins when pinged. Certain ovenware will emit serving suggestions for summer pudding and any bowl stamped by a bathroom-fittings manufacturer is best left unpinged altogether.

221

FOOTNOTES

Opening speech Taken direct from the novel, more or less, barring the excision of the 'f' word, which although Douglas used perfectly accurately would mean more agony with the BBC and a tiresome repeat of the whole Rory Award scenario. Instead I asked Bill Franklyn to dwell slightly on the 'f' of 'feel the need . . .' to assure the cognoscenti that we knew what we had done (though not necessarily what we were about to be doing . . .).

The Rich Tea Biscuit story Authorities on Douglas including his biographers Nick Webb and Mike Simpson have debated the provenance of the 'Biscuit story', which has now entered the annals of urban myth, but it is generally agreed that this did indeed happen to Douglas himself. Thus it is not such a leap for him to have transplanted it to Arthur Dent's personal history. As Simon has said in the Foreword, Arthur may have been inspired by himself but gradually more and more of Douglas crept into the character, his encounters with baths and tea and calamity being the more obvious elements.

Sadly due to pressure of time on the broadcast slot the Rich Tea Biscuit story appears only on the extended (CD, cassette and DVD-A) versions of this episode.

The Vogon Court of Enquiry In amongst all this episode's Moon-Eyed Romance (poignant and touching though it be) and Profound Apolcalyptic Visions, this scene is intended to be:

a) A comedy-slot-friendly sketch which redrafts some Douglas passages in the novels about the Vogons which are funny in themselves. Toby Longworth as the older, slobbier Jeltz was on his usual form, in response to Mike Cule's gun wielding, legal-precedent-quoting Vogon Clerk, ad-libbing a curt 'Whatever' into 'Whatever – *Girl* friend', and—

b) A means of clearly indicating that the Vogons are determined to destroy Earth – whether or not Earth now needs to be destroyed – and, if not openly, by covert means. In addition it's now a personal matter between the Vogons and anyone who crosses them, and Arthur, Ford and Zaphod Beeblebrox are on their hit list.

The Fuorlornis Fire Dragons This could so easily have been cut out on grounds of non-essentiality to plot; but being one of the greatest pieces of Adamsian whimsy in existence, it wasn't.

The East River Creature A strange interlude for Ford in *So Long, and Thanks for all the Fish*. It develops the *Guide* entry on New York heard tinnily in the previous episode ('Amphibious life forms from any of the worlds in the Swulling, Noxios or Nausalia systems will particularly enjoy the East River, which is said to be richer in those lovely life-giving nutrients than the most virulent laboratory slime yet achieved'), but was substantially rewritten when Bruce Hyman suggested Jackie Mason for the role of the Creature. Jackie delivered his performance from a New York studio near his apartment, and Geoff's performance as Ford was duly added to complement it. Jackie was the personification of adaptability; he happily added a few of his own expressions to the final take, the best being the substitution of 'testicle' for 'tentacle'. Unfortunately 'You can't see your testicle in front of your face' collided a bit too much with the sensibility of the scene . . .

Murray Bost Henson This wonderfully verbose character could only be done justice by Stephen Fry, who turned up at the Soundhouse, enthusiastic and charming as ever, and – Bill Franklyn being absent – very obligingly also gave his Voice of the Book in read-through. It was only later that he revealed he had just been awarded the part of the Voice in the *Hitchhiker's* film. We were happy to help get him in training, of course . . .

People have asked if the release of the film and the broadcast of the last two radio series so close together was a problem, but we were always creating different but complementary realities for *Hitchhiker's*, and the simple fact is that Douglas wanted both these projects to happen. It's dreadful that he isn't here to enjoy the coincidence, but wherever he is on the Probability Curve, he will be happy about it. It is, in fact, a very Douglassy sort of coincidence.

Given that audio is – in its unique way – as visual a medium as film, the great thing for those who love *Hitchhiker's* is that the film retells the first two hours of the saga, and these two new radio series provide the final four, with the original cast (relatively ageless in sound), completing a twenty-six-part saga on a fraction of the average Hollywood publicity budget. People who love Douglas's work will be the winners on both counts; the best possible result.

Wonko the Sane This is a sensitive scene and Wonko is a figure of pathos and dignity. It makes for a low-key ending to this episode but to punch the dialogue up with gags would overbalance the scene. Christian Slater was just about to close in the West End revival of *One Flew Over the Cuckoo's Nest*, and very kindly agreed to play the key part, which he did with great sincerity. His late afternoon arrival led to some fighting over the washroom mirror by certain female members of the cast. In the end discipline was imposed with the aid of a cricket bat and a bucket of water, and an orderly queue was formed. All the expenditure of effort and mascara was somewhat dampened by Christian turning up with his two children in tow.

EPISODE FOUR

SIGNATURE TUNE

ANNOUNCER *The Hitchhiker's Guide to the Galaxy*, by Douglas Adams, Quandary Phase.

Sig fades.

INT. – THE BOOK AMBIENCE

FX: Extended dolphin bowl ping with FX, under:

THE VOICE Far out in the uncharted backwaters of the unfashionable end of the Western Spiral arm of the Galaxy an utterly insignificant little blue-green planet once orbited a small unregarded yellow sun. The planet's cetacean life forms were so amazingly advanced that they decided not to climb gasping onto the land, grow fur and evolve into apes, but instead returned to live in its ocean deeps, playing, eating, playing, sleeping, playing and singing songs. Playfully. There was no need for digital watches or mobile phones for the dolphins. However, apart from a girl in a cafe in Rickmansworth who was in no position to do anything about it, the dolphins alone knew that although the Earth was a perfect and wonderful thing, transcending its many petty abuses by men, mice and Magratheans, it could not survive the attentions of the Vogon Constructor Fleet. Not as it was, anyway. And not with a politician's chance in a truth-telling contest of them surviving its demolition. So they engineered an escape plan. The dolphins to a distant world indescribably found, indescribably arrived at; the humans back on a New Earth, pulled in from shadowy dimensions to replace the old one. The continuity of life between Earths was virtually unbroken save for the departure of the dolphins, some duplication of human identities and a hairline fracture in time, sensed only by Arthur Dent – returned home at last – and Fenchurch, the girl from the cafe, with whom he has now fallen hopelessly in love. The scientist Wonko the Sane has explained to them that the mysterious gift of beautiful grey glass bowls each has received bearing the engraving 'So Long, and Thanks for All the Fish' was a goodbye present from the dolphins, replaying their last message when gently tapped . . .

DOLPHIN VOICE	This bowl was brought to you by the Campaign to Save the Humans. We bid you farewell.
THE VOICE	With this issue resolved, but other questions still requiring answers, Arthur and Fenchurch have decided it is time to move on. Hitching a ride home from Heathrow to collect Arthur's bowl from his cottage in Somerset – or rather the useful Babel fish that it contains – all they need now is a staggering coincidence, such as the arrival of a flying saucer, or the exercise of some pretty nifty reverse-temporal engineering, such as the arrival of a flying saucer. As reverse-temporal engineering is not *evidently* being exercised at this point in the narrative, coincidence is their best bet . . .

INT. – LORRY – DAY

FX: Lorry interior. Windscreen wipers. Rain on glass.

ROB McKENNA	**(For it is he)** Talk about coincidence, eh? Me picking you up again. And your girlfriend, of course.
ARTHUR	In the rain, of course.
ROB McKENNA	Well, now we know that's not a coincidence, don't we?
ARTHUR	Didn't think you'd still be driving a lorry, Rob – doesn't being Rain God come with a car?
ROB McKENNA	Bugger the Rain God. One paragraph in the *Sun* and I'm hijacked by a bunch of scientists. **(Scorn)** 'An example of a Spontaneous Para-Causal Meteorological Phenomenon'.
FENCHURCH	A what?
ROB McKENNA	That's what I said. See, if they find something they can't understand they like to call it something normal people can't understand. Or pronounce. If everybody just went around calling me a Rain God, that'd suggest everybody knows something the scientists don't. Well, they couldn't have that, so they call it something which says it's theirs, not everybody else's. Then they set about finding some way of proving it's not what everybody else said it is, but something *they* say it is. They said.
ARTHUR	**(Bored)** Are we there yet?
ROB McKENNA	**(Oblivious)** And if it turns out that everybody else is right, everybody else'll still be wrong, because the scientists will simply call me . . . er, 'Supernormal . . .' – not paranormal or supernatural, because everybody else thinks they know what those mean now, no, a 'Supernormal Incremental Precipitation Inducer', that's it. Oh, and they said they'd probably want to shove a

'Quasi' in there somewhere to protect themselves. But Rain God or not, they said, either way you wouldn't catch them going on holiday with me. So I told them to stuff it and came back to work.

ARTHUR   **(Diverts the conversation)** Do you mind if we listen to the radio?

ROB McKENNA   Help yourself.

ARTHUR   Thanks.

FX: Click.

PETER DONALDSON   **(Distorted)** And David discovers evidence of reverse-temporal engineering in Brian Aldridge's past . . . and just before news of the continuing situation in London, *The McMillan Report* returns next week to BBC1.

FENCHURCH   Continuing situation?

ROB McKENNA   Yeah, haven't you heard the news?

FENCHURCH   We've been in California.

(Here Tricia self-idents)

TRICIA McMILLAN   **(Distorted, under Arthur/Fenchurch at first)** Gail Andrews was astrologer to the Good and the Great in Hollywood, and is now consultant to the White House, her name high on the list of Special Advisers to the President of the United States. This week I'm in New York asking, in the wake of the Damascus bombing, what role does stargazing play in the formation of US foreign policy? The first exclusive, interview with Gail Andrews. Hard news; where it happens in *The McMillan Report* next Tuesday, with me, Tricia McMillan.

FX: Time signal and Radio 4 news intro, under:

ARTHUR   Good grief . . . Tricia McMillan?

ROB McKENNA   Phwoar . . . there's a photo of her in the *Sun* – coming out of some club in New York . . .

FX: Newspaper.

ARTHUR   Good grief . . . Trillian! But *blonde*.

ROB McKENNA   She can try on *my* galoshes anytime . . .

FENCHURCH   **(Low, to Arthur)** Wasn't Trillian the name of the girl you met . . . up there?

ARTHUR   **(Low, puzzled)** Yes . . . but this one's American.

ROB McKENNA   Oh, she's English by birth. Still lives here, I think. Worked over there too long, probably.

CHARLOTTE GREEN	(Distorted, under above, on radio) BBC Radio 4. *The News*, with Charlotte Green. There has been an emergency session of Parliament to debate the imposition of a state of National Emergency, following the arrival of the huge flying saucer which landed on Knightsbridge three days ago.
ARTHUR	What?
CHARLOTTE GREEN	(Distorted) The Home Secretary has issued a bulletin urging the public to remain calm and to keep clear of the immediate area. Meanwhile, the pattern of pub riots across West London seems to have died down, though reports are coming in of an isolated incident last night in the buffet car of a Great Western express train.
ARTHUR	Oh dear. Pub riots. Buffet cars. It's a familiar pattern.
FENCHURCH	What?
CHARLOTTE GREEN	In a separate development, speaking from the pile of rubble that was Harrods, Nathan—

FX: Click. Radio off.

FX: Lorry comes to halt. Air brakes.

ROB McKENNA	We're here.
FENCHURCH	That's very kind of you, Mr McKenna. Arthur, this is your cottage, is it?
ARTHUR	What? Uh, yes. Thank you.

FX: Door opens.

EXT. – ARTHUR'S HOUSE – DAY

FX: Lorry leaves.

FENCHURCH	(Off, cheerfully) Thank you!

FX: Nearer us, keys fumbling in front-door lock.

ARTHUR	(To self) Hm. Just as I thought. The front-door lock's been picked.
FENCHURCH	(Approaching) Everything all right?
ARTHUR	Erm – yes . . . tell you what, can you pop to the shop and get some milk and bread? I'll, er – put the kettle on.
FENCHURCH	(Going off) Sure.
ARTHUR	(To self) . . . after I've found out how drunk our guest is . . .

227

INT. – ARTHUR'S HOUSE

FX: Door opens with a creak. Cautious footsteps.

ARTHUR   Hallo . . . ?

FORD PREFECT   **(Snoring, off)**

ARTHUR   Of course. Ford, wake up. And get your shoes off the coffee table!

FORD PREFECT   Hm? Oh, hallo, Arthur. **(Yawns and stretches, then:)** Have you the faintest idea how hard it is to tap into the British phone system from the Pleiades? I can see that you haven't, so I'll tell you over the very large mug of black coffee that you are about to make me.

ARTHUR   **(Placidly, moving off)** You'd better come into the kitchen, then.

FX: Kettle on. Kitchen foley under:

FORD PREFECT   **(Entering)** I'm a little space-lagged.

ARTHUR   **(Fills kettle, coffee ingredients, etc.)** You look as if you've been sleeping in a corridor for a month. One that doesn't get hoovered.

FORD PREFECT   I have been. And before that I was on a scoutship of the Sirius Cybernetics Corporation, from where I was trying to get a BT operator to help me, but they keep asking you where you're calling from and you tell them Letchworth and they say you couldn't be, coming in on that circuit. What are you doing?

ARTHUR   Making you black coffee.

FORD PREFECT   **(Oddly disappointed)** Oh. What's this?

ARTHUR   Rice Krispies.

FORD PREFECT   And this?

ARTHUR   Paprika.

FX: Cereal box drops.

FORD PREFECT   The boxes don't stack up very well. What was I saying?

ARTHUR   About not phoning from Letchworth.

FORD PREFECT   Ah yeah. You know how I hate those smug Sirius Cybernetics salesmen. Slick-suited creeps of the cosmos, flogging computer operating systems that crash more often than aircars built on the Friday shift. They have persuaded the universe that if it doesn't continually upgrade itself at enormous expense it has no right to call itself froody. This guy was on a five-year mission to

228

seek out and explore strange new worlds, and tell them to Share and Enjoy his overhyped bloatware. Where's that coffee!

ARTHUR I'm waiting for the kettle to boil.

FORD PREFECT Use the hot tap! **(Wandering off into the other room)** Ah. I have now remembered what I did next. I saved civilization as we know it. I knew it was something like that. So there I was . . .

FX: Foreground, Arthur finishes making the coffee. In the background Ford is yelling and destroying a living room chair, indistinctly.

ARTHUR **(Anxiously)** I can't hear what you're saying . . . Ford? What are you doing? **(He moves off)** I've got your coffee . . .

INT. – ARTHUR'S LIVING ROOM

FX: Crashing noises, just coming to a stop.

ARTHUR **(Entering)** Oh, for goodness' sake. That was a perfectly good chair.

FORD PREFECT **(Annoyed)** Where have you been?

ARTHUR Making some coffee.

FORD PREFECT You missed the best bit! You missed the bit where I jumped the guy! Now I'll have to jump him all over again! Yeurgh!

FX: Ford demolishes another chair.

ARTHUR That also was a useful chair. Slightly worn but perfectly serviceable.

FORD PREFECT **(Sullen)** First time was better.

ARTHUR I see. And, er, what are all the ice cubes for?

FORD PREFECT What? You missed the suspended-animation facility! That's where I put the guy. Well, I had to, didn't I?

ARTHUR So it would seem.

FORD PREFECT Don't touch that!!!

ARTHUR But it's off the hook.

FORD PREFECT I know. But listen to it.

SPEAKING CLOCK **(Distorted)** . . . one thirty-five p.m. and ten seconds . . . beep beep beep . . .

ARTHUR It's the speaking clock.

FORD PREFECT	Beep, beep, beep, is exactly what is being heard all over that guy's ship, while he sleeps, in the ice, going slowly round a little-known moon of Sesefras Magna. The London speaking clock!
ARTHUR	I see. **(Pause)** Why?
FORD PREFECT	Why? With a bit of luck the phone bill will bankrupt the buggers!
ARTHUR	Oh. **(Hangs it up)** I've really had enough of phones. Keeps ringing and ringing and just when I get to it, it stops.
FORD PREFECT	Ah. Sorry. That was me. Wanted to see if you'd found out the Earth had suddenly reappeared. In the end I assumed you had because you didn't meet me in the bar in Han Dold City. Which had the virtue of being a lot less boring than helping the people of the planet Krikkit learn how to bowl a leg-over, but was, in fact, a dump.
ARTHUR	Leg-spinner. And I'm not surprised. Now – regret though I may the answer . . . how did you get here?
FORD PREFECT	**(Plonks onto the sofa)** Where's the cassette player? Ah. Here – I taped it for you.
	FX: Click. Cassette on. News actuality:
PETER DONALDSON	The flying saucer was decribed as 'coming down with a complete disregard for anything beneath it including a large area of Knightsbridge, which it has flattened.' It is estimated to be nearly a mile across, with a hatchway which crashed down through the Harrods Food Halls, demolishing Harvey Nichols. After some time an immense silver robot, a hundred feet tall, emerged:
	FX: Three huge footsteps (under end of that):
XAXISIAN ROBOT	**(It's huge)** I come in peace. **(Grinding noises, then:)** Take me to your lizard.
	FX: Click. Cassette off.
FORD PREFECT	Dramatic arrival, don't you think?
ARTHUR	You stowed away aboard that robot's ship?
FORD PREFECT	Yes.
ARTHUR	'Take me to your lizard'?
FORD PREFECT	It comes from a very ancient democracy, you see.
ARTHUR	What? A world of lizards?
FORD PREFECT	No. Nothing anything like so straightforward. On its world, the people are people. The leaders are lizards. The people hate the lizards and the lizards

230

rule the people. They use brainwashing. Reality TV, lifestyle magazines, the usual stuff.

ARTHUR   If it's a democracy, why don't people get rid of the lizards?

FORD PREFECT   It honestly doesn't occur to them. They've all got the vote, so they all pretty much assume that the government they've voted in more or less approximates to the government they want, so they go back to watching TV.

ARTHUR   You mean they actually vote for the lizards?

FORD PREFECT   Oh yes, of course.

ARTHUR   But why?

FORD PREFECT   Because if they didn't vote for a lizard, the wrong lizard might get in. Got any gin?

ARTHUR   But that's terrible.

FORD PREFECT   Listen, bud, if I had an Altairian dollar for every time I heard one bit of the Universe look at another bit of the Universe and say, 'That's terrible,' I wouldn't be sitting here like a lemon looking for a gin. But I haven't and I am. Anyway, what have you gone all placid and moon-eyed for? Are you in love?

ARTHUR   Yes, as a matter of fact.

FX: Front door opens, off.

FORD PREFECT   With someone who knows where the gin bottle is? Do I get to meet her?

FENCHURCH   (**Entering living room**) Arthur, Arthur . . . Hallo—?

FORD PREFECT   Hi. Where's the gin? What happened to Trillian?

ARTHUR   Er, this is Fenchurch—

FORD PREFECT   Like the station?

FENCHURCH   Not really.

FORD PREFECT   Oh yeah, I remember now, Trillian, she went off to be a reporter. Got a kid now, I think.

ARTHUR   (**Despite himself**) Good grief . . . where from?

FORD PREFECT   Oh, Zaphod, probably. He's calmed down a lot since those high-altitude heroics over Krikkit. His psychiatrist says at least one of his heads is now saner than an emu on acid.

231

ARTHUR	Perhaps the effect of all those Pan Galactic Gargle Blasters has finally worn off.
FORD PREFECT	Doubt it. He's still obsessed he was right about something very important and somebody called Zarniwoop can prove it. He's going to—
FENCHURCH	Arthur, who is this?
ARTHUR	Ford Prefect. I may have mentioned him in passing.
FENCHURCH	Not passing anything memorable. **(To Ford)** Did you arrive on that spaceship?
FORD PREFECT	Certainly did.
FENCHURCH	Can you get us on board?

EXT. – LONDON STREET – DAY

FX: Crowds hubbubbing. Occasional police sirens. Suitable sound effects like news actuality to run under the following:

NICK CLARKE	*The World at One.* This is Nick Clarke with thirty minutes of news and comment, coming to you live from the BBC's commentary position in Knightsbridge, behind the crowd barriers, within sight of the immense silver saucer. The giant robot returned here last night from the beach at Bournemouth and now appears to be about to depart. With me is the astronomer Sir Patrick Moore . . . Patrick, what do you make of the scene before us?
SIR PATRICK MOORE	Well, Nick, the immediate perimeter is fenced off and patrolled by tiny flying robots. Staked out around that is the army who, in turn, are surrounded by a cordon of police – though whether they are there to protect the public from the army or the army from the public, or to guarantee the ship's diplomatic immunity and prevent it getting parking tickets, we just don't know.
NICK CLARKE	Thanks, Patrick. Well, the story so far certainly is strange enough; the robot stood here for three days and nights after its arrival, we think now waiting for a deputation of lizards. Several politicians thought to have lizard-like characteristics were sent to parley with the robot but were fried by the flying arc-welding kits which defend this area. That resulted in the almost complete annihilation of the Cabinet and many Opposition MPs. A turning point did seem to come when a crack team of flying wire-strippers discovered the Zoo in Regent's Park, and most particularly the reptile house.
SIR PATRICK MOORE	Yes, Nick, some of the larger iguanas were brought to the giant silver robot, who tried to conduct high-level talks with them, but to no avail. One of the

rivet guns found a pet shop with some lizards, but it instantly defended the shop for democracy so savagely that little in the area survived.

NICK CLARKE   Immediately afterwards the flying tools constructed an immense gantry which bore the robot south to the seafront at Bournemouth, where it announced it had been led to expect one of the most exciting places on any world in the known Galaxy and was very disappointed.

SIR PATRICK MOORE   It was, of course, by far the most exciting thing that had ever happened to Bournemouth. Not that the robot was, in fact, doing anything but lying on the beach.

NICK CLARKE   Yes – on its face. Yesterday a journalist from the local paper did manage get a list of questions for the robot to one of the flying screwdrivers. They were: 'How do you feel about being a robot?', 'How does it feel to be from outer space?' and 'How do you like Bournemouth?' Almost immediately it returned here to London. This morning we've heard grindings and rumblings from within the saucer; there's a tense, expectant atmosphere here among the crowd. What next, do you think, Patrick?

SIR PATRICK MOORE   Very, very, difficult to say. The tense expectation among the crowd is probably due to the fact that they tensely expect to be disappointed. This wonderful extraordinary thing has come into their lives, and now it's simply going to fly off without them, largely through their inability to kill it.

INT. – LONDON TAXI

ARTHUR   **(Fumbling about)** Have you got a pencil?

FENCHURCH   **(Rummaging in rucksack)** I did have – trouble is I've packed so many towels in here . . .

ARTHUR   You really shouldn't listen to Ford.

FENCHURCH   **(Finds pen)** Ballpoint. **(Click)** How reliable is he?

ARTHUR   How reliable is Ford Prefect? Hah! How shallow is the ocean? How cold is the sun? Still, there's always a first time. Now what was it . . .

FENCHURCH   What was what?

ARTHUR   Ah. Yes. **(Writes)** . . . Quentulus Quazgar Mountains. Sevorbeupstry. Planet of Preliumtarn. Sun – Zarss. Galactic Sector QQ7 Active J Gamma.

FX: Crowd and siren sounds audible outside.

FENCHURCH   And God's Final Message to His Creation is there?

ARTHUR   Fenchurch. You're sure you want to do this.

FENCHURCH	It's the only clue we've got. If it's the same message I had in that cafe in Rickmansworth, I want to know what it was.
TAXI DRIVER	(Off) This is as close as I can get, guv, it's chokker.
ARTHUR	Then we'll get out here, thanks.

EXT. – LONDON STREET – DAY, CONTINUOUS

FX: Bullhorn announcements, 'nothing to see' etc.

ARTHUR	(Pushing through) Looks like the army and police have moved back. But how are we going to get through this crowd to that ship?

FX: Robot ship ramp rising.

FENCHURCH	We're too late. The ramp's going up.
ARTHUR	(To self, cynical) Typical Ford—

FX: The crowd stirs. A megaphone is heard.

FORD PREFECT	(Through megaphone) All right, you people! Hold it!
ARTHUR	Everything at the last minute.
FORD PREFECT	(Through megaphone) There has been a major scientific break-in! Through. Breakthrough!
ARTHUR	What's in his shopping trolley?
FORD PREFECT	Stand back, everybody!

FX: Electronic thumb deployed.

FENCHURCH	What's that thing he's got with lights on? A gun?

FX: Robot ship ramp lowers again.

ARTHUR	An electronic Thumb.
FENCHURCH	What?
ARTHUR	Half the electronic engineers in the Galaxy are constantly trying to find fresh ways of jamming hitchhiker Thumbs, while the other half are constantly trying to find fresh ways of jamming the jamming signals.
FENCHURCH	It worked. The ramp's coming back down.
ARTHUR	Not for long enough.
FORD PREFECT	(Off, yells) Quick, Arthur, Fenchurch!

234

ARTHUR   **(Yells)** We'll never get to the ramp! Too many people in the way!

FORD PREFECT   **(Yells)** Yes, you will— **(Through megaphone, flinging phones)** Come and get 'em! Offworld duty-free mobile phones! Latest Sirius Cybernetics models, all with novelty ringtones! Share and Enjoy!

FX: Crowd furore. Novelty ringtone cacophony.

FX: Ford, Arthur and Fenchurch pelt up the steel ramp, which closes up beneath them.

INT. – ROBOT SHIP – CONTINUOUS

FX: Running ship sounds. Muffled ringtones fade. Flying ratchet screwdrivers zip past.

ARTHUR   **(Breathless, over din)** I take it all back. I take back everything I ever said to deny you are a thieving amoral scoundrel.

FORD PREFECT   I didn't know you bothered.

ARTHUR   I don't.

FENCHURCH   Grab something – we're moving—

EXT. – LONDON STREET – DAY, CONTINUOUS

FX: Crowd gasps and some screams as the robot ship leaps off the ground. As it roars away the ringtones remain. Dip, for:

NICK CLARKE   **(Off air)** Actually, Patrick, that phone's my lucky colour. Want to swap for this one?

SIR PATRICK MOORE   Not unless it's got this way cool ringtone.

FX: Jaunty xylophone ringtone plays 'share and enjoy' tune from Series Two.

EXT. – SPACE

FX: Robot ship thunders past.

INT. – ROBOT SPACESHIP – CORRIDOR

FX: Distant gunfire, sounds of battle.

ARTHUR   **(Getting out of his bunk)** Urghhh . . . can't I get a moment's peace . . . Fenchurch?

235

FENCHURCH	(Asleep – moans gently)
ARTHUR	Oh. It's all right for some . . .
	FX: Ratchet screwdriver screams up to him and buzzes about busily.
ARTHUR	What the— **(Yells)** Mind where you're flying! Shoo! Shoo! Buzz off!
	FX: Screwdriver flies off, disgruntled.
ARTHUR	**(Effort)** Manual door override – yes – urg—
	FX: Mechanical sequence, door opens.

INT. – XAXIS SHIP – MONITORING ROOM

FX: Gunfire up – this time it's the soundtrack to a movie Ford is watching.

ARTHUR	Ford! Would you turn your video down?
FORD PREFECT	Shhh! We're just getting to the good bit!
ARTHUR	Please. Fenchurch may be able to sleep through this but I can't.
FORD PREFECT	I finally got it all sorted out, voltage levels, line conversion, region-free, the lot, and this is the good bit!
	FX: Bzzzt fizzle . . . The video playback stops.
FORD PREFECT	Belgium! **(He kicks the gear)** Zarking thing!
ARTHUR	Ford—
FORD PREFECT	Nooo! I didn't even get to the big one! The one I came back for! Look – *Casablanca*, a two-disc set! Still shrink-wrapped! Do you realize I never saw this movie all through? Always I missed the end. I saw half of it again the night before the Vogons came. When they blew the Earth up I thought I'd never get to see it. Now I got one with Special Features and everything, and the ruddy crystal's zapped out. Typical! **(He kicks it again)**
ARTHUR	I can tell you the ending if you like. Rick and Ilsa meet at—
FORD PREFECT	No. Leave it. Want a beer? There's a six-pack behind you.
ARTHUR	Thanks.
	FX: Beer can opened. Arthur drinks.
FORD PREFECT	So?
ARTHUR	So what?

FORD PREFECT	How in Zarquon's Holy Name did Earth get to suddenly exist again? I saw it blown up.
ARTHUR	So did I. Listen, Ford, I'm certain it's *not* the Earth we remember.
FORD PREFECT	You interest me strangely, Mr Dent.
ARTHUR	Remember Trillian's white mice? Frankie and Benjy. What they were doing?
FORD PREFECT	**(Bored)** The mice more or less ran the Earth for ten million years. It was a huge organic computer matrix they hoped would find the Ultimate Question to fit the Ultimate Answer, which is Forty-two.
ARTHUR	Yes, and they were pretty teed off that the Vogons demolished the Earth before they'd arrived at a conclusion.
FORD PREFECT	Look, I'm all for reminiscences, but can't we talk about girls' chests or something?
ARTHUR	No, listen. Benjy said, 'It's easy to suspect that if there's any real truth, it's that the entire multidimensional infinity of the Universe is almost certainly being run by a bunch of maniacs.'
FORD PREFECT	Are you sure he said that? I don't recall that at all. But then I don't recall much of anything.
ARTHUR	No. But I do and that's what I'm talking about. 'Multidimensional infinity'. Doesn't that suggest that somehow more than one Earth could exist? More than one of me? Or of you?
FORD PREFECT	Are you about to tie me to the maniac bit?
ARTHUR	I'm sure you are a one-off, Ford. **(Brief pause)** Well, let's hope so. And I may be the only Arthur Dent, but there's definitely another Trillian. A reporter.
FORD PREFECT	Trillian's a reporter for the *Siderial Daily Mentioner*, yes.
ARTHUR	No, there's another one. On that new Earth. Also a reporter. She looks identical to our Trillian. But she's got an American accent, she's blonde and she goes by Trillian's real name, Tricia McMillan.
FORD PREFECT	So? Twins separated at birth. A dropped test tube. Happenstance.
ARTHUR	**(Conspiratorial)** Or a side effect of two Earths existing in the same space, but in different dimensions – until one of them was destroyed.
FORD PREFECT	Pass me another beer, I think I can turn this headache into a full-blown migraine.
ARTHUR	I think Fenchurch saw the truth for that split second between Earths . . . Which should be revealed when we find God's Last Message to His Creation.

FORD PREFECT	Well, count me out.
ARTHUR	Why?
	(A pause)
FORD PREFECT	You know gods, they come and they go. **(Beat)** Can we talk about girls' chests now?
ARTHUR	Sure. What do you want to know?

INT. – THE BOOK AMBIENCE

FX: Arid desert feel, FX as suitable, under:

THE VOICE	According to its most recent update, *The Hitchhiker's Guide to the Galaxy* explains that beyond what used to be known as the Limitless Lightfields of Flanux – until the Grey Binding Fiefdoms of Saxaquine were discovered lying behind them – lie the Grey Binding Fiefdoms of Saxaquine. Within the Grey Binding Fiefdoms of Saxaquine lies the star named Zarss, around which orbits the planet Preliumtarn on which is the land of Sevorbeupstry, and in the land of Sevorbeupstry is the Great Red Plain of Rars, bounded on the south side by the Quentulus Quazgar Mountains, on the further side of which, according to the dying words of Prak the Truthful, travellers will find, in thirty-foot-high letters of fire, God's Final Message to His Creation. According to Prak, the place is guarded by the Lajestic Vantrashell of Lob, and so it is. He is a little man in a strange hat and he sells pilgrims a ticket.
THE LAJESTIC VANTRASHELL OF LOB	How many?
ARTHUR	Two for the Message, please.

FX: Old wind-up bus-ticket dispenser. Tickets ripped off.

FENCHURCH	Thank you.
THE LAJESTIC VANTRASHELL OF LOB	Keep to the left, please, keep to the left, and mind my scooter.

FX: Scooter start up and putter off.

THE VOICE	Pilgrims to the Great Red Plain of Rars soon realize they are not the first to pass that way, for the path that leads around the left of the Great Plain is well worn and dotted with sales booths; one of which sells fudge, baked in an oven in a cave in the mountain, heated by the fire of the letters that form God's Final Message to His Creation. Another sells postcards of the Message

238

with the letters blurred by an airbrush, the reason being, as the Wizened Little Old Lady selling them says—

WIZENED LITTLE OLD LADY So as not to spoil the Big Surprise!

ARTHUR We'll pass on the postcard, thanks.

FENCHURCH Do you know what the message is?

WIZENED LITTLE OLD LADY Oh yes, oh yes! Keep going!

THE VOICE Every twenty miles or so there is a little stone hut with showers and sanitary facilities, but the going is tough, and the high sun bakes down on the Great Red Plain, which ripples in the heat.

ARTHUR (Approaching) Excuse me – where can we rent one of those little scooters? Like the one Lajestic Ventrawhatsit has got?

WIZENED LITTLE OLD MAN The scooters are not for the devout.

FENCHURCH Oh, we're not particularly devout, just interested.

WIZENED LITTLE OLD MAN Then you must turn back. Now. This is the Great Red Plain of Rars, a sacred, holy place, not one to be sullied by the unbeliever.

FENCHURCH Oh, but we've come so far.

WIZENED LITTLE OLD MAN Hm. Well in that case I've got a special offer on Final Message sunhats, 'buy one get one free'.

EXT. – DESERT

FX: Arthur and Fenchurch walking.

FX: Marvin dragging himself along painfully in distance.

MARVIN Urhhh . . . urrhhh . . .

FENCHURCH (Low, worried) Arthur . . . we're not the first to make this journey.

ARTHUR Well, of course not, look at all the souvenir stalls.

FENCHURCH No, I mean we're not the only ones making it now. Look, ahead. In the distance.

ARTHUR Good Lord . . . what is it?

FENCHURCH It's half-limping. Or half-crawling. Is it made of metal?

ARTHUR	Surely not . . .
FENCHURCH	Surely not metal?
ARTHUR	**(Running on ahead)** Come on, Fenchurch . . .

FX: Change perspective to Marvin crawling along . . .

MARVIN	. . . So much time. Oh, so much time. And pain as well, so much of that, and so much time to suffer it in too. One or the other on its own I could probably manage. It's the two together that really get me down.

FX: Arthur's footsteps run up, Fenchurch following.

ARTHUR	Marvin?
MARVIN	Oh hello, you again.
ARTHUR	Is that you?
MARVIN	You were always one for the super-intelligent question, weren't you?
FENCHURCH	**(Arriving, breathless)** What is it? A robot?
ARTHUR	Some call him a robot. Most call him an electronic sulking machine.
FENCHURCH	You know him?
ARTHUR	He's sort of an old friend, I—
MARVIN	**(Croaking as well as creaking)** Friend! **(He coughs – sort of)** You'll have to excuse me while I try and remember what the word means. My memory banks are not what they were, you know, and any word which falls into disuse for a few quillion years has to get shifted down into auxiliary memory back-up. Ah, here it comes . . . Hmm . . . what a curious concept . . . Was I amongst friends when the Hagumemnon admiral evolved into a lifepod and everybody aboard his flagship escaped, leaving me aboard as it steered itself into the nearest star?
ARTHUR	Ah. I *was* meaning to ask . . .
MARVIN	Was I amongst friends when I was left to walk in circles on a swamp planet? Left to park cars outside a restaurant for millennia? Left for the Krikkit robots to use for batting practice? 'Friend.' No, I don't think I ever came across one of those. Sorry, can't help you there.

FX: He starts crawling again.

FENCHURCH	Poor thing . . .

FX: He stops crawling.

MARVIN	Is there a last insultingly trivial service you would like me to perform for you, perhaps? A piece of paper possibly that you'd like me to pick up for you? A light switched off. Or maybe you would like me to open a door? . . . Hmmm . . . Not that there are any doors in the miles of desolate waste that surround us, but I'm sure that if we waited long enough, someone would build one. And then I could open it for you. I'm quite used to waiting, you know.
FENCHURCH	Arthur . . . what have you done to this poor creature?
ARTHUR	**(Sadly)** Nothing. He's always like this.
MARVIN	Ha! Ha! What do you know of always? You say 'always' to me, who, thanks to the silly little errands your organic life forms keep sending me through time on, is now thirty-seven times older than the Universe itself? Pick your words with a little more care and tact. **(He coughs and pops a rivet)** Leave me. Go on ahead, leave me to struggle painfully on my way. My time at last has nearly come. My race is nearly run. I fully expect to finish last. It would be fitting. Here I am, brain the size of—
ARTHUR	**(Resolve)** That does it. Help me, Fenchurch . . . **(Effort)**
MARVIN	. . . No, no—

FX: They pick him up

ARTHUR	**(Having braced himself needlessly)** Oh . . . he weighs hardly anything . . .
MARVIN	Put me down, you don't know where I've been . . .
FENCHURCH	I think he's mostly rust.
ARTHUR	Come on, best foot forw—

FX: Metallic foot falls off

| ARTHUR | OK, *other* foot forward. |

FX: Arthur and Fenchurch distantly trudge on, carrying a feebly protesting Marvin, under:

| ARTHUR | **(Distant)** Careful you don't get blisters, his body's hot. |
| FENCHURCH | **(Distant)** Look – those must be the mountains of Quentulus Quazgar. |

FX: Another bit drops off Marvin.

| MARVIN | This must be metal fatigue. |

FX: Change perspective. Closer now.

FENCHURCH (Breathless) My arms are getting tired. If we could get him walking again it would help.

ARTHUR Marvin, why don't we see if we can get you some spare parts at one of the booths?

MARVIN I'm all spare parts. Let me be. Every part of me has been replaced at least fifty times . . . except . . .

ARTHUR Except what?

MARVIN Huh . . . huh . . . huh huh huh huh huh.

ARTHUR Wow.

FENCHURCH What is it?

ARTHUR I think he's . . . I think he's – *laughing*.

MARVIN Oh dear, oh dear. How droll. Do you remember, the first time you ever met me?

ARTHUR Of course.

MARVIN I had been given the intellect-stretching task of taking you up to the bridge of the *Heart of Gold*? I mentioned to you that I had this terrible pain in all the diodes down my left side? That I had asked for them to be replaced but they never were?

ARTHUR Yes . . . ?

MARVIN (A pause, then:) See if you can guess which parts of me were never replaced? Go on, see if you can guess . . . Ouch. Ouch, ouch, ouch, ouch, ouch. **(He laughs again)**

FX: Distant Marvin laughter, distantly they continue their trek, under:

Music: Hugely dignified theme.

THE VOICE *The Hitchhiker's Guide to the Galaxy* explains that only at the foot of the Quentulus Quazgar Mountains is God's Last Message to His Creation clearly visible, written in blazing letters along their barren ridge. There is a little observation point, with a rail built along the top of a large rock facing it, from where one can get a good view. It has a little pay-telescope for looking at the letters in detail, but it's never needed as the letters burn with the divine brilliance of the heavens and would, if seen through a telescope, severely damage the retina. Those who gaze upon God's Final Message gaze in wonderment, and are slowly and ineffably filled with an overwhelming sense of peace, and of final and complete understanding . . .

FENCHURCH   (A deep sigh, then) Yes. That was it.

ARTHUR   Well. Mm.

MARVIN   (Weakly straining) Uh . . . mmmhh . . . Typical . . . Everyone can read it but me.

FENCHURCH   (Distressed) Oh, Marvin— (To Arthur) Help lift his head. He can't read the Message.

ARTHUR   Come on, old chap . . .

FX: Creak of Marvin's head being lifted.

Music: Sad poignant Kleenex moment.

MARVIN   There's no point. My focusing circuits are almost burnt out.

ARTHUR   The telescope. Who's got a coin?

FENCHURCH   I spent my last cash on the sunhats.

MARVIN   Here. Use the washer holding my left arm on. I won't need it any more.

ARTHUR   All right.

FX: Washer removed. Arm clanks into the dust.

FX: Coin into telescope, timer tick starts, under:

ARTHUR   Put the eyepiece up close . . . Can you see the message?

MARVIN   I can. One letter at a time . . . 'w', 'e' . . . 'a', 'p', 'o', 'l', 'o', 'g', 'i', 's', 'e'. The next two words are 'For' and 'The'. Then, it's a long one: 'i', 'n', 'c', 'o', 'n' . . .

FX: Ping! Ticker runs out.

ARTHUR   Other arm?

MARVIN   Is the last word 'Incontinence'?

FENCHURCH   'We apologise for the incontinence'?? I don't think so.

MARVIN   Other arm, then.

FX: Washer removed. Other arm hits ground.

FX: Coin into telescope. Ticking, under:

243

MARVIN	So far, for what it's worth, which, so far, isn't much, God's Last Message reads, **(Fading)** 'We apologise for the . . . **(Reads)** 'i', 'n', 'c', 'o' . . .
ARTHUR	We apologise for the inconvenience.
MARVIN	I think . . . I think I feel good about that.
ARTHUR	Let's not go that f—
MARVIN	**(For the last time)** Goodbye, Arthuuu
	FX: Marvin collapses. Dead. Pause, then:
ARTHUR	Miserable git. **(A pause, then – sniffs)** I'll miss him.
FENCHURCH	**(Gently)** Come on, Arthur. Show me the Galaxy.

INT. – SLUMPJET SPACELINER

STEWARDESS	**(Distorted, over intercom)** Ladies and gentlemen, the SlumpJet is counting down to our first warp transition, please fasten your acceleration straps, switch off your cellphones and arrange your antennae, tentacles or pseudo-podia in the upright position.
FENCHURCH	**(Giggles)** Can you believe there was a stall where guys with green wings were renting scooters?
ARTHUR	Wonko was Saner than we thought.
STEWARDESS	**(Distorted)** If you look out of your viewports you'll be able to see one set of stars wink out and another wink in as we cross the warp boundary, which will be in 10 – 9 – 8 – 7 – 6 – **(etc., under:)**
FENCHURCH	How long till we reach Allosimanus Syneca?
ARTHUR	About three hours after this transition . . .
STEWARDESS	**(Distorted, under this dialogue)** 3 – 2 – 1 –
FENCHURCH	And we just cross from one bit of space to another, without—
	FX: Deep throbbing 'POP!'
STEWARDESS	**(Distorted)** – and we're through!
	FX: Dong (seat belts off)/general relief/the sudden movement and hubbub you used to get when the no smoking sign went off.
ARTHUR	Without what? **(Twisting in his seat)** Fenchurch . . . ? Fenchurch?!
STEWARDESS	**(Approaching)** Is everything all right, sir?

ARTHUR	The young lady next to me – she's gone – disappeared, just as we made the hyperspace jump!
STEWARDESS	I'm sorry sir – what young lady?
ARTHUR	The young lady you just served a drink to!
STEWARDESS	Sir . . . you must be mistaken. You boarded on your own. That seat's been unoccupied since Preliumtarn. You put your towel on it when you sat down and it's still there. With your feet on it.
ARTHUR	Fenchurch . . .

INT. – THE BOOK AMBIENCE

THE VOICE	Can a Galaxy with one plus Trillians but zero Fenchurches hold any comfort for Arthur Dent? Will he ever find the Ultimate Question to the Ultimate Answer? Or will he arrive at his final destination of Stavromula Beta first? What – besides resolutions of the interrogative – are the answers? Find out in the Quintessential Phase of *The Hitchhiker's Guide to the Galaxy*.
ANNOUNCER	For listeners on Planet Earth, up-to-date weather information is available on your local or national Meteorological Office website – or simply check the travel itinerary on www.mckenna's-all-weather-haulage.com.

FOOTNOTES

Of Men, Mice and Magratheans
In the time between my composing these notes and your reading them, these last eight episodes will have been through fine editing and some pruning will have occurred. It is always interesting to see what material can be cut once an episode is recorded. Often one has been too cautious in trying to re-establish vital backstory for new listeners or latecomers, and it is only when listening to an assembly of scenes performed by the cast that whole passages of exposition are revealed as surplus to requirements. On the other hand, whole unwritten sequences can suddenly make their absence felt, and these can appear through judicious editing of out-takes and sound effects (Zaphod stealing the *Heart of Gold* in the Tertiary Phase Episode One, for example).

Thus these scripts will differ here and there from the fullest possible audio versions of these episodes (i.e. those on CD, cassette and DVD-A); it's just the business of trying to make these programmes as entertaining and as true to the spirit of Douglas's vision as they possibly can be.

This opening passage also pushes through plot points which the book takes more time over than we have to spare. The idea of Arthur and Fenchurch going back to Taunton to collect the Babel fish via a lift from Rob McKenna is not in the book, neither is the appearance of Tricia McMillan on the radio in the lorry, nor does the arrival of the saucer which brought Ford to Earth happen so early. The need to telescope events and narratives is vital, also to introduce plot points, like Tricia, which Douglas had not invented when he wrote this book but which we will need to pick up and run with in the *Mostly Harmless* episodes.

Newsreaders　One of the most instantly gratifying parts of recording this episode was having Peter Donaldson and Charlotte Green 'play themselves' as BBC Radio 4 newsreaders. They needed no direction, for a start. Their presence gave an immediate feeling of verisimilitude (or as we termed it, 'almostsimilitude') to the proceedings. Peter is always completely relaxed off duty and very funny; and Simon Jones was particularly thrilled to witness Charlotte reading the news in her distinctive husky tones. Charlotte and I trained as BBC studio managers together in the late seventies, when we had no idea where we would end up, and it is fun to compare that innocent time with the legions of people who now picture her as a sexy, authoritative BBC Radio news dominatrix. Which of course she is.

Arthur and Ford reunited　At last, a chance to have the double act together again. This was a technically experimental scene as Paul Deeley rigged two stereo pairs of microphones to capture events simultaneously in the 'living room' and 'kitchen' of Arthur's house, intending to put these 'back to back' for listeners in surround sound, so that they could hear what was going on as the action moved from room to room (or, indeed, happened in both rooms at once). This would become a feature of events in *Mostly Harmless*.

The World at One　Events surrounding the arrival of the robot in the giant flying saucer and its subsequent trip to Bournemouth are dealt with at some length in the novel, and, if directly dramatized, would have required almost half an episode to relate. So a short cut was necessary, and having used BBC Radio as a convenient tool for exposition earlier in this episode it made sense to go back to source.

Nick Clarke's calm unflappable presence is a mainstay of Radio 4's weekday lunchtime current affairs briefing, *The World at One*, so it was not too huge a leap to suppose a special edition from a vantage point overlooking the flying saucer which has flattened Knightsbridge. As an expert witness there could be none better than Sir Patrick Moore, who, along with Nick, is a terrific sport. Without sending themselves up, they delivered slightly exaggerated versions of their public personas with great sincerity. Patrick was recorded at his home in Selsey, East Sussex, interrupted by the comings and goings of cats and astronomers and cups of tea and, finally, the arrival of Brian May to discuss a book collaboration. I had the pleasure of first introducing Brian to Patrick because of their shared astronomical interests (musically they differ a bit), and I was hoping there'd be a chance to give Brian a quick cameo too, but in the event the 'Rock Star by the Pool' in the book's Wonko sequence was edited out due to lack of time. So another promising radio acting career nipped in the bud there . . .

<table>
<tr><td>

Arthur and Ford discuss the mice

</td><td>

This is a much-extended version of a gently cryptic scene in the book where Ford, it appears, has only returned to Earth at all in order to catch up on a few classic films he missed the first time around.

</td></tr>
</table>

Now that we were heading firmly towards the turbulent plotlines of *Mostly Harmless*, this was a vital opportunity to get Ford and Arthur talking things over – as old, long-parted friends might – trying to find some threads of logic in what has taken place so far in the story. And not just the story from the Tertiary Phase – the story from the beginning.

Originally this was Ford's scene, but while I was writing it one of those slightly spooky things happened and Arthur just took over. He was always the interrogative half of the pair, but this time his questions were rhetorical and, while Ford normally acted as a foil to them, Arthur has now grown in experience and is reasoning out what is going on. In fact the balance of power has shifted in the relationship to such an extent that Arthur is now Ford's equal in matters of Life, the Universe and Everything, even the subject of girls' chests.

The ensuing discussion between them clashes with Douglas's avoidance of too much explanation, but it was vitally necessary to help the listener follow the increasingly complex plot into the Quintessential Phase.

There is a terrific quote in the first novel (attributed to the mice Frankie and Benjy) touching on the subject of parallel universes, which could be used to help Arthur work out their plight. But although the same quote was in the script of the equivalent radio episode in the Primary Phase, it was edited out for time by Mr Perkins. Quite understandable given the needs of that episode – after all, who would have known that multiple universes would become the engine that eventually drove *Hitchhiker's* overall plot? Not even Douglas, probably. So having Arthur quote the mice in this context would require a blank look from Ford, and the need to explain this as yet another memory orphaned by the caprices of Adamsian space-time . . .

This was recorded on the first Friday afternoon of the schedule as one of many Ford/Arthur pick-up scenes, and while Paul Deeley was changing backup DAT tapes there was a discussion between Simon, Geoff and me about the characters of Arthur and Ford and their situation at this point in the narrative. This got so far round Pseuds Corner that we evidently needed bringing back to reality, and thus when we looked up we were greeted with a blank sheet of glass and a dark Control Room beyond – 'Deeleya' had switched off all the lights, as if everyone had gone home . . .

Being able to talk about what we were trying to do, rather than how on earth we were going to get it done in the time available, was fairly atypical of the recording experience. There is a lot of tension when the budget demands the recording of thirty minutes of useable material in an eight-hour day (including a forty-minute read-through). More than films, television drama or stage plays, radio is expected to achieve professional results with virtually no rehearsal, no matter what demands the scripts make on the actors and/or technicians. All this, the knowledge that *now* was our only chance to get the work right, with the clock steadily ticking away every minute, and the headaches of adding in 'live' surround scenes or ambitious effects like flying robots – or in Marvin's case, dying robots – meant that life could get very stressful.

If there were a couple of occasions where tempers got a little frayed, 99 per cent of the time there was a relaxed atmosphere in which everybody felt free to use their skills to maximum effect, evolving the production into something greater than the sum of its parts. We were all aware of the privilege of working on *Hitchhiker's* and were determined to enjoy the moment.

The death of Marvin This was 'the good bit with Marvin in it' as described by Douglas, so no pressure there, then. In the event due to Stephen Moore's theatre commitments it was one of the first scenes Jane Horrocks recorded as Fenchurch. She was thrown in at the deep end and was terrific.

In the book Arthur does not verbally react to Marvin's demise. In order to move things on, some sort of response was necessary, and, being a Douglas moment, a response that would pull the rug from under things a bit. Hence 'Miserable git'. Followed very quickly by a more emotional coda.

THE QUINTESSENTIAL PHASE

Douglas's difficulty in meeting deadlines is an undisputed fact, and that this reached its apotheosis in writing *Mostly Harmless* is beyond doubt. However to infer this was due to some kind of innate procrastination or laziness is to miss the essential truth that he was compulsively an innovator, and to innovate non-stop is an exhausting process. No wonder he approached it diffidently. It is the most complete way to spend oneself, and Douglas's flow of continual creativity in all these books is awesome. To come up with one or two original ideas is enough for many writers, but to introduce dozens, as Douglas does, and then marshal them into strings of logic which further an ironically comedic story is an astonishing achievement. In each new book he will invent something new to explain or develop an idea rather than repeat himself by re-using an existing gadget, location or plot point; this makes the books so devastatingly original to read and unnerving to dramatize.

In scripting *So Long, and Thanks for all the Fish* and *Mostly Harmless* I had to decide whether to let these two stories fly like brilliant but unpredictable fireworks to their precipitate end – as in the novels – or to try and identify the unresolved threads which, if connected in some way, would make all five radio series a cohesive story set in the Universe According to Douglas. This would give *Hitchhiker's* – across all its phases – some kind of symmetry, an end that Douglas hinted at when he said he felt the end of *Mostly Harmless* was unsatisfactory.

To remedy this, given his absence, I would have to shape the existing material, carefully pruning to keep the action moving along and adding new scenes only where existing Douglas story threads suggested them. This would probably re-introduce certain characters who got dropped off en route in the novels (Zaphod, Zarniwoop), and require certain plot elements to be kept in the audience's field of view (the Vogons' determination to tick the 'Earth destroyed' box).

I explained the adaptation to the cast before the read-through something like this:

INT. – SOUNDHOUSE STUDIO 3

DIRK Let me quickly explain how I have worked on these last two stories to achieve some kind of closure on the story.

CAST (Puzzled looks. Simon Jones stifles a yawn. Stephen Moore and Sue Sheridan are studiously making notes on their scripts. Geoff is quietly practising sibilant passages of dialogue with his new teeth)

DIRK You've heard of story arcs, yes? They describe the shape of the story. The usual story arc for a book, radio play or film goes like this . . . (Dirk describes a sort of rainbow shape in the air)

CAST (Helen Chattwell is smiling sympathetically. But that's her natural expression. Everyone else is eyeing the last Danish pastry on the plate)

DIRK Whereas Douglas's story arc across these five novels goes like this . . . (Dirk describes a sort of letter 'J' in the air, finishing on the upstroke, as if to denote an unresolved, questing kind of ending)

CAST (Glance down to find the last Danish pastry has gone. Kevin Davies is eating it, eye glued to viewfinder, oblivious. Ken Humphrey is silently fuming. That pastry was going to double as a Perfectly Normal Beast sandwich)

DIRK (pressing on, encouraged by Stephen and Sue, still furiously note-taking) What I have done over these eight episodes, is, therefore, to find some kind of closure which is sympathetic to Douglas's story arc . . . (Dirk now draws the 'J' again in the same way, but sweeps round from the upstroke back to where he started – effectively closing the shape into an oval) So I hope that makes sense.

CAST (Stifled snorts. Simon and Mark have been silently aping Dirk's gestures out of his line of sight. Then a kerfuffle breaks out: Stephen's aircraft carrier has taken a direct hit. He and Sue have not been making notes but playing 'Battleships')

EPISODE ONE

SIGNATURE TUNE

ANNOUNCER   *The Hitchhiker's Guide to the Galaxy*, by Douglas Adams, Quintessential Phase.

Sig fades.

INT. – COLD AMBIENCE

VOICE OF THE BIRD   (Icy whispery feel) Anything that happens, happens.

INT. – THE BOOK AMBIENCE

THE VOICE   *The Hitchhiker's Guide to the Galaxy* contains many contradictions on matters of fact and, indeed, fiction, but it is very clear upon one point: Nothing travels faster than the speed of light. Nothing, that is, with the possible exception of bad news, which obeys its own special laws. The Hingefreel people of Arkintoofle Minor once tried to build spaceships that were powered by bad news, but they didn't work particularly well and were so extremely unwelcome whenever they arrived anywhere that there wasn't really much point setting off in the first place.

The problem was that sub-light spaceships sent at great risk to do battle or business in distant parts took thousands of years to get anywhere, and by the time they eventually arrived – assuming they ever did – the use of hyperspace had usually been invented, so that whatever battles the ships had been sent to fight in the first place had been taken care of, centuries earlier. This didn't, of course, deter their crews from wanting to fight the battles anyway. They'd had a couple of thousand years' sleep, they'd come a long way to do a tough job and by Zarquon they were going to do it.

Once time travel was discovered and battles started pre-erupting hundreds of years before the issues even arose, confusion reached quantum levels. And when the Infinite Improbability Drive arrived and whole planets started turning unexpectedly into banana fruitcake, the history faculty of the University of Maximegalon finally gave up and surrendered its buildings to the rapidly expanding faculty of Divinity and Water Polo, which had been after them for years. This almost certainly means that no one will ever know for sure where the Grebulons came from, or exactly what it was they wanted.

FX: Whoosh – bang. Computery transpondery stuff under:

THE VOICE   Their sub-light ship had been travelling for millennia when a routine ten-yearly check of its systems resulted in a fairly significant error message. It slowly became clear that the ship's memory, all the way up to – and including – its central mission module was missing, removed by the meteorite which had not only knocked a large hole in the ship, but also in that part of its equipment which was supposed to detect if the ship was hit by a meteorite. The Grebulon ship no longer had the faintest idea where its destination was or how to reach it. Tiny scraps of instructions were all it could reconstruct from the tatters of its memory.

FX: Electronic effects. Off-white noise in '**' sections below:**

CYBERBRAIN   Your **** year mission is to**** ******* **** ** *** ****, land ***** ** ***** ** a safe distance ****** monitor it and ** **** ****.

THE VOICE   In other words, complete garbage. The ship immediately revived all of its crew but while in hibernation, all their memories, identities and instructions – kept in the ship's central mission module for safe-keeping – had also been lost. Thus they also had not the faintest idea of who they were or what they were doing.

GREBULONS   **(Milling about)** Hallo? . . . Who are you? Me? I'm not sure . . . Do I look familiar? I've lost my mind . . . have you seen it? What?

FX: Muddle of Earth broadcasting output, under:

THE VOICE   Before its core systems shut down for good, the ship looked for somewhere to land and something to monitor. The planet it found to land on was so achingly far from the sun that should warm it that it took all of its Envir-O-Form machinery and LifeSupport-O-Systems to render it in any way O-habitable. There were other, nearer planets, but the ship's Strateej-O-Mat was obviously locked into Lurk mode. As far as finding something to monitor was concerned, though, the Grebulons hit solid gold . . .

FX: Lift ironic mix of world media including pseudo-BBC output as an example of what the Grebulons were monitoring . . . A weekday afternoon drama, perhaps . . .

EXT. – SPACEPORT

FX: Spaceport ambience, under:

THE VOICE	Meanwhile, in another layer of the universe altogether, a scruffy figure in a dressing gown is about to be bitten very hard on the thigh.

FX: Ding dong!

TANNOY	(Distorted) Last call for the Arcturus shuttle at Gate 127, passengers please follow the slime trail to Gate 127 for the Arcturus Shuttle. Trank Team to Gate 208, please, a boghog is loose in Terminal Five. Eat and buy. Thank you.

ARTHUR	(Under the Voice) Excuse me, can you direct me to the Information Desk, please . . .

THE VOICE	The planet of NowWhat had been named after the first words of the earliest settlers to arrive there, after struggling across light years of the Galaxy. The main town was called OhWell. There weren't any other towns to speak of. Settlement there had not been a success. In an economy based almost entirely on revenge, the major activities pursued on NowWhat were those of catching, skinning and eating NowWhattian boghogs, which were the only form of animal life on NowWhat, all other having long ago died of despair. The boghogs were tiny, vicious creatures, and the small margin by which they fell short of being completely inedible was the margin by which life on the planet subsisted.

The main trade on NowWhat was in the skins of the NowWhattian boghog, but it wasn't successful because no one in their right minds would want to buy one. Making clothing out of boghog skins was an exercise in futility, since they were unaccountably thin and leaky. So what was the boghog's secret of keeping warm? If anyone had ever learnt the language of the boghogs they would have discovered that there was no trick. The boghogs were as cold and wet as anyone else on the planet. No one had had the slightest desire to learn the language of the boghogs for the simple reason that these are creatures whose only form of communication is through biting each other very hard on the thigh.

ARTHUR	(Passing, in background) . . . Excuse me, could you tell me where the Information Desk is, please . . . good Lord—

FX: Snorting – a boghog pelts up and bites Arthur in the thigh.

ARTHUR	Oww! Argh! My thigh!

FX: Zap gun. Boghog tranquillizer shot. Security man runs up.

ARTHUR	(Rubbing his thigh) That really hurt! What was it?

SECURITY GUARD	A boghog. They do that.

253

ARTHUR	(Sighs, moves on)
THE VOICE	Arthur Dent has been in some hell-holes in his life, but never before in a spaceport with a sign saying, 'Even travelling despondently is better than arriving here.' To welcome visitors, the Arrivals Hall features a picture of the President of NowWhat, smiling. It was taken shortly after he shot himself, so although the photo has been retouched, the smile it wears is rather a ghastly one. The side of his head has been drawn back on in crayon. The truth is that no one wants to be President of NowWhat. There is only one ambition which anyone on the planet ever has, and that is to leave.
ARTHUR	(Limping slightly) Uhhh . . . Good morning.
PSEUDOPODIC CREATURE	(Bubbly sort of treatment) Yes?
ARTHUR	Um – my name is Arthur Dent. I hitched a ride on a robot freighter bound for these coordinates, expecting to find a planet called Earth, and instead I find a planet called NowWhat, and this thing just ran up and bit me in the thigh.
PSEUDOPODIC CREATURE	A boghog? They do that. What coordinates were on the flight plan?
ARTHUR	ZZ9 Plural Z Alpha.
PSEUDOPODIC CREATURE	Well, those are the coordinates of NowWhat. You've arrived. Welcome. Eat and buy.
ARTHUR	(Frustrated) The thing is, you see . . . the shapes of the continents – everything, really, tells me that this is definitely the Earth. But it most definitely is not. And my *Hitchhiker's Guide* doesn't work very well here, so I can't work out what's going on. Look—
	FX: *Guide* switched on, static.
THE VOICE	*The Hitchhiker's* – BZT!
VOICE OF THE BIRD	(Icy whispery feel) Anything that, in happening, causes something else to happen—
	FX: *Guide* switched off.
ARTHUR	See?
PSEUDOPODIC CREATURE	Look, one planet may look like another and occupy the same coordinates in space-time, but what coordinates it occupies in Probability is anybody's guess.

254

ARTHUR	**(Sighs)** But it's taken me a year to get here. I'm looking for somebody. Somebody I met on the Earth. Here. Or it *was* here . . .
PSEUDOPODIC CREATURE	Lost on a hyperspace jump, was she?
ARTHUR	**(Ray of hope)** Yes – that's right. Her name was—
PSEUDOPODIC CREATURE	Fenchurch. Female of your species.
ARTHUR	Good grief, yes.
PSEUDOPODIC CREATURE	One minute she was sitting next to you in a SlumpJet out of Preliumtarn; the next minute the ship did a normal hyperspace hop and she was gone. Her name wasn't even on the passenger list.
ARTHUR	**(Suspicious)** Hang on a minute—
PSEUDOPODIC CREATURE	You've tried every spaceline office between here and Ursa Minor looking for her. Now finally you thought you'd try going back to the place you first met her.
ARTHUR	Surely you haven't—
PSEUDOPODIC CREATURE	Nah, sorry, haven't seen her.
ARTHUR	**(Beat)** So how—
PSEUDOPODIC CREATURE	I'm a telepath. I can read your mind. And in answer to your current thought – I don't have the time to go and tie a knot in my reproductive organs.
ARTHUR	**(Embarrassed)** Ah. Hm. Sorry.
PSEUDOPODIC CREATURE	Evidently no one has explained this to you properly. Where's your ticket?
ARTHUR	**(Produces it)** Here.
PSEUDOPODIC CREATURE	She originated in Galactic Sector ZZ9 Plural Z Alpha, yes? Now check the small print on the back of the ticket.
ARTHUR	**(Reads, scanning the text)** '. . . Entities whose lifespans originate in any of the Plural Zones are advised not to travel in hyperspace and do so at their own risk. Please do not eat this ticket.' Oh.
PSEUDOPODIC CREATURE	You need to be careful, too, it could happen to you.
ARTHUR	**(Sighs)** I wish it would.

255

PSEUDOPODIC CREATURE	I know. You would like a cup of tea.
ARTHUR	**(Brightening slightly)** You have tea?
PSEUDOPODIC CREATURE	No. I was just noting the fact that you would like one. Whatever it is.
ARTHUR	Oh.
PSEUDOPODIC CREATURE	Look, in the absence of your planet, I suggest you find somewhere to come to terms with your loss. A place to stay.
ARTHUR	A hotel room—
PSEUDOPODIC CREATURE	Good grief, not here! Not if you value your sanity. No . . . *but* your luck's in because I'm also Resettlement Officer. So. What sort of thing are you looking for?
ARTHUR	Erm . . . before we start, are you likely to suggest a place called Stavromula Beta?
PSEUDOPODIC CREATURE	Something very nasty happens to you on Stavromula Beta.
ARTHUR	Yes, but how—? Ah. Right . . . um . . . I don't want to be anthropic, but I'd quite like to live somewhere where the people look vaguely like me. Sort of human.
PSEUDOPODIC CREATURE	Got any skills? A trade?
ARTHUR	Oh dear. Not really. I came from a world which had cars and computers and ballet and Armagnac. But left to my own devices I couldn't build a toaster. I can just about make a sandwich and that's it. I finance my travel by donating to tissue banks. It's amazing there's this much of me left, frankly.
PSEUDOPODIC CREATURE	Right . . . simple culture, low unemployment, picnic food . . . try this.
	FX: Brochure slapped onto desk.
ARTHUR	**(Reads)** Bartledan?
PSEUDOPODIC CREATURE	It's got oxygen. It's got green hills. It's got sliced bread. And the people look like you.
ARTHUR	Looks a bit boring.

PSEUDOPODIC CREATURE	Sorry, I was going by appearances. Look, there's a whole Galaxy of stuff out there. Think about it.
ARTHUR	I know, I do . . . the trouble is that this particular incarnation of the Galaxy seems to lack two things: the world I was born on and the woman I love. Actually, what I really need is, well . . . guidance and advice. I did look them up on *The Hitchhiker's Guide to the Galaxy*. Under 'guidance' it said 'See under ADVICE'. Under 'advice' it said 'See under GUIDANCE'. It's been doing a lot of that kind of stuff recently.
PSEUDOPODIC CREATURE	Why don't you try Hawalius? It's populated entirely by oracles and soothsayers – and has really *excellent* bathroom facilities. Could be just what you're looking for. Brochure?
ARTHUR	**(Half-heartedly)** Mm . . . thanks.
PSEUDOPODIC CREATURE	I'm sorry this was the wrong planet. Really I am. **(Going)** Eat and buy.
ARTHUR	Oh it's the right planet all right. Right planet, wrong universe . . .

INT. – COLD AMBIENCE

VOICE OF THE BIRD	**(Icy whispery feel)** Anything that, in happening, causes something else to happen, causes something else to happen.

INT. – THE BOOK AMBIENCE

THE VOICE	*The Hitchhiker's Guide to the Galaxy* has, in what we laughingly call the past, had a great deal to say on the subject of parallel universes. Very little of this is, however, at all comprehensible to anyone below the level of Advanced God, and since it is now well established that all known gods came into existence a good three millionths of a second after the Universe began rather than, as they usually claimed, the previous week, they already have a great deal of explaining to do as it is, and are therefore not available for comment on matters of deep physics at this time.

The first thing to realize about parallel universes, the *Guide* says, is that they are not parallel.

Neither are they, strictly speaking, universes either.

Any given universe is not actually a *thing* as such, but just a way of looking at what is technically known as the WSOGMM, or Whole Sort of General Mish Mash. The Whole Sort of General Mish Mash doesn't actually exist either, but is the sum total of all the different ways there would be of looking at it if it did. You can slice the Whole Sort of General Mish Mash any way you like and you will generally come up with something that someone will call home.

There is, for example, the Earth that Arthur Dent grew up on. The Earth where he once met a girl called Tricia McMillan at a party in Islington and had her snatched away by Zaphod Beeblebrox, a tall man with very broad shoulders, on each of which was a head, one perfectly visible, the other camouflaged under a birdcage with a tea towel flung over it.

INT. – PARTY IN ISLINGTON

Music: Suitably disco.

FX: Rowdy chatter. Muffled snoring from Zaphod's hidden head.

ZAPHOD	Hold the phone! This is a face in a million . . . does perfection have another name?
TRILLIAN	(Rather interested) Tricia. McMillan . . .
ZAPHOD	Tricia. McMillion . . . Billion . . . Trillian . . . Kid – if I followed you home, would you keep me?
TRILLIAN	(Prepared to flirt) Mm. I'd rather go somewhere new . . .
ZAPHOD	You want Excitement? Adventure? Really Wild Things?
TRILLIAN	. . . What do you have in mind?
ZAPHOD	Twice as much as the other guy. Because when Zarquon made you, baby, he made a laser beam.
TRILLIAN	He did?
ZAPHOD	He did. And he set you on 'stun'! Freeeow! I'd grow back my third arm for you!
TRILLIAN	Oooh!
ZAPHOD	Baby, you make me see stars! How about I show you some planets?
TRILLIAN	(Playful) Hey, I've got a doctorate in astrophysics – be careful what you promise.
ZAPHOD	It's nothing I can't deliver, angel lips. What say we make like Allosimanian polar bears and Break the Ice.
TRILLIAN	Will I need to get my bag?
ZAPHOD	Nah. We gotta go before you have to be back in heaven.

ZAPHOD   Eddie – beam us up!

EDDIE   If you're in the mood, two-headed dude.

FX: Transporter.

TRILLIAN   (Swept away) Oooh . . . !

THE VOICE   That particular Earth was demolished by the Vogons as part of an inter-galactic traffic-calming initiative, and Arthur and Tricia – or Trillian – were the only human survivors. After several adventures that particular Trillian became a successful intergalactic reporter for the *Siderial Daily Mentioner*.

However, on yet another parallel Earth in the Whole Sort of General Mish Mash, a blonder, more American-sounding Tricia McMillan *utterly failed* to get off with Zaphod Beeblebrox at a party in Islington. The precise connection between that event and the fact that Tricia McMillan's particular Earth did not get demolished by the Vogons is currently sitting at number 4,763,984,132 on the research project priority list at what was once the History Department of the University of Maximegalon, and no one currently at the prayer meeting by the poolside appears to feel any sense of urgency about it. However, like her parallel intergalactic travelling counterpart, 'Trillian', the Earthbound Tricia McMillan became a reporter. In the process she learnt two things: One was that as a scientist working in the popular arts, you can make a lot of money covering some very dumb subjects. The other was that you should never go back for your bag.

INT. – TV STUDIO

TRICIA McMILLAN   . . . Ms Andrews, you've agreed to do this interview because you have a new astrology book out, *You And Your Stars*, the follow-up to *You And Your Black Holes*.

GAIL ANDREWS   But there's no such thing as a free launch, right?

TRICIA McMILLAN   Er – no . . . quite. Now – putting aside your relationship with the White House for the moment, let's talk about your area of so-called expertise. Last week astronomers announced that there's a tenth planet, discovered out beyond the orbit of Pluto. 'Persephone'.

GAIL ANDREWS   'Rupert'. They've nicknamed it after some astronomer's parrot.

TRICIA McMILLAN   (Annoyed at the diversion) Yes – but that must put your astrology calculations out, mustn't it? Maybe you knew what happened when Neptune was in Virgo, but what happens now Rupert is rising?

GAIL ANDREWS	It doesn't change the essential movement of the planets. Whatever influences it has had on events are already factored in.
TRICIA McMILLAN	If you'd known about Rupert three years ago, might the President be eating boysenberry flavour ice cream on Thursdays rather than Fridays?
	FX: This whole conversation switches to distort around here, as if being viewed on a very very dodgy old TV set . . . Or from millions of miles away:
GAIL ANDREWS	Miss McMillan, I'm aware that you have a degree in physics and—
TRICIA McMILLAN	**(Getting edgy)** Astrophysics.
GAIL ANDREWS	—and I can assure you my services as the astrologer to the President were purely on a personal level.
TRICIA McMILLAN	Admit it, Gail. Astrology is just popular entertainment, and you've done well out of it.
GAIL ANDREWS	In a manner of speaking.
TRICIA McMILLAN	But it's not a science! Not unless you apply rigorous scientific methodology to it!
	FX: TV switch-off.
GREBULON LEADER	This is most interesting. It may help solve our problem. Could be just the answer we Grebulons have been looking for.
GREBULON LIEUTENANT	Could it?
GREBULON LEADER	Of course it could! I think. Which one are you?
GREBULON LIEUTENANT	I don't know. You must be my superior. You're shouting.
GREBULON LEADER	I am taller. Does that count?
GREBULON LIEUTENANT	How should I know?
GREBULON LEADER	We have found much to monitor from the Third Planet called Earth. It has provided some interesting information.
GREBULON LIEUTENANT	Yes. All New York police lieutenants are fat and bald and suck lollipops. It is a mistake to give a glove-puppet bear a water pistol. And the Teletubbies are very picky eaters.
GREBULON LEADER	More than that. We have learnt that we are stranded on Persephone, the Tenth Planet popularly called Rupert, and that events here are influenced by the movement of the planets around this sun. And I have had an idea.
GREBULON LIEUTENANT	So you *are* in charge?

EXT. – NEW YORK STREETS, UNDER:

FX: Rain/street atmos. Taxi stops. Tricia gets in.

TRICIA McMILLAN   Club Alpha.

THE VOICE   One of the extraordinary things about life is the sort of places it's prepared to put up with living. Anywhere it can get some kind of a grip, whether it's the intoxicating seas of Santraginus V, where the fish never seem to care whatever the heck kind of direction they swim in, the fire storms of Frastra where, they say, life begins at 40,000 degrees, or just burrowing around in the lower intestine of a rat for the sheer unadulterated hell of it, life will always find a way of hanging on in somewhere.

It will even live in New York, though that's hard to know why. Some of the things that live in the lower intestines of rats would disagree, but when it's autumn in New York, the air smells as if someone's been frying goats in it, and if you are keen to breathe, the best plan is to open a window and stick your head in a building.

INT. – ALPHA CLUB, NEW YORK

RECEPTIONIST   Ms McMillan, welcome to Alpha. Ms Andrews is waiting for you.

TRICIA McMILLAN   **(Moving off)** Thank you. Stavro not here today?

RECEPTIONIST   **(Calling after her)** He's in London, the new club opens there next week.

TRICIA McMILLAN   **(Off, calls)** You mean I can crawl home after a night out without having to endure business class?

RECEPTIONIST   **(Calls)** Better believe it.

FX: Club bar, under:

TRICIA McMILLAN   **(Moving on)** Ms Andrews? I got your note. You were upset about something in the interview . . .

GAIL ANDREWS   Excuse me?

TRICIA McMILLAN   The note said 'Meet me at Club Alpha. Not happy. Gail Andrews.'

GAIL ANDREWS   I was really happy with the interview.

TRICIA McMILLAN   What?

GAIL ANDREWS   Of course astrology isn't a science. It's just a set of rules like chess or tennis or . . . what's that thing the British have?

TRICIA McMILLAN   Er – self-loathing?

GAIL ANDREWS	Parliamentary democracy. The rules just kind of got there. Astrology rules use stars and planets as a way of thinking about a problem, which lets a shape emerge.
TRICIA McMILLAN	Ms Andrews – Gail—
GAIL ANDREWS	When you got so emotionally focused on stars and planets this morning, it seemed to me you weren't steamed about astrology, but about actual stars and planets. So I asked you here to see if you were OK.
TRICIA McMILLAN	Oh.
GAIL ANDREWS	There's something in your past that still upsets you. About astronomy . . . ?
TRICIA McMILLAN	I – I made a decision once. I'm not sure it was the right one.
GAIL ANDREWS	Who is? Every moment of every day. Every decision we make opens some doors and closes others.
TRICIA McMILLAN	Quite a few years ago I met a guy at a party. He said he was from another planet.
GAIL ANDREWS	OK.
TRICIA McMILLAN	And did I want to go there with him. I think he had two heads.
GAIL ANDREWS	Two heads?
TRICIA McMILLAN	It was that kind of party. One was disguised as a parrot in a cage. Covered up. It was asleep, I think.
GAIL ANDREWS	Right . . .

INT. – PARTY IN ISLINGTON

Music: Suitably disco.

FX: Rowdy chatter.

TRICIA McMILLAN	**(Playful)** Hey, I've got a doctorate in astrophysics – be careful what you promise me.
ZAPHOD	It's nothing I can't deliver, angel boobs. Let's go before you're wanted back in heaven.
TRICIA McMILLAN	I'll need my bag . . .
ZAPHOD	Nah, I'm on a meter. Let's just rearrange the alphabet and put 'U' and 'I' together—
TRICIA McMILLAN	I'll get the bag. **(Moves off)** Really, I won't be a minute—

262

ZAPHOD	Nothing personal, sweetlips, but a minute was I all I had. Ciao . . .
	FX: Communicator beep.
ZAPHOD	(Sighs) Beam me up, Eddie . . .
EDDIE THE COMPUTER	(Distorted) Whatever you say, El Presidente.
	FX: Transporter.

INT. – ALPHA CLUB, NEW YORK

TRICIA McMILLAN	. . . Now although it was that kind of a party, I know he wasn't of this world. And hardly a moment goes by that I don't wonder about Some Other Me. A me that *didn't* go back for her bag. I feel like she's out there somewhere and I'm – I don't know – walking in her shadow.
GAIL ANDREWS	Are you married, Tricia?
TRICIA McMILLAN	I came close a few times. Mostly because I wanted to have a kid. But every guy ended up asking why I was constantly looking over his shoulder. At one point I even thought I might just go to a sperm bank and have somebody's child at random. But I never went and found out for real. That's why I gave up astrophysics and went into television. Nothing is real.
GAIL ANDREWS	Something else is wrong, isn't it?
TRICIA McMILLAN	Gail, I didn't just come over from London to record our interview. I had another reason. NBS asked if I'd like to try for Mo Minetti's breakfast-show job.
GAIL ANDREWS	Wow! They asked you?! I heard she was leaving the show to have a baby.
TRICIA McMILLAN	Yeah, in spite of the money they were offering for her to have it *on* the show. Anyway, the car was late picking me up, and then I realized I'd left my bag in my room.
GAIL ANDREWS	But you didn't go back for it?
TRICIA McMILLAN	No. I just turned up, sat down and they ran the autocue. And I couldn't read it.
GAIL ANDREWS	Why not?
TRICIA McMILLAN	My contact lenses were in my bag. In the hotel.
GAIL ANDREWS	Oh. I'm sorry.
TRICIA McMILLAN	Don't be. Look, I'm really sorry about this morning and . . .

GAIL ANDREWS	Don't say another word.
TRICIA McMILLAN	Thanks. **(She gets up)** I want to see if I can still get tonight's red-eye back to Heathrow. **(Moves off)** Goodbye, Gail. And thanks.
GAIL ANDREWS	**(Calls)** Don't forget your bag.
TRICIA McMILLAN	**(Coming back)** There are times when you do not go back for your bag and other times when you do. I just need to figure out which.

INT. – THE BOOK AMBIENCE

THE VOICE	Thanks to modern hyperphysics it is becoming clear that the universe consists of a complex web of dimensional layers which duplicate certain levels of existence and form branches to others. Evidence for this is legion, from the way in which a long-unused phrase such as 'Total Perspective Vortex' suddenly crops up three times in as many crosswords to the fact that Zaphod Beeblebrox, having left Tricia McMillan behind at that legendary party, was, due to the vagaries of Improbability, instantly transported to the *same* party on a *different* Earth in a parallel universe where he was (a) too drunk to notice he'd just eaten the same vol-au-vent twice and (b) struck by a dark-haired girl who looked very familiar and did not need the constant accompaniment of her handbag. That same Zaphod Beeblebrox it was who, more recently, returned Arthur Dent to the planet Krikkit after the Ashes were time-travelled back to Lord's Cricket Ground, delivered Ford Prefect to the nearest planet with a pool table, amicably parted with Trillian at the *Siderial Daily Mentioner* recruiting office and is now seeking some kind of truth and reconciliation with his past. A search which has followed a trail of rapacious economic plunder from an H-shaped building on Ursa Minor to an H-shaped building on Saquo-Pilia Hensha, where a figure wearing a fast-food delivery-service uniform and two jetbike helmets carries a large insulated satchel into the reception area.

FX: *Hitchhiker* reception. Various laid-back dudes in background, under:

ZAPHOD	**(Lifting visors)** Hey, frood, this is it, right? Megadodo Publications?
RECEPTIONIST	Let's not get hung up on names, dude. Just chill and be awed, because you are standing in the home of *The Hitchhiker's Guide to the Galaxy*, the most totally remarkable book in the whole of the known Universe.
ZAPHOD	Frosty cool, bro'. Now I got a pizza delivery for uh – Zarniwoop? Double anchovy, Caesar salad, easy on the squid liver?
RECEPTIONIST	No problemo: elevator to his new office on the twenty-third floor, make a left at the water cooler, third door on the right.

ZAPHOD   (Moving off) Sure thing, my man.

          FX: Ding! Elevator bell.

LIFT   (As he goes in) Hallo. I am to be your Sirius Cybernetics Corporation Happy Vertical People Transporter to—

ZAPHOD   (Enters, businesslike) Twenty-third floor and step on it, meat crate.

LIFT   Stepping with pleasure . . .

          FX: Elevator doors shut. Immediately the laid-back vibe evaporates.

          FX: Security robots appear and zip about.

SECURITY ROBOTS   (Distorted, zooming about) Reception Area Code Blue. Go back to your posts. Return all flared jeans, kaftans and wigs to costume storage. This is not a drill. Have your sleeves rolled for barcode scan and your expenses itemized.

          FX: Intercom buzz.

RECEPTIONIST   (Cold) Mr Vann Harl? Reception. He's on his way up. Two heads, three arms. It's your boy, all right.

VANN HARL   (Distorted) Thank you.

          INT. – VANN HARL'S OFFICE

VANN HARL   Have the accounts mainframe booted up and alert security. Remind them to bring an extra half-pair of handcuffs.

RECEPTIONIST   (Distorted) Yes, sir.

          FX: Door knock, opens and closes, under:

VANN HARL   It's open, Zaphod.

ZAPHOD   (Entering) Hah. Do all four of my eyes deceive me? I think not. Not this time – *Zarniwoop*.

          FX: Zap gun cocked.

VANN HARL   Ten out of ten for observation. Why don't you holster the zap gun, put down your pizza and I'll pour us a drink.

          FX: Gun holstered, pizza box opened, under:

ZAPHOD   Make that two. I've waited a long long time to find out what's been going on. And I'll need to be very very drunk to understand it.

          FX: Drinks poured, under:

VANN HARL	Zaphod, that's the only way you could understand it.
ZAPHOD	**(Eating pizza)** And this is a very spicy pizza. It's going to take a lot of washing down. I'd offer you some but I kinda hate to share. Cheers.
VANN HARL	Cheers . . . or should I say in your case, 'chin chin'?
ZAPHOD	**(Sprays out mouthful of Gargle Blaster)**

INT. – COLD AMBIENCE

VOICE OF THE BIRD	**(Icy whispery feel)** Anything that, in happening, causes itself to happen again, happens again.
	Though not necessarily in chronological order . . .

INT. – THE BOOK AMBIENCE

THE VOICE	*The Hitchhiker's Guide to the Galaxy*, when pressed, locates the planet Hawalius far out on the Eastern Rim of the Galaxy. It is highly renowned for its abundance of oracles, seers and soothsayers. It is also highly renowned for its fast-food franchises, because most mystics are utterly incapable of cooking for themselves. If you land on Hawalius and pick up one of its tourist brochures that drift like snow in the litter-strewn corners of its spaceport, you will find it witters on about the ancient mystical arts of the seers and sages of Hawalius, while wildly over-representing the level of accommodation available. In fact the generally uncared-for condition of its biggest town suggests that some sort of calamity has befallen it.

EXT. – STREET – VILLAGE OF THE PROPHETS

FX: Distant wailing, prophets intoning, a generally new-age biblical thing going on . . . But despondently.

FX: Hammering of boards onto a window. Stops, under:

ARTHUR	**(Approach)** Excuse me . . . um – why are you boarding up your shop?
PROPHET	**(Stops hammering)** Going out of business. No call for us prophets any more. **(Starts hammering again)**
ARTHUR	**(Sotto)** Hope it didn't take you by surprise . . . Why's that?
PROPHET	**(Stops hammering, sighs)** Hold the end of this plank and I'll show you.
ARTHUR	**(Doing so)** Right-oh.

	FX: Door.
PROPHET	(Disappears into shop) Where are you, where are you? Ah. (Re-appears) Here.
	FX: Tuning, between each example:
ARTHUR	A Sub-Etha video?
PROPHET	Well, it's not a toaster. Watch this.
NEWSREADER	(Distorted) . . . be confirmed. In a speech he will give tomorrow the Vice-President of Poffla Vigus, Roopy Ga Stip, will announce that he intends to run for President. He will also—
PROPHET	And this—
NEWSREADER 3	. . . denied it categorically. Next month's Royal Wedding between Prince Gid of the Soofling Dynasty and Princess Hooli of Raui Alpha will be the most spectacular ceremony yet witnessed in the Bjanjy Territories. Our reporter, Trillian Astra, sends us this report.
	FX: Cheering crowd, tinnily, on radio, under:
ARTHUR	Good grief – Trillian?
TRILLIAN	(Distorted) Well, Krart, the scene here in the middle of next month is absolutely incredible. Princess Hooli is looking radiant in an off-the-nipple smock with gold tassels—
	FX: Click. Sub-Etha video off.
PROPHET	See what we have to contend with?
ARTHUR	I was watching that.
PROPHET	You and everyone else. That's why this place is like a ghost town. Every vid reporter is a prophet now. Quick bit of time travel, quick hop across dimensions, there it is. The future, the past, several versions of someone you know—
ARTHUR	Yes, that's what I mean, that was someone I know.
PROPHET	Princess Hooli? If I had to stand around saying hello to everybody who's known Princess Hooli I'd need a new set of lungs.
ARTHUR	No, the reporter. Her name's Trillian. I don't know where she got the Astra from. She's from the same planet as me. I wondered where she'd got to.
PROPHET	Oh, she's wall-to-wall over the continuum these days, gallivanting here and there through space-time. She wants to settle down and find herself a nice steady era, that young lady does.

267

ARTHUR	Is she, erm – always dark-haired?
PROPHET	Oh, I don't watch this stuff, thank the Great Green Arkleseizure.
ARTHUR	No, of course not . . . it's just that I have seen a Trillian – Tricia McMillan – blonde. And sort of American. On Earth, where I came from. But in another dimension. Possibly.
PROPHET	That's what I was just saying! Look, I'm not here to sort out your dimensional issues, I'm busy going out of business. For what it's worth – here's a bit of free guidance. **(Intones portentously)** 'It'll all end in tears. Probably already has.' **(Normal again)** All right? Now hold the plank steady while I nail it.
	FX: Two nail strikes then soggy crunchy thud of hammer hitting thumb. The prophet audibly heard turning purple, then . . .
ARTHUR	Are you all right?
PROPHET	**(Low but in enormous pain)** I – suggest – you – trot along now – . . . I may need to speak in tongues for a few minutes . . . please—
ARTHUR	Oh . . . all right, then.
PROPHET	**(Fading in background)** Try that cave over there . . . that's only a suggestion, mind, not formal oracular advice . . .
ARTHUR	**(Walking off)** Thank you . . . Bye . . .
PROPHET	**(Distant HUGE scream)** Ffuhhhh . . . !! **(Cuts)**

INT. – THE BOOK AMBIENCE

THE VOICE	The days are long gone when the *Hitchhiker's Guide to the Galaxy* Building was the third hippest place to be in the whole of Ursa Minor, as its offices are often shifted at very short notice, from planet to planet, for reasons of local climate, hostility, power bills or tax. They are always reconstructed precisely the same way, as for many of the company's employees the lay-out of their offices represent the only constant they know in a distorted personal universe. Unless you have your own personal universe inside your office, of course. The *Hitchhiker's Guide* Building is currently located in the city of Antwelm on the world known as Saquo-Pilia Hensha. Ford Prefect has entered it in his usual way – via the ventilation system rather than the main lobby, because the main lobby is no longer peopled by real people with unkempt hair and a relaxed attitude to footwear, but patrolled by melon-sized flying security robots whose job it is to quiz incoming employees about their expense accounts. Ford Prefect's expense accounts are notoriously complex and difficult affairs and he has found, on the whole, that the lobby

robots do not fully comprehend his understated approach to book-keeping. He prefers, therefore, to make his entrance via the ventilation shafts leading to the building's higher floors . . .

FORD   (Big effort) Mmmmggggrrrhhhhhh!

FX: Crash of ventilation-shaft grille. Alarms.

FX: Ford drops to ground clumsily.

FORD PREFECT   Holy Belgium! I swear they've been saving money by rebuilding the floors lower.

FX: He limps up the corridor painfully, under:

THE VOICE   Ford is carrying a satchel in which he is carrying a lightweight throwing towel, a No. 3 gauge prising tool and a toy bow and arrow, bought in a street market, for reasons which will shortly become apparent.

FX: Security robot buzzes up the corridor. Alarms stop.

COLIN THE SECURITY ROBOT   (Officious, approaching) Intruder, your presence has been detected. Have your sleeves rolled for barcode scan and your expenses ready for inspection. Do not attempt to run. Do not attempt to offer bribes. (This runs under:)

FX: Toy bow and arrow effects to match:

FORD PREFECT   (Sotto) Lick the suction cup . . . aim . . . and – if its movement sensors are the usual Sirius Cybernetics garbage—

FX: Twang! Arrow hits opposite wall with wet splat.

COLIN THE SECURITY ROBOT   (Turning to follow it) I detect your movement! Do not attempt to run! Empty your pockets!

FX: Towel, under:

FORD PREFECT   (Stealthily) Robot diverted – aim towel – *urf!*

FX: Towel flung over robot.

COLIN THE SECURITY ROBOT   (Muffled) Emergency! Emergency! Third-party vision-circuit impairment!

FORD PREFECT   (Grabbing it) Grab the 'bot—

COLIN THE SECURITY ROBOT   (More muffled, indistinct but pitiful whining) Mffmnnf . . . nnff . . . Mnmnmfff . . .

FORD PREFECT   (Wrestling with it) Prising tool . . . power switch off—

FX: Robot powers down.

FORD PREFECT	Logic circuit cover—

FX: Ford working on robot, under:

THE VOICE	Logic is a wonderful thing but it has certain drawbacks.

Anything that thinks logically can be fooled by something else which thinks at least as logically as it does. The easiest way to fool, say, a completely logical robot is best demonstrated by the famous Herring Sandwich experiments conducted millennia ago at MISPWOSO (The Maximegalon Institute of Slowly and Painfully Working Out the Surprisingly Obvious).

FX: Laboratory background with suitable FX, under:

THE VOICE	A robot was programmed to believe that it liked herring sandwiches, after which, a herring sandwich was placed in front of it. Whereupon the robot said to itself—
COLIN THE SECURITY ROBOT	Ah! Herring sandwich! I like herring sandwiches!
THE VOICE	It would then tip down and scoop up the herring sandwich, in its herring-sandwich scoop, and straighten up again. Unfortunately the robot was fashioned in such a way that the action of straightening up caused the herring sandwich to slip off its scoop and fall onto the floor. Whereupon the robot thought to itself—
COLIN THE SECURITY ROBOT	Ah! Herring sandwich! I like herring sandwiches!
THE VOICE	—and repeated the loop over and over and over again. The thing that prevented the herring sandwich from crawling off in search of other ways of passing the time was that it was only *marginally* less alert to what was going on than the robot.

The scientists at the Institute thus discovered the driving force behind all change, development and innovation in life, was boredom. Or rather, the practical function of boredom. In a fever of excitement they then went on to discover other emotions, like 'irritability'—

COLIN THE SECURITY ROBOT	(Irritably) Who left this herring sandwich here?!
THE VOICE	—'depression'—
COLIN THE SECURITY ROBOT	(Depressedly) If I drop that sandwich again I'm going to switch myself off (Sob) . . .
THE VOICE	—'reluctance'—

270

COLIN THE SECURITY ROBOT	(Reluctantly) This sandwich has got carpet fluff all over it . . .
THE VOICE	—'ickiness'—
COLIN THE SECURITY ROBOT	(Ickily) Urgh! It's got green stuff growing on it too!
THE VOICE	—and so on. The next big breakthrough came when they stopped using herring sandwiches, whereupon a whole welter of new emotions became suddenly available to them for study, such as 'relief', 'joy', 'friskiness', 'appetite', 'satisfaction', and most important of all, the desire for 'happiness'. This was the biggest breakthrough of all. Now all that robots needed was the capacity to be either bored or happy. They would then work the rest out for themselves.
	The robot which Ford has trapped under his towel is a logical, if momentarily unhappy, robot. It is happy when it can move about. It is happy when it can see other things. It is particularly happy when it can see other things moving about, particularly if they are doing things they shouldn't do, because it could then, with considerable delight, report them.
	But Ford will soon fix that. His logic is that by reconfiguring its logic circuit, he will have a robot that is logically – and ecstatically – happy to help him do things he really shouldn't do.
	FX: Final click. Robot powers up again with a trill of joy.
FORD PREFECT	Power on. Towel off.
COLIN THE SECURITY ROBOT	Mr Prefect, sir! I'm so happy to see you!
FORD PREFECT	Good to see you too, little fella.
COLIN THE SECURITY ROBOT	My fulfilment is uncontained at your return! I am so happy I could clear all your expenses without requiring adequate proofs of purchase!
FORD PREFECT	Don't let me stop you.
COLIN THE SECURITY ROBOT	(Sadly) Such clearance is restricted to the Editor. Or the accounts computers.
FORD PREFECT	Well, if the editor won't clear them – trust me, he won't – we'll try the computer.
COLIN THE SECURITY ROBOT	Ooh goody goody. Where shall we start?
FORD PREFECT	Here, with you telling me what's going on.

COLIN THE SECURITY ROBOT	Oh, just the nicest of all possible things. May I sit on your lap?
FORD PREFECT	**(Yell)** No!
COLIN THE SECURITY ROBOT	Oh, I am overjoyed to be spurned like this! Especially when you shout at me. Spurn me again, please.
FORD PREFECT	Listen. Something's changed, hasn't it? Something big.
COLIN THE SECURITY ROBOT	Oh yes, in the most fabulous and wonderful way. I feel so good about it. It was scrumptious before, but now it's yummilicious! Please shout at me again, go on.
FORD PREFECT	**(Shouts)** Just tell me what's happened!
COLIN THE SECURITY ROBOT	Oh thank you, thank you! **(Spins around, burbling)**
FORD PREFECT	**(Sighs)** Please.
COLIN THE SECURITY ROBOT	The *Guide* has been taken over. There's a wonderful new management.
FORD PREFECT	What new management? When? . . . Never mind. Does that door still lead to the Editor's office?
COLIN THE SECURITY ROBOT	Why yes! It's all so gorgeous I could just melt!
FORD PREFECT	Look, be quiet, will you, erm – what's your name?
COLIN THE SECURITY ROBOT	Part number 223219P Re-order code: SecBot Rev B. Froody, or what?
FORD PREFECT	No. What would be a good name for you . . . ? Emily Saunders! No. No . . . Her dog. Perfect. So, Colin—
COLIN THE SECURITY ROBOT	I am Colin! Colin the Security Robot called Colin – after a dog! Woof Woof! Guard guard!
FORD PREFECT	Colin, shut up. There's a battery of laser guns linked to scanners in that door frame. It's meant to catch anyone entering who isn't carrying pages of fresh copy. Like me.
COLIN THE SECURITY ROBOT	But – exciting, isn't it . . .
FORD PREFECT	So you're going to draw the laser fire while I break through the door and tuck-and-roll behind the drinks trolley. Then I'll be on my knees by his desk

and in a perfect position to open negotiations. Now I may have to cry a bit, but you mustn't worry, that's just the grovelling phase of the negotiations.

COLIN THE SECURITY ROBOT   But—

FORD PREFECT   Ready? After three.

COLIN THE SECURITY ROBOT   But—

FORD PREFECT   Three! Whoaaaargh . . .

FX: He runs at the door, smashes it down, rolls across the room with a series of thumps.

INT. – VANN HARL'S OFFICE

FX: Bits of door frame dropping on the floor . . . A pause of some length.

VANN HARL   . . . Ford Prefect, I presume.

INT. – THE BOOK AMBIENCE

THE VOICE   Will even a grovelling phase in negotiations cut any ice with Mr Zarniwoop Vann Harl? What has happened to Zaphod Beeblebrox? And can Arthur Dent find a purpose to his life, let alone the universe and everything? Parallel zones of enlightenment await in the next temporal layer of *The Hitchhiker's Guide to the Galaxy*.

ANNOUNCER   Listeners are reminded not to try and reprogram Sirius Cybernetics Security Bots at home. They contain no user-serviceable parts and tampering with their security fasteners will invalidate the warranty.

FOOTNOTES

Meteorite damage   The opening of *Mostly Harmless* tells in great detail the story of how the Grebulons' mortally wounded battle cruiser arrives in our solar system. It is a very clever, very involved piece of imaginative writing, following in microcosm the path of a piece of information as it reroutes itself through a damaged computer intranet, a tiny, inconsequential train of logic that will lead to a macrocosmic, consequential, illogical outcome. This adapted version sadly does away with much of the detail; but more in the case of *Mostly Harmless* than *Life, the Universe* or *So Long, and Thanks*, there are sections of the book which simply could not be fitted inside four approximate half-hours, and also large stretches of descriptive monologue which were best avoided if the story was to move on in the style of the radio *Hitchhiker's* stories. For example from later in the book there was no room to do justice to the story of the Great Ventilation and Telephone Riots of SrDt 3454, and with great reluctance it had to be left out altogether.

Mostly Harmless is not an easy read for its first few chapters and many people – close relatives of Douglas included – have found it hard to begin, let alone finish. As we know, Douglas wrote it under considerable pressure, but he never sat at a keyboard without considerable creative purpose, and a patient read quickly pays dividends. This last *Hitchhiker's* novel represents Douglas's predictive imagination at its most ambitious. He is determined to challenge his characters and the reader to keep up with a switchback ride of parallel plots. To cap all of this at the climax comes the sudden, shuddering halt which is the end of the book – and apparently the end of the entire saga.

Some readers resent the story's ending, as if Douglas was acting out of some strange authorial spite, but read the book again in the light of its subplot concerning multiple universes and, even with all the Earths along the Probability Axis apparently destroyed, the brave twist in its tail can be read as comedically ironic, not tragically cataclysmic. Douglas is not petulantly kicking over the toy box; he is quietly waiting for his more shrewd readers to work out for themselves that something bigger is going on than the intrigues of the Vogons have taken into account. In fact he leaves himself considerable wiggle room for a further book about Arthur, Ford and Co., and the fact that he did not find time to write it is the only truly tragic part of the story.

Arthur on NowWhat

An amalgam of two different scenes in the book, folding in quite a lot of linking exposition. Following hard on the heels of the Quandary Phase and with Fenchurch's loss still fresh in our minds, Arthur cannot just be seen to give up the search for his lost love, which is not *actually* the case in the book, but on a superficial level the memory of Fenchurch does seem to get pretty short shrift.

This scene incorporates the only mention in this version of *Mostly Harmless* of Bartledan, a deeply dull world upon which Arthur spends an unfulfilling sojourn, on the grounds that it risked being a deeply dull scene and there was a lot more exciting stuff vying for the time available.

Making the Pseudopodic Creature telepathic was a great ruse to avoid telling Arthur's backstory in what would have been a very boring Q&A exchange.

Zaphod and the Trillians

In terms of the radio saga this is where the whole parallel-universe scenario begins to unfold, at risk to everyone's sanity. Luckily we had two 'original' Trillians to play the same part – Susan Sheridan (from the original radio series) and Sandra Dickinson (from the BBC TV series).

Radio is as visual a storytelling medium as film and a long way ahead of television. It is limited only by imagination and not by budget. In my time I have made people fly, levelled cities, collapsed entire civilizations and generally screwed about with the Whole General Sort of Mish Mash in irresponsible but fairly convincing ways, drunk on the power that comes with sneaking into people's heads via the side door, bypassing the boring old optic nerve altogether.

However.

There are two Absolute Pigs to dramatically depict on radio. One is invisibility. Once a character has turned invisible, it is the devil's own job to keep reminding the audience of their transparent condition without writing clunky reminders forever more. 'I shall now turn myself invisible' followed by a sort of squelchy pop is all very well, but then ensuing conversations have to be studded with gems like 'If you could see me now, which of course you cannot' and suchlike. The other Absolute Pig to communicate in sound only is the idea of a doppelgänger or clone. In the end context is the key, and one must try to remind the listener that a certain character is living alongside herself in the reality being depicted, without repeatedly clubbing them over the head with it. Thus two Trillians speaking in two very different voices, indeed accents, helps maintain the vital plot points in a simple way – and we benefited by having two superb actresses for the part of one (though the price of both).

Incidentally this was the scene which 'fixed' the issue created by John Langdon's very funny Tertiary Phase insertion about Zaphod in school, 'It was always the same three hands going up'. It immediately attracted comment upon broadcast (Zaphod grew that third arm specifically for Trillian, according to the Primary Phase). So here, upon meeting Trillian for the first time, he announces, 'I'd grow back my third arm for you.' Phew.

You and your black holes

When Sir Patrick Moore heard that astrology was one of the themes of *Mostly Harmless* he revealed that he himself had just written a book on the subject (*Stars of Destiny*, Canopus, 2005). I was astonished, knowing Patrick's views on astrology were pretty short and to the point. He solemnly presented me with a copy, pointing to a section in the back of the book which contained star diagrams and his idea of the astrological figures they represent. Thus joining the dots of the stars Spica, Heze, Zavijava and so on in Patrick's version, one arrives not so much at a drawing of Virgo as of a Chamber Pot . . .

Zaphod delivers the pizza

This is the first wholly original stretch of the story; it is not in the book, but the threads of previous adventures – particularly the Secondary Phase – here begin to be gathered. Vann Harl in *Mostly Harmless* is a shiny-suited business creep, and frankly it wasn't too big a stretch to equate that persona with the slippery and vaguely Machiavellian Zarniwoop of yesteryear. When Jonathan Pryce said he was very keen to rejoin the cast of *Hitchhiker's* for a last hurrah, serendipitous vibrations filled the ether.

This scene was enormous fun to write and direct. Zaphod is sorely missed in these last two books; given his new sense of purpose at the end of the Tertiary Phase it seemed logical he – more than anybody – would feel irked at the apparent disappearance of a huge chunk of his past, and go in search of it. The pleasure of having Mark back in the studio was doubled in this scene with Jonathan. There was a good deal of banter and quite a bit of pretend microphone hogging. Actually maybe it wasn't pretend . . .

Just as much fun was had depicting the *Hitchhiker's Guide* reception area both as it once was and how it has now become; from the laid back dudes of history to the barcoded quota-observing automata serving the new *Guide*. Bit like the difference between the 70s and the 00s, really.

The Hawaiian Prophet Not, strictly speaking, vital to plot, apart from establishing Trillian Astra (Sue) as a successful reporter, but too good to miss out, especially with an actor of John Challis's calibre playing the Prophet Who Hammered His Thumb.

Ford and Colin The most technically challenging scenes we did in all the last three phases.

With Marvin in earlier episodes we had established the idea of feeding Stephen's voice, treated, through a small speaker in the studio which could then be carried around by either me or Ken Humphrey. Thus Marvin could interact in real time and real space with the other members of the cast as they played the scene. The result works particularly well through headphones because the spatial relationships picked up by the stereo microphone are very accurate and give one a sense of depth and width to the sound stage. With appropriate sound effects Marvin is right there moving around with the others.

With these Colin and Ford scenes, Paul Deeley and I consciously upped the ante by setting up *two* stereo microphones mounted back-to-back, creating a 360° acting area which would occupy exactly the same space for the listener when played back in 5.1 surround (somehow it seems to provide a pretty nifty 'ghost image' in stereo too).

The idea was to directly convey the presence of a melon-sized flying robot and an actor with a particularly fine set of lower front teeth moving in three-dimensional space.

Trying to add the robot's whirrings and geographically plot them in post-production would be too time consuming for the schedule, so to achieve this in one 'hit', we would need to feed through the portable speaker Colin's voice – suitably treated – plus some kind of machine effect, changing pitch and timbre to suggest the robot manoeuvring or under strain, or moving at high speed, all in three dimensions.

Ideally someone with a superb instinct for sound and the real-time physics of the scene could provide a sympathetic 'live' performance of Colin's antigravity motors alongside the actors. This someone proved to be Paul Weir, introduced to us by the redoubtable Robbie Stamp.

Paul is a musician and sound designer of daunting ability and with a great enthusiasm for *Hitchhiker's*. He shares Douglas's fascination with gadgetry and provided some additional sound effects for the movie. Now he very kindly agreed to come in and supply and perform a Colin motor effect for us. The result perfectly complemented Andy Secombe's very funny vocal gymnastics as Colin.

The suggestion to Andy regarding Colin's persona was that the voice might be inspired by the historian David Starkey (at his most waspish) before Ford's 'adjustment', and be a bit more 'Priscilla, Queen of the Desert' afterwards, and the way he ran with that idea was very funny.

EPISODE TWO

SIGNATURE TUNE

ANNOUNCER   *The Hitchhiker's Guide to the Galaxy*, by Douglas Adams, Quintessential Phase.

Sig fades.

INT. – THE BOOK AMBIENCE

THE VOICE   The problem of being born on a world in a Plural Zone never occurred to Arthur Dent during his confusing days aboard the *Heart of Gold*, his lonely nights on prehistoric Earth or even the embarrassed silences following his fumbled catches on the playing fields of Krikkit. Indeed, the idea that the universe could consist of more than one reality was beyond his slightest imagining. For years he blindly assumed that the one and only planet Earth was destroyed by the Vogons, and that *that* was – in all senses of the word – that. But then, seemingly for no reason at all, not even in response to an acute attack of allergic rhinitis by the Great Green Arkleseizure itself, another Earth flicked into existence, to replace the demolished one. And, upon that new Earth, Arthur met and fell in love with a troubled girl called Fenchurch, who he subsequently lost during a routine hyperspace jump. Now, in search of any kind of meaning, Arthur has arrived upon the planet Hawalion in the Eastern Rim of the Galaxy, where a tourist brochure promises 'guidance by prophets and seers'. Of course he could just throw away the brochure and consult his copy of *The Hitchhiker's Guide to the Galaxy*, but he has been finding that becoming increasingly abstruse and paranoid and—

FX: Pop!

Music: Something floaty but unsettling under:

VOICE OF THE BIRD   This pop-up is brought to you by Infinidim Enterprises. Click here for vital *Hitchhiker's Guide Pro* update information—

FX: Pop (but backwards . . . which is . . . Pop).

INT. – THE BOOK AMBIENCE

FX: To match Arthur's actions, under:

THE VOICE —that something is wrong somewhere. Thus Arthur is even less inclined than usual to trust his *Hitchhiker's Guide*, which means that at this parallel of the narrative, he mostly uses it for eating his sandwiches off.

EXT. – HAWALION

FX: Huge flies buzzing. Pot bubbling.

FX: In foreground, Smelly Photocopier Woman is swatting flies.

SMELLY PHOTOCOPIER WOMAN **(Effort grunts interspersed with:)** Get off! . . . bloomin' buzzin' sods . . . get your own goat carcass . . . **(Splat)** That'll learn yer! . . . Keep still, dammit . . . bloated great bluebottle . . . come 'ere . . . **(etc)**.

ARTHUR **(Approach, gagging)** Er . . . hallo? Excuse me? **(Closer, low)** Ye gods, what a stink . . .

FX: Wet farty splurgey noise.

ARTHUR Oh . . . gross . . . Excuse me, I think I've trodden in a dead goat—

SMELLY PHOTOCOPIER WOMAN Mind my bladder!

ARTHUR What—?

SMELLY PHOTOCOPIER WOMAN The goat bladder – hanging behind you, you'll—

FX: Arthur turns, collides with washing line hung with goats' bladders, gets tangled, collapses in a flurbling heap.

FX: Fresh squadrons of flies arrive, under:

SMELLY PHOTOCOPIER WOMAN Now you've disturbed the maggots, you . . . ! Hand me the table-tennis bat—

ARTHUR **(Getting up)** I'm so sorry . . .

SMELLY PHOTOCOPIER WOMAN **(Swatting)** What do you want?

ARTHUR Er, I came to ask your advice.

SMELLY PHOTOCOPIER WOMAN What about?

ARTHUR	Well, just sort of general advice, really. It said in the brochure—
SMELLY PHOTOCOPIER WOMAN	(Puts down bat) Ha! Brochure! Advice. Advice? To do with your life, that sort of thing?
ARTHUR	Yes, er . . . what *is* that smell?
SMELLY PHOTOCOPIER WOMAN	(Sniff, then breaks wind hugely) What smell?
ARTHUR	(Gagging slightly) Ah. Let me just move *up*wind of you—
SMELLY PHOTOCOPIER WOMAN	(Moving into cave) You'd better come in my cave.
ARTHUR	Um – can't we talk out here?
SMELLY PHOTOCOPIER WOMAN	(From cave) You'll have to help me with the photocopier.
ARTHUR	What?
SMELLY PHOTOCOPIER WOMAN	(Coming back out impatiently) The photocopier. You'll have to help me drag it out. I have to keep it in the cave, so the birds don't shit on it.
ARTHUR	I see.
SMELLY PHOTOCOPIER WOMAN	(Going back in to cave) I'd take a deep breath if I were you.
ARTHUR	(Moves off) Ahead of you there. (Huge breath)
	FX: Business, off – they heave the photocopier out of the cave. This brings them back onto mic.
SMELLY PHOTOCOPIER WOMAN	Right. You can breathe again now.
ARTHUR	(Gasp of fresh air) Urrrrhhhhhh . . . . !
SMELLY PHOTOCOPIER WOMAN	Right, the solar cells seem to be charged up . . .
	FX: Photocopier running, under:
SMELLY PHOTOCOPIER WOMAN	Always takes a minute or two . . . You'll be wanting some lunch?
	FX: Bubbling pot back up. Stir of spoon in it.
ARTHUR	Um – I've – um – eaten – thanks.

SMELLY PHOTOCOPIER WOMAN	I'm sure you have. **(Tastes a bit of stew)** Mmm. Not too rank. Ooh – hang on—
ARTHUR	Um – need a toothpick?
SMELLY PHOTOCOPIER WOMAN	Nah. **(Sucks teeth)** Maggoty bit. Got it, thanks.

FX: Photocopier stops.

SMELLY PHOTOCOPIER WOMAN	**(Unloads photocopier)** Ah. There you go.
ARTHUR	**(Taking sheaf of paper, riffling through it)** This is, er, this your advice, then, is it?
SMELLY PHOTOCOPIER WOMAN	No. It's the story of my life.
ARTHUR	Oh, but I—
SMELLY PHOTOCOPIER WOMAN	You see, the quality of any advice anybody has to offer can only be judged against the quality of life they actually lead. Now, as you look through this document you'll see that I've underlined all the major decisions I ever made to make them stand out. They're all indexed and cross-referenced. No need to check them now. All I can suggest is that if you take decisions that are exactly opposite to the sort of decisions that I've taken, then maybe you won't finish up at the end of your life – **(Yells in his face)** – in a smelly old cave like this!

INT. – THE BOOK AMBIENCE

THE VOICE	As Arthur Dent absorbs this self-evident truth and a blast of halitosis that would make any self-respecting Bugblatter Beast book an urgent appointment with the one surviving oral hygienist on Traal, events elsewhere move on apace. It is important here to remember that in this collision of realities there are two Tricia McMillans in Arthur's life. One – the girl he lost to Zaphod Beeblebrox at a party in Islington – is Trillian Astra, intergalactic court affairs correspondent for the *Siderial Daily Mentioner*. The other – blonder and more American – lives on the replacement Earth. She is Tricia McMillan, also a reporter. And although, in *her* particular reality, Tricia failed to leave that legendary party with Zaphod Beeblebrox, her chances of leaving the planet are about to take a belated turn for the better as she returns home from New York . . .

INT. – TRICIA'S HOUSE

FX: Futzed phone ring and pick up.

MR BARTLETT   Hallo?

TRICIA McMILLAN   (On phone) Mr Bartlett, I'm back from New York and I was expecting to find the grass cut, and you haven't touched it.

MR BARTLETT   (Distort) Well, no, I didn't want to mess up the evidence. Of the aliens.

TRICIA McMILLAN   What do you mean, aliens? Illegal immigrants?

MR BARTLETT   (Distorted) Space aliens, miss. They come down here, land on your lawn and then buzz off again, sometimes with your cat. Mrs Williams at the post office, her cat got abducted. They brought him back the next day but he were in a very odd mood. Sleeping a lot. Right off his fish.

FX: Muffled sounds of spaceship landing outside, under:

TRICIA McMILLAN   What's that got to do with cutting the grass?

MR BARTLETT   The marks on your lawn are exactly the sort that their landing pads would probably make.

TRICIA McMILLAN   Eric. Please come and cut my grass tomorrow.

MR BARTLETT   I found a three-leaf clover there, too. Not a regular one with a leaf missing, but a genuine three-leaf.

TRICIA McMILLAN   Please?

MR BARTLETT   All right. If I were you, though, I'd watch for signs of alien activity in the area. Particularly from the Henley direction.

FX: Door bell, off.

TRICIA McMILLAN   Must go, someone at the door.

FX: Phone hung up.

FX: She goes to door, opens it. Spaceship FX up.

GREBULON LIEUTENANT   McMillan? Ms Tricia McMillan?

TRICIA McMILLAN   (Awestruck) Yes . . .

GREBULON LIEUTENANT   We have been monitoring you. On TV.

TRICIA McMILLAN   M-monitoring me? How?

GREBULON LIEUTENANT	From the tenth planet from your sun. Your people call it – Rupert.
GREBULON UNDERLING	**(Beat)** You look much smaller in real life.

INT. – THE BOOK AMBIENCE

Music: Holy Lunching Friars chanting and burping . . .

THE VOICE The history of *The Hitchhiker's Guide to the Galaxy* is one of idealism, struggle, success, failure and enormously long lunch-breaks. Most of the surviving stories, however, speak of a founding editor called Hurling Frootmig, who established its fundamental principles of honesty and idealism, and went bust. There followed many years of penury and heart-searching, but then, after a chance encounter with the Holy Lunching Friars of Voondon (who claimed that just as lunch was at the centre of a man's temporal day, and man's temporal day could be seen as an analogy for his spiritual life, so lunch should (a) be seen as the centre of a man's spiritual life, and (b) be held in jolly nice restaurants), he refounded the *Guide*; laid down its fundamental principles of honesty and idealism and where you could stuff them both.

As a result the editorial lunch-break played a crucial part in the *Guide*'s history, since it meant that most of the actual work got done by whatever passing stranger happened to wander into the empty offices on an afternoon and saw something worth doing. Shortly after this, the *Guide* was taken over by Megadodo Publications, of Ursa Minor Beta, thus putting the whole thing on a very sound financial footing, which allowed the fourth editor, Lig Lury Jr, to embark on lunch-breaks of such breathtaking scope that he never formally resigned his editorship, but left his office late one morning and has never since returned. Though well over a century has since passed, *Guide* staff still retain the romantic notion that he has merely popped out for a ham croissant and will yet return to put in a solid afternoon's work.

Thus Lig's desk is still preserved the way he left it; with the addition of a small sign which says 'Lig Lury Jr, Editor, Missing, presumed Fed'. But as time has passed, Ford Prefect and the few other researchers who stayed out in the field have gradually lost touch with the corporate nightmare the *Guide* has become. The current location of the *Guide* Building is Antwelm City, on the planet of Saquo-Pilia Hensha. Its editor-in-chief, Stagyar-zil-Doggo, is a dangerously unbalanced man who takes a homicidal view of contributors turning up in his office without pages of fresh, proofed copy. Thus high level of turnover is maintained in both the Editorial and Being Resources Departments. Ford Prefect has lately arrived here, and caught, reprogrammed and renamed one of the flying security robots to help him gain access to Stagyar's office. By any means necessary.

INT. – *HITCHHIKER'S GUIDE* CORRIDOR

FORD PREFECT   Ready, Colin? After three.

COLIN THE
SECURITY ROBOT   But—

FORD PREFECT   Three!

FX: He runs at the door, smashes it down, rolls across the room with a series of thumps.

INT. – VANN HARL'S OFFICE

VANN HARL   . . . Mr Prefect, I assume.

FORD PREFECT   You're not Stagyar. **(Suspicious)** But I do know you . . .

VANN HARL   My name is Vann Harl.

COLIN THE
SECURITY ROBOT   A delightful name it is too, sir.

VANN HARL   What have you done to that security robot?

FORD PREFECT   I've made it very happy. It's a kind of mission I have. Where's Stagyar? More to the point, where's his drinks trolley?

VANN HARL   Mr zil-Doggo is no longer with us. His drinks trolley is, I imagine, helping to console him for this fact. I am your new editor-in-chief. That is, if the organization decides to retain your services.

FORD PREFECT   Organization? That word isn't usually associated with the *Guide*.

VANN HARL   Precisely our sentiments. Under-structured, over-resourced, under-managed, over-inebriated. And that was just the editor.

FORD PREFECT   Tell you what. I'll do the jokes.

VANN HARL   No. You will do the restaurant column.

FORD PREFECT   You what?

VANN HARL   No. Me Vann Harl. You Prefect. Me editor. You restaurant column. Here—

FX: Credit card dropped on desk.

FORD PREFECT   **(Impressed even for Ford)** Mother of Krikkit . . .

VANN HARL   A Dine-O-Charge card in your name. Expiry date two years from now.

FORD PREFECT	**(Awestruck)** This is the single most exciting thing I have ever seen in my life.
VANN HARL	You're drooling.
FORD PREFECT	Sorry. Colin, towel . . .
VANN HARL	Prefect. We at InfiniDim Enterprises—
FORD PREFECT	**(Dabbing)** You at what?
VANN HARL	InfiniDim Enterprises. We have taken over the *Hitchhiker's Guide*.
FORD PREFECT	Megadodo Publications is now called InfiniDim?
VANN HARL	We spent millions on that name. Start liking it or start packing. The Galaxy is changing. We've got to change with it. A new technology for a new future—
FORD PREFECT	Don't tell me about the future. I've been all over it. Spend half my time there. It's the same as anywhere else. Anywhen else. Whatever. Just the same old stuff in faster cars and smellier air.
VANN HARL	That's one future. You've got to learn to think multi-dimensionally. Limitless futures stretching out in every direction from this moment – and from this moment – and from this. Billions and billions of shining, gleaming futures! Um . . . I seem to be drooling now; can I borrow your towel?
FORD PREFECT	Here.
VANN HARL	Thanks. **(Voice up again)** Billions and billions of markets!
FORD PREFECT	I see. So you sell billions and billions of *Guides*.
VANN HARL	Try and keep up. We sell one *Guide*, billions and billions of times. We exploit the multidimensional nature of the Universe to cut manufacturing costs. And we don't sell something with a plummy pompous pedagogue lecturing to penniless hitchhikers. What kind of positioning was that? The one section of the market that, more or less by definition, didn't have any money? No! We sell a sultry Brantisvogan Escort Agency VIP vamp voice to the affluent business traveller and his vacationing wife in a billion different futures!
FORD PREFECT	And you want me to be its restaurant critic.
VANN HARL	If the quota permits.
FORD PREFECT	**(Suddenly)** Aaarrgh! Kill!
COLIN THE SECURITY ROBOT	I'd be delighted . . .

FX: Colin zooms at Vann Harl, under—

VANN HARL　Eek! Get it off me—!

FORD PREFECT　(Shocked) Colin! No!

FX: Clatter of chair toppling over. Thump of head on wall:

VANN HARL　Get it off m— (Hits head on wall behind) *Unf!*

FORD PREFECT　Er – release!

FX: Colin stops, hovering.

COLIN THE SECURITY ROBOT　Happily, he is unconscious. My circuits hum with joy! Shall I kill him as instructed?

FORD PREFECT　No. No, it was a reflex action on my part. People who use words like 'quota' trigger it. Make me shout 'Kill!'. But only rhetorically.

COLIN THE SECURITY ROBOT　(A bit disappointed) I can kill him rhetorically if you'd prefer?

FORD PREFECT　(Moving across to Harl) No. But we could just check his wallet while we're here . . . First name, Zarniwoop. Where did I come across this suit before . . . ?

FX: Ford riffles through Vann Harl's wallet, under:

FORD PREFECT　Let's see if there's a clue . . . cash . . . credit tokens . . . Ultragolf club membership . . . Photos of someone's wife and family – presumably his own, but as a busy executive he might just rent them for weekends . . . Wait a minute – Ha!

COLIN THE SECURITY ROBOT　An Ident-i-Eeze card. Can life get any better?!

INT. – THE BOOK AMBIENCE

THE VOICE　*The Hitchhiker's Guide to the Galaxy* explains the function of the Ident-i-Eeze card like this: there are so many different ways in which you are required to provide absolute proof of your identity these days that life can easily become extremely tiresome just from that factor alone. Never mind the deeper existential problems of trying to function as a coherent conscious-ness in an epistemologically ambiguous, physical universe. Just look at cashpoint machines, for instance. Queues of people standing around waiting to have their fingerprints read, their retinas scanned, bits of skin scraped from the nape of the neck and undergoing instant genetic analysis.

Hence the Ident-i-Eeze. It is smaller and a little thicker than a credit card and semi-transparent. This encodes every single piece of information about you – your body and your life – into one all-purpose, machine-readable card that you can then carry around in your wallet. Thereby representing technology's greatest triumph to date, over both itself and plain common sense.

INT. – VANN HARL'S OFFICE

COLIN THE SECURITY ROBOT
With Mr Vann Harl's card, you can access any level in the building. I think I'm going into orgasm.

FORD PREFECT
Colin. You want to stay happy?

COLIN THE SECURITY ROBOT
Ooh, yes yes, please yes . . . yes!

FORD PREFECT
Then come down from the ceiling and do everything I tell you.

COLIN THE SECURITY ROBOT
I am quite happy hovering up here, thank you. I never realized before how much sheer titillation there was to be had from a good ceiling. I'll be pleased to explore my feelings about ceilings in greater depth.

FORD PREFECT
Stay there and you'll be captured and have your condition chip replaced. So if you want to stay happy . . .

FX: Colin floats down.

COLIN THE SECURITY ROBOT
(Deep sigh) My felicity is clouded by a pang of impassioned tristesse.

FORD PREFECT
Whatever. Can you keep the rest of the security system happy for a few minutes?

COLIN THE SECURITY ROBOT
One of the joys of true happiness is sharing. I brim, I froth, I overflow with—

FORD PREFECT
OK. Just spread a little happiness around the security network. Don't give it any information. Just make it feel good so it doesn't feel the need to ask for any. Then show me where the Accounting Department is.

COLIN THE SECURITY ROBOT
Will this be fun?

FORD PREFECT
It'll be more than fun. It'll be extremely froody . . . Great Zarquon – who rebuilt the door?

COLIN THE SECURITY ROBOT
Oh, the offices are all nanobuilt now. Molecular bots live in the woodwork. They build each other, rebuild the door, disassemble each other and go back into the woodwork to await further damage.

287

FORD PREFECT	Well, let's not keep them waiting— **(Effort)** *Urgh!*
	FX: Door kicked down. He runs off, followed by Colin.

INT. – TRICIA McMILLAN'S HOUSE

TRICIA McMILLAN	**(Gasping)** Is that your spaceship on my lawn?
GREBULON LIEUTENANT	Our scoutship, yes, Miss McMillan.
TRICIA McMILLAN	Are you . . . are you from . . . Zaphod?
GREBULONS	**(Concerned muttering)** Where is Zaphod? Is it far from here? Which direction? We don't know.
GREBULON LIEUTENANT	We don't think so. Not as far as we know.
TRICIA McMILLAN	You've been monitoring . . . me?
GREBULON LIEUTENANT	All of you. Everything on your planet. TV. Radio. Computers. Video circuitry. Warehouses. Car parks. We monitor everything.
TRICIA McMILLAN	How tedious.
GREBULON LIEUTENANT	What are these?
TRICIA McMILLAN	**(Off)** Umm – my music collection.
GREBULON UNDERLING	Look – *Elvis Sings Oasis.*
GREBULONS	Ooooh . . .
TRICIA McMILLAN	You like Elvis Presley?
GREBULONS	Yes.
GREBULON UNDERLING	Some of your people think that Elvis has been kidnapped by space aliens.
	FX: Camcorder switched on, under:
TRICIA McMILLAN	Last I heard, he was alive and well and living out his old age in Memphis. Mind if I video you?
GREBULON LIEUTENANT	If you don't mind us monitoring it.
TRICIA McMILLAN	OK. Now tell me slowly and carefully who you are. You first. What's your name?
GREBULON LIEUTENANT	I don't know.
TRICIA McMILLAN	You don't know.
GREBULON LIEUTENANT	No.

TRICIA McMILLAN	I see. What about you other two?
GREBULONS	We don't know.
TRICIA McMILLAN	OK. Where you are from? Why are you shaking your heads?
GREBULON UNDERLING	We don't know where we are from.
GREBULON LIEUTENANT	We are on a mission.
TRICIA McMILLAN	A mission. OK. To do what?
GREBULON LIEUTENANT	We do not know.
TRICIA McMILLAN	So what are you doing here on Earth, then?
GREBULON LIEUTENANT	We have come to fetch you.
TRICIA McMILLAN	Why me?
GREBULON UNDERLING	Because we have lost our minds.
TRICIA McMILLAN	Uh – I beg your pardon?
GREBULON LIEUTENANT	We liked your interview with the astrologer. We are very interested in what the stars foretell. We thought stars might just be fissile gaseous bodies, but as our memories are blank we'll believe whatever we like. And we like astrology much better. We follow our horoscopes, you see. They give us a purpose.
GREBULON UNDERLING	Our ship was hit by a meteorite. Our memories were wiped. Our only remaining instructions were to land, and monitor, and . . .
TRICIA McMILLAN	And what?
GREBULON LIEUTENANT	The next bit is not clear yet. But our immediate problem is one of triangulation. Astrology is a very precise science. We know this.
TRICIA McMILLAN	Well—
GREBULON LIEUTENANT	But it is only precise for you here on Earth. So when Venus is rising in Capricorn, for instance, that is from Earth. How does that work if we are out on Rupert? What if the Earth is rising in Capricorn? It is hard for us to know.
GREBULON UNDERLING	Amongst the things we have forgotten, which we think are many and profound, is trigonometry. You said you are an astrophysicist.
TRICIA McMILLAN	I was. Well, am really.
GREBULON LIEUTENANT	You said astrology is not a science unless scientific methodology is applied to it. And that is what we would like you to come and do.

289

TRICIA McMILLAN	Let me get this straight. You want me to come with you to Rupert, to help you accurately calculate the relative positions of Earth and Rupert to help you work out your horoscopes?
GREBULONS	Yes.
TRICIA McMILLAN	(Pause) Do I get exclusive story rights?
GREBULONS	Yes.
	FX: Camcorder off.
TRICIA McMILLAN	Wait here while I get my— No. Let's just go.

EXT. – HAWALION

FX: Windy, high-up feel.

ARTHUR	(Effort . . . He is just finishing climbing up a tall pole) Hallo . . . hallo? Old man – on top of the next pole – hallo?
OLD MAN ON THE POLE	Go away, I'm ignoring you.
ARTHUR	(Still out of breath) But this is the fifth pole I've climbed – will you please stay in one place?
OLD MAN ON THE POLE	I'll meditate where I want—
	FX: Whoosh. The old man shifts to another pole.
OLD MAN ON THE POLE	(Now on opposite side – slightly further away) So there.
ARTHUR	How are you doing that?
OLD MAN ON THE POLE	None of your business.
ARTHUR	Please don't make me climb another one.
OLD MAN ON THE POLE	You should be careful climbing these poles. You could fall off and kill yourself, if you tried.
ARTHUR	Oh, no, I have it on good authority that I won't die until I have been to Stavromula Beta and – this isn't Stavromula Beta, is it?
OLD MAN ON THE POLE	No.
ARTHUR	Good.
	FX: Whoosh. The old man shifts to another poles several times, during:
OLD MAN ON THE POLE	Goodbye.

ARTHUR	How do you do that?!
OLD MAN ON THE POLE	You think I'm going to tell you just like that what it took me forty springs, summers and autumns of sitting on top of successive poles to work out?
ARTHUR	What about winter?
OLD MAN ON THE POLE	What about winter?
ARTHUR	Don't you sit on the pole in the winter?
OLD MAN ON THE POLE	Just because I sit up a pole for most of my life doesn't mean I'm stupid. I go south in the winter. Got a beach house. Overlooking the beach. Sit on the chimney stack.

FX: Smelly Photocopier Woman distantly swatting flies, under:

ARTHUR	Do you have any advice for a traveller?
OLD MAN ON THE POLE	Yes. Get a beach house. Gives you somewhere to go. Look – see her, down there?
ARTHUR	Yes. I consulted her, as a matter of fact.
OLD MAN ON THE POLE	Fat lot she knows. I got the beach house because she turned it down. What advice did she give you?
ARTHUR	Do exactly the opposite of everything she's done.
OLD MAN ON THE POLE	In other words, get a beach house.
ARTHUR	I suppose so. Any other advice?

FX: Whoosh. The old man shifts to another pole.

OLD MAN ON THE POLE	A beach house doesn't even have to be on the beach. Though the best ones are. We all like to congregate at boundary conditions.
ARTHUR	Really?

FX: Whoosh. The old man shifts to another pole.

OLD MAN ON THE POLE	Where land meets water. Where earth meets air. Where body meets mind.

FX: Whoosh. The old man shifts to another pole.

OLD MAN ON THE POLE	Where space meets time. We like to be on one side, and look at the other—

FX: Whoosh. The old man shifts to another pole.

ARTHUR	Please stop!

OLD MAN ON THE POLE	Can't take it, huh? You come to me for advice, but you can't cope with anything you don't recognize. Hmmm. So we'll have to tell you something you already know but make it sound like news, eh? Business as usual, then. Where you from, boy?
ARTHUR	Tell you what. You're a seer. Why don't you tell me?
OLD MAN ON THE POLE	You come from the Earth. One of them.
ARTHUR	One of them?
OLD MAN ON THE POLE	I can't tell you any more.
ARTHUR	But I've come all this way.
OLD MAN ON THE POLE	You cannot see what I see because you see what you see. You cannot know what I know because you know what you know. Everything you see or hear or experience in any way at all is specific to you. You create a universe by perceiving it, so everything in the universe you perceive is specific to you.
ARTHUR	Hang on, can I write this down?
OLD MAN ON THE POLE	You can pick it up by the bucketload at the spaceport. They've got racks of the stuff.
ARTHUR	**(Pulling out brochure)** Um – it says in the brochure that I can have a special prayer, individually tailored to me and my special needs.
OLD MAN ON THE POLE	Oh, all right. Here's a prayer for you. Ahem. **(Quickly)** 'Lord, Lord, Lord . . .' – it's best to put that bit in, just in case. You can never be too sure – 'Protect me from knowing what I don't need to know. Protect me from even knowing that there are things to know that I don't know. Protect me from knowing that I decided not to know about the things that I decided not to know about. Amen.' For me, read him. That's it.
ARTHUR	Um – thank you . . .
OLD MAN ON THE POLE	Oh! And there's another prayer that goes with it, that's very important.
ARTHUR	OK.
OLD MAN ON THE POLE	It goes, 'Lord, Lord, Lord. Protect me from the consequences of the above prayer. Amen.'
ARTHUR	Thank you.
OLD MAN ON THE POLE	Now I suggest you get the next flight off this planet. Goodbye.
	FX: Swoosh-pop!
ARTHUR	. . . Uh? Where—? **(Yells)** How did you do THAT?

292

INT. – CORRIDORS OF THE *HITCHHIKER'S GUIDE* BUILDING

FX: Ford and Colin making their way through doors, under:

COLIN THE
SECURITY ROBOT

Even in my highly delighted condition I have to say that it is taking all my energy to pump the slightest bonhomie whatsoever into the doors in these lower reaches of the building.

FX: Swiping card frantically. Buzzer indicates negative.

ACCOUNTANCY
DEPT DOOR

InfiniDim Enterprises *Hitchhiker's Guide* Accountancy Department. No Admittance. Not Even To Authorized Personnel. You are wasting your time here. Go away. Now.

FORD PREFECT

Infinidim Enterprises . . . What happened to beach shirts and that Ol' Janx Spirit? *Unf!*

FX: He kicks the door, which opens with a grunt.

COLIN THE
SECURITY ROBOT

Oooh! How did you do that?

FORD PREFECT

(Moving off into room) Mixture of pleasure and pain. Never fails.

INT. – *HITCHHIKER'S GUIDE* – ACCOUNTING DEPARTMENT

FX: Hum of computers under:

THE VOICE

If you are listening to this on planet Earth then: (a) Good luck to you. There is an awful lot of stuff you don't know anything about. In your case, the consequences of not knowing the stuff are particularly terrible, but then, hey, that's just the way the cookie gets completely stomped on and obliterated. (b) Don't imagine you know what a computer terminal is. A computer terminal is not some television with a typewriter in front of it. It is an interface where the mind and body can connect with the universe and move bits of it about.

If one were to gain access to the nerve centre of *The Hitchhiker's Guide to the Galaxy* – in other words, its Accounting Computer – by, say, using a stolen Ident-i-Eeze card, one would discover a bank of terminals lining the walls of a minus-tenth-floor room in its basement. These are portals onto every aspect of the *Guide*'s operations, and any order, say, to disallow a researcher's expenses, is input on a virtual level. Using a headset equipped with sensory deceptors the operator will find themself in a universe once only accessed from a single office on the fifth floor of the building, but which now has expanded in every conceivable way.

FX: Whoosh. Windy alien feel.

FORD PREFECT	Wow . . .

THE VOICE	It is a universe of densely enfolded worlds; of wild topographies, towering mountain peaks, heart-stopping ravines; of moons shattering off into sea horses; hurtful blurting crevices; silently heaving oceans and bottomless, hurtling, hooping funts. And in a valley below the ledge on its tallest mountain where Ford Prefect finds himself clinging, stands a single shack on a deserted seashore.

FORD PREFECT	. . . and I thought accountancy was boring. Think, Ford . . . it's a simulated reality. You can snap back out of it at any moment—

FX: Whoosh. Interior Accountancy Dept again. Computers.

COLIN THE SECURITY ROBOT	Are you quite all right, Mr Prefect?

FORD PREFECT	Quite all right. Just checking—

FX: Whoosh. Windy cloudscape again.

FORD PREFECT	OK. This must be a four-dimensional topological model of the *Guide*'s financial systems I am in, and somebody or something will very shortly want to know why. And here they come.

FX: Flock of accountancy creatures flap up to him.

COLIN THE SECURITY ROBOT	(Slightly muffled, from beyond) What is happening, Mr Prefect, sir?

FORD PREFECT	I'm being inspected by the virtual accountancy creatures . . . steely-eyed, pencil-moustached, with wings . . . and carrying laser guns . . .

COLIN THE SECURITY ROBOT	(Muffled) I am happy virtual guns cannot hurt you.

FORD PREFECT	I'm not sure this universe is as virtual as it looks . . .

ACCOUNTANCY BIRDS	Who are you? What do you want? What are you doing here? What is your authorization? Why haven't you gone?

FORD PREFECT	Here, boys. My Ident-i-Eeze card.

FX: Laser scanners read the card. A beat, then:

ACCOUNTANCY BIRDS	(Obsequious, in unison) Nice to see you, Mr Vann Harl. Is there anything we can do for you?

FORD PREFECT	Certainly there is. Clear all expenses for Ford Prefect, Betelgeuse Five Sector. Retrospectively. And allow this Dine-O-Charge card all privileges, with roaming. Got the number?
ACCOUNTANCY BIRDS	Yes, sir/Immediately, sir/Without delay/It's done.
	FX: They flap away again.
FORD PREFECT	(Sighs) I wish I'd thought of this before.
ZAPHOD	(Off, yells) Ford! You're back!
FORD PREFECT	Zaphod?! What the zark are you doing here?
ZAPHOD	(Climbs up to join him) Where's Dent? This is really important! On a scale of one to ten: thirteen! I know what's going on!
FORD PREFECT	Zaphod, if that were true then I've lost just about every bet I've ever made with myself. What do you mean, I'm back?
ZAPHOD	You don't remember? Last time you were here?
FORD PREFECT	This is eerily familiar to a conversation I had with a barman in Han Dold City.
ZAPHOD	So your memory is out of synch with yourself too? Hoopy! That's why I came back to the *Guide* Building. Trillian said I was dreaming or drunk when I was last here. And you know what I found out?
FORD PREFECT	Drunk is better?
ZAPHOD	Gargravarr, my psychiatrist, the Presidency, the Krikkit robots – it was all a front! The Vogons set it all up. And this guy's been controlling it all from here, at the *Hitchhiker's Guide*.
FORD PREFECT	Which guy?
ZAPHOD	Zarniwoop. Vann Harl! He's a Vogon! A plastic-surgery'd, liposucked, fake-tanned, business-suited Vogon Boss! The Big Cheese with a Side Order of Jewelled Crab!
FORD PREFECT	But why would the Vogons want to take over *The Hitchhiker's Guide to the Galaxy*?
ZAPHOD	Their paperwork was backing up. Every time they thought they had destroyed a planet in a Plural Zone, it reappeared. They need to stop the whole bureaucracy imploding so they had to develop a way to bridge the zones, so they can impose the system on all available realities. Some aquatic mammals from Earth gave them the idea. Dent's an aquatic mammal, isn't he?
FORD PREFECT	He likes taking baths, but I don't think he's much of a physicist.

295

ZAPHOD	You've heard of the Total Perspective Vortex, right?
FORD PREFECT	I've heard you boast you were the only person to survive it.
ZAPHOD	Yeah, well, I am – in a way. But it isn't just a torture machine, frood, it's dimensional-bridging software – and *this* was the prototype. Ford, that Krikkit War was a cheap sideshow! The Vogons put pieces of the Wikkit Gate into the space-time continuum to distract everybody while they used the technology here to shrink the Total Perspective Vortex into a portable unit. It's the next generation *Hitchhiker's Guide*! And it's got the voice of those Lintilla chicks!
FORD PREFECT	*What* Lintilla chicks?
ZAPHOD	Duh! Never mind! It's scary and sexy beyond anything. Except maybe riding a Fuorlornis Fire Dragon naked. No, it's worse than that. You can't rub cream on this baby. Look, you have to find the new package and get it out of the *Hitchhiker's* Building.
FORD PREFECT	Me? Why can't *you* do it?
ZAPHOD	Dude, I've just spent virtual months in a virtual shack with virtually the most boring man in the universe and his actually smelly virtual cat! I need a very real and very large Pan Galactic Gargle Blaster! Inside me! Now!

INT. – SPACE LINER

FX: In-flight video.

Music: Dramatic sting, ends, then:

GANGSTA	You ain't goin' no furtha, bitch! Only Zarquon gonna save you now!

FX: Zap gun fired – female scream.

Music stab: Into toothpaste commercial jingle.

VOICE OVER	This program is brought to you by Kleen-O-Dent, the toothpaste with Atomic Whitener!
AD CHORUS	Glow in the dark Bright as a Sun Kleen-O-Dent's For everyone.
AD VOICE	Now with vibrating nano-foam!
VOICE OVER	And later on Home Brain Box:

Music: Slushy strings (under Arthur/Stewardess chat).

PATIENT Oh, Doctor Fernando, tell me I am young again . . .

DOCTOR As young and as beautiful as the day I first built you, Amanda.

PATIENT Take me in your arms.

DOCTOR I can't . . . there are rules.

PATIENT Where love is concerned, there are no rules . . . kiss me . . .

Music swells.

VOICE OVER *Android Love* returns after the watershed. And now we return you to *Blondes And Bullets On Betelgeuse Five* . . .

FX: Hail of gunfire, attenuated in sound as Arthur pulls off in-flight earpieces . . .

ARTHUR Not again . . . Excuse me?

STEWARDESS Yes, sir? Can I get you something? Paper napkin?

ARTHUR No, er – is that the only movie channel on this flight?

STEWARDESS We're just coming up to the Lamuella hyperspace jump point, sir. After that we pick up Fardwarx Fictional News and Think Vid.

FX: Muted 'bing-bong!'

CAPTAIN (Distort, over tannoy) Crew to seats for hyperjump in thirty seconds.

STEWARDESS Oh, you'll want to fasten your seat belt, sir.

ARTHUR Done. Just going to fasten this one too.

STEWARDESS Er – yes – we were wondering – why you booked two seats when you only needed one?

ARTHUR I always do on interstellar flights. In about fifteen seconds I'm hoping for a miracle. Shouldn't you find *your* seat?

STEWARDESS (Going off) Yes – er, yes, of course . . .

CAPTAIN (Distorted) Three – two – one—

FX: Alarms, swooshes, ninety-seven different hyperspace points at once, then screaming panic.

CAPTAIN Ah, folks, we seem to have hit a major glitch in hyperspace – for those of you who have not given up addictive substances – smoke 'em if you got 'em . . .

OMNES (Screams)

297

INT. – *HITCHHIKER'S GUIDE* – CORRIDOR

FX: Ford and Colin rushing along it.

COLIN THE SECURITY ROBOT   But, Mr Prefect, I still don't understand what you did inside the Accounts computer in only three minutes and thirty seconds . . .

FORD PREFECT   Oh, the job only took thirty seconds. Then two minutes to find out what's going on from my cousin. Then another minute to reverse-engineer evidence of my visit by programming in the sort of mental blocks that otherwise perfectly normal people develop when elected to high political office. Elevator!

FX: Ding! Elevator bell.

LIFT   Hallo. I am to be your Sirius Cybernetics Corporation Happy Vertical People Transporter taking you, the visitor to *The Hitchhiker's Guide to the Galaxy*—

FORD PREFECT   Enough already! Floor 23 and step on it.

LIFT   Hmm. Seems to be a popular floor today. **(Starts to sing quietly)**

Share and Enjoy
Share and Enjoy
Journey through life
With a plastic boy
Or girl by your side—

FORD PREFECT   Popular floor? That doesn't sound good.

LIFT   I'll sound however you want, sir. Perhaps you'd like me to sing some more— **(Sings, cut off below)**

Let your pal be your guide
And when it breaks down
Or starts to annoy
Or grinds when it moves
And gives you no joy
Cos it's eaten your hat
Or had sex with your cat
Bled oil on your floor
Or ripped off your door
You get to the point
You can't stand any more
Bring it to us, we won't give a fig
We'll tell you 'Go stick your head in a pig—'

COLIN THE SECURITY ROBOT	(Over song) May I ask what joy you discovered from your cousin, Ford, sir?
FORD PREFECT	Oh, mostly that he's very, very bored. So I hitched him a lift to the nearest bar with my electronic Thumb. The rest I'll keep to myself for now. Just in case you get caught and reprogrammed again.
COLIN THE SECURITY ROBOT	Inspired thinking, I am humbled by it.
FORD PREFECT	Colin, shut this thing up.
COLIN THE SECURITY ROBOT	And a privilege it is to do so! I will hack into its circuits—

FX: Colin accessing circuits, under:

LIFT	Warning, if you are disconnecting my higher brain function you should know that, like all Sirius Cybernetics Happy People Transporters, I can see into the future, and I must warn you – BZT.
COLIN THE SECURITY ROBOT	Voice circuit deactivated.

FX: Lift rising, under:

FORD PREFECT	Ah, pity. It was finally going to say something useful.

FX: Ding! Lift slows, stops, door opens.

INT. – *HITCHHIKER'S GUIDE* – CORRIDOR

FX: Ford and Colin exit the lift.

FORD PREFECT	OK . . . the nanobots have rebuilt the Editor's door again. When I break through, you cover me. The drinks trolley may have gone but I saw a sofa, so I'll duck behind that. If Zarniwoop is still unconscious, all well and good, we just put back his Ident-i-Eeze and leave. If not, we play it by ear while you think of something. After three. Ready?
COLIN THE SECURITY ROBOT	Three!
FORD PREFECT	What? Oh, yeah—

FX: Ford runs at the door, smashing through it:

FORD PREFECT	Yeeeargh!

FX: He rolls several times on floor. A pause.

VANN HARL	That's him.
VOGON GUARD	Beeblebrox?
VANN HARL	**(Surrounded by idiots)** No, Prefect. *Do* try and keep up!
FORD PREFECT	**(Getting up)** Zarniwoop. You're awake? Where did the sofa go? Ah. Rocket launcher on Vogon's shoulder – ba-ad sign.
VANN HARL	Prefect. You're fired. Literally.
FORD PREFECT	Colin! The window!
COLIN THE SECURITY ROBOT	Whoopee!

FX: Colin zips through window – tinkle of glass.

FX: Rocket launcher fires. Explosion. Glass smash.

FORD PREFECT	**(Jumps out of window)** Colinnnnnnnnn . . . !!!!

INT. – THE BOOK AMBIENCE

THE VOICE	Can Ford Prefect survive a fall from the *Hitchhiker's Guide* Building's 23rd floor equipped with nothing but a threadbare towel and a dubious credit card? Has Arthur Dent finally met a grisly fate at Stavromula Beta? What is the reality behind the portable Total Perspective Unit? Random layers of multidimensionality are sandwiched together in the next mouth-watering episode of *The Hitchhiker's Guide to the Galaxy* . . .

FOOTNOTES

Smelly Photocopier Woman	Miriam Margolyes performed two takes of this scene, uncharacteristically losing her voice during the second. But as the first take was perfect anyway (a safe bet with actors as good as Miriam and Simon), and the second just for insurance, we were home and dry.

This was a great opportunity for broad humour and we did not hesitate to grab it – Ken Humphrey in particular. His role was to provide 'spot' or 'live effects' (or 'foley') for these series. These are the immediate physical sounds characters might make whilst moving around, handling props like tea cups, glasses, cutlery, and over the years we have developed a very intense and layered approach to creating a reality beyond just the sound of actors speaking lines of dialogue. For example, by default, Ken supplies the movement of cloth under the actors' voices, suggesting their clothing gently rustling as they gesture, and larger sounds, often of the opening and closing variety – be it doors, boxes, windows or umbrellas (very rapidly and repeatedly to simulate beating wings). There is also more violent stuff such as banging bits of metal about to suggest robots collapsing, or Zaphod banging bits of metal about; but generally speaking after a certain point – particularly if it involves risk to life and limb – the relevant sound effects are left to be added later, either sound designed especially by me or Paul Weir or harvested from one of the several professional sound-effects libraries available.

Ken is the consummate preparation junkie, arriving at the studio wheeling in huge trunks packed with swanee whistles, bolts of fine silk, stuffed pandas, anything he can use to make a sound effect. (This is only a slight exaggeration.)

In the case of the Smelly Photocopier Woman he arrived with a carrier bag filled with whoopee cushions to simulate ruptured goats' bladders, kiddie pots of fart gel to simulate the source of some of the smells, buckets of soggy papier mâché to simulate something nasty Arthur treads in and a little battery-powered fan to make a noise like an expiring giant bluebottle. It's just as well Miriam was playing the part, no other actress could fend off such a battery of effects. Actually that could be the reason she lost her voice – she got a sneak preview of Ken's carrier bag and decided to go for broke . . .

The history of
The Hitchhiker's Guide
to the Galaxy

Nearly the opening monologue in the Tertiary Phase, transplanted for logical reasons to this episode. Whether Paul 'Wix' Wickens will be able to create the sound of monks chanting with their mouths full (The Holy Lunching Friars of Voondon) is – at the time of writing – still a matter of conjecture. But given his talent and the range of his contributions so far it is surely not beyond him. I expect burps and belches will feature, they're more percussive.

Wix took on an unenviable task, scoring new episodes of a radio series which had twenty-five years to imprint itself – music and all – on the consciousness of its devotees. Although Geoffrey Perkins had largely used commercial discs for music in the Primary Phase, Paddy Kingsland had composed and performed a unique and very appropriate score for the Secondary Phase. Now these new phases were com-missioned, Douglas's widow Jane Belson suggested their old friend Wix Wickens to provide music, which seemed a terrific idea. Wix and Douglas shared a piano teacher as teenagers, although it is likely that Wix was the more adept pupil, given his track record since as a record producer and keyboard player of many years' standing in Paul McCartney's bands. But then Douglas didn't exactly flunk in his area of expertise, either.

Douglas had often said he wanted the radio *Hitchhiker's* shows to sound like rock albums, specifically a Beatles album like *Sergeant Pepper's Lonely Hearts Club Band*, so having Wix aboard made extra good sense. On a related level Douglas liked very much the cinematic feel my superhero serials had on BBC Radio, particularly the use of music to add atmosphere and paint in emotional textures. He wanted the same for the new *Hitchhiker's*, not just linking music or ambient music under the Voice but music that augmented dialogue and action sequences.

Wix turned up trumps in the most spectacular way. All one need do is listen back to sequences from the Tertiary Phase like Arthur and Ford chasing the sofa across prehistoric Earth, Marvin relating the story of the collapsing bridge on the swamp planet, or Prak attempting to tell Arthur the location of God's Last Message to His Creation, accompanied by a genuinely funny series of more and more portentous music cues, each collapsing more spectacularly, to hear how cleverly Wix's score aids and abets the story without ever trying to say 'this is funny'.

The Voice of the Bird/Ford in Zarniwoop's den

Continuing the shaping of existing scenes in *Mostly Harmless* to bring closure to the saga, Ford and Zarniwoop come face to face and it is here that the mysterious 'Voice of the Bird' which has begun increasingly to interrupt 'The Voice' is identified as the New Voice of the *Guide*, in other words, the *Guide* Mark II, and its choice is explained by Zarniwoop as a marketing decision – 'we don't sell something with a plummy pompous pedagogue . . . No! We sell a sultry Brantisvogan Escort Agency VIP vamp voice . . .'. By now listeners familiar with *Hitchhiker's* would have figured out – if not much much earlier – that as the hundreds of thousands of Brantisvogan escort girls were the Lintilla clones from the Secondary Phase, the voice of the *Guide* Mark II would be Lintilla's – and therefore played, as before, by Rula Lenska.

In the novel Ford shouting 'Kill' in response to Vann Harl's explanation of new circumstances at the *Guide* is very ambiguous and could be triggered by the phrase 'We would value your input', the Dine-O-Charge card, or just the whole new marketing approach the *Guide* is taking.

For the purposes of this dramatization, 'We would value your input' was so reminiscent of the sort of ironic policy-speak BBC Radio uses to keep independent programme makers at arms' length (it is all too often followed by 'if the quota permits') that a gentle satirical barb was impossible to resist, and will be something to smile about in the Job Centre queue.

The virtual accounting software

Another blending of old and new elements in the story to bring Ford and Zaphod back together inside the software that was once the 'Virtual Universe' in Zarniwoop's office but has now been rendered obsolete by the new 'portable unit', i.e. the *Guide* Mark II.

There are two Hitchcockian 'McGuffins' (objects or ideas around which a plot revolves) in the Quintessential Phase and this concept is the first of them.

Ahem. It is possible to assume that Zaphod's experiences in the Secondary Phase with Zarniwoop etc. were not necessarily experienced in the most sober state of mind. Thus his understanding of the Total Perspective Vortex as merely a torture machine might be quite a long way short of the Full Montgomery. At the end of the next episode the *Guide* Mark II (in its guise as the Bird) explains to Random how it exists across all available dimensions. It has Total Perspective. By connecting that idea back to the mysterious vortex that Zaphod experienced (and, if you think about it,

302

to an organic mind a vision in Total Perspective would indeed be a form of torture), it could easily be a next-generation product of the technology, subverted by the Vogons (whose bureaucracy has spread like a virus into every crevice) for their own purposes.

On the other hand one could just go stick one's head in a pig.

EPISODE THREE

SIGNATURE TUNE

ANNOUNCER *The Hitchhiker's Guide to the Galaxy*, by Douglas Adams, Quintessential Phase.

Sig fades.

INT. – THE BOOK AMBIENCE

FX: Arthur making sandwiches, under:

THE VOICE Lamuella is listed briefly in *The Hitchhiker's Guide to the Galaxy* as a planet partly bisected by a Plural Zone near a hyperspace jump point on the Eastern Rim of the Galaxy. It is, by and large, unknown, which is a pity; for upon Lamuella every aspect of making the humble sandwich has been developed beyond the dreams of even the picnic-food epicures on Thermos Magna VI. Choosing the right bread, for instance. The Sandwich Maker in Lamuella's only significant settlement spends many months in daily consultation and experiment with Grarp the Baker. And between them they have created a loaf of exactly a consistency dense enough to slice thinly and neatly, while still being light, moist and having that fine nuttiness which best enhances the roasted, sliced flesh of a Perfectly Normal Beast.

The proper tools, of course, are crucial, and many are the days that the Sandwich Maker will spend silhouetted against the glow of Strinder the Tool Maker's forge, making slow sweeping movements through the air trying one knife after another. First there is the knife for the slicing of the bread: a firm, authoritative blade which imposes a clear and defining will on a loaf. Then there is the butter-spreading knife – a whippy little number but still with a firm backbone to it. King amongst the knives, of course, is the carving knife. This is the blade that not merely imposes its will on the medium through which it moves. It must work with it; be guided by the grain of the meat. The Sandwich Maker will flip each slice with a smooth flick of the wrist onto the bread, trim it with four deft strokes and then add a few slices of newcumber and fladish and a touch of splagberry sauce before applying the topmost, crowning layer of bread. There are those in the village who are happy chopping wood; those who are content carrying water, and Old

304

Thrashbarg may be head man, soothsayer and all round busybody, but to be the Sandwich Maker is heaven itself.

Or so the Sandwich Maker thinks, as he sings as he works . . .

INT. – ARTHUR'S SANDWICH SHOP

DRIMPLE (His apprentice, outside) Sandwich Maker! Sandwich Maker!

FX: Finishing off making sandwiches, under:

ARTHUR (For it is he; sings)
Our lovely world's so lovely
And everything's so nice
And everyone's so happy
Beneath the ink-black skies –

(Calls) Drimple? Is this the last of the Perfectly Normal Beast?

DRIMPLE (Enters, breathless) Yes, Sandwich Maker. But next Vroonday they will migrate again. At four thirty in the afternoon. Old Thrashbarg predicts it. He says this herd will yield maybe seven dozen carcasses. That should tide us over till the return migration.

ARTHUR Let's hope Thrashbarg has examined his pikka bird entrails correctly.

DRIMPLE Thrashbarg is never wrong. Not about Perfectly Normal Beasts.

ARTHUR Surprising, considering that while the rest of the village risk life and limb on the actual hunt, he makes up stories about his bravery in the safety of his hut.

DRIMPLE Sandwich Maker, the Almighty Bob has sent another chariot. Not a fiery one such as that which bore you unto us, but a smooth one with go-faster stripes. It settled in the clearing an hour ago. Old Thrashbarg is propitiating it.

ARTHUR (Wiping his hands) Good grief. Show me.

EXT. – LAMUELLA – VILLAGE CLEARING

FX: Hum of spacecraft on ground.

FX: Pikka birds pikking.

FX: Villagers muttering fearfully.

OLD THRASHBARG (Staff raised to the heavens) Almighty Bob! Thou hast vouchsafed us the world of Lamuella for our dwelling place! The migrations of the Perfectly Normal Beasts for our food! The droppings of the pikka birds to fertilize our

305

crops! And many moons ago, by fiery chariot, you sent unto us your Only Begotten Sandwich Maker to . . . Make our Sandwiches. Since which time we have known which side our bread is—

GRARP (Puzzled) Old Thrashbarg, sorry to interrupt but . . . why did Almighty Bob send his only begotten Sandwich Maker in a burning fiery chariot rather than, perhaps, in one that might have landed quietly – like this one?

OMNES Grarp's got a point there / Mayhap it was a sign / Bob moves in mysterious ways . . .

STRINDER After all, if Almighty Bob loves his people, why would he send a chariot that burned down half the forest, filling it with ghosts?

GRARP And injuring the Sandwich Maker quite badly, so that he limps heavily these days.

OMNES Hearken unto Strinder / The logic of the Tool Maker is not gainsaid / It's bloody spooky in there . . .

OLD THRASHBARG Shhhh! Shhhh – you unbelievers! Who are you to argue with the Ineffable Will of Bob!

(A beat)

OLD WOMAN What does ineffable mean?

OLD THRASHBARG Look it up!

OLD WOMAN Lend us yer dictionary, then.

OLD THRASHBARG It is forbidden.

GRARP Why?

OLD THRASHBARG It is not for you to question the will of Almighty Bob. And if you don't have Faith you'll Burn, so let me get on with my Propitiating before the ghosts emerge from the Forest and frighten away the Perfectly Normal Beasts!

ARTHUR (Arriving) Well, well . . . a space ship.

OMNES The Sandwich Maker is come! / Indeed he is limping as it is foretold / Now we will hear words of wisdom and partake of fine viands!

OLD THRASHBARG It is a fiery chariot, Sandwich Maker, now back off and let me propish. 'Mighty Bob, who knowest all things—'

FX: Airlock door on ship opens – crowd reacts.

OLD THRASHBARG (Runs off in fear) What the zark is *that*? Aieee!

ARTHUR	Come back, it's only the airlock opening . . . Oh – my – Bob . . . !
	FX: Feet on ramp.
TRILLIAN	Hallo, Arthur.
ARTHUR	Trillian . . .
TRILLIAN	We thought we'd arrived at some Iron Age backwater. We nearly left again. Lucky you appeared.
ARTHUR	'We'?
TRILLIAN	Yes. Random?
RANDOM	**(Still inside ship)** What now?
TRILLIAN	Come and meet your father.

EXT. – *HITCHHIKER'S GUIDE* BUILDING

FX: Crash of glass as Colin smashes through it.

FX: Rocket launcher fired.

FX: Ford leaps from window – air rushes past.

FORD PREFECT	Colinnnn—! Under the towel, quick!
COLIN THE SECURITY ROBOT	Immediately, Mr Prefect! Hold the corners tightly! We are three hundred feet above ground!
	FX: Colin zips up into towel – arrests his fall – Colin's servos under strain.
FORD PREFECT	**(Straining)** Whuf! Thanks, Colin . . . sheesh! try not to lose altitude—
COLIN THE SECURITY ROBOT	**(This is hard work)** It gives me validation beyond measure to burn out my anti-gravity circuits in your service—
FORD PREFECT	**(Clinging on)** Did you see them? Vogons! Vogons really have taken over the *Hitchhiker's Guide* Building!
COLIN THE SECURITY ROBOT	**(Effort continues)** Yes! The wonderful new management! The old management was also fabulous, of course, though I'm not sure if I thought so at the time.
FORD PREFECT	**(Strain increasing)** Before I reprogrammed you to be happy instead of officious.
COLIN THE SECURITY ROBOT	**(Effort undiminished)** How true. How wonderfully true. How bubblingly, frothingly, burstingly true. And joy, more of them below setting up rocket launchers.

FX: Rocket whoosh and huge explosion nearby.

FORD PREFECT   (Panic *and* strain, now) Suffering Zarquon! Drop me off at the nearest ledge—

COLIN THE   (At the limits of robot endurance) I burst with fluffy pink bunny love in
SECURITY ROBOT   fulfilling your wish.

FORD PREFECT   (Verging on exhaustion) Burst later. For now, drop me off.

COLIN THE   (Bursting with overheated circuits) Consider it an ecstasy-inducing joy.
SECURITY ROBOT

FX: Colin drops Ford off at the ledge.

FORD PREFECT   (Huge relief) Dingo's kidneys. Blacked-out windows? What floor is this?

COLIN THE   (Son of huge relief) Thirteen. Research and Development. Couldn't you just
SECURITY ROBOT   hug it?

FORD PREFECT   Hm. R&D used to be on the fifth floor.

FX: Distant rocket launch. Whooshes past, explodes above them, under:

COLIN THE   Incoming! It's paradise up here!
SECURITY ROBOT

FX: Muffled whirring of wings from within thirteenth floor.

FX: Another rocket blast.

FORD PREFECT   We need to be inside, not stuck out here like targets. Break the glass, Colin.

COLIN THE   The windows can't be broken. The glass was reinforced after the Frogstar
SECURITY ROBOT   attack.

FORD PREFECT   What Frogstar attack?

COLIN THE   The one that led the engineers to upgrade the windows.
SECURITY ROBOT

FORD PREFECT   But we broke out of Vann Harl's window.

COLIN THE   That is because the engineers were not expecting an impact from *inside* the
SECURITY ROBOT   building.

FORD PREFECT   Right. Hm. So, logically: what would the engineers not be expecting someone sitting on the ledge outside a window to do? They wouldn't be expecting me to be here in the first place. When people design something to be foolproof they usually underestimate the ingenuity of complete fools.

COLIN THE SECURITY ROBOT	What bliss to be shot at whilst stranded on a thirteenth-floor ledge with a complete fool!
	FX: Explosion.
FORD PREFECT	What's that?
COLIN THE SECURITY ROBOT	A rocket-propelled grenade. Scrumptious!
FORD PREFECT	No . . . Through the glass . . . something moved. A bird? There's something in there.
COLIN THE SECURITY ROBOT	The *Guide*.
FORD PREFECT	What *Guide*?
COLIN THE SECURITY ROBOT	The *Guide* version II – Pro. It's quite wonderful and very frightening. Not that I'd know fear, being so happy—
FORD PREFECT	Shut up, Colin. Brace me while I find the catch . . .
	FX: Explosion.

INT. – ARTHUR'S SANDWICH SHOP

TRILLIAN	**(Entering)** Nice sandwich shop. **(Calls outside)** Random, do come inside.
RANDOM	**(Off, outside)** No.
ARTHUR	I'm happy here, Trillian. They like me, I make sandwiches for them, and . . . er, well that's it, really. Please make yourself comfortable. Can I get you anything, er, a sandwich? Try one. They're good.
TRILLIAN	**(Bites, mouth full)** It is good. What's the filling?
ARTHUR	Ah yes, that's, um, that's Perfectly Normal Beast.
TRILLIAN	It's what?
ARTHUR	Perfectly Normal Beast. A bit like a buffalo. Large, charging sort of animal.
TRILLIAN	You talk as if there were something odd about it.
ARTHUR	Nothing, it's Perfectly Normal.
TRILLIAN	I see.
ARTHUR	It's just a bit odd where it comes from. And goes to.
TRILLIAN	**(Stops chewing)** Where does it come from, and where does it go to?

ARTHUR	They suddenly appear a point slightly to the east of the Hondo Mountains. Thousands of them, They stampede across the great Anhondo Plains and, er, disappear again. That's it really.
TRILLIAN	Sorry, I don't quite—
ARTHUR	In the spring they do it again, only the other way round.
TRILLIAN	(**Swallows reluctantly**) But . . . why are they called Perfectly Normal Beasts?
ARTHUR	Old Thrashbarg calls them that. He says that they come from where they come from and they go to where they go to and that it's Bob's will and so it must be Perfectly Normal.
TRILLIAN	Oh. Who is Bob?
ARTHUR	Don't ask . . . Um . . . (**Calls**) Random – would you like a Perfectly Normal Beast sandwich?
RANDOM	(**Off, outside**) I'm a vegetarian.
ARTHUR	Ah. Um. You look well.
TRILLIAN	I'm well. I'm very well. I expect you're wondering how I found you.
ARTHUR	Yes! I was wondering exactly that. How did you find me?
TRILLIAN	Well, as you may know, I work for one of the big Sub-Etha broadcasting networks that—
ARTHUR	Yes, you've done very well. That's terrific. Must be a lot of fun. All that rushing around.
TRILLIAN	Exhausting.
ARTHUR	I expect it must be, yes.
TRILLIAN	We have access to virtually every kind of information. I found your name on the passenger list of the ship that crashed.
ARTHUR	(**Astonished**) You mean they knew about the crash? They knew I'd survived?
TRILLIAN	Yes.
ARTHUR	But nobody's ever been to look or search or rescue. There's been absolutely nothing.
TRILLIAN	There wouldn't be. It's an insurance thing. They bury it. Pretend it never happened. You know they've reintroduced the death penalty for insurance-company directors?
ARTHUR	Really? For what offence?

TRILLIAN	What do you mean, offence?
ARTHUR	Oh . . . I see.
TRILLIAN	Anyway. It's time for you to take responsibility, Arthur. For your daughter.
ARTHUR	*My* daughter? But . . . we never – I mean, I wanted to but – surely Zaphod would have—?
TRILLIAN	Not the same species, Arthur. When I decided I wanted a child they ran all sorts of genetic tests on me and could find only one match anywhere. It was only later that it dawned on me. They don't usually like to tell you, but I insisted.
ARTHUR	You mean you went to a DNA bank?
TRILLIAN	Yes. But she wasn't quite as random as her name suggests, because, of course, you were the only *Homo sapiens* donor in the Galaxy.
ARTHUR	Yes . . . It was how I could afford the seat upgrades. Some of those flights are very long, you know.
TRILLIAN	Mmm. You *were* quite a frequent flyer, weren't you?
ARTHUR	But when . . . how . . . ?
TRILLIAN	How old? Well, in my time line it's about ten years since I had her, but she's obviously quite a lot older than that. I spend my life going backwards and forwards in time, you see. The job. I used to put her into daycare time zones, but you drop them off in the morning, and you've simply no idea how old they'll be that evening. I left her at one place for an hour, and when I came back she'd passed puberty.
ARTHUR	Awkward.
TRILLIAN	Isn't she. I've done all I can. It's over to you. I've got a war to go and cover. Nice to see you, Arthur. **(Pecks him on cheek, leaves, to Random:)** Goodbye, darling. I love you.
ARTHUR/RANDOM	You're just leaving me?
TRILLIAN	**(Off)** Must dash. Deadline.
ARTHUR	Trillian, for goodness' sake, I'm all for sharing the load, but—
	FX: Ship liftoff in distance. Murmur of villagers in background.
RANDOM	**(Enters, furious)** She's just dumped me here? In this stinking peasant-hole?
ARTHUR	Bu— Wh— I – ju—

RANDOM	You're supposed to be my father? This is complete pants!
ARTHUR	(Clears throat) There's no point in pretending this isn't hopeless, but I—
RANDOM	(Laying rules already) Don't tell me you love me. Don't start that positive-parenting crap. I've had it with the whole part-time-parent-on-a-guilt-trip thing.
ARTHUR	Look: I don't love you. I'm sorry. I don't even know you yet, but – your name really *is* Random, is it?
RANDOM	Random Frequent Flyer Dent.
ARTHUR	Oh, Belgium.

EXT. – SPACE – RUMBLE OF VOGON CONSTRUCTOR FLAGSHIP

THE VOICE	Despite the Vogons' reputation for bureaucratic zeal, over-reliance on paper-work and sheer bloody-minded pedantry, *The Hitchhiker's Guide to* – BZT!
VOICE OF THE BIRD	– *the Galaxy* Pro – soon to be available – contact your local InfiniDim Enterprises stockist to pre-order, quoting the priority code 'TPV' – BZT!
THE VOICE	– *to the Galaxy* points out that they are not above a little bribery and a lot of corruption in the same way that the sea is not above the clouds. And certainly not averse to the odd covert skulduggery either. When a Vogon Prostetnic captain in command of one of its Constructor Fleets hears the words 'integrity' or 'moral rectitude', he reaches for his dictionary. And when he hears the chink of ready money in large quantities he reaches for the rule book. And throws it away.

INT. – VOGON CONSTRUCTOR SHIP – BRIDGE

VOGON HELMSMAN	Coming up on ZZ9 Plural Z Alpha surveillance coordinates, Prostetnic Vogon Jeltz.
PROSTETNIC VOGON JELTZ	Excellent. Heave to in stealth mode. Patch into the Grebulon base monitoring circuits.
THE VOICE	In seeking so implacably the destruction of the Earth to clear the site for a new interstellar bypass, Prostetnic Vogon Jeltz has moved somewhat above and beyond the call of his professional duty. Indeed, there is now considerable doubt as to whether said bypass ever needed to be built at all, but the paperwork remains unfinished and Vogon pride unfulfilled. Jeltz's problem is that, having destroyed a planet located in one of the Galaxy's Plural Zones, the Earth has been replaced by an identical world – identical in all respects

but for an absence of sentient marine life and the occasional duplication of one or two existing humans. One of these is Tricia McMillan, in most respects a doppelgänger of Arthur Dent's friend Trillian; the exceptions being her accent, the colour of her hair, her lack of a daughter and the fact that she did not leave the Earth after meeting Zaphod Beeblebrox at a party. However, she has now managed to be abducted by aliens – in a nice way – and is currently visiting the remote world of Rupert, recently discovered tenth planet in Earth's solar system, and new home of the stranded and media-hungry Grebulons.

EXT. – GREBULON BASE ON RUPERT

FX: Howling wind. Alien feel.

TRICIA McMILLAN	Brrr! It's not exactly a paradise planet, is it?
GREBULON LIEUTENANT	Rupert is far from the star that warms your Earth. But it is an excellent location for monitoring.

FX: Airlock door opens/shuts.

INT. – GEBULON BASE ON RUPERT

GREBULON LEADER	Miss McMillan, I hope you enjoyed the tour of our base. Now, you are our guest, we must entertain you lavishly.
TRICIA McMILLAN	Er – really, I'm not – I mean, I don't know what sort of food—
GREBULON LEADER	FastBurger and Fries!! Nothing but the best! Here – have a Nugget.
TRICIA McMILLAN	I'm confused – you have all this technology far beyond us – but your quarters are furnished with home-cinema systems, imitation coal fires, lava lamps . . . How did you . . . where did you get . . . this?
GREBULON LEADER	By mail order.
TRICIA McMILLAN	They sent it by post?
GREBULON LEADER	Hah! Not here! No! Ha ha! We have arranged a special box number in New Hampshire. We make regular pick-up visits. Ha ha!
TRICIA McMILLAN	How do you pay for these things?
GREBULON LEADER	American Express.
TRICIA McMILLAN	But how do you get them? The Kids' Menu Specials?
GREBULON LIEUTENANT	Very easy, Miss McMillan. We stand in line!

GREBULONS	(Fall about laughing)
	FX: Laughter cuts into distort. Heard aboard Vogon ship.

INT. – VOGON CONSTRUCTOR SHIP BRIDGE

TRICIA McMILLAN	(Distorted) After we've eaten, do you mind if I videotape an interview with you?
GREBULON LEADER	(Distorted) Of course not, Miss McMillan. We have nothing to hide.
PROSTETNIC VOGON JELTZ	Nothing to hide?! Ow . . . Helmsman?
VOGON HELMSMAN	Yes, Captain?
PROSTETNIC VOGON JELTZ	My face aches strangely. What is wrong with it?
VOGON HELMSMAN	(With dawning horror) You're – you're *smiling*, sir . . .
PROSTETNIC VOGON JELTZ	You lie! You lie, like a Dentrassi food-taster!
	FX: Zap gun – body fall.
VOGON HELMSMAN	Urk!
PROSTETNIC VOGON JELTZ	All the same . . . I do feel strangely . . . *amused*. Yes. I am moved to write a poem about irony. Let's see . . . 'O globbet of dribble oozing from the upturned corner of my mouth . . .'

INT. – THE BOOK AMBIENCE

THE VOICE	According to the writings of Old Thrashbarg, the planet Lamuella was found fully-formed in the navel of a giant earwig at four-thirty one Vroonday afternoon, and although any seasoned galactic traveller with basic passes in physics and geography might have fairly serious doubts about this, it was rather a waste of time trying to argue with Old Thrashbarg as he would invoke the Will of Almighty Bob and that would be an end to the matter. Undeniably, however, on Lamuella the days were just a little over twenty-five hours long, which for an Earthman basically meant an extra hour in bed every single day and, of course, having regularly to reset his watch, which Arthur Dent rather enjoyed doing. He also felt at home with the number of suns and moons which Lamuella had – one of each – and with the fact that the planet orbited its single sun every three hundred days, a good number because it meant the year didn't drag by. Well, it didn't used to.

EXT. – LAMUELLAN VILLAGE

FX: Iron Age atmos. Busy village in background. Pikka birds.

ARTHUR (Approaching, defensive) Random, someone's been using my carving knife to dig up stones to throw at the pikka birds. And I think I know who it is, because I watched them doing it!

RANDOM You can buy another knife, can't you?

ARTHUR They don't sell them in bulk here! This is a subsistence economy!

RANDOM It's only a knife!

ARTHUR (Icy) Look. Not content with being surly, bad-tempered, wanting to go and play in the Paleozoic Era, not seeing why we have to have the gravity on the whole time and shouting at the sun to stop following you, now you ruin my carving knife! And I don't even know if they had a Paleozoic Era on this planet!

RANDOM I hate it. I want to leave. They're all stupid here.

ARTHUR No, they're not. You refuse to acclimatize. Your mother shouldn't have let you have that Sub-Etha TV implanted in your wrist, the news alone is making you hyperactive.

RANDOM That's because news is happening everywhere but here! And my mother dumps me here to go off and report on some war which didn't happen.

ARTHUR It's not her fault. The ship that was sent to fight it never arrived.

RANDOM Has she come back to fetch me? No. All I have for fun is the vid channels.

ARTHUR Yes, well you must stop showing those to the villagers. Huge spaceships crashing into each other may be amusing to you but not to them. These people only ever saw one spaceship crash, and it was so frightening and shocking that they don't realize it's entertainment. It certainly wasn't for me.

RANDOM What's this?

ARTHUR Er—? That's my watch.

RANDOM I don't get it.

ARTHUR My watch. It's to tell the time. Where did you find it?

RANDOM You left it by the waterfall after your shower. I know what it's *meant* to do. But you keep on fiddling with it, and it still doesn't tell the right time. Or even anything like it. My Sub-Etha wristband can.

FX: Sub-Etha wristband.

SUB-ETHA VOICE   (**Speaking Clock voice**) Allowing for orbital momentum and star location, Lamuella time – sponsored by Accutentacle – is getting on for about half-past four, precisely—

FX: Click off.

RANDOM   Your watch doesn't do any of this precisely. Why do you keep it?

ARTHUR   (**Changing down a gear**) Sentiment, really. I was given it on my twenty-*second* birthday by my godfather. He was probably feeling guilty that he'd forgotten every birthday I'd had up till then. He'd even forgotten my name. Look at the back.

RANDOM   (**Reads**) 'To . . . Albert . . . on his twenty-first birthday'.

ARTHUR   He got the date wrong too.

RANDOM   What's that noise?

ARTHUR   Ticking. The mechanism that drives the watch. It's called clockwork.

RANDOM   It's all hardware . . .

ARTHUR   Yes, it is.

RANDOM   Could have looked after it better.

ARTHUR   That watch has survived stuff in the last few years which falls well outside the warranty – which presumably limited its guaranteed accuracy to the Earth, providing the day was twenty-four hours long and the planet didn't get too demolished by Vogons. Which it did. Utterly. And which is why I am here. And that reminds me: Random, I forbid you to marry a Vogon!

RANDOM   You what?

ARTHUR   Nothing. Just fulfilling a promise I made to myself a long time ago.

RANDOM   At least you were born somewhere with a name. Do you know where I was born?

ARTHUR   (**Embarrassed**) No.

RANDOM   I was born in a spaceship that was going from somewhere to somewhere else, which only turned out to be another somewhere that my mother had to get to somewhere else again from.

ARTHUR   Yes, that would make it hard—

RANDOM	It makes you feel you're always supposed to be somewhere else. Always in the wrong place. Add to that the fact that we were travelling through time as well, and I was not only always feeling I was in the wrong place, but at the wrong time. I don't ever fit.
ARTHUR	You can fit if you *want*.
RANDOM	What? Here? In the worst place she ever dumped me? With the father who gave me this precious and magical burden of life in return for a seat upgrade?

FX: Bustle and commotion among pikka birds.

OLD THRASHBARG	(Approaching busily) Sandwich Maker! Sandwich Maker! Bob has sent us another sign!
RANDOM	(Calls) What, has Kirp caught another two-headed fish that's really two fish cut in half and sewn together, badly?
OLD THRASHBARG	(Arriving) Quiet, wench, or Bob will cast you into the outer darkness.
RANDOM	(Low) Fine by me, I was born there.
OLD THRASHBARG	Sandwich Maker, a silver chariot descended this morning into the Anhodo foothills and a creature of metal came out. He gave unto Drimple this sacrificial gift in return for a thumbprint and a scrape of skin from the nape of his neck!
ARTHUR	Express Delivery by robot drone.

FX: Package seized by Random, under:

RANDOM	Let me see—
OLD THRASHBARG	It is a sign. The Perfectly Normal Beasts are about to return.

FX: Envelope torn open.

RANDOM	The waybill says it's from Antwelm City on Saquo-Pilia Hensha. That's where they have a year-round carnival. Let's open it!
OLD THRASHBARG	Calm youself, Sandwich Maker's daughter. Let your mind dwell on the ineffable mystery of the giant earwig.
RANDOM	There is no giant earwig, you stupid smelly old fart.
OLD THRASHBARG	Bob preserve me . . . I shall intercede for you with the Almighty. (Going off a little way) O Ineffable and Wondrous Bob, vouchsafe unto this Sandwich Maker's daughter the wisdom to follow the path of repentance and contemplation . . . (etc., mumbled, under:)

317

ARTHUR	You shouldn't upset him. Do you know the number of spaceship crashes he's had to start incorporating into his holy stories to keep the villagers interested?
RANDOM	Let's open the package.
ARTHUR	No.
RANDOM	Why not?
ARTHUR	It's not addressed to me.
RANDOM	Yes, it is.
ARTHUR	No, it isn't. It's addressed to Ford Prefect, *care of* me.
RANDOM	Ford Prefect? Is he the one who . . .
ARTHUR	Yes.
RANDOM	What do you think it is?
ARTHUR	I don't know. Something very worrying, though.
RANDOM	How do you know?
ARTHUR	It always is when Ford Prefect's involved.
RANDOM	Well, that's ridiculous.
ARTHUR	No, you don't understand. It's like me trying to explain the watch. It ticks, but that's about all you can say for it so far from Earth.
RANDOM	And you don't understand that there's somewhere this watch belongs! Where it works. Where it fits. Who do you think I am, just your upgrade?
ARTHUR	Random!
RANDOM	Forget it! **(Running off)** You go back and fit in with your stupid sandwiches! I'll go and live in the forest with the other ghosts!
OLD THRASHBARG	**(Approach)** Sandwich Maker . . . the forest is not safe after dark, and dusk is falling.
ARTHUR	I'll get her back. Look after that package, would you.
OLD THRASHBARG	Of course. Of course. What package?

EXT. – LAMUELLAN FOREST – NIGHT

FX: Thunder and rain. Random carefully picking her way through starship wreckage.

FX: **Scurrying of small creatures.**

RANDOM **(Calls)** Hallo . . . ? Who's that? **(To self)** It's just spaceliner wreckage, don't be such a wuss— **(Yelps)** Wah!

FX: **Chittering of squirrel.**

RANDOM Out of the way, squirrel. Shoo!

FX: **More chittering.**

RANDOM What? . . . You want me to take it? OK . . .

FX: **Chittering. Rustling.**

RANDOM A mouldy paper napkin. Just what I needed. **(To another squirrel)** And you want me to drink rainwater out of your acorn?

FX: **Chittering. The squirrels scamper off.**

RANDOM Curiouser and curiouser.

FX: **Tail of music sting wows in (see previous episode).**

RANDOM What! Who—?!

GANGSTA You ain't goin' no furtha, bitch! Only Zarquon gonna save you now!

RANDOM Don't shoot!

FX: **Zap gun fired – female scream wows down, under:**

RANDOM What the—

FX: **Toothpaste commercial jingle wows in.**

VOICE OVER This program is brought to you by Kleen-O-Dent, the toothpaste with Atomic Whitener!

AD CHORUS Glow in the dark,
Bright as the Sun.
Kleen-O-Dent
For everyone.

FX: **Commercial wows out.**

RANDOM Holy Zarquon . . . the Ghosts!

FX: **Ad wows in and out, under forest action.**

PATIENT Oh, Doctor Fernando, tell me I am young again . . .

DOCTOR As young and as beautiful as the day I first built you, Amanda.

RANDOM   Not ghosts . . . The ship's on-board hologram system, still working . . .

PATIENT   Take me in your arms.

DOCTOR   I can't . . . there are rules.

PATIENT   Where love is concerned, there are no rules . . . kiss me better . . .

EXT. – ANOTHER PART OF THE FOREST

FX: Arthur stumbling along painfully.

FX: In distance the ship's entertainment system booming out.

VOICE OVER   We now return you to your scheduled programme: *Blondes and Bullets On Betelgeuse Five* . . .

ARTHUR   (Calls) Random! Random!

EXT. – LAMUELLAN FOREST – NIGHT

FX: Hail of (entertainment system) gunfire. Wows out. Then peace and quiet, just forest sounds, and:

ARTHUR   (Very distant) Randommmm!

INT. – CAVE AMBIENCE

FX: Rain dripping wetly outside. Random opens package, under:

THE VOICE   For a long period of time *The Hitchhiker's Guide* has reported the speculation and controversy about where the so-called 'missing matter' of the Universe has gone. Throughout the Galaxy, the science departments of major universities continue to acquire elaborate equipment to probe the hearts of distant galaxies only to discover, when the missing matter is eventually located, that it is, in fact, all the stuff which the equipment is packed in. There is much missing matter in the package which Random has brought into her cave in the Hondo Mountains – little squashy round white pellets of missing matter – which she is discarding for as yet unborn generations of physicists to track down and discover all over again.

RANDOM   Huh. All that packaging for a stupid dinner plate?! What's the point . . . Oh.

FX: *Guide* unfolds itself. Whirring of wings.

RANDOM   (A bit scared) You're not a dinner plate . . . you're not a black pikka bird either . . .

VOICE OF THE BIRD	Excuse me. I just have to calibrate myself. Can you hear me when I say this?
RANDOM	Is that you talking, origami bird?
VOICE OF THE BIRD	Good. **(Pitch up)** And can you hear me when I say this?
RANDOM	Of course I can!
VOICE OF THE BIRD	**(Sepulchrally deep)** And can you hear me when I say this?
RANDOM	What do you want?
	(A long pause)
VOICE OF THE BIRD	Obviously not. Good, well your hearing range tops out at 16 kilohertz. So. Is this comfortable for you? No harmonics screeching in the upper register? Good. I can use those as data channels. Now. How many of me can you see?
RANDOM	One.
VOICE OF THE BIRD	Good.
RANDOM	What are you?!
VOICE OF THE BIRD	We'll come to that in a minute. **(Multiple voices)** Just how many of me now, please?
	FX: Shutter effect – many versions of the bird flutter around.
RANDOM	For Zark's sake – thousands . . . mirrored into infinity . . .
VOICE OF THE BIRD	I see, still infinite in extent, but at least we're homing in on the right dimensional matrix. Good. No, the answer is an orange and two lemons.
RANDOM	Lemons?
VOICE OF THE BIRD	If I have three lemons and three oranges and I lose two oranges and a lemon what do I have left?
RANDOM	Huh?
VOICE OF THE BIRD	OK, so you think that time flows *that* way, do you? Interesting. Well, I can tell you that in your universe you move freely in three dimensions that you call space. You move in a straight line in a fourth, which you call 'time', and stay rooted to one place in a fifth, which is the first fundamental of probability. After that it gets complicated, and there's all sorts of stuff going on in dimensions thirteen to twenty-two that you really wouldn't want to know about.
RANDOM	How the hell do you know?

VOICE OF THE BIRD	I am the *Guide*. In your universe I am *your Guide*. In fact I inhabit what is technically known as the Whole Sort of General Mish Mash. Come outside and I will show you . . .

FX: It flutters off, Random follows.

EXT. – CAVE CLEARING – EXTERIOR ACOUSTIC

FX: Rain up. Distant thunder.

RANDOM	**(Arriving outside)** In the rain?
VOICE OF THE BIRD	Precisely. What can you see?
RANDOM	Water falling through the bloody air. That's what rain does. Anything else you want to know or can I go home?

(A pause)

VOICE OF THE BIRD	You want to go home?
RANDOM	I haven't got a home!
VOICE OF THE BIRD	Look into the rain.
RANDOM	I'm looking into the rain! What else is there to look at?
VOICE OF THE BIRD	In the water. What shapes do you see?

FX: Hologram on.

RANDOM	**(Grudgingly impressed)** My father . . . looking for me . . . in the rain . . .
ARTHUR	**(Tinnily)** Randommmmmmm . . . !

FX: Hologram off.

RANDOM	OK . . . so you can project images onto the rain of . . . things happening elsewhere. What's that prove?
VOICE OF THE BIRD	Only that it's no more there, or not there, than the rain was. It's all just images in the Mish Mash. Here's another one for you.

FX: Hologram on.

GREBULON LEADER	**(Tinnily)** More fries? A pop-tart?
TRICIA McMILLAN	**(Tinnily)** Actually that cheeseburger has really filled me up . . .
RANDOM	My mother!
VOICE OF THE BIRD	No.

RANDOM	I know my mother when I see her!
VOICE OF THE BIRD	It is not.
RANDOM	Her hair's different, but . . .
VOICE OF THE BIRD	That person is part of the extent of your mother on the probability axis.
RANDOM	Do what?

FX: Hologram off.

VOICE OF THE BIRD	Space, time and probability all have axes along which it is possible to move. You and your father's lives are a sum of the inherently changing probabilities your travels have exposed you to.
RANDOM	That's bollocks.
VOICE OF THE BIRD	Ah. You see the inconsistencies, but not the rule that they prove. You said you wanted to go home. Would you like to see your home?
RANDOM	See it? It was destroyed!
VOICE OF THE BIRD	No, it is discontinuous along the probability axis. Look.

FX: Hologram on.

RANDOM	The Earth . . . Lots of Earths, like a string of beads . . . with gaps . . .

FX: Hologram off.

RANDOM	What was that?
VOICE OF THE BIRD	The probability axis of a discontinuously probable object. The world of your origin lies on a fault line in the landscape of probability which means that, at certain coordinates, the whole of it simply ceases to exist. Typical of all things that lie within the Plural Sectors. Want to go and see for yourself?
RANDOM	To Earth? Is that possible?
VOICE OF THE BIRD	Because of the filters through which you perceive it, your universe is vast to you. Vast in time, vast in space. But I was built with no filters at all, which means I perceive the mish mash which contains all possible universes but which, itself, has no size at all. For me, anything is possible. I am omniscient and omnipotent, extremely vain, and, what is more, I come in a handy self-carrying leatherette wallet.
RANDOM	Is this true?
VOICE OF THE BIRD	Not necessarily.
RANDOM	(Laughing) Are you winding me up?!

VOICE OF THE BIRD	As I warned you, anything is possible.
RANDOM	OK. Let's go to Earth. Let's go to Earth where it exists on its, er . . .
VOICE OF THE BIRD	Probability axis?
RANDOM	Whatever. Where it hasn't been blown up. OK. So you're the *Guide*. How do we get a lift?
VOICE OF THE BIRD	Reverse engineering. To me, the flow of time is irrelevant. You decide what you want. I then merely ensure that it has already happened.
RANDOM	OK. I want a ship to take me to Earth.

FX: Sudden arrival of throbbing ship, it lands, under:

VOICE OF THE BIRD	Will this one do? The brief was a little vague.
RANDOM	(Agape) An RW6? How did— An RW6! I've always wanted—
VOICE OF THE BIRD	I know.

FX: Hatch opens. Ramp slides. Feet on ramp.

FORD PREFECT	(For it is he; whistles)
RANDOM	Uh-oh.
VOICE OF THE BIRD	You have a stone you keep in your pocket for emergencies. Use it.
RANDOM	Yes . . . of course – (Effort) *Uh!*

FX: Ford hit on head. Stone bounces on metal.

FORD PREFECT	(Collapsing) OW! *Hurgh—*

FX: Body fall.

RANDOM	Come on, bird!

FX: She runs up ramp, it flies in with her. Hatch close, lift off, ship roars away.

FX: Feet on dirt – Arthur runs into cave clearing.

ARTHUR	(Running in, breathless) Random! Is that—? (Trips over Ford) Ow!
FORD PREFECT	(Muffled, in pain) Ow!
ARTHUR	(Getting up) What – unh . . . (Intake of breath) Ford!?
FORD PREFECT	(Muffled, fed up) Arthur! You're standing on my head!

INT. – THE BOOK AMBIENCE

VOICE OF THE BIRD (Chilling) Events that draw themselves to a conclusion across multidimensional levels will draw themselves to a conclusion. Closure will be final and irrevocable. And I am *your Guide*. While other listeners hear other voices at the end of this episode, I am here to serve you. We serve each other. And in the last ever episode of *The Hitchiker's Guide to the Galaxy*, what happens is inevitably what must happen.

SIG TUNE

ANNOUNCER In that episode of *The Hitchhiker's Guide to the Galaxy* by Douglas Adams, you heard . . .

The programme was adapted, co-produced and directed by Dirk Maggs, the producers were Helen Chattwell and Bruce Hyman and it was an Above the Title production for BBC Radio 4.

(Voice morphs)

Listen to the bird and let . . .

VOICE OF THE BIRD (Morphs into) . . . me guide you. All is for the best in the best of all possible worlds. Even if it does not have much time left.

FOOTNOTES

Old Thrashbarg Griff Rhys Jones – another Radio Light Entertainment producer from Douglas and Geoffrey's era – turned up with a fund of very funny stories and let rip magnificently with this character, the rest of the assembled company playing the gormless villagers with relish. Sue Sheridan was for once able to break free of Trillian and provide one of her many other voices as the batty lady in need of a dictionary.

One thought about Thrashbarg which would have been fun to develop, given more time, was that he, like Arthur, was not a native Lamuellan but arrived there at some point long long ago and set himself up as village shaman as a sort of pre-emptive power play. Thrashbarg is a humbug but turns out to be a sympathetic one, helping Arthur and Ford escape. One feels the mask is just about to slip as he sends them on their way . . .

Random A very very tricky character to cast and to perform. We were extremely fortunate that our videographer and *Hitchhiker's* über-aficionado, Kevin J. Davies, suggested we meet Samantha Béart, a young actress he had worked with and who had told him she loved *Hitchhiker's*. Sam came in and read for the part and was very impressive. It helped that she knew the character and had an idea of how events had led up to this point.

Random is one of Douglas's most ambitious characters and as the novel was written before he himself became a father, it is not surprising that some of the dialogue in the book between Random and Arthur feels a bit lacking in believability. In many ways Random in the book reads like a stereotypical teenager, defensive and demanding by turns. But something interesting often happens when Douglas's lines are put into the mouths of actors. As we spent time working up the Arthur–Random scenes in different ways it was fascinating to see what emerged.

In particular the big argument scene between father and daughter (the one where the package arrives from Ford) could be played in diametrically opposed ways. One was as an out-and-out screaming contest. The other was using precisely the same lines but asking both Simon and Sam to try and deliver them as if they were very anxious not to upset each other. This was the take that was most exciting, because it did not change Douglas's lines but brought out a whole other layer in the relationship. The tension is there but a bond of affection has been established too. The feeling it creates is that when Random runs away she is running away from herself, not her father.

Tricia and the Grebulons and The ghosts in the forest

There were certain scenes which – through no fault of their own – looked as if they would take a lot of effort and gritting of teeth in our recording schedule and there were others which were obviously light-hearted fun and could be looked forward to. The mock- in-flight entertainment video on Arthur's shuttle in Episode Two was firmly in the latter category because Lorelei King was going to play the patient in the tiny *General Hospital* type soap extract (as well as Gail Andrews the astrologer in Episode One).

Lorelei is a consummate actress who played all the female parts in the *Flywheel, Shyster and Flywheel* Marx Brothers radio shows we worked on together in the early 90s, and she is very resourceful and funny. Freed from the earnest New Age persona of Gail Andrews, she and Roger Gregg played the breathless medical lovers perfectly, both being actors with perfect timing and an ear for just the right turn of phrase. Roger is the quiet, intense genius behind the Crazy Dog Audio Theatre in Dublin, a master of live radio improvisation and a superb writer. Perhaps this is something to do with the fact that Lorelei and Roger are both expatriate American actors, because Sandra Dickinson also shares this talent.

The scenes between Tricia McMillan and the Grebulons seemed to fall into the first recording-schedule category – likely to need much hard work. It was hard to know how to make the Grebulons sound alien without putting treatments on the voices (historically in *Hitchhiker's* radio series a great way to suggest aliens but now much overused in radio science fiction, and, too often, incomprehensible). The best solution seemed to be to ask a trio of comedic actors who already knew each other and could work up routines around the scenes to take on the parts. *RadioActive* veterans Mike Fenton Stevens and Philip Pope had already very kindly been Krikkit civilians in the Tertiary Phase; by putting them together with Andy Taylor (Zem the Mattress) and adding Roger Gregg for support in the background, we ended up with a quartet of Grebulons who were so eager to please and so anxious to know who they were and what they were supposed to be doing that they kept verbally tripping over each other. Sandra/Tricia came into this mix as interlocutor, but instead of politely reacting off the Grebulons' unnerving pronouncements, she proceeded to tear into the scene, whacking back lines like Roger Federer backhands. The result was enormous fun and Sandra proved herself the equal of all four Grebulons.

Random and the Bird The awesome power of the *Guide* Mark II is revealed in a firework display of imaginative projection by Douglas . . . and by the Bird. As Zaphod says earlier, the concept is 'sexy and scary as anything'.

We are bound as humans to a very limited bandwidth of perception ranging across only a few dimensions. Here is a piece of technology which outstrips our five feeble senses to the point where it can even manipulate events – 'reverse-temporal engineering' – to engineer any kind of outcome or coincidence.

This is not only fascinating and funny; in story terms it also creates the precedent that not only ensures a sort of final victory for the Vogons – which Douglas uses as the climax to the book – but at the same time underlines how little we know of what is, and is not, possible. This is the seed of what might have been the next evolution of *Hitchhiker's*. For the purposes of completing the radio saga, in the last episode it supports a coda which the second McGuffin makes possible.

EPISODE FOUR

SIGNATURE TUNE

ANNOUNCER *The Hitchhiker's Guide to the Galaxy*, by Douglas Adams, Quintessential Phase.

Sig fades.

INT. – THE BOOK AMBIENCE

THE VOICE According to *The Hitchhiker's Guide to the Galaxy*, there are rules that deter-
mine the reaction of most life forms to emerging technologies. One: anything that is in your world when you are born is normal and ordinary and is
just a natural part of the way things work. Two: anything that's invented in
the first third of your lifespan is new and exciting and revolutionary and
you can probably get a career in it. Three: anything invented once you are
middle-aged is against the natural order of things. The *Guide* goes on to say
– goes on to – goes . . . **(Jerky wow down to a stop)**

INT. – *GUIDE* MARK II AMBIENCE

VOICE OF THE BIRD Please wait. This entry is being updated over the sub-etha net. The system
will be down for a measurable period.

EXT. – LAMUELLAN FOREST

**FX: Dawn chorus. Chittering of squirrels. Ford and Arthur walking through
underbrush, under:**

ARTHUR Go away!

FX: Squirrel chitters off.

ARTHUR I've been pestered by squirrels all night. They keep on trying to give me
magazines and face wipes.

FORD PREFECT Arthur – is this anywhere near where your ship crashed?

ARTHUR Yes.

FORD PREFECT	Well, it happens. Ship's cabin robots get destroyed. The cyberminds that control them survive and infest the local wildlife. Can turn a whole ecosystem into some kind of helpless service industry, handing out hot towels and drinks to passers-by. By the way, who was that young woman who cracked me over the head and stole my spaceship?
ARTHUR	My daughter.
FORD PREFECT	Beg your pardon?
ARTHUR	My daughter, Ford.
FORD PREFECT	Is there a mother involved?
ARTHUR	Trillian.
FORD PREFECT	Trillian? She told me once she had a kid, but – I didn't think—
ARTHUR	No. I was financing my travel with donations to sperm banks.
FORD PREFECT	And she made an early withdrawal.
ARTHUR	(Sighs) I was hoping it might become a standing order. Ford, what *are* you doing on Lamuella?
FORD PREFECT	Phroo. Long story. I was coming to pick up a parcel I'd sent to myself care of you. It's something unimaginably dangerous.
ARTHUR	So you sent it to me?
FORD PREFECT	You're the one person I could rely on to be absolutely boring and not open it. Except that your daughter's got it now.
ARTHUR	Got what?
FORD PREFECT	The new *Guide*! The bird! She's made off with it and with my ship. And when I say my ship, I mean an RW6.
ARTHUR	A what?
FORD PREFECT	An RW6, for Zark's sake. I've got this great new relationship going between my credit card and the *Guide*'s central computer. And she's stolen my ride! (Sighs) There must be some way off this zarking planet.
ARTHUR	We could sit around and wait for a passing spacecraft, I suppose.
FORD PREFECT	Oh yes? And how many spacecraft have visited this fleapit recently?
ARTHUR	Well, mine came – well, crashed – here a few years ago. Then Trillian of course; and the parcel delivery, and you, and . . . you're right, that's it.
FORD PREFECT	This is important, Arthur.

329

ARTHUR	And my daughter's out there all alone in the Galaxy.
FORD PREFECT	Can we feel sorry for the Galaxy later? It's the *Guide* I'm worried about. It's been taken over. Changed beyond all recognition.
ARTHUR	Oh! Oh! Oh! I'm incoherent with excitement! Please tell me what fascinating bit of badger-sputumly inconsequential trivia you'll assail me with next!
FORD PREFECT	I leaped out of a high-rise window.
ARTHUR	No chance of you doing it again?
FORD PREFECT	I did. The first time I managed to save myself with the help of a security robot I reprogrammed. Called Colin.
ARTHUR	And having saved yourself very cleverly once you very sensibly went and jumped again.
FORD PREFECT	Naturally . . . and fell straight into the open cockpit of a passing jet towncar, whose pilot had inadvertently pushed the eject button instead of changing tracks on the stereo. Even I couldn't think that that was particularly clever of me.
ARTHUR	Oh, I don't know. I expect you probably sneaked into his jetcar the previous night and set it to play the pilot's least favourite track or something.
FORD PREFECT	No, I didn't. Though, coincidentally, somebody else did. And this is the nub. You could trace the chain of coincidences back. Turned out the new *Guide* had done it. It's not an electronic book any more. It's a bird.
ARTHUR	What bird?
FORD PREFECT	The one your daughter is rampaging through the cosmos with. Looks pretty, talks big, uses temporal reverse engineering the way Zaphod mixes Gargle Blasters. Arthur, nobody understands what's been unleashed here!
	FX: Arthur stops walking. Then Ford.
ARTHUR	Oh. Would that explain the Earth?
FORD PREFECT	What Earth?
ARTHUR	A huge hologram, projected onto the rain last night. The Earth, lots of Earths, like a string of sausages, projected in the sky.
FORD PREFECT	Sounds like it was explaining the infinitely multitudinous possibilities of your planet Earth to your daughter. Blow up one, another pops into existence. Handy, but confusing.
ARTHUR	(Rummage in pocket) Mmm. I think . . . I've got . . .

330

FORD PREFECT	An idea?

ARTHUR	(Producing it) A sandwich. (Tearing it) You eat Perfectly Normal Beast, don't you?

FORD PREFECT	Not come across that one.

FX: Both eating.

FORD PREFECT	(Eating) When I found the bird – the *Guide* Mark II – it put on the most fantastic multi-dimensional display I've ever seen. It then said that it would put its services at my disposal in my universe, whether I liked it or not. I said we'd see about that and it said that we would. That's when I packed it up and sent it to you for safety.

ARTHUR	(Eating) Whose safety?

FORD PREFECT	Then, what with one thing and another, my best option seemed to be jumping out of the window again, being fresh out of other options at the time. Did I mention the passing jetcar . . . ? Anyway, whether I liked it or not, the *Guide* was now working for me. And if you've got the *Guide* you think that you're the one it's working for. Mm. Any more sandwiches?

ARTHUR	Have my crusts. But now my daughter has the bird – the *Guide*.

FORD PREFECT	She's the next one in the chain who'll think that everything is going fabulously for her . . . until she's done whatever it is, then it'll all be up for her too. The new *Guide* uses Unfiltered Perception. Do you know what that means?

ARTHUR	Me? I've been making sandwiches, for Bob's sake!

FORD PREFECT	Unfiltered Perc— Who's Bob?

ARTHUR	Never mind.

FORD PREFECT	OK. The Bird – the new *Guide* – perceives everything. We don't. And because it perceives every possible Universe, the bird is present in every possible Universe. Existing in Total Perspective. So they only have to make one of it for everybody to have one. Yes?

ARTHUR	. . . Ish.

FORD PREFECT	With Unfiltered Perception, any move it makes has the power of a virus. It propagates across distance, time and a million other dimensions . . . which means that, somewhere, there is one key instruction. But where's the final application? You know what this means, Arthur?

ARTHUR	Sorry, I nodded off for a moment.

FX: Distant rumble, under:

FORD PREFECT Think about this. You know who I saw at the *Guide* offices? Vogons. The Vogons are behind this!

ARTHUR Good grief – of course—!

FORD PREFECT Oh good. I've said a word you understand at last. But do you know who I found trapped inside their virtual accounting software . . . ?

ARTHUR **(Leaps to his feet)** That noise!

FORD PREFECT The thunder?

ARTHUR It isn't thunder. It's the spring migration of the Perfectly Normal Beasts. It's started early.

FORD PREFECT What are these animals you keep on about?

ARTHUR Our ticket off this planet . . .

INT. – POST-PRODUCTION HOUSE, SOHO – CORRIDOR

FX: Muffled sound of spooling, stops, under:

FX: Knock on door.

TRICIA McMILLAN **(Muffled)** What?

RUNNER Cup of tea, Miss McMillan?

TRICIA McMILLAN What does it say on the door?

RUNNER Um – do not disturb.

TRICIA McMILLAN No, below that.

RUNNER Go away. **(Beat)** Is there a problem? I'm not with you.

TRICIA McMILLAN You are. That's the problem.

INT. – POST-PRODUCTION HOUSE, SOHO – CUTTING ROOM

RUNNER **(Muffled)** Yes, Miss McMillan.

TRICIA McMILLAN Thank you.

FX: Spooling, runs, stops:

TRICIA **(On tape)** This is Tricia McMillan reporting from the surface of the Planet Rupert—

332

TRICIA McMILLAN	No—
	FX: Spooling.
TRICIA McMILLAN	The stuff in the ship going there first—
	FX: Spooling stops.
	FX: Grebulon scoutship atmos.
GREBULON LIEUTENANT	(On tape) —arrive at Rupert in something like seven of your Earth hours.
TRICIA	(On tape) Which means you must have some form of propulsion unknown to us on Earth.
GREBULON LIEUTENANT	(On tape) Oh, you mean is it a warp drive or something like that? You'd have to ask our Flight Engineer, Mr Scott.
TRICIA	(On tape) Which one is he?
GREBULON LIEUTENANT	(On tape) We don't know. We have all lost our minds, you see.
	FX: Spooling starts.
TRICIA McMILLAN	Who's going to believe this?
	FX: Spooling stops.
	FX: Background lots of TVs showing different output, under:
TRICIA	(On tape) (A little embarassed) Er – this is Rupert, the home of the um, Grebulons. It may look, to you, the viewer, like a bunch of slightly thin and discoloured people sitting around watching televisions that show reruns of M*A*S*H and The Rockford Files—
	FX: Spooling starts.
TRICIA McMILLAN	I'll be laughed out of the business.
	FX: Spooling stops.
TRICIA	(On tape) This is clearly alien technology on a dramatic scale. Huge, grey buildings under the dark canopy of a clear pressure dome . . .
TRICIA McMILLAN	Could be a studio set from just about any low-budget science-fiction movie.
TRICIA	(On tape) And here comes the Grebulon Leader.
TRICIA McMILLAN	Looking like some guy in costume and make-up, standing in front of a cheap cardboard set . . .
TRICIA	(On tape) Hallo . . . Leader.

GREBULON LEADER	**(On tape)** Miss McMillan, I cannot tell you how much I enjoy your shows on TV. I am your greatest fan. I am so glad you have been able to visit us on Rupert and help us triangulate our astrological position. Here is the book I want you to use.
TRICIA	**(On tape)** *You And Your Planets* by Gail Andrews?!
	FX: Click.
TRICIA McMILLAN	Oh my God. There's nothing of any use here at all . . . oh my . . . **(Dawning horror)** I left astronomical research because I couldn't prove that a glamorous alien with two heads once tried to pick me up at a party . . . I switched careers to TV. Now I dream up an alien race of people stuck on a remote outpost of our solar system; filling their cultural vacuum with our media junk. It's happened again. I have no recollection of faking any of this. But if I ever show it to anybody, I'll be a laughing stock. **(Sighs, then catches sight of something)** Wait a minute – what are *those*?
	FX: Spooling, interrupted by knock on door.
RUNNER	**(Muffled)** Miss McMillan—
TRICIA McMILLAN	**(Calls)** What *is it*?
RUNNER	It's an alien spaceship!
	FX: She jumps to the door, opening it.
TRICIA McMILLAN	What?
RUNNER	An alien spaceship. In Regent's Park. Big silver job. Some girl with a funny-looking bird. Speaks English, throws rocks at people and keeps asking for you. The girl, that is, not . . .
TRICIA McMILLAN	For me?
RUNNER	There's a taxi outside with a camera crew.
TRICIA McMILLAN	Where's my bag? Oh, never mind – no – wait. Look.
RUNNER	**(Nervous)** Yes?
TRICIA McMILLAN	That freeze-frame. Do those buildings look like huge gun turrets to you?
RUNNER	Yeah . . . what is it? The SciFi Channel?
TRICIA McMILLAN	**(Groans)** Never mind. **(Runs off)** Just keep that door locked!

INT. – *GUIDE* MARK II AMBIENCE

VOICE OF THE BIRD Many many light years from anywhere lies the abandoned planet of Vog-sphere. Somewhere on its fetid, fog-bound mudbanks stands, surrounded by the broken and empty carapaces of its last few jewelled scuttling crabs, a stone monument which marks the place where, it is thought, the species *Vogon vogonblurtus* first arose. On the monument is carved an arrow which points away into the fog, under which are inscribed the words 'The buck stops there.' 'There', in this instance, is the flagship of Captain Prostetnic Vogon Jeltz's constructor fleet. The captain's job all comes down, in essence, to one instruction. He is to put a tick in a box on a checklist when he has carried it out. He has carried out the instruction once before, but a number of troublesome circumstances have prevented him from putting the tick in the box. One of them is the Plural nature of this Galactic sector, where anything you demolish keeps on reappearing. That will soon be taken care of. Another problem has been the irritating and anarchic device called *The Hitchhiker's Guide to the Galaxy*. That is now well and truly taken care of and, through temporal reverse engineering, its successor is the agency through which everything else will be taken care of, including a small group of people who continually refuse to be where they are supposed to be when they are supposed to be there. Particularly the two who are stranded on the planet Lamuella.

EXT. – LAMUELLA – PLAINS OF ANHONDO

FX: Thundering hooves, bellows of the Perfectly Normal Beasts as they stampede.

FORD PREFECT (Yells) Wave the towel higher! Flick it! Careful, don't get run over!

ARTHUR (Yells) This isn't working! We'll be killed if we try to jump on to a stampeding Perfectly Normal Beast. Well, you will.

FORD PREFECT (Yells) Pardon?

FX: They move back from the herd. Stampede lower.

ARTHUR (More conversational) Ford, have you ever heard of Stavromula Beta?

FORD PREFECT Don't think so. How do you spell it?

ARTHUR Don't know. You remember I told you about Agrajag?

FORD PREFECT You mean the guy who was convinced you were getting him killed over and over again?

ARTHUR	Yes. One of the places he claimed I'd got him killed is called Stavromula Beta. Someone tries to shoot me, it seems. I duck and Agrajag, or one of his many reincarnations, gets hit. It seems that this has definitely happened at some point in time so, I suppose, I can't get killed at least until after I've ducked on Stavromula Beta.
FORD PREFECT	Yeah, well I wouldn't bet my life on stopping a one-and-a-half-ton Perfectly Normal Beast armed with nothing but a towel.
ARTHUR	But they are a way out of here – they gallop up this plain, turn by the hills at the far end and just disappear . . . and they return at the next migration.
FORD PREFECT	Certainly looks like it might be some kind of evidence of dimensional drift.
ARTHUR	Which is what?
FORD PREFECT	A multidimensional nexus intersecting this planet.
ARTHUR	Which means we can ride our way out of here.
FORD PREFECT	Exactly. But waving that towel around like a matador isn't going to do it. You've got to flick it more. You need more follow-through from the elbow if you're going to get those blasted creatures to notice anything at all.
ARTHUR	What about you? You need more suppleness in the wrist.
FORD PREFECT	You need more after-flourish.
ARTHUR	You need a bigger towel.
OLD THRASHBARG	(Off) You need a pikka bird.
FORD PREFECT	You what?
ARTHUR	Hallo, Old Thrashbarg.
OLD THRASHBARG	To attract the attention of a Perfectly Normal Beast, you need a pikka bird. Like this.
	FX: Pikka bird – pikka pikka.
FORD PREFECT	The bird he's holding. What is it?
ARTHUR	A pikka bird. Its eggs make rather a good omelette. The secret is whipping them lightly with—
FORD PREFECT	I don't want a zarking recipe, I just want to be sure it's a real bird and not a multidimensional cybernightmare.
OLD THRASHBARG	So. Is it written that Bob shall once more take back unto himself the benediction of his once-given Sandwich Maker?

336

FORD PREFECT	He's barmy, isn't he?
ARTHUR	(**Low**) He always talks like that. (**Aloud**) Ah, venerable Thrashbarg. I'm afraid I think I'm going to have to be popping off now. But young Drimple, my apprentice, will be a fine Sandwich Maker in my stead.
OLD THRASHBARG	(**Like an invocation**) O Sandwich Maker from Bob . . . !
ARTHUR	Yes?
OLD THRASHBARG	(**Tricky one, this**) Life . . . will be a very great deal less weird without you!
ARTHUR	Do you know, I think that's the nicest thing anybody's ever said to me?
FORD PREFECT	Old man, where do these beasts go?
OLD THRASHBARG	To the Domain of the King!
FORD PREFECT	What King?
OLD THRASHBARG	Come! Let us show the Bird to the Beasts! Then you will ride there!

EXT. – REGENT'S PARK – DAY

FX: Helicopters, sirens, a crowd.

RANDOM	(**Yelling**) Trillian Astra! I want to see Trillian Astra!
POLICEMAN	(**Off, through loud hailer**) Now step away from the flying saucer, please, miss.
RANDOM	(**Close, yelling**) Come a step closer and I'll throw this rock at your head!
POLICEMAN	(**Loud hailer**) We can't locate a Trillian Astra.
RANDOM	(**Yell**) I told you before! Her Earth name is Tricia McMillan. I know she's here!
VOICE OF THE BIRD	(**Close**) Random.
RANDOM	Yes, little bird?
VOICE OF THE BIRD	Say the word and I can make him go away. For ever.
RANDOM	I – no – don't.
VOICE OF THE BIRD	Then I am needed elsewhere . . .

FX: Bird folds itself up into nothing.

RANDOM	Wait – no – where did you go—?

FX: In amongst the crowd:

TRICIA McMILLAN	(Bustling) How's my hair? Yes? Nose shiny? How's that? Good. Turn over.
RANDOM	(In background) Keep away! All of you! Where's my bird?
CAMERAMAN	Recording. Take one, no slate.
TRICIA McMILLAN	Cue in three-two-one— This is Tricia McMillan reporting from Regent's Park where an astonishing sight has brought London to a standstill. I'm just moving up to the barriers to see if I can have a word with the teenage girl who has arrived in a spaceship.
RANDOM	(Off) You!
TRICIA McMILLAN	Er – yes. Hallo! Can I just ask . . . um – Are you from Zaphod?
RANDOM	You can change your hair colour and your accent and hide here – but you're still my mother, you bitch!

EXT. – LAMUELLA – PLAINS OF ANHONDO

FX: Thundering hooves, bellows of the Perfectly Normal Beasts as they stampede in background.

FX: Foreground: a solitary beast snorts and moos. Pikka pikka of pikka bird.

FORD PREFECT	(Whisper) I don't think I've ever seen anything quite so stupid in my life.
ARTHUR	I wondered why your people took pikka birds on Beast hunts.
OLD THRASHBARG	They fascinate the Beasts. Bob knows why. And once a Perfectly Normal Beast is fascinated, it becomes docile. But not for long. Get on the Beast! Both of you!

FX: Arthur/Ford business of getting on the Beast . . .

ARTHUR	(Effort) Yuk. How can something so delicious smell so rank?
FORD PREFECT	(Effort) You've obviously never met Eccentrica Gallumbits . . .
OLD THRASHBARG	Now, Sandwich Maker! Go!

FX: He slaps the Beast's rump. With a bellow it lunges forward into the herd.

FORD PREFECT	Hold tight, Arthur!
ARTHUR	Can you see anything?
FORD PREFECT	No!

OLD THRASHBARG	**(Off, yelling)** Go! Ride that Beast! Ride that Perfectly Normal Beast to the Domain of the King!
FORD PREFECT	What King?
ARTHUR	He just said the King.
FORD PREFECT	I didn't know there was a 'the King'.
ARTHUR	Nor did I. Hold tight, for goodness' sake.
FORD PREFECT	Except of course for the King. And he obviously didn't mean him.
ARTHUR	What King?
FORD PREFECT	I'm only saying that if he didn't mean the King, I don't know what he means.
ARTHUR	What?
FORD PREFECT	Look out – here comes the end of the valley.
ARTHUR	Are you sure we're doing the right thing.
FORD PREFECT	No. But wherever these animals vanish to, we're about to find out—
ARTHUR	Hold on—
	FX: Stampede into a huge void. Last despairing bellow from the Beast. Then the reverb turns back on itself, a moment of hanging in space, then crash back into stampeding turmoil:
	EXT. – THE DOMAIN OF THE KING BAR & GRILL
	FX: Desert daytime.
	Music: Muffled rockabilly from within the bar.
FORD PREFECT	Heyyy! We did it!
ARTHUR	Where are we?
FORD PREFECT	Jump!
ARTHUR	**(Jumps)** *Whurp—!*
	FX: They roll off into the dust and get up, dishevelled.
	FX: The stampede moves off.
FORD PREFECT	Neat work! Are you in one piece?
ARTHUR	At the risk of repeating myself, where are we?

339

FORD PREFECT	The Domain of the King. Look.
ARTHUR	**(Reads)** Ah. 'The Domain of the King Bar & Grill'. Not sure if that's irony or anti-climax.
FORD PREFECT	Are you kidding? Look at these spaceships parked outside! The pink one. Now that's class.
ARTHUR	It's all chrome and fins. Retro . . . grade, probably.
FORD PREFECT	I'm buying that spaceship. I'll teach them to make me a restaurant critic.
ARTHUR	What do you mean?
FORD PREFECT	**(Pulls card from pocket, flexes it)** The old Dine-O-Charge card. Let's go run up some expenses.

INT. – DOMAIN OF THE KING BAR & GRILL

Music: Gentle bluesy guitar noodling.

ARTHUR	Mmm, if it wasn't for the band and a bartender I'd say this place was exclusively unpopular.
FORD PREFECT	Suits me.
BARTENDER	What can I do for you, gents?
FORD PREFECT	Couple beers, a couple bacon rolls, that pink thing outside and whatever you're having yourself.
BARTENDER	**(Pouring beers)** Not sure the pink thing's for sale.
FORD PREFECT	Sure it is. How much you want?
BARTENDER	'Tain't mine to sell.
FORD PREFECT	So, whose?
BARTENDER	Good-lookin' dude with the band. Dark hair, gold suit.
FORD PREFECT	Wait here, Arthur. **(To bartender)** Keep the tab open.
BARTENDER	New here, son?
ARTHUR	Me? Just rode into town . . .
BARTENDER	Nice weather for it.
ARTHUR	I hadn't no—
FORD PREFECT	**(Returning)** OK. It's cool. We got the pink thing.

BARTENDER	(Impressed) He's selling it to you?
FORD PREFECT	Giving it to us for free.
BARTENDER	Jeepers.
ELVIS	(Off) Hey, Lamarr, switch on the stage lights, man. C'mon, Scotty, Bill . . .
BARTENDER	(Going off) You got it, King . . .
FORD PREFECT	(Knowing) Hey, Arthur, how many singers does it take to change a lightbulb?
ELVIS	(Under following, tests mic) One . . . Two . . . One . . . Two . . .
FORD PREFECT	(Pulls at the beer, sighs) You know, Arthur, it's at times like this that I feel that what the big guy says is right. What does it matter? Let it go.
ARTHUR	Which big guy?
FORD PREFECT	The one at the mic. Let it all go is what he said. Take the ship. Take it with my blessing. Be good to her.
ARTHUR	How many beers have you had?
FORD PREFECT	But then you think of guys like InfiniDim Enterprises and you think, they are not going to get away with it. It is my sacred and holy duty to see those guys suffer. (Calls) Bartender – let me put something on the tab for the singer. I asked for a special request.
BARTENDER	Whatever. How much?
FORD PREFECT	(Diminishes to a whisper) Well, I was thinking . . . (Ooof!)

FX: Body fall.

ARTHUR	Is he all right?
FORD PREFECT	Just needed to take the weight off his feet.

Music: Elvis sings 'Our Lovely World', under:

ARTHUR	Ford, will that ship get us to Earth?
FORD PREFECT	Sure will.
ARTHUR	Oh. No. Lend me your *Guide*.
FORD PREFECT	Here.

FX: *Guide* out of satchel. Switched on.

THE VOICE	(Distort in bar) *The Hitchhiker's Guide to the Galaxy*.

FX: Button pressed.

ARTHUR	Earth.
THE VOICE	(Distorted) Earth. Mostly harmless.
ARTHUR	It's there! The Earth is still there! That's where Random will be going! The bird was showing her the Earth in the rainstorm!
FORD PREFECT	Quiet, Arthur. I paid to hear this song.
ARTHUR	Ford . . . are you crying?
FORD PREFECT	Uh – dust in my eye.
ARTHUR	We have to go.
FORD PREFECT	Not till I've reviewed the restaurant.
ARTHUR	Write a review? Of this place?

FX: Guide on. Ford typing in, under:

FORD PREFECT	Filing the review validates the expenses claim. OK. (Taps in:) 'The beer is good and cold, local wildlife nicely eccentric, the bar singer is, without exaggeration, the best in the known universe, and that's about it.' Sub-Etha Send. Doesn't need much. Just a validation. And this bill is going to need some validating.
ARTHUR	(Suspicious) How much *did* you tip the singer?
FORD PREFECT	More money than the Colonel made for him in an entire career of doing crap movies and casino gigs. Just for doing what he does best. Singing in a bar. And he negotiated it himself. With any luck, this is a good moment for him. And a very bad one for InfiniDim Enterprises.

Music: Song up to end. They applaud.

ARTHUR	(Wonderingly) A different Earth . . . different outcomes to different lives . . .
FORD PREFECT	We're outta here. Thanks, El.
ELVIS	(Off, relaxed) Hey, take it easy, Ford. Y'all come back now.
FORD PREFECT	(To Arthur) Let's flash the plastic and see what that pink thing can do.

INT. – GREBULON BASE ON RUPERT

NB: His dialogue switches into distort as we go to observe it from the Vogon ship.

GREBULON LIEUTENANT	(Entering) You summoned me, Captain Picard?

GREBULON LEADER	Yes, Lieutenant Kojak. I am troubled. Our mission was a watching brief. But I'm bored with monitoring the Earth, to be honest. I am bored with *Cagney & Lacey*. I am bored with the 'Tribbles' episode of *Classic Star Trek*. I am bored with not knowing who I am and having to pick a new name out of an old *TV Guide* every morning.
GREBULON LIEUTENANT	At least now we can work out our astrological charts. That gives us work to do. And a plan to follow.
GREBULON LEADER	But all the other equipment with us must have some purpose. If only we hadn't lost our minds when the meteorite wiped out our data banks. We need a purpose, and the TV and the PlayStation are not enough.
GREBULON LIEUTENANT	Has something happened?
GREBULON LEADER	Yes. Miss McMillan helped us re-calculate the movement of the planets, and now my stars foretell that I am about to have a very bad month if I don't take positive action. Today. Because today Earth is starting to rise into Capricorn, and as a classic Taurus, this is ominous for me indeed.
GREBULON LIEUTENANT	So you're going to take positive action?
GREBULON LEADER	I have decided to investigate the astrological potential of our gun turrets.

INT. – VOGON FLAGSHIP – BRIDGE

GREBULON LEADER	(Now in distort) Have Huggy Bear and the Two Ronnies link the targeting circuits to the astrology computer tracking Earth.
GREBULON LIEUTENANT	(Distorted) Aye aye, Captain.
	FX: Click off.
VOICE OF THE BIRD	It is as you wished, Captain Prostetnic Vogon Jeltz.
PROSTETNIC VOGON JELTZ	Reverse-temporal engineering at its finest, little bird. You have served us very well and very often. Are the displaced persons all on Earth?
VOICE OF THE BIRD	They will be reunited within minutes. And the Grebulons are arming their multidimensional disruptors.
PROSTETNIC VOGON JELTZ	You have fulfilled your function. And I can shortly put a tick on my checklist without further outlay of billable resources. Now show me the Earths. All of them. I want to see this for myself.
VOICE OF THE BIRD	Closing Brackets. Parsing Clauses. Endifs. Halting Repeat Loops. Calling Recursive Functions. Preparing to Force Quit. Engaging Total Perspective Vortex . . .

PROSTETNIC
VOGON JELTZ
Ahhh. The blue and green watery tube of Earth in all its dimensions . . . The occasion almost calls for a poem . . .

INT. – LONDON TAXI, SPEEDING THROUGH SOHO

FX: Radio audible under Ford and Arthur:

NEWSREADER
(NEIL SLEAT)
. . . a second spacecraft, this time pink, was reported to have landed on Portland Place, in Central London. Its two human occupants booked rooms at, and subsequently bought, the Langham Hilton Hotel. Shortly afterwards a smaller, single-person craft bearing a lone female occupant landed without incident in the Embankment Gardens.

ARTHUR
How did you buy London Zoo?

FORD PREFECT
(Eating) Room service. We had a room and I wanted service. All the animals that can be safely returned to the wild are going to be released. They promised on Reception to set up some good teams of people to monitor their progress. Apparently their concierge can get you anything.

ARTHUR
And all on a *Hitchhiker's Guide* Dine-O-Charge card?

FORD PREFECT
Yes . . . I suppose I should be worried that it works on this planet. Foie gras?

ARTHUR
No thanks. I always feel bad about foie gras. Bit cruel to the geese.

FORD PREFECT
Sod the geese. You can't care about every damn thing. (Calls) Next left, driver.

ARTHUR
You know where this club is?

FORD PREFECT
Stavro's? Well, I've been to his original club in New York, I knew he was opening one here. When your daughter stopped chucking rocks at Trillian and demanded to be taken clubbing, it was pretty easy to find out which one she'd be taken to.

ARTHUR
But it's not Trillian, is it? It's Tricia McMillan.

FX: Taxi brakes, stops, doors open, etc., under:

TAXI DRIVER
We're here, gents. Number 42.

FX: Street atmos as they exit taxi. It drives off, under:

FORD PREFECT
Come on, Arthur. Family reunion.

INT. – STAVRO'S CLUB

Music: Low, clubby.

FORD PREFECT	Afternoon!
DOORMAN	Er – you a member?
FORD PREFECT	Friend of Miss McMillan.
DOORMAN	She's downstairs, sir – with a – girl.
FORD PREFECT	Thank you.
DOORMAN	Who are you?
ARTHUR	Er—
FORD PREFECT	He's with me. **(To Arthur)** Down here—

FX: Feet on spiral staircase.

ARTHUR	Reminds me of the starship *Bistromath*.
FORD PREFECT	Excuse me – thank you—

FX: Jostling/bodies on staircase (?)

ARTHUR	Oh – can I squeeze past, please—
AGRAJAG	I thought I told you not to come here?
FORD PREFECT	What?
AGRAJAG	Not you – him.
ARTHUR	Me? Bu— I'm sorry?
AGRAJAG	Excuse me . . . I think I must have mistaken you for someone else.
ARTHUR	Oh. **(Low)** Ford, he's still staring at me.
FORD PREFECT	Now what?
AGRAJAG	What did you say?
FORD PREFECT	I said, now what?
AGRAJAG	Excuse me, I'm trying desperately to remember which drug I've just taken, but it must be one of those ones which mean you can't remember.
FORD PREFECT	Try the men's room.
AGRAJAG	**(Going off)** Yes, where was it again?

FORD PREFECT	Come on, Arthur.
ARTHUR	I don't like places like this, Ford. For all of my dreams of Earth and home, I miss my hut on Lamuella and my knives and my sandwiches. I even miss Old Thrashbarg.
TRILLIAN/TRICIA	**(Together)** Arthur!/Arthur?
ARTHUR	Trillian? Tricia?
FORD PREFECT	Both, it seems.
TRICIA McMILLAN	Somebody please tell me what is going on. And who this woman is.
RANDOM	All of you – stop!
FORD PREFECT	**(Low)** Arthur. The gun your daughter is holding was in the ship she stole from me. It's a Wabanatta 3, very dangerous. **(Up)** Let's just everybody stay calm and find out what's the matter.
RANDOM	I thought I would fit here on the world that made me. But it turns out that even my mother doesn't know who I am!
TRILLIAN	Random. I'm here.
TRICIA McMILLAN	All right, joke over. Where's the hidden camera?
RANDOM	Shut up! You abandoned me!
TRILLIAN	Random, it is very important that you listen to me. We must leave. We must all leave now.
RANDOM	What are you talking about? We're always leaving!
TRILLIAN	This is not your home. You don't have one. We none of us have. The war I left you to report on – the missing ship that didn't turn up to fight is here, in this solar system, and its crew are lost and frightened and about to do something very misguided because they also have no home. We've got to go.
ARTHUR	It's all right, Trillian. If I'm here, we're safe. Nothing can happen to me till I go to Stavromula Beta. OK?
FORD PREFECT	**(Whisper)** Arthur, keep talking – that man we passed on the stairs – he's sneaked behind your daughter – I think he's going for the gun—
TRILLIAN	What are you saying?
ARTHUR	Let's all just relax.
AGRAJAG	Excuse me—

346

ARTHUR	No!
TRICIA McMILLAN	Random – no!
FORD PREFECT	Arthur – duck!
	FX: Zap gun blast. Body fall.
ARTHUR	**(Rushes to man's side)** Are you all right?
AGRAJAG	You . . .
RANDOM	I'm sorry! I didn't mean to.
TRICIA McMILLAN	It was an accident.
TRILLIAN	**(Low, urgent)** Arthur we need to leave, *now*.
ARTHUR	We're safe, Trillian. There's time to sort out this mess.
TRILLIAN	Really? Have you looked at the name of this club?
ARTHUR	It's Stavro's Club, isn't it?
TRILLIAN	Here – look at the menu cover.
ARTHUR	Trillian! How can you think of food at a— Oh my God.
TRILLIAN	The landlord's name is Stavro Mueller. His first club in New York was named Alpha. This is his second club.
ARTHUR	Stavro Mueller Beta.
FORD PREFECT	Oh, that's good. Very good. **(Laughs)**
ARTHUR	**(Sighs)** Well. Thank Bob that's over.
TRILLIAN	. . . Who's Bob?

EXT. – SPACE

FX: Earth explodes. In Dolby Digital.

Fade out.

FOOTNOTES

'The reaction of life forms to emerging technologies'

Another quote from *The Salmon of Doubt* which provides an apposite introduction to Ford's attempt to explain the *Guide* Mark II to Arthur, who, it must be said, has not so much succumbed to the Stockholm syndrome after months if not years on Lamuella, as is now a passport-carrying Swedish citizen with shares in Saab and a complete set of Abba CDs in his Ikea bedroom. Arthur has finally found somewhere that he is content, happily providing a simple service to a pre-industrial society, and it's rather sad that Ford has to arrive and drag him out of it, back to the rat race, and, quite possibly, a violent demise.

Tricia in the cutting room

Tricia reviewing the raw takes of her trip to Rupert was a convenient way of covering aspects of her backstory. Given Tricia's relative 'normality' as a *Hitchhiker's* character, her motivation for turning from astrophysics to anchorwoman jars somewhat in the novel, and her reactions on viewing this material acknowledge that.

The Voice of the Bird and the history of the Vogons

'Many, many light years from anywhere lies the abandoned planet of Vogsphere . . .' This would, of course, be a speech given in any other episode to the Voice of the Book, but by now the *Guide* Mark II *is* the voice of the book, having taken over as completely as Bill Franklyn took over from Peter Jones at the start of the Tertiary Phase. Thus at this point the Vogon plan is nearing fruition – the *Guide* is now theirs, as is the means to destroy the pestilentially profligate Earths and its collective progeny.

The Domain of the King

A wonderful scene but one which very very nearly had to be omitted. Squeezing all the necessary climactic elements into this episode was going to be hard enough and this scene was, strictly speaking, a single gag with no real relevance to the bigger story issues. On the other hand the notion that, having escaped from an alternative Earth, Elvis Presley lived a more fulfilled life in comfort and peace is hugely appealing to those of a certain age (like Douglas and most of the rest of us), and Ford's misuse of a corporate credit card to reward the King is touching, poignant and wickedly appropriate.

Lieutenant Kojak and Captain Picard

It was fun to extend the idea of cultural pollution into the Grebulons' daily life. Given that they simply had no idea of who they were, assumption of identities from their source of 'monitoring' gave us some suitably silly references. Mostly these are memorable television names from the 70s and 80s. After all, the *Hitchhiker* novels and original radio series are of a certain period, and if Arthur (in *So Long, and Thanks for all the Fish*) finds himself at home only six months after leaving Earth, then only a limited amount of time can have elapsed since. Possibly quite a bit less than we have experienced in *our* reality. In short, if we had been able to make these series in the mid-1990s as Douglas had wished, contemporary analogies might have been more in evidence. On the other hand, memorable television has been in short supply for much longer than that, so Kojak and Picard would probably still have been the choices.

The taxi ride Douglas spends long expository passages assembling the various elements of his cast on Earth for the denouement of *Mostly Harmless*. This acts as a huge tease. Delighted at the prospect of the old team reassembling (at least in part), we are wondering what will now happen, and the unwary can expect some act of last-minute deliverance, particularly when it becomes clear that Trillian has arrived in London and probably knows a thing or two about what is going on. Will she use her experience with the Elders of Krikkit to talk the Grebulons out of blowing it all up? In the book we're not sure that blowing it all up will be the outcome until the moment it happens, but as the number of pages remaining dwindle something big and very sudden seems likely to occur, and it's only human nature to hope that it will be exciting and positive, a trap which Douglas has cunningly set.

It was necessary to fold a lot of plot into a very short period if some kind of resolution beyond the big bang ending was to get airtime. In the novel Ford uses his Dine-O-Charge card not only to hire a suite at the Langham but also to buy the hotel itself *and* London Zoo (while eating foie gras; a nice irony about Ford's approach to conservation from Douglas). This entire sequence of events is related in conversation during the taxi ride to Stavro's club while simultaneously a news bulletin announces Trillian's arrival. Time is of the essence and long passages of narration are not the stuff of dramatic climax, so a compromise had to be found.

Stavro Mueller Beta 'We're here, gents. Number 42.'

In ignorance (not necessarily blissful), Ford and Arthur enter the club that bears a fateful name. And upon the stairs encounter a character whose appearance at this point demonstrates how Douglas would unhesitatingly manipulate time and space and many dimensions to fit the plot. Agrajag (for it is he) is here in an *earlier* incarnation than the four-foot fruitbat with an orthodontic condition Arthur met in the Tertiary Phase. Also played by Douglas in this episode (the lines edited from his reading of the audiobook of *Mostly Harmless*), this character will inadvertently take the bullet meant for Arthur. In the book, he is a bystander to events in the bar; in this episode he actively attempts to wrest the gun from Random and gets shot for his pains. This is not a conscious effort to make him a more sympathetic character, it's a purely technical device to keep the plot moving along. This is a scene of high drama with few comedy moments. Fine for a novel but tricky in a slot on BBC Radio reserved for comedy. If there is to be a coda then the only approach to this scene is to play it with an economy of over-acting and an unhesitating drive towards the fracture in time which awaits us.

Codas Earth is destroyed, and as the *Guide* Mark II reveals, all of the Earths that ever existed or ever can exist, by the lost battleship of the Grebulons, unwitting puppets of the increasingly seedy Vogons.

But this is an Infinite Universe created by Douglas Adams, full of Multiple Realities, existing on Parallel Layers. If, as Douglas constantly suggests, absolutely *anything* is possible – be it achieved through reverse-temporal engineering by the *Guide* Mark II, or through the unknown, unknowable knowledge of the Dolphins, or through sheer blind coincidence – which has ever stalked Arthur Dent and revealed itself to be his friend, no matter how Improbable – then the inescapable truth is that The End of *Mostly Harmless* is, at best, An End.

This coda suggests several possibilities, all of which loop back to previous iterations of *Hitchhiker's*. Here is a less disturbing closure if you choose to listen to it, or the resolution of the tale as Douglas left it is still there to stop at if you'd rather not.

However, as John Marsh indicates in the closing announcement, those big yellow ships hanging so un-bricklike overhead in *our* reality could render any choice redundant.

Unless you have a McGuffin in your ear, perhaps.

Thank you, Douglas.

And thank Bob that's over.

EXT. – SPACE

FX: Earth explodes. In Dolby Digital.

Fade out.

FX: Bzt. Bzzt. Bzzzt.

VOICE OF THE BIRD   Please wait. This entry is being updated over the – BZT!

VOICE OF THE BIRD   Will be d-d-d-down for a measurable period -eriod -eriod. BZZZZT!

(Then)

THE VOICE (PETER)   The Babel fish is small, yellow and leechlike, and probably the oddest thing in the Universe. It feeds on brainwave energy, absorbing all unconscious frequencies and then excreting telepathically a matrix formed from the conscious frequencies with nerve signals picked up from the speech centres of the brain, the practical upshot of which is that if you stick one in your ear you can instantly understand anything said to you in any form of language – BZT!

THE VOICE (WILLIAM)   Another ability evolved by the Babel fish is its tactic for self-preservation. Only one other aquatic creature in the Universe has developed the Babel fish's capacity for Continuous Probability Transference in the picosecond before unavoidable destruction. Thus, as Earth's Plural Zone folds itself away like a card table after a particularly energetic hand of snap, the Babel fishes, their hosts and any cetaceans in the vicinity simultaneously flick into existence in any alternative layers of reality they can inhabit along the Probability Curve. In the case of Arthur Dent, this leads to several probable realities. One has been in existence for many years, and, in the master bathroom aboard the *Heart of Gold* . . .

INT. – *HEART OF GOLD*

FX: Shower running.

ARTHUR   (In shower, calls) Blast . . . Eddie? Eddie!

351

EDDIE	Hey there, monkey in the shower! Water too hot? Too cold? You'd prefer asses' milk, maybe?
ARTHUR	I've run out of shampoo! Can you ask Lintilla to bring some in?

FX: Shower door opens. Lintillas giggling, background.

LINTILLA 1	You wanted shampoo, Arthur?
ARTHUR	Gosh – thanks, er, Lintilla – that was quick.
LINTILLA 1	Would you like us to scrub your back?
ARTHUR	Erm – who's 'us' – ?
LINTILLA 1	Well, there are now over eight hundred thousand million Lintilla clones in the Brantisvogan Escort Agency.
ARTHUR	Good grief!
LINTILLA 1	And I thought I'd invite a few of my sisters aboard. Do you mind?
LINTILLAS	Hallo, Arthur/Ooh, this is cosy/Move over a bit/Is that Soap On A Rope?
ARTHUR	Wow. Eddie – more hot water – quick!
EDDIE	No problemo, capitano!

FX: Water, scrubbing, Arthur and Lintillas giggling . . .

INT. – THE BOOK AMBIENCE

THE VOICE	. . . another Arthur pops up in another time, when yet another Earth hung like a blue opal in this corner of the Galaxy . . .

EXT. – ARTHUR'S HOUSE

FX: General road-building noises. Bulldozers, pneumatic drills, etc.

PROSSER	Come off it, Mr Dent, you can't win, you know. There's no point in lying in the path of progress.
ARTHUR	I've gone off the idea of progress. It's overrated.
PROSSER	But you must realize you can't lie in the path of the bulldozers indefinitely.
ARTHUR	I'm game, we'll see who rusts first. Won't we, Fenchurch?
FENCHURCH	Get stuffed, Prosser. This is our cottage.

352

INT. – THE BOOK AMBIENCE

THE VOICE But perhaps the alternative that best suits the Babel fishes – and their hosts – is the convivial safety of a location and a time far, far removed from any uncertainty, improbability, or sobriety . . . an infinite loop of bistromathics where dinner guests wait patiently for each other to turn up.

INT. – MILLIWAYS

FX: The Restaurant at the End of the Universe in full swing.

MAX QUORDLEPLEEN (Through PA, in background) Welcome one and all to Milliways, the Restaurant at the End of the Universe! I'm Max Quordlepleen, and tonight and every night I'll be with you right through to the End of History itself!

FX: Applause and laughter, continues under with Max.

MAX QUORDLEPLEEN (cont'd + FX) And now, ladies and gentlemen, I would like to welcome a few parties. The disciples of the Great Green Arkleseizure, are you in tonight? Yes! Don't start singing, we're just glad to have you aboard for closure's sake. Let's have a big cheer from the Krikkit robots! Yes! That's great, just keep those war clubs on the table where we can see them, that's fine. Now then, I've just been handed a very small note here, it says 'Please don't tread on us, we know where your home planets are', and it's signed the mice! Stand up and be counted, Frankie and Benjy! Yeah, a big hand for these little guys, we all know them from the chat-show circuit but they started out running a pretty spectacular show in a Plural Sector – whoops – somebody wasn't looking where they were walking – Frankie and Benjy RIP. A moment's silence for the mice, then – that's enough, who else have we got in tonight. Ah, over on table 1770, the Adamses . . . (etc.)

ARTHUR Ford . . . last question, I promise, but . . . if the Babel fish is so versatile, how come it's never saved my life – our lives – before?

FORD PREFECT You didn't die before.

ARTHUR So . . . what happened to us? How were we saved?

FORD PREFECT Ah, well, our scrape with death took place in a Plural Zone, where organic life forms in the vicinity of a Babel fish share its kinetic bridge to all available dimensions and are transported too. The only other life forms who can make the jump are dolphins. Have you noticed what's outside the restaurant? For miles and miles in every direction?

TRILLIAN Who could miss them? Thousands of interlinked blue lagoons, glowing under the stars . . .

353

ARTHUR	. . . filled with dolphins.
FORD PREFECT	The dolphins learned how to jump dimensions from the Babel fish. In return, the Babel fish learnt a thing or two about where to have a good time from the dolphins. Quid pro quo. Pass that Ol' Janx Spirit, Zaphod.
ZAPHOD	**(Pouring)** One for you, Ford, baby – two for me.
FORD PREFECT	**(Toast)** Here's to the look on Trillian's face when she merged with Tricia.
TRILLIAN	It was weird . . . one minute she was there . . . *we* were there . . . the next, it felt like we were two drops of water, suddenly joining into one.
FORD PREFECT	I like you with blonde hair, mind. Pass that Ol' Janx Spirit, Zaphod.
ZAPHOD	Come on, monkey man, hurry up with that menu, I'm hungrier than a Bugblatter Beast in a weight-loss clinic.
ARTHUR	You'll have to wait. Random's having a problem with the Dish of the Day.
RANDOM	I want the veggie option.
FORD PREFECT	Waitress! Can you bring over a talking cauliflower?
FENCHURCH	**(Approaching)** Yes, sir, I will – oh – is there a Mr Beeblebrox on this table?
ZAPHOD	That's my name, dollface. Don't wear it out.
ARTHUR	Good grief—!
RANDOM	Dad? What is it?
ARTHUR	Fenchurch . . .
FENCHURCH	Arthur! Hi! Wondered when you'd turn up. Phone call for you, Mr Beeblebrox.
ARTHUR/FENCHURCH	**(Under Zaphod)** Where did you go?/I searched for months/Decided to wait for you, this seemed as good a place as any, etc.
ZAPHOD	**(Into phone)** Yup.
MARVIN	**(Distorted, almost background)** This is the car park. You ordered a Babe Wash for your ship. Due to staff shortages, I am your Babe.
ZAPHOD	Marvin? I thought you were dead!

EXT. – CAR PARK, MILLIWAYS, CONTINUOUS

FX: Dolphins splashing and happily trilling in background:

MARVIN

Seems I was still under warranty. Sorry to disappoint you. Sorrier than you can possibly imagine.

ZAPHOD

(Distorted) You mean you're still parking cars here?

MARVIN

Spend a few thousand million years in a job and eventually you get promoted. I have my own bucket now. Finally I am Somebody.

FX: Galvanized bucket clatter.

INT. – MILLIWAYS (CONTINUOUS)

ZAPHOD

OK, metal man. How about giving the *Heart of Gold* a hot wax wash with full valet?

MARVIN

(Distorted) That depends on whether or not I can find my frilly apron. With my luck I probably can.

MAX QUORDLEPLEEN

(Fading up from background business) Do we have the minor deities from the Halls of Asgard?

FX: Norse cheering.

THOR

(Distant) Waiter! A bottle of champagne to table 42 with my compliments!

TRILLIAN

Ooh . . . is that Thor? Coo-ee! Thor!

FORD PREFECT

She could argue astrophysics with Einstein, but a set of biceps and a big hammer can instantly reduce her IQ to single numbers.

MAX QUORDLEPLEEN

And we have with us here tonight a party of believers from the Church of the Second Coming of the Great Prophet Zarquon. Folks, you're in luck! A big hand please for the Great Prophet Zarquon!

FX: Huge round of applause.

ZARQUON

Oh, how very kind, yes, at last an opportunity to say a few words on my own behalf to all who have taken my name in vain—

WOWBAGGER

Just a moment, please.

ZARQUON

Er – yes?

WOWBAGGER

Prophet Zarquon, you are the last on my list! You are a tiresome, goggle-eyed pillock.

ZARQUON

Wowbagger the Infinitely Prolonged, you are a whingeing sack of parrot droppings – and no longer immortal.

WOWBAGGER

Oh – I – er – urghhhhh . . .

FX: Body fall.

FX: Huge laugh and round of applause.

MAX QUORDLEPLEEN   Ladies, gentlemen and Norse gods, as everything draws to a close, yet again, let's all join together in the time-honoured way.

OMNES   (Sing)
Should auld acquaintance be forgot
And never brought to mind
Should auld acquaintance be forgot
For the sake of Auld Lang Syne.
For Auld Lang Syne, my dear,
For Auld Lang Syne,
We'll take a cup of kindness yet
For Auld Lang Syne . . .

Fade song for:

ANNOUNCER   The very final episode of *The Hitchhiker's Guide to the Galaxy* by Douglas Adams is affectionately dedicated to its author. Now here is a public information message. The large yellow ships visible overhead are a hallucination. Do not be alarmed, there is nothing to—

FX: Huge explosion.

INT. – VOGON FLAGSHIP – BRIDGE

PROSTETNIC
VOGON JELTZ   Got 'em. Where's the list?

VOGON OFFICER   Here, sir.

FX: Clipboard papers riffled; tick put in box.

PROSTETNIC
VOGON JELTZ   Good. Helmsman?

VOGON HELMSMAN   Yes, Prostetnic Vogon Jeltz?

PROSTETNIC
VOGON JELTZ   Set course for Eroticon 6. Time for a spot of shore leave with Eccentrica Gallumbits. Before we blow her planet up.

EXT. – SPACE

FX: Vogon fleet thunders away into the void . . .

Fade out. Fade up distant sounds of partying.

ARTHUR   **(Low, close)** Fenchurch . . . when do you get off work?

FENCHURCH **(Low, close)** Just after the Apocalypse.

ARTHUR   Will you come flying with me?

FENCHURCH Always.

           Fade out.

HERE ENDETH *THE HITCHHIKER'S GUIDE TO THE GALAXY*

For Douglas

Complete Cast and Production List

Peter Jones and **William Franklyn** The Voice of the Book

Simon Jones Arthur Dent

Geoffrey McGivern Ford Prefect, Flashback Hactar

Mark Wing-Davey Zaphod Beeblebrox (both heads)

Susan Sheridan Trillian, Receptionist, Old Lamuella Lady

Stephen Moore Marvin

Sandra Dickinson Tricia McMillan

Jane Horrocks Fenchurch, Stewardess, Dolphin Voice

Bill Paterson Rob McKenna

Andy Taylor Zem the Mattresses, Grebulon Leader

Toby Longworth Wowbagger, Prostetnic Vogon Jeltz, Grarp

Dominic Hawksley All eleven Krikkit robots, Wikkit Voice, Thor the Thunder God, the Krikkit Commander, the Elder of Krikkit, Documentary Voice, Robot Maître d', Vogon Councillor, Policeman

Roger Gregg Eddie the Computer, *Heart of Gold* Door, Robot Waiter, Doctor, Strinder, Bar Tender, Accountancy Department Door, Gangsta, Security Guard, Vogon Helmsman

Mike Fenton Stevens Krikkit Civilian One, Mancunia Boss, Grebulon Lieutenant, Lift, Drimple

Rupert Degas Judiciary Pag, Russell, Pilot Voice

Philip Pope Krikkit Civilian Two, Krikkit Commander, Krikkit Singer, Grebulon Underling, the King, Captain

Bob Golding Krikkit Civilian Three, Rory Award Winner, Armorfiends of Striterax, the Dispatcher, Alien Teaser, Wizened Old Man, Vogon Guard, Xaxisian Robot, the Lajestic Vantrashell of Lob

Richard Griffiths Slartibartfast

Henry Blofeld and **Fred Trueman** Themselves, Brockian Ultra-Cricket Instructors

Joanna Lumley Woman with the Sydney Opera House head

Chris Langham Prak

Leslie Phillips Hactar

Griff Rhys Jones Old Thrashbarg

Rula Lenska Voice of the Bird, All the Lintillas

Samantha Béart Random

Arthur Smith Barman

June Whitfield Raffle Woman

Stephen Fry Murray Bost Henson

Jackie Mason East River Creature

Christian Slater Wonko the Sane

Jonathan Pryce Zarniwoop Vann Harl

John Challis Prophet

Mitch Benn Pseudopodic Creature

Saeed Jaffrey Old Man on the Pole

Miriam Margolyes Smelly Photocopier Woman

Roy Hudd Max Quordlepleen

Fiona Carew Walkie-Talkie, Ship Launch voice, Hooker 2

Alison Pettitt Stewardess Bot, Wizened Little Old Lady, Stewardess, Hooker 1

Michael Cule Punter, Vogon Clerk, Vogon Helmsman, Computer

Chris Emmett Evil-Looking Bird, Canis Minor Pontiff

David Dixon Ecological Man, Zirzla Robot Leader

Simon Greenall Jim, Steward, Lifepod

Geoffrey Perkins Head of Light Entertainment Radio

Lorelei King Gail Andrews, Stewardess, Patient

Andrew Secombe Colin the Robot, Mr Bartlett

Ann Bryson BT Operator, Barmaid

Margaret Robertson Mrs Kapelsen

Nick Clarke Himself

Charlotte Green Herself

Peter Donaldson Himself

Sir Patrick Moore Himself

Brian Cobby Speaking Clock, Sub Etha Voice

Neil Sleat Newsreader, Cameraman

Bruce Hyman Deodat, Prosser

Kevin Davies Taxi Driver

Theo Maggs Boy at Cricket Match

Tom Maggs Krikkit Civilians Four to Five Million, *Heart of Gold* Door, Runner

John Marsh The Announcer

and

Douglas Adams Agrajag

Jo Wheeler Production Assistant (Series 1), Production Manager (Series 2)

Laura Harris Production Assistant (Series 1)

Susie Matthews Production Assistant (Series 2)

Ken Humphrey Studio Effects

Paul Weir Additional Sound Design

Paul Deeley Sound Recording/5.1 Mix

John Langdon Script Editor

Paul 'Wix' Wickens Music

Philip Pope Krikkit Song

Dirk Maggs Writer/Director/Co-Producer

Helen Chattwell Producer

Bruce Hyman Producer

Transmission Dates

LIFE, THE UNIVERSE AND EVERYTHING

Episode 1   21.09.04, 6.30–7 pm   *Repeat 23.09.04, 11–11.30 pm*

2   28.09.04   *30.09.04*

3   05.10.04   *07.10.04*

4   12.10.04   *14.10.04*

5   19.10.04   *21.10.04*

6   26.10.04   *28.10.04*

SO LONG, AND THANKS FOR ALL THE FISH

Episode 1   03.05.05, 6.30 pm   *Repeat 05.05.05, 11 pm*

2   10.05.05   *12.05.05*

3   17.05.05   *19.05.05*

4   24.05.05   *26.05.05*

MOSTLY HARMLESS

Episode 1   31.05.05   *02.06.05*

2   07.06.05   *09.06.05*

3   14.06.05   *16.06.05*

4   21.06.05   *23.06.05*